LEX TALIONIS

R. S. A. GARCIA

Dragonwell Publishing

This is a work of fiction. All of the characters, organizations, and events portrayed in this novel are either products of the author's imagination or are used fictitiously.

Cover design by Olga Karengina

Published by Dragonwell Publishing
(www.dragonwellpublishing.com)

ISBN 978-1-940076-12-6

CONTENTS

▪ ▪ ▪   ▬ ▬ ▬   ▪ ▪ ▪

For Andrea, who believed in me first,
and Granny, who believed in me most.

 PART ONE

...The Roulon have offered to sponsor Earth's entry into the DiploCore in return for certain trade rights to be divided between them and their Dak business partners. In particular, they are interested in the natural resources offered to them at a special price by Conway Enterprises of the U.K. Given the fact that they have dealt with us fairly in every way since their arrival, and the clear necessity for Earth to have representation in the DiploCore if it is not to become a pawn between more powerful civilizations, I recommend that we accept their offer...

—Address to the General Assembly of the United Nations
by Vincent Purcell, Special Liaison to the Roulon Trade Mission,
May 28th, Year One After Arrival

Five there shall be, if all holds to the Pattern,
but the Third controls the Balance.
—Chapter 425, Roulon Book of Fate:
Origin of The Weaver

NOW

Serron

CHAPTER 1

Death is the breath between one Life and the Next.
—*Message of the Will*
Book of the Seven Holies
Ancient Dak Scripture

I

Death came for Michael while he slept.

He woke, gasping and trembling, from a dream of being pushed out the airlock. His fingers were cold and numb; the weight of his head on his arm had cut off his circulation. Michael sat up, wiping sweaty strands of hair off his forehead. Shifting his feet out from under him, he cursed as pain lanced up his leg.

Shit. I fell asleep. I can't sleep. How long was I out?

Michael crawled along the vent to the grille that covered its entrance, stopping once to catch his breath. Despite having dozed, he was exhausted and cold. The air in the vent left a metallic taste in his dry mouth and he couldn't stop shaking. The wound in his leg, which he'd bandaged with cloth ripped from his pants, made a white-hot line down his shin.

God, it hurts. If I don't find some meds soon…

He had to figure a way out before he was incapable of going on, or lost consciousness again—maybe for good. Michael pulled himself onto his knees, inching his way toward the harsh light that shone through the grille. Dust motes danced in the path of square patches of illumination.

Then he heard it.

Faint, a mere whisper: the brief sound of air being expelled from lungs. And it came from outside, from the corridor below the vent. Despite the fact that he was freezing, sweat broke out all over his body.

Fuck. Oh, fuck no. Please, no.

Michael strained to hear, ignoring the pain in his wounded leg, which had become twisted beneath him. There was nothing but the impossibly loud sound of his own breathing. Seconds ticked by, then minutes. He blinked as sweat dripped into his eyes.

Still nothing.

Heart tripping, he decided he must have imagined it all. He began to shift his weight in a careful movement.

Tap, tap, tap.

All the air left his lungs. The grille wavered and darkened before his eyes.

Tap…tap…tap.

The sound came from right below him, on the wall just under his hiding place.

Tap, tap, tap.

He recognized the rhythm. It had been centuries since anyone had used it on a military vessel, but everyone had studied the same vids in their naval history holobooks during basic training.

Three short, three long, three short. SOS. Save Our Souls. A cruel jibe. The only soul left to save was his, and the very thing he tried to escape stood right outside, mocking him with the ancient distress signal none of them, least of all him, would ever be able to send.

The tapping stopped. Michael stared at the opening in front of him, seeing the grille being yanked off like paper as if it were already happening, seeing the light falling fully into the narrow vent, revealing him where he crouched, helpless and too terrified to move.

Not that he would be able to escape even if he could.

The silence pushed at his ears. The grille in front of him continued to filter the light into shapes on the inside of the vent. He waited, certain he was a dead man; wanting it to be over now, because he was tired, so very tired.

Eventually, it dawned on him that it had been silent too long. It took a few more minutes before he worked up enough courage to make his way to the front of the vent and look down to see the empty corridor stretching out on either side.

After he opened the grille and slid down from his hiding place, his legs gave way below him and he crumpled to the floor.

I'm still alive. I'm still alive

But not for long if he just sat there. He had to find medication. That meant Med Bay—and the bridge.

He shuddered, his mind shying away from the endless corridors that waited for him, lights flickering while darkness edged their walls.

Don't think. Just go. Go now.

Leaning on the wall, Michael pushed himself to his feet. He started limping down the corridor, slow at first, and then faster. The way to the bridge would be long and dangerous, and if he was right, he had very little time to get there.

II

Desmond Obuki was not particularly kind or generous. He gave to charity for the tax breaks and avoided fund-raisers like the plagues they were usually trying to eradicate. He was a businessman, not a meal ticket. But he was also something else.

Human.

And if the shoe on the unmoving foot he had spotted told him anything, it was that the Elutheran had a human down on the ground. It kept lashing out viciously, its muscular proboscis waving between its short, sharp beak as it chirped away to itself. The feathered red ball of its body rippled every now and again, as if caught in a stiff breeze. It was at least knee-high; definitely an adult.

After that, he couldn't very well walk away. The warren of alleys surrounding Bradley was dangerous. Not so much for a former soldier like himself, but even he wouldn't be here now if he wasn't trying to beat the clock.

He had no idea how the Elutheran had managed to overpower the human, but a mudsucker couldn't be up to any good in an area like this one. The guy had probably fallen asleep drunk in the gutter, and the Elutheran must have come across him. Humans were few and far between in this part of PortCity; the least he could do was drive off the little mudsucker and help the poor bastard up out of the gutter.

He didn't need to check the dim street for friends of the alien. The alley finished in a dead-end beyond the spot where the Elutheran had the human backed up against the building. The smooth seventy-foot walls of the ore factories on either side offered no hiding places.

"Hey! Get the fuck off him!"

The Elutheran panicked. It sucked its feeding tube back into its head, rolled across the narrow alley, bounced along the lower edge of the wall and shot past Obuki before the man could grab hold of it. Shrugging his shoulders, Obuki walked over to the gutter and bent over the shape clad in a dark jumpsuit and a pair of spacer's boots. There was a faint smell in the air—like rust.

"Hey, you, wake up. This is no place to sleep off…"

He rolled the body over and sucked in his breath.

His hands were wet. He looked at them and it dawned on him that the top half of the jumpsuit was not red. It only looked that way because of the blood.

"Oh, shit."

He'd lost his comm panel on the flight back. Hadn't thought much of it at the time as he had a replacement at the office, but that wouldn't help him contact the police now.

He looked at the battered face again and sighed. *It* had *to be a woman*. And she was still breathing.

Well, he thought, no good deed goes unpunished. He would be late for sure now. Grumbling under his breath, he picked up the unconscious woman and strode out of the alleyway.

III

Colin usually knew who wouldn't make it. After a while, you got a sense. Not the patients that yelled and moaned, cried and complained—they had a chance. But the quiet ones—they were the ones you had to see to first.

Today, Colin had a sick feeling in his gut the minute he walked into the trauma room. It didn't stop him from doing his job, but in the back of his mind, the objective part of him whispered, *waste of time*. Less than fifteen minutes later, bloody clothes in a pile on the floor at his feet and the slim, still body on the floating gurney before him, he watched as the medbot withdrew glimmering threads from the monitor patches on the girl's body. Gray tentacles folded the sensors into its spherical body before the bot floated up to its ceiling station.

"Patient has expired," the medbot said in a soft, unisex voice. The yellow dot of its camera swiveled its circumference until it found him. "Time of death noted for the record."

He did so as the new attendant stared, her face saying: how did this happen? How did I fail?

"It wasn't your fault," he said as he stuck his hands in the sanitizer built into the wall and felt it suck away his gloves. A blast of coldness followed as it cleaned his hands. Colin focused on it, trying to ignore the dull frustration, the come-down from the adrenalin rush of action to the reality of failure.

She looked up at him, shaking her head. "But she died."

"She was dead before she got here. You want to start the paperwork?"

She nodded, hesitant, but starting to pull herself together now. He remembered those days, when he had been brand new to the job and had never had a patient die on him. A million years before, in another life.

"She your first?"

She looked up, nodded, her lips a thin bloodless line.

Colin sighed. "I'm sorry. But she won't be your last. There's nothing we can do for her now, so we'd better get on with it."

With one last look at the gurney, she turned her back and gave him a firm nod. *That's it, Doc. Back to work. Nothing else to see here.*

The doors slid open as the new attendant exited, comm in hand, ready to begin recording her report. He glanced back at the prone body as he withdrew his dry hands from the sanitizer, sadness washing over him. The dead girl looked young—too young to be so broken. And he hadn't saved her. *God, I hate this job sometimes.*

He turned to go, but the tinted doors to the corridor slid open again on a whisper. Something small and green flashed past him. There was a crash as a tray went down. The medbot sounded a high-pitched whine that made him cover his ears. He swung around in time to see its yellow eye spark and go dark a second before the noise came to a blessed end.

What the hell...?

A biped sat on the dead girl's chest. Hairless, it had green skin stretched paper-thin over an almost human skeletal structure, void of genitalia. Its arms and legs ended in four long, thin digits. Its large, round head had enormous black orbs over two tiny holes Colin took for nostrils, and a lipless mouth. It sat in a lotus position,

9

head lowered, with long arms wrapped around its torso and clasped together in the middle of its back.

He reached out to haul the thing off and the next thing he knew, he had slammed into the crash cart in the corner of the room. He sat up with a grunt, his back screaming where he'd impacted on a sharp corner—and barely had time to get his legs out of the way as a huge gray figure strode into the room.

Seven feet tall, the Algaran marched past Colin toward the gurney. The brown toga he wore—which left the breathe flaps on his wide chest exposed—made a sibilant sound as he passed.

"Come now, come to Andraju," the Algaran growled in Universal to the creature sitting on the girl. Andraju stood next to the gurney as though unsure how to proceed. "You've caused enough fucking trouble. Let's go before security arrives."

The creature did not move. Colin pulled himself to his feet, ignoring a sharp, unpleasant tingling under his skin.

"Come on, I said. If we leave now, together, I will forget this when we get back to camp."

The creature remained motionless.

"Sir," Colin began, but Andraju hissed, oblivious to all but the unmoving creature.

"You fucking useless little—" The Algaran reached out and grabbed the animal's shoulder. A second later, his muscular arm shot up and back as though slapped away. He cried out, a shocked look on his gray face, his black, marble-sized eyes wide. Grabbing his arm, Andraju cursed fluently in his own language.

So that's what happened to me. It looked as painful as it felt.

"Is this…animal yours?" Colin asked. "If so, you'd better get it out of here. Neither of you are allowed—"

His voice died as his gaze fell on the girl again. The sitting alien had not moved an inch. But the girl had. Her chest rose, then fell. Rose, then fell. The creature rode her breathing, its arms still wrapped around itself.

She's dead. She has to be. The medbot's never wrong.

The girl arched away from the bed, her body making an impossible curve, like a bow. Her head dug into the plastic sheet under her and the veins in her bruised neck stood out like cords. The white sheet they had half-pulled over her fell away from lean arms as her fists dug into the gurney. One of the monitor patches peeled off and fell to the floor. A strangled gargle came from between her puffed lips.

Still straddling her, the creature stretched one stick thin arm toward the girl's head and touched the center of her forehead. Her body collapsed as if a string had been cut…

…and then she was holding the outstretched finger, her hand clutching the alien's in what looked like a death grip. Her whole body shook from the effort. Her eyes were green, Colin realized, bloodshot, but incredibly green.

"By the sacred Host," Andraju whispered. "What does this mean?"

Colin did not, could not, reply. *She was dead. I watched her die.*

The girl's breaths sounded harsh, each one a faint moan. She struggled to get an elbow under her, but fell back onto the gurney, still clutching the alien's hand. Gasping with pain, she did not break eye contact with the alien on her chest.

The creature leaned down, as if listening for something. Seconds passed before the girl choked out two short words Colin could just barely hear. Her eyes closed and her hand fell back on the gurney, still holding her savior's finger.

"Fucking pest," the Algaran said, but Colin caught an undertone of confusion and fear. The Algaran had no idea what had just happened. Neither did he, for that matter. *But he knows this…thing. He can help.*

Above them, the medbot suddenly whirred to life, flexing tentacles and swiveling its camera eye.

"Patient revived," it announced. "Prepping for surgery." It began reattaching the sensors to the monitor patches.

"Aida me", she said. "Aida me". "Help me", in Latin. Who uses Latin anymore outside of medicine and law school?

The creature leaped from the bed with surprising agility and landed on Andraju, its long arms encircling his short, fat neck. He sneered and cursed it in his own language.

"Troublemaker! You're going back to the fucking cage and will remain there until that bastard son of a prostitute comes back for you. I've had enough."

"Wait." Colin grabbed the Algaran's arm. With the other, he touched the wall sensor that would summon the nurse. "Stay where you are. I have to speak with you."

"So you will help me?" Andraju asked, his Universal sounding thick and heavy through his growling vocal cords. "The receptionist said this was a human hospital. But this thing won't eat and I can't afford a vet." He paused and Colin saw something else in his black, black eyes

(fear? Algarans fear nothing)

before he went on. "I can't have it die on me. The owner will never...forgive me. I run a sideshow and if the performers think they can't trust their animals with me..."

Colin's smile was grim. "Rest assured, Mr...Andraju, is it?"

The Algaran grunted in assent.

"I'll help you figure out what this thing eats, if you allow me to examine it. Something very strange happened here. If I'm going to treat this patient properly, I have to find out what. I'm going to be busy here for a while, so have a seat outside and for God's sake, don't go anywhere."

IV

In the clean, pale-blue corridors of the hospital, Andraju placed the alien on a chair and backed away from it, studying it suspiciously.

Chris had not left instructions on what to do with the fucking thing. In fact, he'd suggested that Andraju would be well advised to leave it alone. But he had to feed it, and that was where the trouble began.

"After everything I tried to do for you," he spat at the motionless green creature, "you repay me with pain? You are worse than a female."

The creature did not move; its enormous eyes held a flat shine, like onyx or marble.

*If it dies on me, Chris will blame me. But if it dies here...*Andraju bared his teeth, thinking hard. Then he sneered at the alien.

"You can understand me, can't you," he said, rather than asked. "I've seen your shows with Chris. You're good money. But I have my limits. I won't have that bastard blaming me when you die. He won't play his nasty tricks on me."

Still the eyes held their unmoving shine. The Algaran fought off a shudder, unnerved, as he always was, by the thing's intelligent silence. He knew that if he walked away and Chris found him, it would not be pretty. The animal was all that fucking human had in the world; without it, his act was worth nothing. But after all the trouble Chris had caused him the past year, maybe it would be good to give him a taste of his own medicine.

"I won't spend another minute with you. You're dangerous and…" he fought for the word, the flaps on his torso sucking air, "…strange. If that fucking doctor wants to study you, he can have you. I wash my claws of you."

He turned to go, thought of something and turned back.

"Don't bother following me, either. Just wait for the human in there. He wants you. I don't."

With that, he stomped away, part of him relieved to be rid of the silent presence of the beast, the other part more than a little disturbed over what Chris might do to him if he found out.

"But he'll have to find me first," he muttered to himself, already planning how best to pack up camp and be gone within hours. Chris wasn't due back for a couple of weeks, but the more distance he could put between himself and both members of his prize act, the better.

Behind him, the tiny alien watched him go. Then it turned its head back to the closed doors of the trauma room, wrapped its arms around itself and waited.

CHAPTER 2

This love that tears me apart!
Memory is a curse of my sentience.
— *Holograffti in No Man's Land, Serron*

I

"You must go now."

"But I don't want to."

"Don't be afraid. You can do it. You won't always be alone."

"I'm not afraid. I don't want to leave you."

A brief caress of her cheek.

"It doesn't matter. It's too late now. You have to go back no matter what we want or think. You have to—"

Murmurs…

"—go back—"

Stronger, getting louder…

"—now."

Lex. Lex Talionis.

She opened her eyes.

Next to her, something moved, coming closer. She turned her head and blinked, trying to focus. A man's face emerged from the blur. Blond hair flopped into his blue eyes. He pushed it back and smiled a little. "Hello there. Welcome back."

You need a haircut. It was a curious thought, and it sounded loud in her head.

14

"Can you understand what I'm saying? Nod if you do."

She nodded, the world tilting off its axis. *"Thirsty."* Talking confirmed it. Her throat was a sandy corridor, her words dusty winds blowing through it.

He gave her water and placed the glass on the table when she finished.

"Do you know where you are?"

She looked around her. Besides the conform chair the man sat in, the windowless room was furnished with one other bed, two side tables and a holoprojector mounted on the pale yellow walls opposite her. A closed door stood across from the other bed. "Hospital?"

"You're at the Mathis Clinic in PortCity, ten kilometres west of Bradley Spaceport. I'm your doctor, Colin Mayfeld. You've been here nine days now and for five of those, you were in a coma. You took quite a beating. You're lucky to be alive at all."

She raised a hand to her head; it felt like someone else had hold of her body and was moving it with strings.

"My face…"

"It feels stiff like that because of the healing patch. Your right cheekbone was broken, as well as your nose. It should all heal well. The cosmetic surgeon assured me there would be no facial scarring."

She lay back, too tired to speak for a while. Then, "I feel strange. Floating."

"It's the painkillers. Right now we have you on quite a bit. When you feel better and your mind is clearer, we'll discuss your injuries and treatment in more detail. Right now, it's imperative that you rest."

The door opened and she turned her head. "What is that?"

Dr. Mayfeld turned to look as the green biped behind him loped over and hunched itself at the foot of the bed, staring up at her.

A painted skeleton, she thought.

"You don't know?"

"Should I?"

He frowned. "I guess not. It's just that—well, the way you responded to it—"

"Responded?" He wasn't making sense anymore, and she was so sleepy.

"Never mind. We'll talk about it later. I just need a couple of things from you before I let you rest. Do you remember what happened to you?"

She made a weak attempt to shake her head, and failed.

R. S. A. GARCIA

"No."

"Then you don't remember who did this to you?"

"No."

"Okay, that's to be expected. Can you tell me your name?"

Name. He wants names. But her mind couldn't process the logic behind the question. *So tired.* "What?"

"Your name. I'd like to contact your family or a friend. Normally we'd get it from your ID, but you didn't have any on you when you were brought in."

"I'm not sure."

"Are you new in town? Is that it?"

She opened her mouth—and froze. *Family. Friends.* But nothing came to her. *My name then.* The truth dawned on her, even as her eyes fought to remain open.

"Do you know anyone in PortCity?"

"I…not that. My name."

"What about your name?"

She glanced away, focusing on the alien. *What are you? Why are you here?* It stared back, immobile, as she stammered, "I don't know."

"Excuse me?" the doctor said.

"I can't remember. It's all blank."

She swallowed and closed her eyes, mumbling, "White. It's all white and I don't remember. I don't…"

She fell asleep.

II

Michael couldn't believe his eyes.

He'd doubled back to Med Bay for the serum. Just a few hours before, he had narrowly missed being killed there. Only instinct kept him from walking into a trap. He hadn't been able to treat his leg at the time, but he'd come back because everything depended on him finding the serum.

Now he stood in front of the open Med Bay doors and saw the last thing he'd expected.

Blood. A small trail of droplets that led away from the doors and down the corridor to his right.

Michael stared at it, unable to look away. Impossible. There's no one else. This must be from before.

16

LEX TALIONIS

He hesitated a moment longer before entering.

Equipment lay everywhere. Gurneys had been overturned. Recessed medicine shelves were torn open, the contents tossed out. Bed-sheets had been ripped to shreds and shards of glass, crystal and plastic covered everything. Hypoguns crunched underfoot. Gaping black holes punctured diagnostic tables, and exposed electronics blinked at him like so many stars in space. The air smelled of smoke and chemicals.

At the back of the circular room, the door to Quarantine was a half-open, dented panel. A crash cart lay on its side nearby. It had been shoved against the Quarantine door until the panel had given way.

Just a few steps from the door, he found the trail and followed it to the one bed still standing. It was almost clear of debris and several vials of painkillers lay empty on the sheet. At the foot of the bed was a small puddle of blood. In that puddle was the clear print of the underside of a boot.

Michael put his foot alongside the print, careful not to step in the puddle. It was a couple of inches shorter than his own. There could be no doubt about it now. Someone else had been through here.

The blood hasn't even dried yet. It's fresh.

Someone else had survived.

The crazy elation that sped through him almost made him dizzy. I'm not alone. I'm not the only person left to screw up.

"Okay," he whispered to himself, "But you have to think. You can't afford to lose focus."

Kneeling, brown eyes narrowed, he studied the footprint.

"Who?" he said. "Who do you belong to?"

Hanson was short and went through the airlocks easier than most because of it. But then he remembered a crumpled body outside the weapons locker on Level Two. No. It couldn't be Hanson.

Murdoch and Ganesh had been below average height as well, but they too were dead, among the first to go, their mutilated bodies sprawled in the brig.

And then it occurred to him.

"Oh shit, Raydell!" he whispered.

He'd completely forgotten about the Lieutenant Commander. She had changed shifts with Lieutenant Matka and had spent most of her time in the brig over the last week. He'd gotten used to not seeing her on a regular basis.

And Michael hadn't seen her today.

"Shit! Shit!"

Excited, he started to rummage through the devastated drug panels and the surrounding debris. It was even more important now that he find the serum. He needed the ability to think free of pain.

III

"When can this mask come off?"

Colin looked up from her chart, startled.

"You're awake."

"For a while now." Her voice was still raspy though the bruises on her throat were beginning to fade.

He replaced the panel at the foot of the bed. "Probably within the next couple of days."

"Now. I want it off now." Her tone was neutral, but there was no mistaking her intent. It was a command, not a request. *Interesting. She's a tough one all right*, he thought with grudging respect.

"Why the hurry?"

"Why wait?"

"If you're worried about the way your face will look, I assure you—"

"It's not that. Please. Just get it off."

What the hell. It won't hurt and might help. "Okay. I'll get a nurse."

Fifteen minutes later, the nurse smiled as she tossed the mask in a metal bowl and handed her a mirror.

"You're almost good as new. See for yourself."

She stared into the surface of the glass for a long time without moving. Raising a hand, she touched her face, her pale cheeks, her lips. Her fingers probed the dark sunken area under each eye, the smooth, high brow marred by splotchy bruises and the synth-skin bandage that covered her right temple. It was a young face, free of lines and wrinkles, by all appearances no older than twenty. But Colin could see age in her eyes. She lowered the mirror.

"Well, what do you think?" the nurse asked.

"There are no scars."

"There won't be any on your face," Colin said. "We did our best to minimize them elsewhere too."

"It was a good job." The nurse looked up at him, a confused frown on her face. Colin knew she was trying to understand the girl's lack of emotion. He nodded to her and she collected the equipment and left. He drew closer to the bed.

"Does the bruising bother you? It will be gone in a few days."

"No." She met his gaze and he saw again the intense green of her eyes; an unusual shade, almost like jade.

"I had hoped. I thought." She looked away as if frustrated.

"Tell me."

She sighed. "I wanted it off because I thought if I could see my face, that maybe I would remember something. Remember who I am."

"And?"

She shook her head. "It was like looking at a picture of someone you've never met."

"That's not surprising. Amnesia is complicated. You've been through a terrible ordeal and to cope with that, your mind blocked off everything connected to the incident, including your identity."

"What will bring back my memory?"

"That depends on a lot of things, including how hard you're willing to work to remember, how extensive the damage was and how long it will take for you to heal, physically and mentally."

"Heal from what?"

Colin paused. *You have to tell her sometime, you know.* But instead he said, "You need to rest. You're very lucid, but you can't overdo it. You just woke up two days ago."

"I'm strong enough now. I can talk now."

"I'd still advise you—"

"Doctor." Her voice cut across his like a scalpel. "I'm living this. I have a right to know what's wrong with me and I want to hear it, all of it. Every last detail."

Well, there go your good intentions. He sat on the bed, knowing that she might need comfort when she heard the truth.

"You were found in an alley eleven days ago by a businessman on his way to a meeting. He ran off an Elutheran that was attacking you at the time. However, only your head injury is consistent with the attack he described. The alien caused the physical damage that may be linked to your amnesia, but Elutherans are too small to have inflicted the other wounds you have. And there are indications that you fought back...hard.

"You have a broken left collarbone and right ankle. Six of your ribs were also broken and that caused the collapse of one of your lungs. Your spleen and liver were lacerated and you had been choked badly enough to damage your vocal chords. You were stabbed once in the back, just grazing your left kidney. Your nose had been broken in two places and we had to repair a skull fracture in the area of your right temple where you were hit by the Elutheran's tentacles. Some of your fingers were broken and your left shoulder was dislocated."

He paused and she took a shaky breath. "Didn't miss much, did they?"

Whoever *they* are, he thought. "Most of your broken bones have already set and the sprains have healed. Your internal injuries will take more time and there was some damage to your spinal cord, but treatment has been very effective and you should have full mobility."

He paused to give her time, but she said, "Everything. Please. Just tell me everything."

He looked at her, willing her to see how much he hated to do this.

"We know you were attacked by at least five different men. We know this because we tested the semen we recovered."

"Semen?"

"I'm so sorry," he said slowly, "but there is evidence that you were raped by at least five men, about forty-eight hours before you were found and brought to this hospital."

There were no words to describe the look on her face before she turned away her head away.

"I'm sorry," he repeated.

"Why?" she replied without looking at him. "You didn't do this to me." A slow pained smile spread across her face. "And I can't remember who did."

"You will."

"You can't guarantee me that."

"The odds are—"

"Not in my favor." She leaned her head back and closed her eyes. "It seems they haven't been for quite a while. Please go now."

"If there's anything you need…"

"I just need you to leave. I'm sorry but I can't. I can't talk to anyone right now."

He knew better than to say anything. He glanced back once at her still form before walking out the door.

IV

"Anything?"

"Nothing. She hasn't spoken since you left her yesterday. I don't even know if she slept. She refused the sleep aid."

Colin sighed and rubbed the bridge of his nose. He'd been in emergency surgery for the last ten hours and another doctor had made his rounds for him. His Jane Doe, as he called her, was the first person he was checking on. She was his most serious case. And his most interesting.

"Do you want me to get Psych down here?"

"All right, schedule it for this afternoon. Try to get Ranie. She's good with the silent ones."

Behind the nurse, the station started to beep. "Code Blue, room 1067. Equipment malfunction. Patient has no detectable life signs. Code Blue, room 1067."

"Doctor, that's—" the nurse began, but Colin was already gone.

As he entered her room, his heart tripped when he saw her empty bed and tiny monitor patches lying on the rumpled sheets. Then movement caught his eye.

She was sitting against the side of the second bed, her back supported by the frame. Both legs were stretched straight out in front of her, her right ankle encased in the flesh-colored shrink cast. The sheets had been dragged off the bed she leaned against, and her paper-thin hospital gown was racked up past her knees. Colin realized that she must have ripped off the monitors, tried to stand up and fallen instead. She sat there now, head lowered, dark hair hiding her face as her breasts heaved with the exertion of what had gone before. *How the hell did you get off the bed on your own?*

"Are you okay?" he asked. She didn't answer, didn't look up or even move. He hunkered down in front of her.

"You shouldn't be doing this. You have to get back to bed." He put out his hand as the door opened and the nurse appeared.

"Here, let me help you." His hand touched her shoulder. Her head came up so fast he hardly had time to register the blank expression on her face before her right arm hit him a solid blow to his cheek.

The nurse gasped as he fell back onto his butt, his face numb. *Goddamn it, she's strong!*

As his cheek started to tingle, his eyes met hers and he saw that they were as glassy and devoid of emotion as her face.

She's not here at all. What is this? A dream? Sleepwalking?

She bared her teeth and spat something at him in a strange, hissing language he'd never heard before.

"Doctor, are you okay?" the nurse asked.

Whatever this is, it isn't sleepwalking. "I'll be fine. Get me a tranq— we'll need some help here."

She disappeared in search of the medication and the orderlies. He turned his attention back to his patient. She was still muttering and had started trying to push herself to her feet again. She kept slipping on the smooth floor. *If she keeps that up she'll break something again. Or worse.*

"Listen to me," he said. "It's okay. Everything's okay."

She hissed at him again, in Latin this time, but too fast for him to understand.

"Let me help," he said, trying to be soothing.

She looked at him, *through* him, her lip curled in contempt. "Never. I'll never scream. You won't make me scream."

He pushed himself onto his knees and moved a little closer to her. She tensed, her head swinging wildly from side to side. *She's terrified*, he thought, with a wave of pity and understanding.

"I'm not going to make you scream. It's a dream, a bad dream. I won't hurt you. Listen to my voice. I don't want to hurt you."

She swung at him, but he was able to duck the blow. Behind him, the door slid open again, but he did not see the nurse when he glanced up. Instead, the bed shook and the alien appeared above her head. It reached down one thin finger and touched the center of her forehead.

Her eyes rolled upward, her lids drifted closed and she slid sideways, unconscious.

CHAPTER 3

Our contacts in the military have been successful in handing over the subjects to the new subsidiary, Tec Solutions. ME&E of Mars will continue the experiments and return the results to Tec Solutions, if the Commission does not find in our favor. Gilene Conway's people should be satisfied with what they've received, although I suspect she will be far too busy trying to retain control of Conway Enterprises to be unduly suspicious.
—Excerpt from an e-mail to Bruce Martin III, CEO of InGene Inc., from David Rosenbaum, Head of Research and Development, August 1st, 244 A.A.

I

Pain. So much pain.

She opened her eyes with a groan and blinked, trying to clear her blurry vision.

"You're awake." The voice sounded relieved. She turned toward it.

"Doctor?" The last syllable cracked. She cleared her throat and a gentle hand cupped the back of her neck, lifting. A straw bumped against her lips and she drank from it. He took it away too soon, but at least when she swallowed again, her throat didn't feel like hay had been packed down into it and set afire. She tried to lift her hand to rub her eyes but it moved only a little way.

"Hold on."

There was a soft clink and her arm felt lighter. She cleared the sleep out of her eyes in time to see him toss a thick silver bracelet onto her bedside table. When he noticed what she was looking at, he said, "Sorry, but you're very strong and you just broke out of the normal restraints. We had to use the gravity bracelets."

Dr. Mayfeld leaned across and took the bracelet off her other arm. Briefly, she caught the citrus scent of some body cleanser, almost buried under the antiseptic smell peculiar to hospitals.

"Why?" she asked.

"You fell out of bed and we had some trouble getting you back in. You got a little violent."

"How long?"

"You mean, how long have you been asleep?"

She nodded.

"Twenty-four hours. We gave you sedatives to keep you quiet, but we didn't want you hurting yourself, hence the jewelry." There was a heavy clink of metal on metal as the second bracelet joined the first. She noticed the bruise on his left cheek. *Oh, shit.*

"Did I hurt you?"

He touched the bruise, as though surprised it was still there. "I'll live."

"I'm sorry."

"Forget about it. You didn't do it on purpose."

"Why are you here, anyway?" she asked, knowing it sounded like an accusation. "Don't you have rounds to make or something?"

"Not for another," he looked at his watch, "three hours."

"Have you been sitting here all day?"

"It was my day off. I didn't have anything better to do."

"Really." She stared at the wall, hoping he would take the hint. "Well, you can go now."

"I just thought you might appreciate the company."

"I'd prefer to be alone."

She could feel him studying her. "You really think being alone is the best thing for you right now?"

She looked at him, unable to tell him how hollow she felt in her chest and

(between her legs)

in her head, and how talking made her feel like every nerve she had was focused on keeping her from screaming. "I'm not going to go crazy again. I don't need you to watch me."

"That's not why I'm here—"

"Look, Dr. Mayfeld—shit!"

A blurred form had jumped up from the floor and was now perched on the end of her bed. As she watched, it wrapped thin arms around bony legs and rested a small chin on pointed knees. *Why does it look so expectant? As if it's waiting for me to do something?*

"What is *that* doing here?"

Mayfeld shrugged and sighed. "I wish I knew. It likes you, I guess. It's been here most of the time since it knocked you out."

"Knocked me out?" Tense now, she kept her eyes on the creature.

"After you punched me, you tried to attack me a second time. It touched you in the middle of your forehead and you were down for the count."

"You're kidding, right?"

"No. And that's not all. We sedated you but the sedatives didn't last long and you would get violent again. That is, until it came and stayed with you. Then you calmed down and fell into a deep sleep."

She looked at him, her eyes narrowed. "What are you saying? I have some kind of connection with this animal? That it can control me somehow?"

"You do seem to have some kind of connection with it. That's been pretty evident from the beginning. Even though I'm almost certain that the two of you have never met before. It won't go very far from you and it definitely won't let anyone take it away, so I've been letting it stay in the room next door, or in here. It seems to be helping you. I don't know how yet—it won't let itself be tested—but it's done some other interesting things since you got here."

"What things?"

He told her about Andraju, the escape and what he called her "reawakening". She listened, surprising herself with her own calmness, the desperate need to be alone on hold in the face of his revelations. "Where's Andraju now?"

"God knows." Colin propped one leg against the side of the bed frame and folded his arms. "He seems to have abandoned it here. He left no contact information. I tried looking up side-shows—he said he ran one—but it didn't help. Truth is, I'm not surprised. He didn't seem to care about anything except not having to answer to the owner for starving it to death."

"He's afraid of the owner?"

Mayfeld nodded. "I got the impression he was human, but nothing else."

He must have seen the look on her face because he shrugged

and added, "I know, I know. An Algaran afraid of a human. Doesn't make much sense, does it?"

Yeah, well, I don't think we can exactly rely on his word. He abandoned it after all. "Wish I could have talked to the owner."

"Because maybe he could tell you something that would explain what's happening?" Colin nodded. "I thought about that too."

They grew quiet as she paused again to catch her breath. Slivers of pain sunk into her body the way they had before, when she'd refused her meds so that she could keep a clear mind. She stared at the alien as she concentrated on breathing, a tight frown on her face. "You haven't figured out what it is yet?"

"Not much. Every time I try to do some preliminary tests or take it near any diagnostic machines, it goes crazy and starts zapping anyone that touches it. The last time I tried, the charge damaged some of our computers. Took four hours to fix."

She smiled a bitter smile at the motionless green figure. "So you don't like being poked and prodded? Well, good for you."

"Not so good for you." Colin leaned forward, his arms resting loosely on his knees. "The less we know about it, the less we know about how and why it's so attached to you. And what it's doing to you."

"You said yourself, it's helping. Maybe it just felt sorry for me."

"It's a possibility. Anything is."

"Well, if you're so worried, why are you letting it stay here? I'm sure it's not hospital policy to have animals running around."

He paused for a second, and folded his fingers together. "You're right, animals aren't usually allowed in here. But nothing about your case has been normal. You have to understand, I tried everything I could, and you died. This creature brought you back. There has to be a reason why it wants to be close to you. Whatever it is, as long as it is helping you and not interfering with anyone else, I'm willing to let it stay."

Silence fell again. She studied the alien and it was unmoving under her gaze. *What the hell are you?*

"Tomorrow," Dr. Mayfeld began, "someone from Psych will be down to—"

"No." Her refusal was sharp. The animal flinched as though it had been hit. *They will not put me under a microscope. My mind— what's left of it—is my own.* "No head doctors."

"You need someone to help you deal with what happened to you."

"All I need is to be left alone."

"Listen…"

"No, you listen." She tried to keep her voice firm, despite the fact that she could not speak very loud. "I was attacked and raped, but I'm not crazy. I don't need a psychiatrist."

The look on his face was both sympathetic and firm. "It's not about being crazy."

"You're right. It's about me. I'm the one in this bed and I'm the one with the problem, not you or your head doctors. I don't need your psychology or your pity. I need to find out who did this to me and why. I need to remember who I am." She stopped, too tired to go on.

Colin studied her for a moment. "Okay, if that's the way you feel, Psych at this point is optional. But you will need some form of counseling and I can't see you out of this hospital before that happens."

"You do what you have to and I'll do what I have to," she said and turned her head away. "I'm tired."

"All right," he said, "we won't talk anymore."

And they didn't. An hour or so later, when she'd succeeded in making him think that she'd gone back to sleep, he got up and left. She felt a moment of regret for dealing with him so harshly—he was, after all, just trying to help—before she reminded herself that regret was a waste of time. She had to be strong and cautious of everyone. *Someone in your position can't afford to worry about others.* After a few minutes, she opened her eyes and looked at the alien still sitting at the foot of her bed.

"Oh, God. Please, please go away."

For an answer, it moved over her, feather-light, and sat next to her shoulder. It stretched out its hand and started to stroke the dark hair tangled on the pillow. She watched it for a while, trying to understand why the gesture felt so human, so comforting. "Can't you understand me?" she said in a voice tinged with frustration. "Go away."

There was no response to her question. She had not expected one, but she persisted all the same. "What do you want?"

It didn't answer; it just continued to stroke her hair in gentle, reverent movements.

"Whatever it is, I can't help you."

It kept stroking.

"Do you hear me? I can't help you." And in a low, tired voice: "I can't even help myself."

The coolness on her cheeks came without warning. She made no sound, just allowed the teardrops to roll down her cheeks, hardly moving because it hurt to do so.

When she pulled herself together and could speak again, she said, "You did that, didn't you? You made me cry because you knew. You knew I wanted to and couldn't."

It stopped stroking her hair and took her right hand in both its warm, dry palms. The feeling that flooded her was nameless and calming. For a few seconds, she didn't even feel the ever-present pain. But most important, she felt...cared about. Afterward, she would look back and realize it was then she began to trust the alien. It was in that moment that the burden of being alone began to lift from her shoulders.

"What are you?" she whispered, but the shiny black orbs of its eyes held no answers and no voice acknowledged her question. Instead, it sat, radiating well-being and eventually, a thought began to go round in her mind. A flowing, melodious phrase that sounded as calm as the alien made her feel, but that she somehow knew was her own thought. A thought that had nothing to do with peace.

Lex Talionis.

II

He was sweating by the time he worked his way out from under the bed, the precious, intact vial clutched safely in his right hand. His arms bore scratches from the chunks of crystal and glass all over the floor and his leg throbbed. For a moment he paused and checked the open doorway, just in case, but the entrance remained empty. No time to lose then.

Pulling himself upright, Michael swept aside the debris on the bed and sat. He lifted his leg with both hands, gritting his teeth as he did so. Untying the makeshift bandage, he checked the wound. It looked clean and the bleeding had stopped a while ago. He picked up a small bottle with a spray nozzle, and a cloying medicinal smell tickled his nose as he misted his leg with the antiseptic-antibiotic spray. Dropping the bottle, his fingertips made dimples in his thigh as he waited for the stinging to pass.

A few seconds later, Michael flicked the yellow plastic cap off the plastic vial. He had seen it used only once before on a crew-member who had been so hurt in an accident during a maintenance exercise, he was transferred to a med ship for treatment on-world. He sniffed it out of curiosity, but there was no scent.

Now. Do it now. Before you lose your nerve.

He upended the vial over his wound. Clear liquid ran out onto his raw flesh with a burning sensation so intense, he almost screamed. Michael dropped the vial as he clenched his teeth.

Oh, shit!

He looked at his leg through watering eyes. The liquid was expanding over his exposed flesh. Its consistency and color had changed—now it was a reflective sliver-gray, like mercury, only it moved much slower. And still it hurt.

Can't go on much longer. Just ride it out—ride it out.

The slash in his leg was almost completely covered now. He could feel the flesh beneath the hot touch of the liquid puckering and pulling as if trying to come together. There was a sudden bolt of pain that lanced through his flesh into his bones and the world went gray.

When Michael came to, his cheek was aching and he was lying twisted on the bed on his right side. He sat up carefully, feeling a new abrasion on his cheek where a piece of plastic he had landed on scraped his face. Med Bay. I'm in Med Bay. My leg…

He looked down. Gray webbing made minute crisscrossings over the length of his wound. When he poked it with his finger gently, the dense material gave easily, the feel of it almost like a rough sponge. But the most important thing was that there was no pain.

He swung his leg down and stood, testing it by putting his weight on it a bit. There was a faint tingling, and nothing else. For all intents and purposes, his leg felt normal. The painkillers in the wound filler had done their job even better than he'd expected. He would be able to walk comfortably now, maybe even run, with no constant pain to distract him.

He knew it wouldn't be a good idea to push it too much—the synthetic filler was meant to be a temporary stabilizer, good only for a couple of days at the most. If he did too much, he would damage his leg even more, whether he felt pain or not. Still, two days would be enough. He had to check the star charts, but he doubted the nearest port was more than a few days away. And that would be all the time he needed.

He would keep an eye out for Raydell, but now that he'd executed the first part of his plan, he felt a lot more confident about the rest of it.

He'd been lucky so far, but he couldn't be so forever. The ship was small; he would be discovered sooner or later.

Next stop, the bridge, he told himself.

III

Fifteen days after her discovery in a filthy back alley, Colin Mayfeld declared his patient fit to have visitors. The Troopers had finally sent someone over to interview her about the attack. Colin had no real hope that they would be able to find the perpetrators so long after the incident. He did have some hope that they would be able to find out his patient's identity.

Or so he thought, until he walked past room 1067 that afternoon and was almost hit in the head by a flying tray.

A Trooper—a tall, thin human of the type born on low-grav planets—ducked out of the doorway, colliding with Colin. Behind him, there was a sharp clang as something hit the closing door.

"What the hell?" Colin frowned at the Trooper. "What happened in there?"

"Your patient attacked me, that's what." The officer's voice was calm, but his eyes checked the door as if to reassure himself that it was still closed.

"Attacked you? She can hardly stand."

"Lucky thing for me. I wouldn't have gotten out alive otherwise." The officer tucked his panel under his arm and raked his hands through his black hair.

"What did you do to her?" Colin demanded.

The Trooper looked at him, his gaze cold. "I tried to ask her a few questions and she went crazy on me. I can't do my job when things are being thrown at me. I have her file and the physical evidence you were able to collect. I'll do what I can with that. You can contact me when she's ready to talk. Until then, I have other cases."

The officer stalked past Colin, looking neither left or right.

Frowning, Colin entered the room, almost tripping over the cover from the food tray.

"I said get the hell...! Oh." His patient lowered her arm, surprise replacing anger. "It's you."

"You can put the glass down. He already left."

She looked at the water glass in her hand as if seeing it for the first time before resting it on the bedside table.

"Good," she said, her voice tight, "because if I have to see his smug face again, I swear I'll break it in half."

Bedridden or not, I think I actually believe you. Colin took a few quick steps and punched up her chart on the touch-panel at the foot of the bed.

"Want to talk about it?" he asked as his eyes scanned her readings.

"No," she said. She leaned back against the pillows, her green eyes dark with emotion. "Holo on."

Behind him, he heard the faint sounds of a rowdy crowd and a cheerful voice said, "…And the stars are out tonight at the launch of the new Systems Media Company! The celebrity studded Board of Directors includes a who's who of Galactic movers and shakers."

Out of the corner of his eye, Colin glimpsed a severe looking woman, dressed in a conservative black dress that reached mid-thigh. Recognizing her, he turned to take in the report. The woman's red hair was cut short against her head, like a scarlet cap. One thin, muscular arm was hooked over the arm of her companion. He was dark-haired, handsome and at least half her age. Dressed in an impeccable white tuxedo, he smiled and nodded at the screaming crowd around them. Through the shimmering pair, Colin could just discern the blank yellow walls of the hospital room.

"We are in luck today, viewers! Here comes Gilene Conway herself, CEO of one of the most powerful companies in the Universe, Conway Enterprises, in a rare public appearance. She has been seen on just four occasions since taking over the family business ten years ago and now E Holovision is streaming her to you, live—"

"Holo off."

The scene melted away. Colin glanced back at the bed.

"Not interested?"

The look she gave him was odd, as if she was in the throes of some strong emotion that she could not articulate. "No. She…the whole thing just annoyed me. I'm not in the mood for celebrities and their stupid functions."

Colin made a non-committal sound in his throat and sat in his chair. *Sure. That's why you look like someone just slapped you. Still angry over the Trooper.*

"I've offended you." She didn't sound like the idea bothered her at all.

"No. It's not that. It's…well, it's kind of ironic. Gilene Conway is one of the clinic's biggest benefactors."

"Oh." She shrugged as if it didn't matter.

Patience, Colin, she's had a hard time of it. "Dr. Exley told me he spoke with you after I left yesterday."

"The neurologist? He spoke *to* me if that's what you mean."

"Did he explain your condition to you?"

She shrugged and intoned, "The damage to my head is healing well and is not the cause of my amnesia. Most likely, I'm suffering from dissociative amnesia as a result of my traumatic experience. Might be addressed by certain recall techniques, but such a total loss of identity means the trauma was severe and I should not be reminded of it before I'm ready to absorb the reality of the incident, blah blah blah. In other words, my brain is screwed up and he can't do anything about it."

She cocked her head at him with a thin smile. "See doctor, I have a good memory. It's just on the fritz at the moment."

Colin drummed his fingers against a knee. "That Trooper must have really upset you."

"All he did was suggest I brought this attack on myself, so why the hell should I be upset?"

That bastard, Colin thought, deciding a change of subject might be a good idea.

"I got the results of your initial tests."

"What tests?"

"Well, we did the usual work-up on you when you came in—blood, tissue, DNA—and we did some neurological and chest cavity scans, of course. But the results came back somewhat abnormal."

"Abnormal?" She met his gaze directly for the first time. It was strange, Colin thought; whatever he told her, she never went into hysterics, never broke down in tears. *Maybe all that pent up emotion is why you act out in your sleep.*

"What are you saying—that I'm even more screwed up than we thought?" Her tone was flippant, but her expression was serious.

"Not exactly. You're an N-gene. Do you know what that means?"

She nodded. "My genes have been enhanced. No big deal—lots of people have had their genes tweaked a little."

"Yes, and you're an N-gene baby—someone who was altered before birth, probably even designed before conception. The DNA tags indicate that, as well as your age."

She became very still. "You know how old I am?"

Colin cursed himself mentally. He should have mentioned it long ago. Of course, she would be grateful for any bit of information about herself. "You're about seventeen."

She breathed out. "Seventeen. Strange. I don't feel so…young." She looked at him, her expression unreadable. "But that's not what you wanted to tell me."

Colin shook his head. "What you said before is correct. There are millions of N-gene babies and it's no big deal, but I've never encountered anyone before with the level of enhancement that your DNA shows. It's really quite incredible. It accounts for how fast you've been healing at least."

She raised an eyebrow. "I've been healing fast? I feel like I've been here forever."

"Well, you haven't. Your broken bones had set days before you woke up. All your organs showed at least a 40% improvement after you'd been here a week. That's how you were able to walk when you should have been bed-ridden. I've seen and treated a lot of N-gene babies before, but I've never seen anything quite like you. I'd even venture to say your genetic manipulation was way beyond anything available to the general public."

She lay silent for a moment, as if thinking over what he had said. "This is good, right? If someone invested this much in me, then you should be able to find out who pretty easily. They'll be looking for me."

"It should have narrowed our search, yes. You see, when a lab or a geneticist works on an N-gene, they usually leave a chromosome tag, an indelible DNA tattoo, something to identify the geneticist and lab responsible for the work and to give limited information about the patient they tagged. For example, the age of the patient when the work was done, or the patient's physical condition. There's a solar system database of tags, so that someone's physician and medical center can be referenced. From there, it's usually an easy matter to get a hold of the patient's file and any info that might be required for effective medical treatment."

"Then what's the problem?" She leaned forward, her body tense now. "If you can find out who I am so easily, why are we just talking about this?"

"Because our lab couldn't identify the tag. We were able to read your age, and that your gene therapy had been done as part of an in-vitro process, but that was it. There was no physician recorded.

The tag we found didn't match anything in the Medsys database. When we ran it through the translation process, all we ended up with was the ancient Terran symbol for eternal. Do you know what that looks like?"

For an answer, she extended a finger and drew a figure eight on its side. Colin nodded.

"Does it mean anything to you?"

She thought about it before shaking her head. "Nothing." She sighed. "So we're back to square one. No idea who I am, where I came from, or how to find out anything."

"Well, that's not strictly true. I can tell you that you're very well educated. You've spoken several languages while you were out of it, including English, a few snatches of Madinah and Latin. That last one really is surprising. It's basically a forgotten Terran language."

She frowned, biting her lip a little. For a brief second, she almost looked her age. "I don't feel as if I know all those languages. Are you sure about that?"

"Pretty sure. We can do testing later to confirm it, if you like."

"Yes, I'd like that." Her voice was firm, certain.

Colin continued. "You were brought in dressed in a standard spacer suit, but it got lost in the clean-up before we could examine or test it. The first thing the Troopers did was run an ID trace on you in their database—they came up with nothing. You have marked calcium loss and a few other signs of space fatigue, so we know you recently spent some time in space, but you're apparently not a spacer, or you would have taken special supplements to counteract those effects. Customs doesn't have you entering PortCity, so we're checking commercial ships and military vessels for any reports of stowaways.

"I can also tell you that you're quite a fighter. Not only is your body in superb shape, but that clip you gave me on the face packed a real punch." He smiled a little and was rewarded by a slight curving of her lips. "Plus your reflexes are fast—faster than anything I've seen anyway. For someone in a semi-conscious state, you seemed pretty competent to me.

"Anyway, therein lies the mystery. You have all the hallmarks of military personnel. Multilingual, recent space travel, signs of intense, regular physical training—but we can't find any record of you anywhere, and you know how the military likes to catalogue things."

"Maybe I work for a secret branch of the military or something. Maybe that's why there's no record of me."

Colin shrugged. *A bit young, but not inconceivable. They take them younger and younger these days. We hardly have enough personnel to meet DiploCore requirements for maintaining human law enforcement away from Earth as it is.* "Well, I guess that's a possibility. It's also a possibility that you have nothing to do with the military at all. You could be a linguist who trains in order to keep fit, for all we know. And of course, none of this brings us any closer to finding the men who left you for dead. For now, I'm having the lab here check your DNA against all the public databases. There must be something in one of them."

He paused. *I thought you were going to be professional and detached about this. You get sucked in every single time, Colin, do you realize that?* Determined, he ignored his inner voice. "But I'm also considering getting a friend of mine to help."

"What kind of friend?" Her voice was cautious.

"An old friend. We were in medical school together. Only I was the student and he was my anatomy professor. His name's Dr. Anton Slake and he's a forensic pathologist over at the city morgue."

"How can he help me? I'm not dead," she pointed out.

"Anton has what he calls the gift of observation. You can give him the physical evidence in a case or get him an interview with a victim and he can sometimes postulate the events surrounding a crime in a way that moves the investigation forward. He's worked on a few cases for the Troopers.

"I think if he sees your files and talks to you, he might be able to tell you something about yourself. At the very least, he might help us find a lead on either your identity or your attackers. But I wanted to talk to you first, get your okay and clear it with the Trooper on your case, Officer Linkow."

"You really believe talking to this Dr. Slake will help?"

"Well, let's face it. There's not a whole lot the Troopers can do while you still can't remember anything, or if they don't manage to match the semen and DNA we recovered against the criminal and public databases. At least this way, we're not just relying on over-worked, under-paid military personnel in a system that doesn't have much interest in human affairs. Officer Linkow gave me the impression that they don't have much time to help individuals. Whatever we do on our own can't hurt."

She thought about it for a while. "Okay. If you think it will help, I'll talk to your friend."

"I'll clear it with the Troopers and set up an appointment with Anton. On one condition." He paused. *Please don't fight me on this.* "You have to have at least two sessions with our psychologist."

Her smile did not reach her eyes. "You're blackmailing me now?"

"I'm trying to help you. It's not just your body that needs healing."

"And why are you so interested in helping me? I asked the nurse—you're the orthopedic surgeon that operated on me when I came in. You didn't have to take an interest in me beyond charting my progress afterward. You're a busy man, in charge of a busy clinic. So why are you going out of your way for me?"

How the hell do I answer that? She wasn't his first rape victim, and she wasn't the sickest person he'd ever treated. But he knew she was hurt beyond her injuries, hurt beyond his skill as a physician to treat her. It bothered him—and it drove him to do everything he could to prove to himself that she wasn't beyond his help.

"You're a mystery, I guess," he said finally. "As a doctor, I can heal your body but that isn't all that you need. I just want you to recover fully from what happened to you, or to at least start the process."

"And that's all?"

"Well...it might not be what you want to hear, but although dissociative amnesia is not unheard of, a case like yours is still fairly rare." *And I think I just...like you,* he thought, but did not say.

She glanced away. "It's okay. I'm fine with that." She looked back at him, green eyes serious. "I'll see your psychologist, but only for two sessions, is that understood?"

For now. If you check out okay. "Understood. When do you want to see her?"

She waved a tanned hand, and the paler skin on her wrist made her look strangely vulnerable. "Whenever. Tomorrow if you like. I'm tired. Are we done now?"

He rose to his feet. "I have rounds so I'll leave you to rest, but I wanted to ask you one more thing."

"What?"

"I'm tired of thinking of you as 'Jane Doe'. Don't you think you should give yourself a name, at least for the time being?"

She shrugged. "Yeah, sure, why not?"

"Any thoughts on what you'd like to be called?"

She paused and then looked up at him, her expression indecipherable. "Actually, yes. I think I'd like to be called Lex. Is that okay?"

He nodded. "That's fine." He extended his hand. "Hello, Lex. Since we're going to be spending some time together, maybe you should call me Colin instead of Dr. Mayfeld."

"Fine," she said. But he couldn't help noticing she shook his hand and let it go in almost the same movement.

CHAPTER 4

The subjects have arrived safely. Train Colony has confirmed their
order and transferred payment. The first shipment will leave once
preliminary flight training has been completed. Handover of transport
system to our security personnel should be viable in six months.
— *Transmission to ME&E Headquarters on Mars, from Tec Solutions
(transmission origin blocked), September 13th, 245 A.A.*

I

"Hey, Linkow."

Lieutenant Marakesh Linkow looked up from the awful
vegetarian sandwich he was trying to consume. The round, ruddy
face of Ian St. Germaine filled the screen of his comm panel.

"What do you want?"

"Those Customs arrival records you asked for? I downloaded
them to your panel while you were out, together with the crime
scene report."

"And the IR's for Spaceport security?"

"Sent that too. Every one for the last week." Ian smiled, more
a show of teeth than an expression of pleasure. "You and Helene
should have lots of fun." His image winked out.

"Stupid tub of guts," Linkow muttered under his breath. The
head of records also doubled as an inter-departmental liaison, and
he thought that meant he was somebody. Linkow knew that was
nothing more than a fantasy. Nobody was anybody in PortCity
unless they were brass, and even the brass was only a collection

of human problems to the alien dominated DiploCore. The rest—with the exception of the few Terrans rich enough to matter—were drones. Unlucky bastards that had the pleasure of dealing every day with crap that the brass wouldn't know how to get off the bottom of their shoes.

He crumpled sanipaper around the squishy ball of his sandwich and pushed back his chair. A one handed dunk sent the remains of his sandwich down the garbage chute behind his desk. The cubicle he shared with his partner was located at the back of the windowless squad room. If he stood up, he could see the transparent door that separated the squad room from the landing in front of the lifts.

Sonja Helene's plexiglas desk faced his. Their comm panels were black rectangles above the confusion of data clips on their desktops. Her high backed blue conform chair was the same as his own and matched the dark blue partitions of the cubicle. The squad room smelled of a hundred stale meals and recycled air. The low murmur of voices was as ever present as the hum of a spaceship's engine.

As he stretched in his chair, his comm panel beeped. "Incoming call. Lieutenant Sonja Helene for Lieutenant Marakesh Linkow."

"Go."

Sonja's short dark hair stood up as though she had been running her fingers through it and there was a pinched look about her thin lips.

"Mark, I just got done at Bradley. Did Ian forward the files?"

"Yeah, I got them. Didn't get a chance to go through them yet. The interview took longer than I thought."

"Sorry about sticking you with that, but it's a good thing I went. Port Security made a huge stink about the files. If I didn't have a contact in Records, I wouldn't have gotten a thing. They should pay me for doing Ian's job."

"Yeah, well, at least no one threw trays at your head."

She raised an eyebrow. "What?"

"Tell you about it when you get here."

"I'm on my way in now—if I can get this shitty runner going, that is. I told Transport the damn thing wasn't working right, but they obviously didn't get around to fixing it."

"What else is new?" Linkow snorted. "Probably had a more urgent ordinance from the Algaran or Dak Troopers. Humans might be the engine of Serron's damn economy, but we still get zero respect. What I wouldn't give for my transfer to come through right this second."

"Just be the same shit, different city," Sonja pointed out.

"Different city's the whole point. Do me a favor. Get me a veggie sandwich from that Roulon deli on the way in. I got one at a diner near the Clinic and it was a complete waste of credits."

"Okay, but you still owe me for last week's breakfast." She winked out.

Linkow leaned back in his chair and propped a foot against the leg of his table.

"Computer, access downloads from Ian St. Germaine."

"Accessed," the computer replied in a no-nonsense male voice. "Three downloads. PortCity Incident Reports, PortCity Customs Arrivals and Case Number P186S0397TT Lab Crime Scene Report. Please indicate preference."

"Incident reports."

The file opened and he started skimming through data. He was still annoyed with the way his interview had gone earlier, and felt no real impetus to bust his balls.

Crazy bitch, he thought. *A simple question like what she was doing in an alley at that time of night, and she flips out.* He had very little patience with hysterical females and he was certain the girl at Mathis Clinic knew a lot more than she was telling. He'd read the hospital reports. This wasn't just gang rape. Someone had tried to kill her. And in that part of PortCity, at that time of night—well, maybe she wasn't as innocent as she put on.

Amnesia my ass.

He was surprised when she hadn't showed up in the criminal, or the global, DNA databases. His gut told him she was more than just a victim. He flagged all the stowaway and unsolved petty crime reports as he read. There was no guarantee he would find anything useful, but with luck, he might be able to find clues to her identity.

And why killing her had been so important to someone.

II

Anton Slake propped his elbows on the edge of his desk and made a steeple of his fingers. "Are you sure you want to go through all the trouble of cleaning up, Colin? I'm afraid I might have to disappoint you," he said, his voice a mild rumble.

Colin paused in the act of transferring a pile of data clips from the only chair in front of the desk to the already overflowing orange sofa.

"What do you mean?" he asked, shifting pillows out of the way. *He's still sleeping on this thing. Why he even bothers to keep an apartment is beyond me.*

"If you're here for a favor, I'd like to help you, but I really don't have the time." The pathologist leaned back and Colin heard the tiniest of squeaks. Anton's six foot seven frame was too much even for the conform sponge. He placed his hands on top of his head as if trying to flatten the close cap of his hair.

"At least let me try to change your mind." Colin settled into a chair that smelled of antiseptics and floral cleaners and pushed another rack of data clips on the desk aside so that he could rest his elbows on the smooth wood.

"A few minutes then." Anton gestured over his shoulder, the expression in his dark brown eyes apologetic. "The bot should be done soon."

Colin looked through the window behind him and into the autopsy room. Banks of glimmering metal cabinets took up two of three walls; a mix of the typical freezer units and a range of oddly shaped containers meant for aliens. The third wall was dominated by surgical and cleansing equipment.

On a gleaming metal table, a med-drone carefully prepared a cadaver. The squat spider-like robot crawled over the red-brown corpse of a Dak, then levitated for a moment as it shifted position, moving to inspect the head of the massive, limbless body. Daks were giants, well over eight feet, with bodies that resembled a Terran slug's.

"Asphyxiated."

"What?" Colin broke his gaze. His friend was looking at him with a wry smile that exposed very white teeth in his dark brown face. Anton took his hands off his head.

"The Dak. The autopsy is just a formality because it was a Spaceway Guild factor. It was heading to a meeting when its runner went over a bump too hard. Its head impacted on the roof, the atmosphere filter broke and it asphyxiated."

"Sounds like a hard way to go."

"Not really. It was probably already unconscious from the blow. Daks don't have much in the way of a cranium."

Colin nodded and shifted in his chair. "So since when are you too busy to help a friend?"

"Since I agreed to help with another case. I'm due to leave for Greater Polcar in a week."

"You're kidding me." Disappointment surged through him.

Anton studied his face for a moment. "Is this about one of your patients?"

"Yes. She was attacked, left for dead. The Troopers are investigating, but she was in a coma for some time. I'm afraid the trail has grown too cold for them to do much, even if they wanted to."

"What does she remember about the attack?"

"Nothing. She's been diagnosed with dissociative amnesia."

Anton's eyebrows went up a fraction. "But that's not all, is it? This woman, she was raped, wasn't she?"

Colin hesitated before nodding. "And probably tortured before that." He waved a dismissive hand. "I know what you're thinking. That I'm a sucker for the old damsel in distress bit."

"Colin." Anton shook his head. "Of course you're a sucker. You think you can help everyone—you never think about how getting involved wears on you."

"Yes, well, this isn't about me. It's about Lex." Colin could hear the tightness in his voice but he couldn't help himself.

Anton laced his fingers together on top of his desk and studied the pattern they made. "You call her Lex?"

"She named herself. I got tired of Jane Doe."

"Indeed." Anton seemed to find the flat, shiny opals of his fingernails very interesting. When the pathologist was thinking deeply, it was his habit to find some small thing to concentrate on while his brain worked.

"I'm sorry, Colin, but I must refuse you this time. I have seven days before my flight leaves, and a back-load of official cases to clear. I will be gone for at least a month. What I can accomplish in a few days—"

"Would go a long way to helping the Troopers. Maybe even help Lex remember who she is, and what happened to her." Colin leaned forward. "There's something else."

Anton looked up. "Another patient?"

"Sort of. I'm not sure what to call it, but the creature was brought to me for help."

"Since when do you treat extraterrestrials?"

"Since they bring my patients back from the dead."

42

That seemed to give him real pause. Anton frowned a little before saying, "Let me guess. The patient it brought back from the dead was this Lex woman?"

Colin nodded. "I need your help to figure out what it eats, before it starves to death. It hasn't consumed anything for the last three weeks. And if that doesn't get your attention, consider this: Lex is an N-gene, but her DNA sequence is not in the database. In fact, her chromosome tag translates into a symbol not recognized by the Soltem database. The Terran symbol for eternal."

For the first time since he had known him, Colin saw a genuine look of surprise cross his old professor's face. *Finally, I've got his attention.*

"You are sure about this? That she is an unregistered N-gene?"

"I'm positive. Why? Do you know something?"

But Anton was leaning back in his chair, his hands on his head again. He remained silent for a long time, his eyes focused on some point behind Colin's head.

"I cannot promise anything. But I will do what I can before I leave. What I need from you is everything you have on her and the mystery alien. Their admission records, medical reports—everything."

"For Lex, sure. I can transfer that from my panel now. As for the alien—I have no information other than what I've gleaned for myself. It won't let itself be analyzed or studied. In fact, every time it gets near a diagnostic machine—"

Anton waved a hand. "Just download what you have and I will set up a meeting later. I'm sorry to be so curt, but I must attend to this case before the day ends."

Colin frowned. "Is something wrong, Anton?"

Anton lowered his hands to his desk and stood, leaning forward slightly. "Colin, in all my time, I've never heard of an unregistered N-gene, or a sentient life form that can survive as long as this creature without any form of sustenance. You have intrigued me, and I will help you any way I can, but for now, I have too little information. I must fill in the gaps before I proceed." Colin stood as well, a little bewildered.

"Anton…"

"Colin, you have always trusted me. Trust me now. I will do everything in my power to help. But you must wait till I come to you."

III

He was at the intersection of two corridors, halfway to the bridge, when he heard it again.

Tap tap tap. Tap…tap…tap. Tap tap tap.

The faint echo floated down the corridor to his right. Instead of the stark white light that illuminated the path to the bridge, that corridor held only the flickering yellow glow of the emergency lights. Fear put his feet into action before he had time to think. He backed up, his boots as quiet as possible against the metal floor panels, the stink of his own sweat in his nostrils.

What I wouldn't give for a weapon. Any weapon.

But what had been passed out to the crew when the massacre began had been taken, destroyed or even used against them. Michael's own gun had skittered away from him into the darkness when he had been ambushed and thrown to the ground not far from the brig. On a patrol unit this size, too many guns had never been a good idea. In the aftermath of this though, he suspected the regs would be changed.

He stopped in front of a door and waved his hand over the lock. With a tiny ping that echoed in his ears, it clicked open. Michael slid inside and the door whispered shut behind him, leaving him in absolute darkness. The blackness was like dark cotton—a soft presence against his unseeing eyes.

In front of him were rows of tightly packed shelves. He could barely move or breathe because the shelves took up most of the space. Wiggling around to face the door, he felt the cold, smooth walls on either side of it, searching for the inside lock release. He found it to the left of the entrance, at shoulder height. Relieved he wouldn't be trapped there, he stood on his toes, tried to find the ceiling above, hoping against hope that there would be a vent he could hide in.

His fingers touched nothing. He twisted sideways carefully, praying the shelf could hold his weight, then climbed up it. Placing one hand on the top shelf, he reached for the ceiling again, his fingers trembling with the adrenaline rushing through his system. Finally, he felt metal. But there was no telltale crease, no opening to indicate a vent.

Michael got down, his mind spinning with the fear that he'd trapped himself in a place he couldn't escape from. Breathing hard, he placed one hand against the wall to steady himself.

Outside, a faint, rhythmic thudding began. He held his breath, listening as it grew louder, came closer.

Feet. It was the sound of feet running. And it came from roughly the same direction as the signal he'd heard.

44

Raydell? Could it be?

His hand hovered over the lock release before he lowered it again. Outside, feet pounded past his corridor, headed along the hallway that crossed right to left.

Silence descended again. The tapping had stopped. Not a good sign. The tapping stopped for only one thing.

Pursuit.

Michael waited, the seconds ticking over in his head as every minute crawled along his hypersensitive skin in a rash of goose bumps.

He never heard the approach.

Ping, ping.

He jumped, startled.

Fuck! Oh, fuck!

Silence.

Ping, ping.

So silent, he thought. So very silent. He had not heard a thing. Not a single step. But there was no mistaking the double ping of denied access. Someone was trying to get into his storage unit. Someone who did not have authorized access. Someone who wasn't part of the crew.

Chaotic thoughts ran through his mind, but he could make sense of only one thing.

Trapped. I'm trapped. I'm trapped, I'm trappedI'mtrappedI'mtrapped.

Ping, ping.

There came a low sound of frustration, almost a snarl.

Thunk!

Michael's eyes opened wide as an impact shook the door panel. Two more thuds followed, and he felt each one vibrate in the floor beneath his feet, in the shelves against his back.

There was a horrible rending sound of metal being torn from metal. A clatter as something was tossed aside. He heard the sound of wires sparking, smelled smoke and realized what it must mean.

The lock panel had been torn off.

The sparking came again, followed by more silence. He clenched his fists, preparing to lunge out of the door if it opened. If he died, he would die fighting. His breathing was heavy in his ears.

The wall shuddered again, but the impact appeared to be lower this time. A kick, he guessed. Another followed, along with a shout of anger and frustration.

From somewhere else, a faint bang echoed.

No! Oh, shit, no!

The kicking stopped. Michael strained to hear but minutes passed and there was nothing else.

This time, he didn't wait long to try the lock release. Amazingly, it still worked when he thumbed it, the panel sliding back halfway before sticking. The corridor outside was empty again, except for the crumpled rectangle of the lock lying on the floor. As he looked at it, a vulnerable memento of his near capture, a stray spark from the damaged panel on the wall stung him on his upper arm, burning through the sleeve of his suit.

He took it as a cue to get moving.

Michael tried his hardest not to think of what must be happening down that corridor. Tried not to see Raydell's face contorted in fear as she looked over her shoulder.

He tried—but he did not succeed.

IV

"Useless human!"

The cup slid from nerveless fingers, spilling tangy, fake orange juice over the sheets before rolling onto the floor with a sharp clatter.

"Not one credit! Not one!"

Her side burns where it has hit her. She can't open her eyes anymore. There's no doubt in her mind. She's dying. This creature will kill her as she lies here, on the street, unable to move.

Lex opened her eyes, her breath coming loud from her open mouth. *Stop it! You're not dying. You're not dying.*

Fumbling, she managed to find the button that moved the bedside table her lunch rested on. It swung away to the left in a smooth arc. On the floor, at the foot of her bed, the small green creature that had saved her life rose from its crouching position, the black orbs of its eyes focused on her face. Lex stared into them, holding her side as she breathed in harsh gasps.

What is this? What's happening to me?

She had to call the nurse. Had to get help.

There's an explosion of pain against the side of her head. She cannot think. The pain stops, enveloped in a soothing darkness that pulls her down, down, into the deepest recesses of her mind where something glimmers, winks at her. Calls her on into the—

—middle of a dark green paradise. She is standing in a primitive forest, with foliage so rich and diverse, she can hardly separate tree from shrub. She is bent over, looking into the glistening heart of a bead of water, studying the hues and the dance of light it projects.

Everything around her is damp. Water drips in soothing rhythms somewhere in the distance. The grass beneath her feet is dew-slick. The air smells of earth, vegetation and moisture; it is a heavy thing. It pushes against her nostrils like the wet, welcoming tongue of a pet.

She straightens up, spreads her arms as she closes her eyes. Breathes deep as she feels the air settle against her bare arms.

"You are beautiful."

She opens her eyes, twists to her right. A shape is there, almost hidden by the overhang of leaves that shades the path she took to this clearing. It's tall, much taller than she is. She cannot see a face, but the voice is deep, definitely male.

He's followed me, she thinks, and part of her is pleased, gleeful. The other part of her feels—trapped. A small, vulnerable confusion whirls in her. She doesn't understand that part of her—doesn't want to understand.

"You say that to all the girls." She smiles, but she has no control over herself. She speaks without thinking, as though reading from a script. The whirlpool in her spins faster, tries to assert control. It fails.

"Don't say that. You know it is not true."

"You deny there are other girls?" Her smile is wider. She is enjoying his discomfort. He deserves it, she thinks, and again, does not know why.

"I don't tell them they are beautiful."

"Why not?" She takes a step in his direction. She can feel the air whisper past her, an echo of her movement. "Aren't they pretty enough for you?"

"Nothing is beautiful for me. Except you."

She crosses her arms. The light material of her vest scratches her skin. "You're lying. I know one other thing that's beautiful to you."

He's silent as she draws closer, almost close enough to see his face, to make out the indistinct lines beneath dim, tree-filtered light and shifting shadows.

"Power. I think…I know, it is much more beautiful to you than I am."

He is so still, it's as if he's stopped breathing. The colors in her mind are spinning fast now. The whirlpool has begun to make a sound. A whisper trails softly inside her head, too thin yet to understand. She stands her ground. She will not move closer. He must come to her. If he wants to.

"You are…different today. Why do you say these things to me?"

"You know why."

The whisper is rising in her mind, like the roar of the sea in a seashell as it's brought closer to an ear. Neither of them moves. She takes another breath and feels the cool life of the forest expand in her chest, like liquid.

"No." His refusal is soft, unconvincing.

"Coward," she taunts. Smiling, she raises her arms, runs her fingers through her hair. She throws her head back and closes her eyes as she does so. She can feel him looking at her. Feel her vest stretch tight across her breasts. But the sound…the sound is rising in her head. It's a low, churning noise now, the syllables in it almost clear. Without intending to, she is listening, trying to make it out, turn it into words. She is listening so hard, she almost misses what he says.

"Not cowardice. Self-preservation."

His voice is very close. Her eyes open, but it's too late. She's missed his approach. His arms slide around her, cool and unbreakable as metal bands. Before she can see his face, focus on his features, his head dips.

The whisper is a scream now…

His lips are soft against hers, the pressure of them firm, insistent. Her head falls back as he presses her mouth open. Her blood sings with his touch. Her arms circle his neck and pull him closer. She has made him submit, she thinks, triumphant.

Be…Be…

He pulls back, says something as his hands tighten on her body. But she cannot hear, cannot see for the spinning colors in her mind.

Be…trayal. Be…trayal. Betrayal.

Bright, savage shards of memory pierce her. She opens her mouth to scream and the world swirls away, rushes back from her. She is going up, spiraling toward something. A presence that waits, pulling, tugging her into—

—her head. Her breath sounded loud in her ears. Pain throbbed along her nerves. She opened her eyes and realized that she was sitting up, bent forward over the edge of the bed, her hand clenched over her stomach.

She could not think. Bile rose suddenly in her throat and she retched for long moments, bringing up what little she had eaten of her lunch. It made multicolored splatters on the white, clean floor that smelled of ammonia.

Mess. I'm making a mess, she thought, but it was a while before she could stop.

When she finally finished, she pulled back from the edge of the bed, wiping her hand over her mouth. Her vision wavered, the tears in her eyes making it hard to see.

Something. I saw something. Remembered something. But her mind was too chaotic, too hurt, to latch on to meaning. She shied away from the memory.

Focused instead on the small green figure still watching her. The black orbs of its eyes shone like polished stone. She was angry suddenly, tired of pain, tired of being watched. Tired of not understanding, and so, so tired of not knowing.

"Are you doing this?" she whispered. It did not move. Anger twisted her insides and though she had no real reason for doing so, she shouted at it, *"Are you doing this to me?"*

It hopped up onto the end of her bed, the movement lithe and graceful. A hand reached out, touched her right foot.

"No," it said.

CHAPTER 5

The search for truth can be easily diverted by the hunt for a scapegoat.
— *Gilene Conway, President of Conway Enterprises*

I

For a second, Lex was incapable of speech. She could only stare, a sour taste in her mouth, her head throbbing, but all of it so insignificant in relation to the shift that had just taken place in her world.

It can't...I didn't...

"You can speak?" she whispered, unwilling—unable—to believe her ears.

"Yes," the creature said, its voice soft and hollow. A dying breeze in an empty tunnel.

The door slid open.

"I think she's having lunch—" The nurse entering the room stopped in surprise as she noticed the mess on the floor. Lex tore her gaze away from the alien.

"Sorry," she said, the words leaving her mouth independently of her brain. "Went down the wrong way."

"Computer, I need clean-up."

"Dispatching unit," the computer acknowledged.

"Are you sure it's nothing more? Are you experiencing pain? Dizziness?" the nurse asked as she walked over to Lex's bed.

"I'm fine. Ate too fast, I guess." Lex tried to smile, hoping to reassure the woman. "Sorry to cause you so much trouble."

"Don't worry about it." The nurse nodded toward the alien. "You know, it really shouldn't be on the bed with you."

"I wouldn't worry about it, Miriam. It's been here for weeks. What harm could come of it now?"

Lex started. She'd been so distracted, she hadn't heard anyone else enter. The woman that had spoken was tall and thin and she smiled at Lex, a genuine flash that crinkled laugh lines around her mouth. A touch panel was tucked under her right arm; it added creases to the plain white blouse she wore loose over a pair of dark green pants. A heavy blonde braid slid over her shoulder as she approached Lex. She flicked it back with an impatient movement of her left hand.

"You must be wondering who I am," she said. She shifted her panel to the other arm and extended her hand. Lex took it without thinking. The woman's grip was firm, warm and brief. A light floral scent surrounded her.

"Dr. Ranie Sangborn. I'm a psychiatrist with the Psych department here. Dr. Mayfeld was supposed to tell you I would be dropping by this afternoon, but I'm guessing he didn't get around to it."

"No, he mentioned it. I just forgot." Lex tried to keep her voice from betraying the frustration she felt building inside her. *Lady, you have got to have the worst timing ever.*

"Look, I'm not really in a talking mood right now. Couldn't we schedule this for another day?"

A small cleaning unit slid into the room, positioned itself between the empty bed and her visitors, deployed a hose from its squat, metallic body and got to work on the floor.

"Sorry, but I don't have much room to shift around my appointments." Dr. Sangborn studied the alien. "Do you want it to stay here while we talk? Will that help you feel better?"

Lex hesitated. She wanted to say that she'd rather have both Dr. Sangborn and the nurse leave, but she sensed that she was faced with two very determined women. She would not be able to fend them off the way she had Colin.

The nurse took her hesitation the wrong way. "Would you like me to stay as well?" she asked kindly.

So we can all talk about my rape together? Thanks, but I'm not the sharing type.

"Thank you, but no."

The cleaning unit finished and left the room as silently as it had entered.

51

Ranie smiled at the nurse. "I think you can leave us alone."

"I'll be outside if you need me."

Lex nodded, a brief movement. *If only I could get this woman off my back and out of here just as easily.*

Without warning, the creature spoke again.

<<*Not mouth/say now. Othertime. Headfixer here. Keep hush/still of our mouth/say. Headfixer must not know.*>>

The alien leapt down off the bed and loped out the door, startling Ranie with its sudden movement.

"Whoa!" she said, trying to mask her surprise. "Does it always just run off like that?"

Lex didn't answer. In a split second, her headache had intensified, as though trying to match her shock. A tremor she barely managed to hide ran through her.

That the creature could talk had been revelation enough. But its last statements to her had not been said out loud.

She had heard them in her mind.

II

The chill of the night air penetrated Anton's open coat, forcing him to pull it closed around him as he walked. The road to his left hummed with the passage of low-slung runners. Aircars swished by and the wind created by them tugged at his coat as though trying to rip it off. The city smelled of dirt and damp tarmac mingled with the tang of people. Sweet or sour, musty or sharp, acrid or mossy, he did not have to look up to separate his species from others. Years of Terran and extraterrestrial autopsies had gifted his nose with more identities—and accuracy in discerning them—than he cared to remember.

It had rained earlier, so when he looked up at the night sky as he left the morgue, the tallest domes, spires and smooth geometrical angles of the city's buildings sparkled a blinding, colorful light show back at him. Rain drops had washed the transperiwalls clean and they caught and reflected the headlights of the sleek zip cars that cruised at different levels hundreds of feet above his head, following the twisting blue glow of the zip rails. The sound of their passage drifted down to him as a low, thrumming vibration against his eardrums.

Anton started to cross another street, only to take a step back as a runner rounded the corner and was forced to brake. The woman driving glared at him as the man next to her continued talking as if nothing had happened.

"Hey, you stupid asshole! Watch where you're going next time, okay?"

With an apologetic shrug of his shoulders, Anton took another step back and allowed her to continue. The runner sped past him. He did not watch it go. He wanted to be inside, away from the possibility of social contact.

He was not entirely comfortable out here. Getting too close to the everyday dance of the world overloaded his acute senses in a way that he could not explain to anyone. So he did not try. He simply kept to himself and lived his life in a way that would ease his discomfort as much as possible. He no longer cared what others thought of his ways; the few friends he had understood him. Everything else was unimportant. Except his job. The one thing he could excel at just by being himself.

Someone stepped into his path.

"Good night, sir, and what a beautiful evening it is!"

The man was short, portly, with white hair parted smoothly to the left. He wore a cheerful smile and a white high-collared suit. Anton could see right through him to the faint outline of the building ahead.

"You look like a man of distinction and taste, but when you go shopping, I'm sure you have trouble finding your size. Well, look no further than—" He waved a hand at the store on Anton's right. "Paget's Emporium! Inside we have the widest selection of—"

He sighed, side-stepped the holo-ad and continued on his way.

"Sir! You are missing out on the chance to be well-dressed in the most comfortable—"

Anton did not look back. He knew the ad could only follow him as far as the boundaries of the store front's holoprojector. Sure enough, the voice was cut off in mid-sentence, only to start up again in growling Universal as the ad changed to suit the newcomer's species. "Want to send the females crazy? Want to make a statement without pheromones?"

Ahead of him was a small, hexagonal building on the corner of a long block dedicated to nightspots and restaurants. The walls of the building rippled with pictures of the diverse crowd inside, partying to music that could not be heard. At regular intervals, the pictures faded to a swirling turquoise and the words "Welcome to the Cosmos!" appeared in yellow curving script, followed by a shot of a sexy female gyrating on the stage. The door slid open for him when he paused in front of it. Music drifted out on invitingly warm air. In the gloom inside, shapes moved back and forth between a crowded bar and an equally crowded dance floor. Anton entered, nodding briefly to the tentacled bouncer standing in the shadows to his right.

He went through a door into the dining area. The music was softer here, the ambience antique wood and brass. Arc lights floated around the room like fairy lamps. Tables dotted the small space; most of those not in secluded corners had green privacy cones shimmering over them.

Anton spotted Troi seated near the door. Drawing his coat off and throwing it over one arm, he strode over to the table and slid into the seat, shifting it so that he would have a better view of the entrance.

Troi Marcas coughed softly. "Hey, Anton. On time, as usual."

Anton dipped his head by way of greeting and flicked the switch for the privacy cone that would signal to the establishment that they wished to be left alone. "You look well, Troi."

She laughed, the action exposing her slightly elongated, very white teeth. She had removed her veil as soon as she gained the safety of the establishment. Large, unlashed, midnight blue eyes, set far apart in a bone white face, looked at him cynically. The rest of her features were small, delicate, unmarred by her mutations.

"As well as I can, you mean."

"I understand that I've inconvenienced you, but it was unavoidable. Are you hungry? Thirsty?"

She shook her head and her straight, pale blonde hair wisped around her face, as if caught by static electricity. Her scent, a clean musk free of perfumes, filled his nostrils. "I'm fine, so let's just get to why I'm here at this hour."

Anton reached into his pants pocket and tossed a transparent yellow data clip onto the table. Troi picked it up. The four fingers of her left hand were tipped with flat, claw-like nails, buffed to a shine. Long and thin, they twirled the clip as she studied it.

"I think you have an idea what I need."

The mutant tilted her head to the left. "A search. Thorough?"

54

"No. More detailed than that. There is one DNA sequence on the clip. I need an identity. Anything you can find. Be warned, though, it's already been run through the Soltem database and the criminal database, with negative results. As far as I can ascertain, this woman is an unregistered N-gene."

Troi flicked the clip into the voluminous sleeves of the black robe she wore. "Impossible. Whoever you've been working with is looking in the wrong place. I'll find your lady for you, no problem."

Troi's right hand rested, relaxed, on the table top. Under almost translucent skin, Anton could see the branching of bluish veins. *It must be so very soft. Like spider cloth.*

"The rest of the clip contains a description and what little information I have on an alien that seems to be connected to her. I would like a similar search on it—anything you can find."

Troi nodded, her full lips spread in a knowing smile. "But you wouldn't be talking to me for a simple search."

Smart girl.

"You're correct. You have two days, three at the most, and you can't alert the authorities, or use official channels. You have to do this on your own."

She hissed softly. "Anton, that's a lot to ask."

"I know. But if anyone can do it…"

One thin brow arched. "Flattery doesn't work on me. What's this about?"

"I can't answer your question yet. My information is limited, my theory unproved. Until you accomplish this for me, and I do a little research of my own, I can't be sure of anything, except the less you know, the better."

Troi considered what he had said, her eyes narrowing as she thought. "That's why you didn't want to do this over the Net?"

"Precisely. Safer to meet face to face. I'm a regular here. They can be very discreet." He paused for a moment. "Troi…"

She met his eyes. He could feel her leg beginning to shake rhythmically under the table, a sure sign she was anxious to be out of there. Anton understood the feeling and it was part of why he liked Troi. They were both solitary creatures—she because of her looks and her allergies, and he because of the quirks his sensitivity had imbued him with. He had often thought, if things had been just a little different. If she had been less fragile, or he less closed off and set in his ways, maybe…

"You don't have to do this," he continued. "If you're busy, or you'd rather not, I'd understand."

She laughed again. "Please, Anton. Who else would be able to pull this off? No, I'll do it." She smiled and reached out toward him, but he shifted his arm away slightly. Her ghostly hand, so different from his own huge palms, hesitated, and then drifted back toward her lap.

"This is another favor for a friend, isn't it?"

She knew him so well. He nodded.

She sighed. "I will have Asja call you when I'm ready. We'll meet again, but I'll choose the place."

He inclined his head. "Of course."

She rose, pulling her hood up on the robe as she did so and affixing the filter veil across her nose and mouth. She turned to go.

"Troi."

She looked back at him, her eyes questioning.

I was wondering—would you like to have dinner with me before I leave for Polcar? A proper dinner, with no work involved? Just the two of us?

But in the end he said, "Thank you. Be careful," and watched her walk away.

III

"You're a real jerk, you know that Linkow?"

"Come on, Sonja. Tell me you're not the least bit suspicious."

Sonja threw him a brief, cutting glance as she sent the runner into another tight curve around a building.

"Let me ask you something, oh brilliant one," she said, hands on the panel. Sonja always drove on manual. A control freak, she couldn't bear to trust the runner's navigator. "If it's true what you say, that someone was trying to kill our Jane Doe, why beat her so bad and not finish the job?"

"Maybe they were interrupted." Linkow braced his hand against the dashboard, readying himself for another sharp turn.

"Five men got interrupted at the same time? And besides, in this town if you want someone dead, you don't rape and torture them first. You just kill them."

"Unless you wanted to teach them a lesson. Maybe that's why she was left out there—as a lesson to anyone else that got out of line."

"Got out of whose line?" Sonja arched her eyebrows at him. "And how does that tie in with the evidence that she'd just recently returned from an interstellar trip, and that she was attacked elsewhere and brought to where she was found? No, this isn't a local thing."

Linkow frowned, annoyed that she had been able to poke holes in his theory so easily. Helene had a habit of doing that. He went on instincts, she went on facts. They tended to finish their cases somewhere in the middle. "Okay, I'll accept that. It happened somewhere off planet. That doesn't mean the motives can't be the same. Someone went through a lot of trouble to drop her off outside Bradley. Does this smell like a simple gang rape to you?"

"Hell no," Sonja replied, speeding up as she hit a straightway, brightly lit buildings and the flash of passing headlights going by them in a blur. "I think your instincts are right. There's something else going on here. I just don't think the victim is to blame. Not yet, anyway."

"But it *feels* wrong, and you didn't meet her. She's no push-over. She's plenty dangerous herself."

Sonja barked a short laugh. "So she had a couple of nightmares and she threw a tray at you. Don't take this the wrong way, Linkow, but you're an asshole. Lots of people would like to throw a tray at you."

Linkow snorted. "Bitch."

"You're just mad because I'm making you think. Come on, Linkow. We've got to go where the evidence leads us. You can't lock up everyone you don't trust or like. Everyone we know would be in jail."

Something moved out into the street and she slammed on her brakes. "Shit!"

Linkow barely glanced at the big man in the dark coat standing on the glistening tarmac. "So what do you want to do? Start on the spaceport tomorrow? Or go see Desmond Obuki again, since he's our only lead until Jane Doe gets her memory back?"

Sonja lowered the window. "Hey, you stupid asshole! Watch where you're going next time, okay?"

Shaking her head, she sped past the man before speaking again. "I think Obuki might be a dead end. But we may as well pay him the follow-up visit, get it out of the way."

Linkow braced his feet against the floor as she swung down another street. "Hey, could I get home in one piece today?"

"Oh, please. Fucking coward. You never complained about my driving before."

"It's wet out here."

"I hear that happens when water falls from the sky. As I was saying before you started whining—"

The vidphone beeped. "Incoming call. Dr. Phillips for Sonja Helene."

"Put it through."

The small, wrinkled face of the lab tech filled the dashboard vidscreen. "Hey, sweetie. You wanted me to call if I finished the initial DNA sweep today."

"You're my man, Phillips. What did you get?"

"Bad news. Nothing. The samples were too degraded for accurate matches."

"Nothing?" Linkow couldn't believe it. *Shit, does anything ever go right in this frigged up city?* "Didn't you get any partial matches?"

"Sure. You want to go interview about 200,000 possible rapists, be my guest. *I'm* on a government paycheck here. You want I should forward the report to you now?"

"In the morning's fine. What about the Jane Doe?"

"Still working on it. We're on the military databases now. Should have something by tomorrow, if my assistant gets over her flu."

"Whatever you can do, as soon as you can do it," Sonja said, flashing a brilliant smile. "Later, Phillips. End."

Linkow gave her a sideways glance, his lip curling in derision. "You're kissing up to the lab tech now?"

"Well, if we relied on your charm, we'd get precisely nowhere." She pulled up in front of Linkow's housing unit, a drab building so old it wasn't even made of transperiwall.

Linkow looked up at the dark windows of his tiny apartment, thinking how shitty it was. How shitty everything was. "So, no match on the guys that raped her. That leaves us with our Jane Doe again."

"We've got the IR list down to twelve. After the Obuki visit, we could start at the spaceport. Maybe we'll have better luck there."

She touched the dashboard and Linkow's door retracted. "Now would you get the hell out? I've got a date."

"The asylums let you in? Their standards have dropped." He clambered out, his feet splashing into a tiny puddle. The air was colder than in the car. *Fucking rain.* Weather like this generally messed up his sinuses.

Sonja leaned over a little and smiled a beatific smile. "Better than staying at home and spanking it with Mrs. Hand and her five kids. Till tomorrow then."

He watched her pull off, swerving to avoid another runner that honked its distress.

IV

Michael stood outside the mess hall and stared at the door. He was just beyond the reach of the sensors, so it remained closed, an impassive metal panel.

You should get a move on. The bridge is not far now, *he thought. But he was thirsty. So thirsty.*

Had it really been only hours since the alarm had gone off?

You could get a drink. Get some energy. You won't be able to, pretty soon. *He took a hesitant step closer.*

But what if it's not empty? What if there's someone in there? What if...?

Enough, *he thought, and breached the distance to the sensors. The door slid open.*

Pristine. Just as he'd left it.

The small room glimmered under the stark white lights. Two low metal tables stood in the center with benches on either side. Abandoned plates of food rested in two places on one table; a third plate sat at the end of the table to his left. The food dispenser made a dark, square hole in the right wall. The touch panel on its left blinked the bright green "ready" light.

Against the left wall, beyond the tables and below a small digital clock, stood a truly incongruous thing for a space patrol unit. A compact silver mini-fridge stocked, he knew, with what Captain Marchand had considered indispensable. His favorite brand of spring water—

Trust me, no comparison to recycled water. You know what you're drinking when you sip that shit, right?

—and a bottle or two of wine. Orgalian wine. He wondered at first how Marchand had gotten his hands on alcohol. He hadn't wondered for long.

Michael stepped into the room cautiously, his senses on the alert for anything out of place. He shivered from the chill in the air. The room had been empty for some time; the temperature had dropped automatically to save energy. If he stayed long enough, it would kick back in. But he couldn't stay that long if he valued his life.

Michael stopped next to the table, reached out a hand to touch its cold surface. The reflection of his fingers wavered across the gray metal tabletop, closed around the stainless steel mug next to the plate. The bitter nut smell of coffee drifted upward as he tilted it to see the dark dregs within.

Coffee. Ganesh had been addicted to it. Wouldn't even hear of using decaf. And since it was the legal drug of choice in the Confederated Troops, he had his fill of it, every day...

"You got a problem?"

He started, looked around but even as he did so, he knew it was futile. There was nothing here but memories.

I was having dinner. Thinking about settling in early for the next shift. And Ganesh asked me that stupid question. As if it was me that started it. As if they hadn't closed me out from the very beginning.

A few scraps of egg remained on the plate on the next table. He'd been finishing up alone when Ganesh and Matka came in. He tended to eat alone, not because he enjoyed it, but because so few of the crew wanted anything to do with him after he'd made clear his position on their unauthorized stop-over. He had openly disagreed with Captain Marchand. Marchand had been nasty in his own underhanded way. Lots of double shifts and black marks for supposedly shoddy performance. But the crew—they shut him out. Ignored or ridiculed him for the entire week.

It didn't make him want to change his mind. But he'd become more and more aware that he'd been transferred to the kind of ship he'd dreaded his entire career. What the service called a junk ship. One that had been in deep space too long. It was a nation unto itself; the crew disdainful of rules when no one was around to see them broken. Anxious for any opportunity to kill time. Or make money.

Ganesh and Matka hadn't even looked at him when they entered. Just settled down to their meal with ribald jokes and loud laughs. He could feel the frost from the cold shoulder all the way across the room. But he didn't care. He didn't want to know any of them either. Not after what they'd done.

Dipping his head, Michael pushed the eggs around on his plate a bit, and sipped juice from his half-empty cup. The eggs tasted pretty good—not as powdery as sims usually were. But the juice. Well, he had yet to taste sim juice that went well with recycled water.

Ganesh and Matka smelled of sweat...and something else. They must have just come from the Brig.

Bastards. Fucked up low-lifes. *He'd stared at them without realizing* it. But Ganesh noticed, his hazel eyes narrowing. Slim and dark, he made up for his small size with quick reflexes and an even quicker temper.

"You got a problem?"

Michael shook his head, but of course, it wasn't enough to head off the argument.

"Then what is it? Looking for something else to write up, law man?"

As if I could. As if they'd believe me with all of you standing against me, giving your side of it. *Anger burned inside him.*

"Fuck off."

Ganesh stood as Matka turned on his bench and swept his lank, blond hair out of icy blue eyes.

"Fuck you and the high horse you rode in on," Matka said in his deliberate drawl.

"You know what your problem is?" Ganesh began. But Michael cut across him, unable to keep quiet any longer.

"My problem? My problem is very simple. And it has to do with you, and Matka and the rest of this goddamn crew. We shouldn't be doing this! Any of this! For a few bottles of wine, you all let that old man compromise everything we're supposed to stand for!"

"I swear," Ganesh ground out. "Either you shut that blow hole of yours or I'll shut it for you. You're just trying to protect your precious commission at our expense. Did you forget what we have to do to collect a few credits? I haven't seen my daughter in over a year!"

"And how will you look her in the face when you do see her again? Will you tell her what Daddy did while he was supposed to be out making the spaceways safe? How easy it was for him to sell his integrity?"

"Please," Matka scoffed. "Like you've got any. It makes you feel better to be up there, breathing all that righteousness air, but guess what—you're no better than us. You'll get your cut, which makes you an accomplice too."

"Fuck that!" Ganesh said, swinging one leg, then the other over the bench to stand free. "I'm tired of your whining. You want out, I'll give you an out."

The Comm sounded. Three tones—high alert.

"Warning, warning, weapons fire on Deck Three. Hull damage on Deck Three. All hands to battle stations. Repeat, all hands to battle stations. This is not a simulation."

They stared at each. The shock on Ganesh and Matka's face would have been comical if he wasn't feeling it himself. *Shit,* he had thought. *Oh shit... Deck Three. The brig. What if—what if the brig had been breached? What if—*

And then they had all run for the door. The fight had been forgotten. Would be forgotten for good now, with both Matka and Ganesh dead.

Michael put down the cup and went to the fridge. Cold air washed over his knees as he opened the door. The backlit shelves were crowded with blue water bottles and golden glass globes of Orgalian wine. His hand hovered over the water for only a second before he picked up the wine instead. Breaking the seal and pulling the easycork, he upended the bottle. Let the cool, lavender liquid wash down his throat. Tried to drown his memories in it; burn them away in the warm fire that started in the pit of his stomach as the alcohol hit. He lowered the bottle, a sweet, tangy aftertaste filling his mouth as he looked at the clock.

It was amazing, he thought, studying the yellow numbers. Only six hours. That was all. Six hours, and his entire life had changed completely. Yesterday, the worst thing he could imagine was being stuck here for the rest of his three month deep space tour. Now, the worst thing he could imagine stalked the corridors, looking for any sign of life to crush, destroy.

They had no one to blame but themselves.

Michael turned, bottle in hand, and raised it to his lips again before his hand froze. His eyes widened as, for the first time, he noticed the shadow under the table behind him.

CHAPTER 6

The children have taken to passing their downtime by learning obscure Earth history and languages. Subject Ru-ad has requested permission to develop a language for the older subjects based on Latin. He's planning to use it to keep their internal communications secret once they are hired offworld. I think it's a good idea to keep employers ignorant, and it should keep them occupied. They seem to be restless of late.
—*Diary entry dated May 5th 256 A.A. by Dr. Xavier Murdoch,*
Head of Education and Development, Phoenix Facility
(formerly Tec Solutions), Planet Orgala

I

Colin groaned and ran his fingers through his hair. Tiredness made his vision blurry, turned his thoughts into mush. Still, he didn't want to sleep. Indeed, he couldn't sleep. There was simply too much to do, and he hadn't even checked on Lex yet.

Light from vehicles on the streets below slid across his desk and onto the wall of the room before fading into the ceiling. He swung his chair around to look out of the large, untinted square of transperiwall behind him. The city glistened in a slight drizzle that was beginning to taper off. The control towers at both ends of the landing field were thin, blue spires, jabbing up at the dark evening sky like accusing fingers. He could see the flashing lights of spacecraft as they descended and ascended. Further out, to the west of the spaceport, the night sky glowed with the pale light of the atmosphere shields that protected the cluster of alien alternate habitats jokingly nicknamed No Man's Land.

Sighing, knowing he had to get back to work, he said, "Tint window." The view faded away and he turned his chair around again. Blinking, he tried to focus on his glowing comm panel, only to look up as the door to his office opened and Ranie Sangborn walked in.

She dropped into the chair in front of him, crooked an eyebrow at his cluttered desk, cleared a space for her touch panel and leaned back.

"You look like crap."

Colin sighed, rubbed his face vigorously for a moment. "Good evening to you too."

"Uh-huh. You're leaving, and right now," Ranie said, her voice firm, her blue eyes giving him their no-nonsense glare.

"I can't. I've got forms to file, the report to the Foundation to vet and—"

"And nothing. You'll have all those things to do in the morning too. Aren't you tired of sleeping in this cramped office?" She waved a hand around her. "Do you even remember what your apartment looks like?"

Not really, he thought, but didn't say. "I've got a lot on my plate, Ranie."

"That may be true, but you'll never get out of here if you keep thinking about work. You have to let it go sometimes."

Colin rested his chin on his hand and gave her a wry glance. "Pot calling kettle, Ranie? After all, what are *you* doing here at this hour?"

"Your fault, actually. I went to see your amnesiac this afternoon."

He sat up straight. "Lex? How did it go?"

Ranie wiggled her hand from side to side. "Better than I expected, but you're right. She's a tough nut to crack."

"You managed it, though." Colin smiled. "I knew you would."

"I wouldn't say I've cracked her. I wouldn't even say I've scratched the surface. I got my foot in the door, is all."

Colin frowned a little. "She didn't trust you?"

"It's complicated." Ranie leaned forward a bit. "Lex is in a lot of pain, and she's going through the usual anger and self-loathing, but she's also very guarded. I'm not so sure that's just the result of what she's been through. I'm starting to think her amnesia might be an extension of an unhealthy tendency to hold her emotions in. It's too early to come to any concrete conclusions yet, but definitely it will take a lot to get her to the point where she trusts me enough to open up."

"That's what I thought too. She interacts with me well enough, but the nurses say she hardly talks otherwise."

"That doesn't surprise me, given what I've seen. More than anything else, I think she wants to avoid letting anyone see how she truly feels. We started okay today. She talked about her feelings as well as I think she can at the moment. I'll see her again tomorrow and hopefully, we'll be able to make more progress."

"Anything I can do to help?"

Ranie's stare was direct and apologetic. "I'm not sure there's anything a man can do right now that you haven't already done."

Colin raised his eyebrows. "A man? What do you mean by that?"

"Colin, you do realize that she's in a bad place right now where men are concerned?"

He blinked, surprised. "But—"

"She hasn't said so directly, but I think Lex has serious trust issues with men in particular. She understands what you've done and are trying to do for her, but you should know that people on the whole are anathema to her at this stage.

"And men? Men are the devil, the reason why she's in this pain. As long as she sees you as her doctor, she can cope with your presence, but based on what I've seen and the way she dealt with the officer the other day, I think the less she deals with men right now, the better. She has some things to resolve before she can start interacting normally."

Colin was silent for a moment. "It makes sense, but I really didn't see it that way, you know?"

"That's what I'm here for." Ranie got up from her chair and came around the desk. "Don't worry about it. She's smart and tough. She'll move past this eventually. It won't be easy, though."

She moved behind Colin's chair and started to massage his shoulders with gentle fingers. Colin sighed and leaned back, grateful for her soft touch. His eyes drifted closed against his will. The scent of her perfume embraced him, sweet and light. Without warning, he found himself thinking: *Would Lex wear perfume? Would her hands be this light on me? Would her green eyes ever grow bright with a smile?*

Stop it. She's seventeen to my twenty-eight years. She's a patient and that's all there is to it.

"Like that?" Ranie murmured.

Colin nodded slightly and put all thoughts of his patient firmly away. "You know I do." Ranie leaned over him, her hands gliding down from his shoulders. He opened his eyes, twisted his head so he could see her. The mischievous glint in her blue eyes made him smile. Her braid tickled his face.

"What if someone walks in?"

Ranie frowned, considering his point. "You might be right." She stopped touching him and walked around the desk with a slow sensual movement. She drew her right index finger along the top of the desk as she went, stopping only to pick up her touch panel.

"I guess we should continue this somewhere a little more private. Your apartment, for example." She smiled sweetly at him and walked out of the office.

Colin laughed to himself. *All right. You win.* With a rueful shake of his head, he rose from his desk.

II

For long agonizing seconds, Michael stared. He lowered his arm, fingers trembling around the bottle he held. The light from the open fridge door had thrown into relief a dark, hunched shape under the table. His mind hit upon the worst before he told himself that he was being ridiculous. Otherwise, he would have been dead by now.

Do it. Before you lose your nerve. Michael placed the bottle on the fridge, took a few quick steps and bent over. He expelled his breath in a rush.

Fayn. Dr. Fayn. Fayn's eyes were wide open. He was curled on his side, his right arm outstretched and his left across his stomach, the fingers curved into claws. A grimace twisted blue lips, and his hair stood up in short gray spikes.

Overcoming his revulsion, Michael grabbed the cool, smooth cloth of Fayn's navy jumpsuit and dragged the rigid body out from under the table. A gentle whisper filled his ears as the cloth dragged on the floor. He kicked the fridge door shut with his foot and turned back to his task, examining the body with careful fingers. Rigor mortis had already set in, so he found it impossible to move the limbs much.

There wasn't a single mark of violence on Fayn's body. No surprise there. He had already guessed what killed the doctor from the grimace on his face, the claw of his fingers. The medic had recently been diagnosed with a heart problem of some sort, but had decided to serve out his last tour before retiring from active duty.

LEX TALIONIS

When it started to go bad, he must have hid in here. He had probably been terrified by everything that was going on outside—the screams, the fighting, the bloodshed—and his heart just gave out.

Michael stared at the old man's body for a long time before his shoulders started to shake. The tremor built in him until it escaped in the form of sputtering, almost girlish giggles and he was forced to cover his mouth with his hands to hold them in.

It was just so funny, he thought. So goddamned funny. Here was Fayn, crouched under a table like a little kid playing hide and seek. He could see the moment when the old ticker must have imploded. Could see him grab his chest, his eyes opening wide as he fell over on his side. A painful death, all alone.

"And you...you're the lucky one," he gasped at the cold, still form, tears beginning to run out of the corners of his eyes. "That's the funny thing. You're the lucky one. You cowardly fuck. You get to die of natural causes. And I get stuck with all this shit."

It was a while before he stopped laughing, before the tears stopped leaking from his eyes. He sat, breathing heavily, looking around him as if seeing the room for the first time.

When he glanced at the clock, he realized that almost ten minutes had passed. Shit. What the fuck was I thinking? *The answer came to him in grim tones.* You weren't thinking at all, idiot. Better move on. You've been in one spot too long now. *A thrill of fear coursed through him as he realized how easily he'd slipped. How easily he could have been discovered. He looked back at the body. It seemed to him that Fayn was no longer grimacing—he was smirking.*

You're losing it. You're fucking losing it.

He scrambled to his feet. Fuck yes, I'm losing it. So what? No one here cares anyway.

He laughed at that, a short bark that he bit off when he realized how loud it sounded.

No noise now. No noise. Maybe I'm going crazy, and maybe I'm not. But I'm going to get off this ship. I'm not going to die hiding under some fucking table. No way.

Michael looked at Fayn one last time. Smirk away, good doctor, but I know one thing. I'm still alive, and you're still fucking dead. So maybe you're not so lucky after all.

With that, he strode toward the door.

III

Lex waited for hours after Ranie left. Waited until she could feel the change in the rhythm of the building around her. The palpable slowdown that meant everyone had settled in for the night.

She sat up carefully, the muscles in her torso under her bandages stretching and pulling. Ignoring the soreness, she flung back the sheets and swung her legs over the edge of the bed. Her feet dangled, a naked, vulnerable white, aside from the cast on her right ankle. With slow movements, she inched her legs down onto the smooth floor. Transferring her weight to her left leg, she rose from the bed, wincing as her body protested and pain shot upward. Lex gritted her teeth, steadied herself with a hand on the bed, gathered her white hospital gown behind her and took a hesitant step.

The first step was the worst. *Come on, you can do this. You have to do this.* She drew her mind away from the pain, focused instead on the door. Colin had told her the alien—she could no longer call it an animal—stayed in a room next to hers. She wasn't sure which room, but she would find it, whatever it took. Limping in a creeping, steady rhythm, she made her way past the second bed and over to the door.

When it slid open, she stuck her head out and looked left. The corridor opened out to a nurses' station. Several people moved quietly back and forth between brightly lit consoles. To her right, the corridor continued around a corner. Doors were set at regular intervals along the hallway, but she only cared about the one next to hers.

Getting to the next room was nothing compared to what had gone before. After she entered, she leaned against the inside wall, breathing hard as the door slid shut next to her. The room was bright, stark. A bed stood in front of her. The alien crouched opposite it, under the holoprojector on the right wall, knees against its chest, arms encircling its feet. Its obsidian eyes met hers as she caught her breath and wiped sweat from her damp forehead. The room held a familiar smell, yet she could not figure out what it was exactly. Like so much else, the memory remained elusive. It occurred to her that she'd never caught any smell from this creature before.

"Don't just stare at me," she said, her voice weak and trembling a little from tension and exertion. "Talk to me!"

"Say." the creature left its mouth open, lifted its hand in an odd gesture that Lex realized was meant to be questioning.

"You know why I'm here." She pushed herself off the wall and half stumbled, half walked to the bed, pain jolting through her as she collapsed on it.

<<Know. Have much pain. Sorrow. Headfixer not help?>>

Lex's head began to ache, but she ignored it. "I don't know her, don't trust her."

<<Headfixer not harm.>>

"Not help either," she bit out. "How do you do this? How can you talk to me without speaking?"

<<Way of Oux. HurtOne first to mind/say.>>

Lex blinked, wincing at the intensifying pain in her head. "Are you saying I'm the first one to understand you?"

<<One other. Not here.>>

"Your keeper?" she ventured, but the alien didn't answer. "If Ranie can be trusted, why didn't you want me to tell her about you?"

<<Tell others. More machines. Oux hurt.>>

Lex's smile was grim. "You're not dumb, I'll give you that." She leaned forward. "Have you been in my mind? Do you know what I want?"

"You must go now."

"Must I? Isn't there another way? Something else that can be done?"

"No. No other way. You must go."

Lex gasped, grabbed her stomach. The memory had been sudden and sharp. The air smelled of wet vegetation, a brief whiff that passed as quickly as it had come. She looked up, her green eyes dark as jade.

"You? You woke me?"

Its mouth opened. "Yes." The voice was a sigh.

"How?"

<<Dream/feel past/mind. Use to shift/pull mind back to shell.>>

Her mind reeled. "A memory? You used my memories?"

"Yes."

Her breath caught. "Then you gave me that memory of the jungle."

"No." The alien made a whispering noise. <<HurtOne do this. Oux only heal.>> It raised its left hand and a waft of pale light shifted around its arm, spiraled its way to its wrist before puffing out, like smoke in the wind.

Lex felt wetness trickle out of her left nostril; she wiped her hand across her mouth, still trying to absorb what she had just seen. "What the hell are you?"

"Oux," it whispered and its small hands fluttered like butterflies. "Oux."

"But what does that mean?" Lex pushed, determined to understand. "How do you do this? Why did you wake—save me?"

<<*Oux, not mouth/say. HurtOne pain/ache. Must hush/still.*>>

"No!" she cried. "Talk to me, damn it! Don't you dare put me off! Don't you dare—"

Dizziness swept over her. Pain blossomed behind her eyes. She gasped as wetness flooded from her nose. She looked down to see dark red liquid sinking into the white gown like water into the sand of a desert. There was a pat, pat of drops hitting the floor. She tried to catch her breath, but couldn't. Raising her hand, she stared at the red streak across the back of her palm.

"Oh," she whispered, but the sound was very far off. Before her eyes, the room wavered then darkness closed off her vision.

IV

"So you never noticed anyone or anything else but the Elutheran?"

"No."

"Did you pass anyone getting to the alley?" Sonja asked, but Desmond Obuki shook his head.

"No one. I remember being relieved." He noticed Linkow's questioning look and added, "Less chance of an ambush."

"You worry a lot about things like that?" Linkow asked, letting a trace of sarcasm trickle into his voice.

Obuki gave no indication he'd noticed. "In that neighborhood, definitely." A slight, unusually tall Asian man, he had a double fold in his eyelids that spoke of either surgery or a mixed heritage. His glossy hair shone blue-black in the bright morning sunlight and his perfect tan contrasted beautifully with his high-necked ivory business suit. He had a broad, serious face; Linkow had yet to see him smile. He spoke with an accent that told Linkow he'd been born Earthside.

They were in a corner suite on the 110th floor of Combined Systems Inc., where Obuki was the Vice President in charge of mergers and acquisitions. The room was spacious, with plush red carpeting so thick, Linkow's shoes disappeared into it. Behind them, the rest of the office worked away in front of tiny consoles behind head-high cubicles.

"If it was that dangerous, why risk it?" Sonja asked.

"I had a very important meeting with an official from a subsidiary of Conway Enterprises," Desmond Obuki replied, the tone of his voice pointed. "You don't keep someone from Conway waiting unless you have a damn good reason. I did some time in the military and I know how to protect myself."

"So you scared the Elutheran off and took the victim to the Mathis Clinic where you made a report to the first officer on the scene. You left rather quickly though, didn't you?"

"I still had time to make my meeting. I gave the officer all the information I had and he told me someone would talk to me again. There was no need for me to stay." Desmond shifted in his chair and glanced at his comm panel. "Listen, I have other meetings today and another flight to catch. If there's nothing else...?" He raised his eyebrows.

"Of course. Thank you for your time." Sonja flicked a fingernail at the touch panel in her hand, turning off the recording device. "If you remember anything else, please call us." She handed him her ID chit. He took it with a brief, acknowledging nod. Linkow scoffed inwardly. *Like he'll really call us. These guys never have time for anything but meetings.*

Something bothered him though. Something Obuki had said.

"No problem," Obuki said to Sonja and rose to his feet to escort them out.

"So the woman actually survived?" he asked Sonja as they went to the door.

"Yes, you saved her life. She was badly hurt, but she'll make a full recovery," Sonja said with a quick smile. Ass kisser, Linkow thought.

And immediately remembered what had struck him about Desmond's statement. He spun on his heel just inside the door.

"Mr. Obuki, one more thing."

The man's expression was a mixture of exasperation and resignation, while Sonja shot him a quelling stare. Linkow ignored her.

"You said you were taking a shortcut to your meeting at JetWays. But you didn't take a taxi, did you?"

Desmond shook his head. "No. JetWays isn't that far from Bradley and I'd been feeling cramped after spending all day on a ship. I walked."

"So you're telling me you walked from the alley, with an unconscious woman, almost a mile to the Mathis Clinic?"

Desmond smiled again. "I'm in pretty good shape, but not that good. I used the runner of course."

"Runner?" Sonja said, her voice sharp. "What runner?"

"The one I found a little way from the alley. I thought it belonged to the woman. I parked it outside the Clinic, but I must have parked in the wrong zone, because when I came out it was gone—towed. I had to call a taxi to get to JetWays. I forgot to mention it to the officer when I was in the Clinic, but I called the station later and left a message about it for Officer Hexlan."

Desmond looked from one startled face to the other. "What?" he asked. "Didn't he tell you?"

CHAPTER 7

There are no flaws in the Pattern.
—*Message of the Will*
Book of the Seven Holies
Ancient Dak Scripture

I

Colin could not sleep. He lay awake well past midnight, staring up at the dim ceiling overhead. Beside him, he could hear Ranie's soft breathing as she slept; the clean smell of her soap filled his nostrils. She had a late shift tomorrow, and would sleep soundly, comfortable in the knowledge that she would not have to be up early. She'd promised she would see Lex as soon as she went in to work the next day.

Lex. Her face filled his mind's eye, surprisingly clear. Wavy dark hair, lips that softened into curves when she smiled...and green eyes full of pain and suspicion.

Stop it, he told himself. I have Ranie. A sweet, smart woman who understands me and doesn't ask for what I can't give. *Not to mention Lex is Conor's age, for crying out loud.*

Conor. Fun-loving, ambitious Conor. He'd checked his messages while Ranie took a shower, and had been surprised to find one from his brother. Conor's usually serious face had been all smiles. He shook dark blond hair—too long and slightly mussed—out of eyes the same shade as Colin's.

"Hey, bro. Just wanted to let you know I aced my finals today. Looks like I'll be graduating two years early. Yeah, yeah, I know you did it in three, but you didn't have any fun while you were at it.

"Call me when you get this. I want to know if you'd be okay with me doing my internship at Mathis. I'm considering focusing on human medicine, maybe neurosurgery. Mathis would be perfect, and you'd get to yell at me in person. Tell Ranie hi for me. Later."

He'd forgotten Conor knew about Ranie. It had been that long since he'd found the time to think about anything but work. Now Conor wanted to come to PortCity.

How much of that is his own decision, and how much of it is him emulating me?

Who knew? Conor had been following in his footsteps so long now it was a running joke between them. They had been inseparable until Conor decided to do his degree at his father's alma mater on the eastern continent of Maynor. Colin agreed and paid his way.

He'd been taking care of his brother from the moment he opened the door of his parent's house thirteen years ago and found two Troopers and his uncle Josiah standing on his doorstep. He took one look at his uncle's old, sad face and knew something terrible had happened.

"We need to speak with you, son," Josiah said, and Colin nodded, his throat tight, more aware than ever that his Mom and Dad were late coming back from dinner, something that never happened. He led them into the living room, glad that Conor was in bed with a cold, and sat quietly while they tried to tell him gently the kind of news no one should ever have to hear.

His father, Maxwell Mayfeld, so robust and alive when he left the house that evening, was already dead by then. Shot to death by a robber as he and his wife sat in their runner outside the restaurant, preparing to pull away. Janine Mayfeld had barely survived being shot in the head and was rushed to the nearest hospital.

Three days later, she died without regaining consciousness. The hospital she'd been admitted to first had no resident trained in human medicine, and the doctors had done their best to stabilize her before moving her to another institution. In the crowded conditions, she'd been put in a room with an injured alien that none of the hospital staff knew carried a dormant virus potentially fatal to humans. The resulting infection killed her. At least, that's what her death certificate said. Colin knew the real killer had been the robber—who was never found—and ignorance.

Until then, he'd wanted to be a psychiatrist, like his mother. But after her death, he'd decided that he never again wanted anybody to die like that. Colin's parents had left more than enough money for their children to live comfortably, and Josiah Mayfeld had been appointed their guardian until his death when Colin was nineteen and Conor just eight. At that point, Colin had gone from being the big brother to a father figure as well. The shift didn't change much. Colin had already graduated from med school and soon after completing his internship, he gathered enough funds to start the Clinic while still working at PortCity General. A year after that, he left to run Mathis full time.

Now here he was after working another hundred hour week, lying in bed with a wonderful woman, and finding his thoughts coming full circle to another woman, a girl really, in whose eyes he could see the ghost of the shell-shocked feeling that had settled inside him that evening, so many years ago.

That's probably why you're so attracted to her, because you can understand her pain—her loss—a little. That horrible tilting feeling of your whole world coming off its axis.

Sure. And maybe you could try being honest with yourself for a change. If you really saw her as a child, you wouldn't be lying here giving yourself a pep talk.

Next to him, Ranie sighed and stretched a leg out, kicking him under the covers. He turned his head to look at her and noticed the blinking yellow light on his panel. *The hospital.* He eased himself out from between the sheets, satiny material slipping against his legs as he tried not to wake Ranie. Padding across the carpet in his shorts, he collected the panel from the bedside table and went into the darkened living room. The door closed behind him and the lights came on bright enough to see, but not to hurt his eyes. He held the panel up and said, "I'm here."

The panel beeped. "Dr. Anton Slake for Dr. Colin Mayfeld."

Relief flowed over him. *Not a problem at the hospital then.* "Transmit."

Anton's dark brown face filled the screen.

"Colin. Good. You're still up."

"Yes, well, even when I try to sleep, it seems fate has other ideas." Colin settled into a chair. The soft material grabbed and held him like hands.

Anton smiled briefly. "Sorry about that."

"What's up? Anything for me on—what we discussed yet?"

"No, not yet. I'm working on it and I should have something for you soon. However, I was wondering if you had any objection if I came by the Clinic tomorrow before I went in to work. I have those dataclips you asked me for."

Translation, he wants to see Lex. Colin shrugged. "Don't see why not. I—"

The panel sounded two quick tones. "Incoming call from Mathis Clinic for Dr. Colin Mayfeld. Designation, urgent."

Shit. "Anton, hang on a moment, I'm getting another call."

Anton nodded and Colin instructed the panel, "Hold Anton, transmit Mathis."

The head nurse came up on screen, looking grim. "Dr. Mayfeld, it's Lex. She had a blackout and she's lost a lot of blood. Dr. Exley's examining her now."

A cold feeling settled in the pit of his stomach. "Tell him I'm coming in and I'll want to consult with him as soon as I arrive."

"Yes, doctor." The screen went blank.

"Transmit Anton?" asked the panel.

"Yes."

Anton took one look at his face and said, "What is it? What has happened?"

"I'm not sure. The hospital just called about Lex. I'm going in to see her now."

Anton tapped a finger against his lower lip. "I might not be able to see you tomorrow morning after all."

"At this point, I can't say if that will be possible." *I'm just hoping she'll be okay…*

"No matter. Find out if your patient is all right. Call me back later and let me know when I can drop those clips off."

"It may be quite late, or very early. You sure you want me to call?"

Anton smiled briefly. "You forget, I sleep less than you do."

··· — — — ···

"Take a look." Dr. Exley waved a hand at the console. Colin bent down a little as he studied the holo scan of a skull with the brain exposed while it turned slowly above the touch-panel of the console. A lock of his blond hair fell into his eyes and he pushed it back. The image of the skull, with its gray brain and white bone appeared sharp and real as a severed head in the semi-darkness of the tiny room. Five other consoles stood around them in a rough semi-circle. Only one of them glowed with a blue ready light.

"It looks fine to me."

"Precisely," Exley answered, folding his arms across his broad chest. A short, powerful man, Exley ran double marathons for a hobby, sometimes taking his vacation time to compete in the South islands of Serron or even offworld. He was also the best neurologist in PortCity.

Colin asked cautiously, "And that's good, right?"

"Good, bad and remarkable."

"Explain." Colin glanced across at Exley.

"Well, there's no trauma to the patient's brain…"

"Lex," Colin corrected. Exley gave him a considering glance before continuing.

"There's no trauma to *Lex*'s brain from the initial attack or from today's incident, no indication that she's been physically hurt in any way."

"That's great news." *The nurses said she was with the alien when she collapsed, but maybe it didn't have anything to do with what happened.*

"Yes, well, the problem is that isn't possible. We don't know what caused the bleed. There are no signs of hemorrhaging in her brain. Her blood pressure's never tested anything other than normal, but there's a good chance, with that much blood, that a vessel or two burst. Only there's no indication of that either. There is no indication of anything. These scans show a perfectly healthy, undamaged brain. We scanned her several times, with several different machines and got the same results."

Colin frowned. "So you have no idea what happened."

"No," Exley said flatly. "That's the bad part—at this point, there's nothing to say it can't happen again. She's physically fine now, but without a clear idea of what caused the blackout or the nose bleed, I can't promise you she'll stay that way."

Just as long as she doesn't die on me again. Colin sighed. "So what's the remarkable part?"

Exley turned to the console. "Full body scans on patient Lex, please."

"Loading now," the computer replied in neutral feminine tones. The skull disappeared, replaced by a frontal view of a naked female— Lex. Exley touched the panel, and the computer focused on several key areas, dissolving away layers of skin and muscle to display bone.

Colin studied the images for a few moments. His eyes widened. *What the hell?*

"These can't be right," he said looking up at Exley. The neurologist shook his dark head.

"No, they shouldn't be right. However, I can assure you that they are completely accurate."

"But this is—unbelievable."

"My sentiments exactly."

II

How could a small airlock look so beautiful?

Adrenaline flooding his body, making his heart beat faster, Michael stepped in front of the entrance to the bridge, breaching the sensors.

The door remained closed.

Shit. Of course. *Marchand would have locked it down as soon as he realized what was happening. He placed his hand over the key pad and his palm tingled briefly as a DNA sample was taken. A small tone sounded.*

"Identify."

"Acting Lieutenant Michael Flax Zorida," he said, looking around him nervously. Don't be ridiculous. It's just the door. It's not that loud.

"Acknowledged."

His breath was a harsh outflow. Hurry and open up, damn it!

"Acting Lieutenant Zorida, please be advised that security protocol has been changed as per Captain Marchand's instructions—"

His heart tripped. No…no…

"—please insert override key and confirm authorization."

Fuck! Oh, you fucking asshole! You son-of-a-bitch!

He leaned his head against the cold, hard metal of the airlock and bit back tears.

To have come this far…He raised his hand and slammed it down next to the key pad, smearing blood on the sharp edges of the airlock.

"Awaiting authorization, Lieutenant Zorida."

"Cancel," Michael choked out. A tone acknowledged his instruction and the computer fell silent.

Get it together. Come on. You have to think. You have to find a way around this.

As hard as he tried to tell himself it wasn't about him, that Marchand had just tried to ensure only crew would have access to the bridge, the bitter taste of disappointment in his mouth and the terrible fear pounding in his chest, would not let him focus past an inescapable fact.

To get into the bridge, he would need the override key.

The same key that hung around Marchand's neck as he lay dead on Deck Three, next to the brig.

III

Lex looked up as the door opened and Colin walked into the small scan room. He paused for a moment, the door sliding shut behind him.

"You're up," he said in an odd tone that she couldn't quite place. She spun on the cold metal scan table, swinging her legs around so she could face him, relishing the lack of pain.

"I feel much better."

Colin slid his panel into the deep pockets of his white coat as he came toward her. His movements were careful, measured. Too much so. He's nervous, she thought. Why? What's changed?

Everything. You know it. You can feel it.

As if he'd read her thoughts, Colin said, "You should. You are better."

"But I passed out, didn't I?"

"You did, but your scans came back normal." He paused. "All your scans came back normal."

She met his gaze, searched his blue eyes for confirmation. He did not look away. Her breath caught slightly.

I knew it. As soon as I woke up, I knew it. "I'm—"

"Cured. Bones knitted, bruises healed, everything. Overnight." He shook his head. "I've never seen or heard of anything like it before. After yesterday's scans, you had another week to go before I'd let you out of here. Today, you're in perfect health. It might be your own immune system since you have been healing fast." He paused. "But then again, it might not."

You mean it might be the alien. But what's really bothering you is that you can't explain it. I don't care, though. Because it means that I'm finally free, that I'll finally be able to...

"Leave," she said, her voice just above a whisper. *Is that what you want?* came the sly thought. *Is it really? Because you'll be leaving the only person you can trust behind too, you know.*

"You want me to leave?" he said, surprised.

"No. I mean, I'll be able to leave now."

He nodded. "Yes."

Good, said a tiny, nasty voice inside her. *After everything he's done for you, all the concern he's shown for you, you've lied to him. He doesn't know about the Oux; he doesn't know about your memories. He certainly doesn't know that you've thought about getting well and leaving here—so you can find the men who hurt you and make them feel the pain you felt.*

He doesn't need someone like you around. Someone who'll only tell him lies and cause him trouble.

But I don't want to lie to him. I just can't tell him about the (woman on the holoshow) *Oux yet. I have to know more. I have to know the whole story before I go to him. I have to sort things out in my head. I'm tired of being half a person to him and everyone else.*

"I can go outside? See the sky?" Lex didn't try to hide the relief in her voice. She'd worked hard not to think of the outside over the past few weeks, knowing if she thought about it too much, she would go stir crazy. But now…

Colin smiled and for a moment, she was struck by how handsome he was. *Better get off that track. He's your doctor and you're just a kid to him. A patient he cares about, nothing more.*

"Yes, you can see the sky," he answered. "And anything else you'd like, I guess. It will be up to you now."

She sighed and savored the promise of freedom. *All well and good, but what am I going to do? I've got no money, no family, no identity. The only person who cares whether I live or die is my doctor. Where the hell am I going to go?*

"I'd like it if you didn't leave at once, though," he said slowly. Lex looked at him, surprised.

"Why? If I'm not sick, why stay here?"

"You can't just rush back out into the world after what your body's been through, especially when it might be a world you don't even know. There are still issues we need to address."

She raised an eyebrow. "Like?"

"You still want me to give you those neuro and intellect tests, don't you?"

She thought about it and then nodded. "I guess so. It'll be even more important now. I have to know what I'm capable of for when

I go"—*after the men who hurt me*—"out there. What I can do." She smiled briefly. "I might have to get a job real soon if we don't find any of my family."

"Exactly. My friend Anton called me earlier, wanting to know if he could see you tomorrow. Are you up for that?"

Shit. More exams. She waved a hand. "If I'm going to get poked and prodded, might as well get it all out of the way."

"Then there's Ranie. You have another appointment with her."

Lex shook her head. "Uh-uh. No way am I staying here just so that she can psychoanalyze me."

"It's for your own good. You know that. If you'll just give me another day or so, I can arrange with Ranie to find a place for you to stay until we get you back on your feet."

She looked at him suspiciously. "I'm not staying with her, if that's what you mean."

"No, of course not. She works with a couple of shelters here. I'm sure if I ask, she'll find a bed for you at one of them. I will expect you to have at least one more session with Ranie." The look on his face told her he knew exactly what he was doing. "A fair trade off, don't you think?"

She shook her head, smiling slightly. "You sure you're a doctor? Because you're really good at this arm-twisting thing."

"I'm not letting you out of my sight until I'm satisfied you're going to be okay."

For a silent, endless moment, their eyes met. She felt a vague sense of astonishment. *Am I reading him right? He...likes me?* An emotion made her shiver—surprise mixed with

(*panic*)

uncertainty. Then he looked away and she decided she was being ridiculous. She took a deep breath and considered what he'd said instead. "Colin, is the alien okay? You didn't—"

"It's fine," he reassured her. "The head nurse didn't know what to think at first, when it dragged him to where you'd collapsed. We just kept it in its room until we could be sure you were out of danger."

Thank God they didn't take it away. Relaxing a little, Lex stretched her arms above her head, enjoying the pull on her little used muscles before she lowered her hands. "Okay, I'll accept your offer, but on one condition. Wherever you place me, they have to be comfortable with the alien. I don't think I want to leave without it."

Colin nodded. "I understand. I'll see to it." He smiled again, looking relieved. "You're doing the right thing, Lex."

But she was no longer listening. One word came through to her, hit her like a physical force; an echo that surged over her like waves. She gasped a little, squeezing her eyes shut. *Lex. Lex. Law. Law.*

Lex Talionis.

Law of revenge.

"…A system of justice practiced widely during the Middle Ages on Old Earth, it works on the eye for an eye, tooth for a tooth principle. Remember it, children. It formed the basis for what we do here today…"

"…Here comes Gilene Conway herself, CEO of one of the most powerful companies in the Universe, Conway Enterprises, in a rare public appearance…"

"Lex!"

Her eyes flew open. She realized that Colin had grabbed her arms; his hands were cool, his palms smooth on her bare skin. "Colin. I—"

"You went away there for a second. What happened? Did you feel faint?"

She shook her head, allowing a slight dizziness to pass. The first voice she'd heard resonated in her head. A man's voice, speaking in hard, authoritative tones. Familiar tones. *Who the hell was it? Who did I remember?* A terrible feeling coiled tight in her stomach. *It's important. I've remembered something very important. So why am I so afraid?* She forced herself to move past that, to calm herself.

Why, when Colin tells me—when I know*—I can speak Latin, did I block out the meaning of those words? And what the hell does Gilene Conway have to do with any of this?* She searched inside herself for something, anything, but all she felt was a vague disquiet. A sense that something about the woman in the black dress was…wrong.

"I'm fine," she said, her tongue suddenly feeling heavy and dry. "I'm just tired."

"Of course." Colin let go of her arms. "That was exactly what I was about to say. You need to rest now. Tomorrow morning's going to be very busy for you."

She nodded, thinking, *You have no idea. I have a lot of questions. One way or another, in the morning, I start getting answers.*

··· —— ···

By the time she'd returned to her room, Lex was tired, but there was something she wanted to do, something that had occurred to her on her way back from seeing Colin. When Dr. Exley examined her, he had used the holoprojector in a way she had never seen before. He used it to search for information on possible causes for her condition. Holoprojectors were more than vidscreens; they were libraries as well. So she waited until the nurse had gone and settled herself at the foot of the bed.

"Holoprojector. Network query mode." A tone sounded and the image of a middle aged, dark haired woman, dressed in a shimmering pale blue business suit, appeared.

"Ready," it said with a surprisingly realistic movement of its lips.

"Who is Gilene Conway?"

The woman clasped her hands in front of her skirt. "Gilene Conway is the main benefactor of the Mathis Clinic."

"In what way?"

"She provides funds for the operation of the Clinic by way of grants from the Jason Conway Memorial Fund."

"Do you have any specific or personal data on Gilene Conway?"

Another pause. "Gilene Conway was born on Terra. Date withheld. She is believed to be in her late fifties. She is the CEO and President of Conway Enterprises, the fourth largest company in the known galaxies. Her education includes several degrees and doctorates in intergalactic corporate governance, politics and linguistics.

"She first achieved the post of CEO during the Colonial Troubles, when Jason Conway, her younger half-brother and the sole heir to Conway Enterprises, was called to serve in the DiploCore. Upon his return, she stepped down and allowed him to reclaim his post. Eight years later, Jason Conway, his wife, Falon Conway, his only child and two of his cousins were killed in a yachting accident in Whiteway Sector. Gilene Conway was returned to the CEO position which she still holds. Her personal net worth is many times more than all of Terra's economies and offworld holdings combined. She is unmarried."

Strange. I don't know her, but we have a lot of the same interests. But she shook that off. She had seen Gilene Conway and the woman did not look familiar. In fact, nothing the holoprojector had said sounded familiar. *But would I remember just because I heard something I once knew?*

"Is that all the information you have on Gilene Conway?"

"Yes."

She thought for a second. "Please provide any personal or specific data on the Conways as a family."

The holoimage wavered as if a hand had passed over it. "This unit is not equipped to handle such a request."

"Explain."

"This unit is a general search engine based on the Mathis Clinic Network. It is not linked to outside networks with more specific data. The Conway family is made up of several hundred individuals, making the volume of information too heavy for the present network database capabilities. Any information on these individuals is highly restricted and not available to this unit at this time."

Damn it. "Where can I get such information?"

"There are many libraries, network information sites and government centers devoted to public information on the Conways and Conway Enterprises. A search in any one of these areas should yield accurate results."

Lex considered this and sighed. "Holoprojector query mode, off."

The image disappeared and she stared into the space it had occupied, refusing to let her tired eyes close.

So I can't get the information here. Fine. If I do find a shelter when I leave, I'll have to do some more searches on Gilene Conway.

But why? Why am I so interested in her?

I don't know. But I have nothing to lose. Nothing else to do.

She climbed into the bed, planning to lie still just until she felt strong enough to go in search of Oux. Her head barely hit the pillow before she was asleep and dreaming.

Of a cool, green place. Water dripping everywhere and the scent of rich earth and vegetation. She is facing a path where overhanging leaves shade a nook beneath a tree. A form is hidden there. A man. But it's not the same man who was here before. The body is the same, yet the essence she feels is different. Very different.

"I'm sorry."

The same deep voice, but not the same. She is confused. "For what?"

"Hurt...hurting you."

There is a familiar hesitance. She tries hard to pin it down.

"You hurt me?"

"Yes. I did not realize how...undeveloped you were."

And it dawns on her, with the brilliance and suddenness of the last second of sunrise. "Oux? Oux is it you?"

A pause. "Yes."

His word is a stone in the lake of her mind; shock ripples through her. "How?"

"You are dreaming. I can enter. Without hurting you so badly."

"You mean my nose bleed? You think you're responsible for that?" She smiles. "Don't worry about it. I'm fine. Completely cured."

"I know. I healed you." A very human sigh drifts out to her. "The damage was too great. I did not realize that you were not as strong as I hoped. I spoke with you too long. Your mind...broke."

Her breath catches, her lungs fill with rich, scented air. He was responsible. And her recovery—it hadn't been due to her own genes. It had been him fixing a terrible mistake. "You almost killed me, didn't you?"

"Yes. But it will not happen again. I will speak with you this way, or... out loud you call it? Until I'm finished growing—" He breaks off.

She persists. "What? Growing what?"

"It's not important. I'm forgetting myself."

"I find that hard to believe, somehow." She tilts her head a little, takes a step forward. Leaves rustle.

"Stop. Come no closer."

She freezes. "Why?"

"This is not my face. You are not—you cannot—"

She understands. "I'm not ready to see who you are?"

"No. You will remember this conversation. I have made sure of this. To know all too soon would...destroy you. Your mind is not ready to remember."

"I want to remember. Doesn't that count for something?"

"No. You must be patient."

She snorts, shakes her head. "You know, it's strange, hearing you talk so well. You're taking things from my mind again, aren't you? But if you could heal me all this time, why didn't you do it before all of this? Were you afraid you'd attract too much attention to yourself?"

"Yes."

She frowns. "Yes to which question?"

A sigh. "It is almost time for me to go. I must warn you."

"Warn me?"

"Yes," and the sound of his voice changes, seems disturbed. Fainter. "You must be careful, you must prepare yourself. He is coming for you."

Fear thrills through her even as she asks, "Who? Who's coming for me?"

"Your enemy. The Angry One."

Frustration fills her. "Can't you be a bit more specific?"

"No. It is not my place. I can only warn you. The time approaches quickly and his anger is very deep. Keep me by your side. Trust me. I will help you, when the time comes."

His voice is very faint now; her sight wavers, growing misty, everything blurring into a mixture of green and shadows. She feels herself slipping away.

"Why is he angry? What does he want from me?"

Far away now. "To hurt...kill you."

Darkness seeps into her vision from the right, a hand closing over her eyes. She shouts, "How do I stop him?" but it is too late. Blackness falls and she is caught in it, like a fish in a net, turns and twists and finally drifts in it for a while, a frond of seaweed in a dark sea...

...before she opened her eyes, awake.

Thoughts spun through her mind as she stared up at the pale ceiling, dimly visible in the glow of the room's lowest illumination setting. She remembered the dream, the Oux, the way the vegetation—

that's it. That's what I remembered before Ranie came in—was it only yesterday? That's what I

—smelled; the way the air surrounded her. But most of all, she remembered the warning. Puzzled over it.

Who, she wondered? Who was coming for her? Who wanted to kill her?

"Why do you want to kill me?" she whispered to herself.

But the room had no answer.

IV

"Chief Security Officer Poujade is in a meeting right now. He might be busy for some time." The secretary smiled apologetically but couldn't quite meet Sonja's eyes. Linkow noted that the man's hands were folded together on the slick metal surface of his desk as if he were trying to restrain himself from fidgeting.

Busy for some time, or just long enough to get rid of us?

"Does he understand that we're on Trooper business here?" Sonja asked.

"Yes, and he regrets that he has to—"

"If he was in a meeting, why didn't you tell us that when we called to say we were on our way?" Linkow broke in.

"He wasn't *in* a meeting then." A note of frustration crept into his voice. "Maybe if you'd let me reschedule?"

"You're obstructing two officers in the performance of their duties," Sonja said. "Either you get him out of that meeting or you direct us to someone who can explain why Spaceport Security didn't see fit to report a stolen runner to us."

For a second, the man could say nothing. "I'm not—"

"Drake," a brusque growl broke in. The secretary looked at his panel.

"Sir?"

"Send them in."

"Yes, sir."

Poujade, an eight foot Algaran with the dark blue stripes of age banding his short neck, did not stand as they entered his small, spotless office. The metal walls shone with a purple tint that complimented the lilac carpet. On the left wall, a bank of monitors displayed holo scenes from all over the Spaceport. The flickering light from the images stopped just short of the broad metal desk the Algaran sat behind.

Two conform chairs stood in front of the desk, one of them occupied by a slender, efficient-looking man dressed in a dark blue uniform. Linkow glanced at the man, surprised at the presence of another Trooper.

"Lieutenant Sonja Helene and Lieutenant Marakesh Linkow to see you, sir," Drake said, and Linkow noted how he studiously avoided looking at the Trooper as he spoke.

"That will be all, Drake."

Poujade waited till the man left, then gestured to the empty chair next to the Trooper. "If one of you wants to sit—"

"We're fine standing," Sonja said. The Algaran made a short dismissive growl. He hasn't introduced us to the Trooper, Linkow thought, and knew it was not an oversight. He could feel the officer studying them both and steeled himself not to look in his direction.

"You want to tell us what the hell that was all about?" Linkow said. *The best thing about talking to Algarans. No need to be polite.*

"I was in a meeting," Poujade said. "*You're* the ones that should explain to me what was so fucking important."

"Unless you're deaf," Sonja replied, "you heard us out there. We have impounded one of your spaceport runners. It was found at the scene of a crime and we suspect it was used to transport the victim. Yet we have had no reports of missing runners in our daily incident reports from your department. You want to explain that, Poujade?"

"We sent you everything we had. It must have been left out by accident." Poujade's tone was unconcerned, but Linkow noted how the Algaran's tiny black eyes studied them carefully.

"Bullshit," he said.

Sonja threw him a warning glance before saying, "Well, that's easily rectified. Just fill us in now so we can continue with our investigation."

The Algaran paused and his gaze darted across to the Trooper. The Trooper did not meet the CSO's gaze, but he leaned back in his chair and the fingers of his right hand tapped against the metal desk once, twice, before stilling again. *They're holding something back from us.*

"And if I can't?" Poujade said. Sonja raised her eyebrows at that.

"It's called obstruction of justice, Poujade, and you know it as well as I do."

"What the hell is it you can't tell us?" Linkow asked, coming forward to rest his hands on the back of the conform chair. The smooth, malleable plastic cover gave slowly beneath his fingers like wet sand. "So you lost a runner, so what? We're not here to make you look bad. We want to find out who took your runner and maybe catch some rapists."

"As they say on Terra," the Trooper said suddenly, "that's the tip of the iceberg, Officer Linkow." His voice was measured, but firm. Linkow looked at him and noticed the tiny gold emblems that decorated the seal strip on the left side of the man's jacket. An animal in full flight, bushy tail trailing behind it. *Shit. A Fox. He's IU.* And that disturbed Linkow, because the Foxes didn't investigate just any case. *If he's here, there's a much bigger fuck-up somewhere behind all this. And it involves the Troopers.*

"And you are?" Sonja asked.

"Lieutenant Commander Jamal E. Vernon of the Trooper Investigative Unit." The man studied Linkow while he answered Sonja. His hazel eyes reminded Linkow of chips of glittering stone. His dark brown hair was neatly trimmed and parted on the left.

"Nice to meet you," Sonja said. "You want to tell us what the hell you're doing in the middle of our investigation?"

"Actually," Vernon said, "you're in the middle of mine."

Something clicked in Linkow's head. "You told the CSO to leave that report out, didn't you?"

The Lieutenant Commander looked him over as if seeing him for the first time. "You're smarter than you look."

"And you withheld information vital to an ongoing criminal investigation. The physical evidence in that runner is gone now,"

Sonja pointed out. "Is that the kind of method the IU sanctions?"

"I don't think I have to explain the IU to you, *Lieutenant*."

Oh, he's good. Reminding us just how far down the pecking order we are.

"You can't seriously think we're going to back off because you tell us to?" Linkow said. "We do have a job to do, whether you like it or not."

"Right. You were tracking some rapists." Poujade gave a short growling laugh. "You have no idea how fucking irrelevant that is."

"It's not irrelevant to the victim," Sonja shot back. Her black eyes had narrowed to slits and the spikes of her short, dark hair seemed stiff with the strength of her anger.

"Perhaps," Vernon said. "However, I'm warning you. This is a matter of DiploCore Security and I can only tell you what's not classified."

"Spare us the espionage shit," Sonja said. Vernon made a slight acquiescing motion of his head.

"We've been looking for the runner you found for days now. It's one of two that disappeared from the Spaceport several weeks ago. The first runner was found abandoned in an obscure sector just inside the Spaceport last week."

"Well, maybe if you'd informed us, we might have found the second one sooner," Linkow interjected. Vernon made a brief downward movement with his hand, as to cut him off.

"Not your jurisdiction, and you know it. Oversight and Spaceport Security are responsible for all ports of call. They assigned the case to a colleague of mine, but he was delayed by the Destra Spacelane strike. I was assigned three days ago. My flight from Polcar landed only yesterday. Before that, Oversight informed Spaceport Security that unless more crimes that were…comparable to what happened occurred again, it should withhold all information from outsiders until they'd had a chance to decide on a course of action. You found Poujade and me in the process of figuring out the best way to share information with the Department here."

I'll bet, Linkow thought. *Those arrogant bastards at Oversight. This is their screw up and they endangered the entire population just so they could cover their ass.*

"We had no idea that the missing runner had already been linked to another case. I will tell you it's impossible that my lone suspect gang-raped your victim. However, if what you say is true, and I have no doubt it is, then you will only be able to continue your case as part of my larger investigation and perhaps find the link between your attackers and my murderer."

"Murderer?" Sonja echoed.

"Yes," Vernon said. "Somewhere in PortCity is a cold blooded murderer with unmatched skill and strength and I think the only thing that has kept your population safe is the single-mindedness of its mission."

It. So the killer's probably not human. "What mission?" Linkow bit out.

Vernon paused before answering. "To find and kill the last survivor of a massacre. The only living witness to the crime."

"Linkow," Sonja said, her voice taut, "tell me he didn't just say that HQ let some psychotic killer loose in PortCity *and didn't bother to inform us.*"

"We didn't want to keep our own out of the loop, but you must understand—anything the precincts knew, the press could find out," Vernon said in a tone so calm, Linkow's fist itched to hit him. Out of the corner of his eye, he saw a self-satisfied sneer spread across Poujade's face. Through the window behind the Algaran's flat head, he glimpsed a slender spacecraft rising slowly, like the finger he longed to give the CSO.

"It would have meant panicking an entire city needlessly."

"Needlessly?" Linkow bit out. "People are dead. I'd say panic is a pretty good response to that."

"Not if we are able to prevent another massacre without tipping anyone off to the first."

"You mean tip off the killer."

Vernon inclined his head.

"So you want to fill us in on your case, or do we just continue to bump up against each other in the dark while the suspect slips out the door?" Sonja asked.

"You can start with this so-called massacre. When and where it occurred, who died. You know—the stuff you usually put in an APB." Linkow's smile dripped the sarcasm of his words.

"Lieutenant, as I said before, when it comes to ports of call and the spacelanes, what HQ chooses to do and who they choose to inform is up to them. You're in no position to second-guess them."

"And you're in no position to take the high ground," Sonja said. "When and where, Major?"

Vernon leaned back in his chair and crossed his legs at the ankle.

"Eighteen days ago, on a deep space patrol unit—the *DSS Meridian*. Eight people were mutilated and killed. The *Meridian* limped here on autopilot and was admitted to a Quarantine Bay. My guess is—"

A tone interrupted him. Vernon sat forward and reached into his pocket. The palm-sized panel he pulled out had a shifting rainbow of colors running across its flat screen. Vernon tapped it once, studied the message and looked up, his face a mask.

"I must take this." He stood and strode past Sonja into the hallway.

She threw a glance at Linkow as the door closed. "Is he for real?"

"Fucked if I know what he is, besides some HQ ass-kisser," Linkow replied.

Poujade grunted. "You speak ill of your superior. I will never understand this human failing."

"Yeah, well," Linkow said, "it beats stabbing them in the back, like Algarans usually do."

The door opened again and this time, Vernon remained in the doorway. Sliding the panel back into his pocket, he said, "I'm sorry, but I have urgent business to attend to. Poujade, I'll meet with you tomorrow."

The Algaran nodded even as Sonja said quickly, "Oh, hell no."

"Lieutenant." The anger in his eyes brooked no argument and killed the words in Linkow's throat. "I will contact you both tomorrow. We'll compare notes and I will even take you on a tour of the crime scene, but we won't be having any further discussion today. If you wish to continue your meeting with Poujade, it's up to you, but I'm leaving."

Without a second glance, he turned and did just that.

Linkow looked at Sonja. "Now what in the fuck was *that* all about?"

"I have no idea," Sonja replied, still looking at the closed door. "But we'll find out tomorrow. Because come hell or high water, that's when that bastard is going to stop stalling and start talking."

Without another glance at the CSO, they left the office. As they passed the secretary's desk, Linkow noticed Drake trying to ignore them, his eyes firmly fixed on his panel.

He stopped and waited till Drake reluctantly acknowledged his presence. "I have a question for you."

The man looked nervous. His eyes refused to rise above the level of Linkow's chest. "Officer?"

"Did you hear Major Vernon answer his panel when he came out of the office a few minutes ago?"

Drake tried not to look alarmed and failed.

"Look, I'm not here to get you in trouble. I'm just wondering where the Major went off to."

The man looked doubtful.

"If you help me, I owe you a favor. I know a few people who might be able to get you a better job than a shit post under an Algaran. Am I right?"

Drake looked nervous, glancing over his shoulder at the closed door. "He's not so bad."

"Compared to what? You think you'll ever get out from behind that desk? You work under an Algaran, you stay under them. You want a future in a posting a human can get ahead in, you help me out. I have contacts, you have information. What do you say?"

Drake hesitated a moment longer. "I didn't hear most of it. He was standing too far away."

"Anything you can tell me would help."

"I think it was a hospital or something. It was about a patient who woke up. He got really upset because no one told him. He said he'd be right there. That's all I heard."

Linkow forced himself to smile. "Thanks. I'll call you with those names tomorrow."

Drake glanced at the door once more. "I look forward to it."

CHAPTER 8

Truth is the most expensive commodity there is.
Is it any wonder it's so hard to find and even harder to recognize?
—*Gilene Conway, President of Conway Enterprises*
Address to the DiploCore (297 AA)

I

Andraju shifted the panel in his right hand to his left and keyed open the lock to his temporary home, a white, plastic, pre-fab dome. The circus had set up camp on a cliff near the sea and behind him waves struck the rocks below with a rhythmic crash and ebb. The smell of sea salt and damp sand surrounded him. Andraju's mind was distracted as he calculated the night's take—which was why he didn't sense anything out of the ordinary until the door closed behind him.

It was then he caught the subtle scent of damp fabric, and beneath it, a whiff of human sweat. But by then a hand had caught him by the throat and shoved him against the wall next to the entrance. The tiny dwelling shivered and his traveling cot creaked. Andraju tried to bring his arms up and realized it was too late. He could not move a muscle.

"Nice to see you, Andraju. You certainly took your time. It must have been a good night."

The smooth, baritone drawl belied the firm grip on Andraju's neck. The man was tall for a human, a foot shorter than Andraju's seven and a half feet. Dressed in a thick, brown cloak against the night chill, his long, deep red hair glowed in the stark light of the dome. A thin smile curved his lips and brown eyes glittered as he pulled Andraju down to kneel at his feet.

"Chris!" Andraju tried to smile, but his breathing had become erratic despite the fact that the flaps on his torso had not been harmed. "You came back."

"You seem surprised. Perhaps that's because you tried so hard to leave me behind. You were supposed to move east after PortCity, and I find you here, in the south instead." Chris shook his head. "Bad decision, Andraju. Very bad decision."

A horrible weakness flooded Andraju's body. His panel fell from his fingers, raising a puff of dust from the white sand beneath their feet. "You don't understand. Let me explain."

"Oh, I think I understand." Chris smiled, perfect white teeth glimmering like the edge of a knife. "I can't find my pet and I notice the cage is missing. You wouldn't happen to know its whereabouts, would you?"

Andraju couldn't breathe properly. His chest felt heavy, his arms and legs leaden. Once Chris had hold of someone, he could do anything to them. Make them do anything. And despite the fact that he was a human, he was far stronger than even a Madinah warrior, much less an Algaran. Terrified, he began to babble.

"It wouldn't fucking eat. What was I supposed to do? You just took off, never said a word about when you'd be back. I had no fucking choice! I had to do something, find someone that could help me figure out what the hell it ate!"

Dark eyes narrowed and the grip on Andraju's throat tightened. The Algaran felt as if he were trying to breathe through plastic.

"Tell me what you did. Quickly now. I can make this last a long, long time."

"Can't." Andraju gasped helplessly. The pressure on his chest eased a bit.

"I took it to…hospital."

A hiss escaped the man's mouth. "You left it with *people*? With strangers?"

"I had to. After the woman. The doctor wouldn't let it go."

"And you thought you'd just be rid of it, then throw me off track by leaving PortCity." His voice reflected no anger, only a chilling calm.

Chris flexed the broad hand closed around the width of the Algaran's short neck as he stared down at the alien. "Sorry, Andraju, but you don't get rid of me that easy. We'll have to chat about what happens to those who don't respect other people's property. But first, you're going to tell me exactly what happened or I will crush the breath out of your worthless fucking body."

II

Michael stood still, back to the wall, chest heaving. Sweat trickled down his back. Thoughts chased themselves around his brain, like dogs after their tails.

I can't. Shit, I can't go there.

But he had to. The key to the bridge lay just beyond his hiding place, in the main corridor. Without it, he would not get into the bridge. And without access to the bridge, he would simply be marking time until he was discovered and killed.

So stop feeling sorry for yourself! Stop standing around and move!

He clenched his hands, too scared to move. Sure that he had no other choice.

Don't think about it. Just go!

Michael took a deep breath and peeped out around the corner.

Blood. So much blood. The air stank with that iron smell. His throat felt coated with it. Great red splashes marred the gray walls. Drying puddles made maroon shapes on the floor under the yellow emergency lights. But blood no longer dripped from the ceiling into puddles, and the hiss of the air changers was the only sound.

No thinking back. Focus. Look down.

I don't want to. Fuck. I can't.

Look.

He lowered his gaze.

Three or four bodies lay tossed on the floor, the scattered toys of a bored child. One seemed whole, but the rest...

Unaware he made a sound, he whimpered in his throat, and swallowed.

Fuck it, look!

Deliberately, he let his gaze sweep over the scattered bodies; the blasted, torn remains of his crewmates. He stared past the deck access ladder a few feet to his left. Shadows huddled like a murder of crows at the other end of the tunnel, where the overhead lights had been destroyed. He didn't dare swing his gaze right, did not want to see what the shadows half concealed. Instead, he turned his attention back to the bodies in the corridor, strained his senses to try and pick up any sound, any movement—a smell, a vibration. There was nothing.

Now. Go now.

What if it's a trap?

GO!

Pushing away from the wall, he stepped into the corridor. His boots made a faint clang but to Michael, the sound echoed off the walls like a shout. Gritting his teeth, heart racing in his chest, he took another step into the gumminess of a blood puddle. His foot slid and he tripped over the clawed, bloodied hand of a body that lay face down. A twisted, multicolored snake tattoo marked the back of the hand.

Fuck. That's Matka's hand. *Michael shivered as incomprehensible thoughts screamed through his mind. Still, it was too late to stop. He continued scanning the bodies around him.*

He took five more steps before he recognized Marchand's battered face on his left. The hawk-like nose had been smashed into the broad face. Clumps of silver-gray hair were missing from the scalp, leaving bloody, naked spots. The neck ended in a jagged stump that trailed ragged ends of tissue and muscle. Michael looked away from it quickly. The urge to vomit was a hot burning at the base of his throat.

There's no help for it. You have to search them all. Move them. It could be anywhere.

He didn't bother to think about it, didn't bother to try and stifle the hysteria seething inside him. There was no time. Turning, he started to kick at body parts, overturned heavy torsos with his gore covered hands, poked fingers into two cool, slick piles of entrails. Methodically, without thought, he worked his way down the corridor, all the while feeling the pull of the darkness at its end and the gaping nothingness to the right. Where he did not want to go.

And where he ended up anyway.

Marchand's body lay a few feet before the end of the corridor, half in and half out of the lightless area. Michael recognized the insignia still pinned to his chest. He stood a few steps away and battled the urge to run.

Why there? Why the fuck there?

You're wasting time.

Against his will, his gaze went to where the shadows of the corridor melded with the darkness of the hole in the wall. He could just make out the dented edges of the ruined airlock in dim outline. Could almost feel a difference in the air here. As if it was colder somehow. The airlock waited like a snake in a hole, ready to strike. His breath shuddered in his chest as he stared, remembering.

Blood. So much blood, and silence. Terror pounds in his chest as he moves forward, eyes wide, gun extended in numb fingers, seeing and not wanting to see. Smelling and not wanting to smell. And then a sound, so soft. He looks toward the doorway—

—and snapped back to the present, gasping as if he'd just run a race.

I can't do this. I have to go. Have to get out of here...

Frantic now, he bent and searched the body. The skin felt unreal under his fingers, like a mannequin, the uniform stiff with dried blood. But this mannequin had only a ragged sleeve where the right arm should have been, and just one foot wore a shoe.

Michael ran his hands over the body, refusing to look at the broken end of the neck, where a bit of spine poked out, the tip of it white and vulnerable. The key did not hang on what little neck remained. Nor had it slipped down into the front of the uniform, which he was forced to unfasten so he could search the bruised and battered body. It wasn't in the pockets of the pants, or on the ground around him.

He could feel the darkness in the hole just in front of him reaching out, like the flickering tongue of a viper. Tears of frustration began to blur his vision and air hissed out from his open mouth as he scrabbled fingers across the small rectangles of the grilled flooring, slick with blood and tissue.

What if it fell in? What if it slipped beneath the flooring and oh shit I feel as if it's not empty as if the brig is NOT EMPTY...

He glanced up at the dark hole, his breath coming in nervous hitches. His nerves sang a bitter tune as he rocked back on his heels. His injured right leg twinged sharply as he stared at the body, unable to think what to do next, only aware that he had to leave, had to leave now or go mad.

He put his hand out one more time and lifted the body back against the wall.

With a soft clink, the grimy rectangular key dropped out from the back of the uniform collar, the silver chain pooling and glinting on the grill like a strand of precious pearls.

III

"Oh, Colin, I don't know," Ranie said, biting her lip, a small crease between her eyes. "That's a tall order. Lex *and* the alien? The shelter will only take women. And the alien shelters don't allow humans."

"I know, but you realize why I have to ask you?" Colin gave her a persuasive smile and Ranie rolled her eyes.

"I don't know why I bother with you."

"So you'll do it?" he asked.

Ranie sighed in a show of martyrdom and flipped her ever-present braid back over her shoulder. "Has anyone ever said no to you? Hello—look who's here."

Colin glanced over his shoulder. Anton stood behind him, his large body draped in a brown overcoat, his hands shoved into the pockets. Ranie smiled at him.

"Hey, stranger. What wind blew you this way?"

Anton gave her a rare smile and inclined his head toward her. "A fortunate one. It brought me into your presence. Good morning, Ranie."

"Good morning to you too." Ranie laughed and glanced at Colin. "See? That's how you charm a woman into doing what you want." To Anton she said, "So, are you here for business or pleasure?"

"Business, unfortunately."

"Hmmm. Well, if PortCity's esteemed forensic pathologist has come all the way down here, us mere mortals had better let him go about his business."

"On the contrary, it appears I'm the one interrupting."

"No, we're finished here." Ranie turned to Colin. "I'll get back to you on those shelters by this evening."

"Knew I could count on you."

She made a derisive sound in her throat and said to Anton, "You should get out of the morgue more. Pay Colin a visit."

"I'll do my best," Anton replied.

Ranie took a step back. "Colin?"

"Ms. Sangborn?"

She pointed a finger at her head and then at him. "Haircut, okay?"

He sighed. "Tomorrow, I promise."

She rolled her eyes in a "yeah, right" gesture and walked away, her plait bouncing against her back.

Anton watched her go. "I gather you're still seeing each other. It must be serious by now."

"We're not getting married if that's what you mean. Ranie and I understand each other. For now, that's more than enough." *Would she understand Lex?* his traitor mind wondered, but Colin pushed the thought away, reminding himself that there was nothing to understand about Lex.

Anton glanced at him with his "I'm missing nothing" look.

"What?" Colin asked.

Anton shook his head and took a slow breath. "May I see Lex now?"

"I suppose so. I had hoped to have some intellect and skill tests done before you showed up, but the senior med tech isn't in today and he's the only one qualified to administer them."

Anton titled his head to the right and tapped a forefinger against his lips. "Would you still like to get the tests done?"

"I could wait till tomorrow, but Lex is not so patient. She had her heart set on today."

"We don't have to disappoint her. I can administer the tests. But I'd rather not meet with her before we're done, so can you find a junior VR tech to stand in for me in the room?"

"I'm sure I can find a tech." Colin was relieved.

Anton nodded as if coming to a decision. "Then, by all means, lead the way."

IV

Colin watched through the transperiwall as the tech, a portly young man barely in his twenties, powered down the interface with a tap on the panel in front of him. The hologram above the table dissipated like vapor in a breeze as he stood up from his chair.

The room was used primarily for specialized training simulations. It held a table, the two chairs and the interface panel; its only occupants were the tech and Lex. As the man rose, Lex removed her VR glasses and looked straight at the transperiwall. For a moment, Colin felt like she was looking right at him.

Don't be stupid. She can't see through tinted walls. She just knows someone has to be watching.

Despite the ridiculous hospital gown, Lex had an air about her that was both demanding and impatient. She seemed much more confident. As if her body being healed gave her direction. Something to push back the waiting.

Anton came up alongside him.

"So," Colin asked, trying to sound casual, "What are your findings?"

Anton breathed out, as if releasing a great weight. "She's everything we suspected and more. She ran through those tests in a third of the time they usually take."

"Details please."

"She has a photographic memory, with perfect understanding. Do you know how rare that is? Most people with photographic memories don't understand what they're seeing immediately. They just remember it very well. Lex, however, can see, remember and understand at the same time. Her intellect tests in the high genius range. Her language skills are astonishing."

"I know. She spoke five or six languages while she was delirious."

"That's the tip of the iceberg. Lex is fluent in over seventy languages."

Colin raised his eyebrows. "You're kidding."

"Not at all. She also understands twenty-three more, though not necessarily well enough to speak them."

Colin looked back at the room and the woman ignoring the tech who was trying to make conversation with her. "She's practically a damn translator."

"That would be exaggerating—even a basic portable translator has thousands of languages in its database—but for a human, it is amazing. Naturally, her unusual memory contributed to it. In addition to her language skills, she's picked up quite a bit on the culture, alien or otherwise, behind the languages she knows. She displays an unusual level of knowledge regarding current events, particularly those that relate to corporate and political intrigue. It's almost as if she's been studying up on such things."

"So she's a genius, very educated and cultured. A well-rounded individual." *So how the hell did you end up here, almost dead and badly beaten?*

"There's one other thing. She has a psi rating. She's a low-level telepath."

Holy shit. Colin looked at Anton, a frown creasing his brow. "Do you think she knows? That maybe she's been—"

"Eavesdropping? I doubt it. She's not strong enough for that. But if she doesn't know now," Anton rose from his chair, "she's about to find out."

V

Anton held back a little as his friend strode into the room where Lex waited, trying to prepare himself for what he knew would come next.

It didn't work. The emotions he had picked up on behind the transperiwall became impossible to ignore in Lex's presence. Eyes green as gems met his with curiosity and wariness. Beneath that, her impatience swirled about him like an undertow. She was not frightened by his size, like most people. "This is Anton Slake, the man I told you about," Colin said.

Trying to put her at ease. It would work better if you weren't so keyed up around her yourself, old friend.

Anton could sense Lex's heightened interest.

"You're the part-time detective? You're not exactly what I expected."

"I think it's safe to say you're not what I expected either," Anton replied. He did not offer his hand, and was surprised when he got a fleeting sense that she had noted and understood the omission. *Could she have picked up on my sensitivity? No. Impossible. She's not strong enough.*

"You don't look like a doctor."

"So I've been told. But this isn't about me. It's about you."

"Anton has some things he wants to discuss, so I should probably leave you two to it," Colin said.

Lex's consternation tugged at Anton's senses. "You're not staying?"

"Not in here. I'll be in the next room if you need me."

"We'll be fine," Anton said, taking the seat in front of Lex. She watched him sit, her emotions ebbing and flowing around him like a tide. "Won't we, Lex?"

She was silent, looking from him to Colin and back again. *Oh my, I was afraid of that. This might complicate things later.*

"Yes," she said finally.

After Colin left, Lex sat in silence as Anton explained her results to her. She made no move to speak until he was finished. "Well, at least I don't have to worry about being able to find a job."

"It would appear so," he agreed.

"You're sure about the psi rating?"

"Yes. But I'm more interested in your fields of study."

She slanted a glance at him. "Why?"

"Because soldiers your age are usually grunts. And someone like you is no grunt."

"You're so sure I'm a soldier?" Her voice held just a suggestion of a question, but her desire for answers touched him like fingers.

"Turn your hands over."

She frowned, confusion a brief flash in her eyes. "My hands?"

"Please. Turn them over."

She hesitated before placing them palm upward, fingertips toward him.

"See the calluses?"

"Yes."

"Consistent with hard work and possibly gripping a weapon often. Look at your arms."

She glanced down. "What about them?"

"The tan lines. I'm sure you've noticed one on your neck as well. Your face and hands are tanned. And that's it. Your wrists, arms and feet are not tanned at all."

"So I've been to a beach sometime, what of it?"

"You wouldn't have tanned just on your face and arms at a beach. No, I think you've been near sand all right, but in the desert. You were in a place hot enough to burn your exposed limbs, but so hot you had to cover the rest. Serron has only one small desert to the east, but no one has settled it. As a matter of fact, there are no other deserts on the habitable planets in this system." He paused.

"However, beyond this galaxy—where you might expect to find a combat soldier—is another matter. And then there's this."

Anton could be fast when he wanted to. He used that speed now, raising his right hand, and darting it toward Lex's eyes. His hand barely moved before slender fingers clutched his wrist like grav-cuffs.

Lex looked at him over the V of his fingers, astonishment spreading across her features. He barely noticed. His entire being was focused on the spot where her flesh met his. On the feelings and thoughts that washed over him, drowning his mind in drifting miasma.

Pain. Painpainpainsomuchpain. Had never felt so much in his life. And sorrow. Heart-rending. Mind-numbing. The body's pain is bad, but the mind. The pain there is worse. Born of betrayal.

Someone close. Someone. Someone.

It's too dark. Even the feelings are hidden from him. Can't see beyond the burning. Can't remember the cause.

But there's something in the dark. Something angry.

He's hurting and angry. And hiding something. From Colin. Something about the alien. It's...it's...

...coming. Rushing up to him from the deep is something large, yet small. Completely new, but familiar. Soft as a breeze it touches his mind, coils in him, pushing out everything but the soft insistent command to

<<Leave.>>

One voice, soft but loud. Too loud to be one voice. Many sounds behind it now. Murmuring. Cajoling.

<<This is not your place, feeler. She is not yours to heal.>>

Pain is blossoming, but far off. Noise shifts through his awareness, but he does not care. He must listen. Must

<<Leave. Let go. Let go.>>

She'd let go of his hand. Time crawled as he looked at Lex, took in the shock on her face, thought to himself, *she felt it. She must have felt part of it. Must have.* Realized that her face had begun to pull back and away from him.

Falling. Because I'm falling.

His eyes drifted closed and his thoughts fell away with him.

··· —— — ···

When he opened them again, he lay on his back, a tremendous headache pounding behind eyes dazzled by the light. He blinked several times before he managed to focus enough to see both Colin and Lex hanging over him. Colin's lips were moving.

"...okay?" he asked, his voice coming through loud and clear with a suddenness that made Anton gag. He tried to sit up, feeling a vague soreness throughout his body.

"I'm fine. I'll be fine."

Colin extended a hand to help him up, and Anton took it gratefully. Relief, both Colin's and his, washed over him. *What happened? What did I see? Feel?* But his memory had shattered into a hundred pieces and he could not make sense of what was left. He remembered impressions, sounds, but little else.

"What happened? One minute Lex grabbed your hand, the next she let go and you were falling." Colin's voice sounded a little rough and Anton could feel the concern coming off him. But Lex's turmoil drowned him out.

"I didn't mean to let you fall," she said. "I didn't realize..."

"It's okay," Anton said, and even managed a smile for her. "I'm a big guy. It didn't hurt that much."

"But what happened?" Lex asked, concerned.

Anton waved a dismissive hand and made himself stay upright as he let go of Colin's arm.

"Dizzy spell. Not enough sleep lately, I guess. I get them from time to time." He turned to Colin, ignoring the disbelief that Lex projected. *Too smart to believe that, but at least it buys me an exit line.*

"I think I'll have to leave now and return at another time.

When I have a chance to finish my research, I should have some more information for you both."

With a nod to Lex, he walked off. *That was the clumsiest you've ever been, Anton. In more ways than one.*

A short while later, Colin caught up to him, a frown marring his brow.

"Okay, what the hell was that all about? You scared the shit out of me in there—and don't tell me it was a dizzy spell."

"I'm sorry I had to lie, but I didn't want to talk to you in front of Lex. Not just yet. She hid something from you and I'm not sure what that means." *If only I had come sooner.*

"Hid what? What are you talking about?"

"The alien. It did more than just heal her, Colin. She's been talking to it and I'm guessing she hasn't told you about that. I'm not so sure it's just an alien animal anymore."

"You're not—what the hell else would it be?"

"I can tell you this. It's not alone. When I touched her, I picked up on something. A residue. I'm having trouble remembering exactly what. But I believe there's more than one consciousness connected to that alien. There was a—plurality that I can't quite put my finger on."

"You're telling me the alien can *communicate*?"

"Yes. It, or something like it, was connected to her, Colin. And whatever it was pushed me out. Hard. I have never felt anything like that before. I'm no telepath, but I think that while I was in there, it spoke to me." The memory of something brushing against his mind sent goosebumps rushing across his skin. *Hurry. If you're right, whatever it is, it knows what you know now.*

"Colin, I need you to show me this alien."

"Now?" Colin raised an eyebrow. Anton nodded firmly.

"I have to figure out what kind of connection it made with Lex— maybe use that to help her regain her memory."

Colin's eyes brightened with sudden understanding. "Follow me."

It wasn't far to the alien's room, but Anton's senses alerted them to what they would find before the door opened.

They stepped into an empty room. The alien was gone.

CHAPTER 9

These soldiers are so damn weird. They're always practicing,
sleeping, or chattering in that damn language they've invented.
They never smile or really relax unless they think we're not looking.
And they know about the cameras.
I'm starting to think it might be better to just let you guys handle
the transport thing again instead of the soldiers—but every time I
try to talk to Murdoch about it, he shuts me down.
　*—Vid-transmission from Daniel Ryner, Head of Security for Phoenix
Facility, to his wife, Abigail Ryner, Junior Vice-President at ME&E,
July 260 A.A.*

I

What the hell just happened?

Lex sat slowly, her brow furrowed, alone now that Colin had
gone after Anton.

Anton. The big, soft-spoken pathologist who fainted after
touching her. She didn't know what to think about that. One minute,
he was talking to her, the next, he'd tried to poke her eyes out, she'd
grabbed his hand—

Do ordinary soldiers even move that fast?

—and he looked at her like—

He could see right through me.

She had felt so many things. Emotions wisped through her like
fog—too insubstantial to hold on to. Her mind went blank. Then the
thought came to her that she should let go, just let go. And she had,

never expecting what happened next. Never expecting him to look at her with such bewilderment, such utter confusion and just tip over.

He'd tried to pass the whole thing off as some fainting spell, but Lex knew better.

He picked up on something. Damn it, Colin. You could have warned me he was an empath. Not that it mattered. She'd guessed the moment he politely avoided shaking her hand.

Does he know? Does he know about Oux, about the Angry One? She dreaded the idea of telling Colin, but what if Anton Slake got there first? It would not be the ideal situation. Colin would want to push for answers, and she had a feeling Oux didn't appreciate being pressured.

You're being paranoid. Maybe Anton didn't get anything. He's just an empath. He can't read your mind.

He sure can read clues though.

She breathed out and decided worrying about it could do no good. Whatever happened, she would deal with it. She'd done nothing wrong, just kept a few things to herself. Considering her position, Colin would understand, right? *Relax. You're chasing shadows.*

The door swished open and Colin came back into the room. She saw the grim expression on his face and knew something had happened.

He planted his hands on the desk and leaned over slightly.

"How long have you been lying to me."

"Lying to you?"

"Anton knows. He told me you and the alien have been communicating." The accusing look in his eyes made her stomach twist.

Shit. Thanks a lot, Sherlock.

"Colin, what are you asking me?" she said cautiously.

"I'm asking you, why? Why did you lie to me? We're on the same side, Lex. I've done nothing but try to help you."

"Don't you think I know that?" she burst out. *Damn it, stop looking at me like I killed your pet. I didn't do this to hurt you. This isn't even* about *you.*

He glared for long minutes. She refused to turn away. Tension shivered between them. Finally, he sighed and sat in the chair. Running his hand through his hair, he said, "You don't trust me, is that it?"

If there's one person I think I can trust in this whole thing, it's you. But you can't help me as much as Oux can.

And—for whatever reason—I trust Oux too.

"No, that's not it. The alien didn't want me to tell anyone. It was afraid it would be taken away and studied. You remembered what happened to your diagnostic machines. I think being examined hurts it."

"And you decided I didn't need to know this?" Colin's voice sounded curt, professional. It stung, but Lex did not let herself show it. "I spoke to it for the first time yesterday. Before then, I had no idea it could speak either."

"So why did it talk then? What did it say?"

Lex made a quick decision. Until she could speak to the Oux again and find out more about the Angry One, she would delay telling Colin everything. It would only alarm him and there was nothing anyone could do right now anyway. *Besides, it's never a good idea to show your whole hand.* The thought was odd—but felt right.

"I think I remembered something, but I couldn't hold on to it. It helped me get it back. I was planning to let you know later, after I figured out a way to get back the rest of my memories."

Colin started to speak, stopped and tried again. "You had a memory and you didn't tell me about that either?"

"It all happened yesterday, okay? I didn't have time to process it yet."

"What is there to process? When I saw you this morning and I asked you how you were feeling, you could have said 'Fine, Colin, and by the way, I had a memory'."

"Well, I didn't and I'm sorry, okay?"

Colin searched her face. She wanted to cringe inside, knowing she was lying to him again, but she steeled herself instead.

He shook his head. "Okay, but understand, I'm trying to help here."

She nodded, the action brief.

"I mean it, Lex. You don't need to keep secrets from me. I'm your doctor. I only have your best interests at heart. And starting now, I'd like you to tell me the truth. Beginning with where it went."

"What do you mean, where it went?"

He frowned. "I thought you knew. The alien is missing. Anton and I went to see it and it wasn't in the room. I don't know how it got past the nurses or the cameras, but Security made a complete check and it's nowhere in this hospital."

Shock made her mute. *Oux, you son-of-bitch. Where the hell have you got to?*

But deep inside, Lex knew there was really only one thing she cared about.

Are you coming back?

II

"So, is she telling the truth?"

Anton turned away from the transperiwall as Colin walked into the observation room. "For the most part. The alien asked her to keep its abilities a secret."

"But she's still lying about something." Colin moved to stand beside him.

"Unfortunately, yes. I don't believe she really wants to lie to you, but she's convinced herself it's necessary. She's afraid. Without the alien, she feels exposed."

Colin sighed and Anton watched as he tucked one hand into the pocket of his white coat. "Why is she hiding things from me?"

"You and the alien are her only friends. And she likes you. More than she realizes. She doesn't want you to see her as a victim. She wants you to stop pitying her."

"I don't pity her."

"I know. You like her and not just the way a doctor likes a patient." Anton leveled a gaze at him. "I'm sorry, but it was fairly obvious the whole time Ranie was with us. I didn't mean to pry."

Colin groaned, frustrated. "Am I turning into a pervert? She's a teenager for goodness sake."

Anton shrugged. "I don't think so. Lex is very mature for her age. But there can't be anything between you. Not now."

"Believe me, I get that. I'm not that much of a cretin."

If only it were that simple. "There's more to it, Colin. There's a lot of unfinished business there. A lot of—danger. Whatever that alien did, there's something else with her now. You shouldn't get too close."

Colin gave him a wry smile. "Are you trying to protect me from a seventeen year old girl?"

Anton studied the unmoving figure beyond the transperiwall. "Yes, Colin, that's exactly what I'm trying to do. I asked a friend to check every database she could find for anything on Lex, and there was nothing. Nothing at all. We're processing the Dead files now—just in case she was reported MIA or KIA."

And if I'm right, that puts Troi in a very risky position. But if it comes to that, if my suspicions are correct and they trace it back to Troi, I'll get her out.

What if I'm right, though? What happens if the truth Troi finds leads back to my past? Can she still be friends with me once she knows what I did?

Anton pushed the thought away, unwilling to deal with the ramifications.

"Take my advice, Colin. Be careful. Help her all you want, but when the time comes, when she's better, let her go. Lex—"

(is not yours to heal)

"—doesn't belong here. Her path lies elsewhere."

III

The last corridor was the hardest. Michael kept thinking he heard someone sneaking up behind him, and he spun around twice, gripping the key in his hands so hard the edges dug into his palm.

Nothing came out of the accessways. Nothing grabbed at him from closed airlocks. But the hairs on his neck stood up all the same.

Just jumpy from the trip to the brig. Forget about it. You're almost done. Almost safe.

Mere hours before, making it to the bridge seemed an impossible task.

Now, I'm here.

He checked both sides of the empty corridor. Then, for the second time that long, horrible day, he stood in front of the entrance and palmed the lock.

"Identify."

"Acting Lieutenant Michael Flax Zorida."

"Acknowledged."

The pause seemed interminable. His breath sounded as loud as the instructions.

"Acting Lieutenant Zorida, please be advised that security protocol has been changed as per Captain Marchand's instructions. Please insert override key and confirm authorization."

Fingers trembling, he slid the key into the slit below the palm lock. The necklace swung from side to side like a pendulum. A chime sounded.

Michael placed his hand on the palm lock.

"Acting Lieutenant Michael Flax Zorida, emergency clearance Alpha, Alpha, three, six, two, two, Sierra."

Two chimes sounded. Michael had never heard anything more wonderful.
"Acknowledged."

The airlock in front of him irised open and the small bridge was laid out before him, bright light striking off the gleaming surface of the consoles.

The relief flooding through him almost buckled his knees. For the first time, hope became something more.

So far, so good. Just one more thing. Hold on just a bit longer, and everything will be all right.

He heard another soft sound. His right hand gripped the airlock tighter as he twisted to squint down the dim corridor.

His head was still turning, his leg tensing to go over the airlock rim, when something slammed into his left side. A horrible ache seared its way across his ribs and the arm holding on to the frame twisted painfully as his legs went out from under him and he half fell into the airlock. His leg came awake to sharp, unforgiving pain. Michael cried out and tried to pull himself upright with the hand that still held on to the door.

That was when he felt himself effortlessly picked up and thrown across the bridge and into one of the consoles.

IV

The ticket agent frowned at the panel in front of him. "I'm sorry, but it looks like you're out of luck. The last connecting flight to PortCity just finished boarding and the next one will be two days from now." He smiled apologetically at the tall man standing in front of him.

"Maybe I could book you on that one instead?"

The man shook his head and a dark red ponytail bobbed into view. "It has to be today. It's a day's travel to PortCity as it is. Three days will be too long for my business to wait."

Behind him, the terminal had quieted down after the initial early evening rush. Travelers waited in covered yellow lounge seats, most of them asleep until their chairs woke them to catch their flight.

"Well, there's not much I can do. We have no more flights available and they're closing the gate."

"Keith," the man interrupted, and the agent blinked, surprised at the change of tone in the man's voice. It sounded very—soothing. That was probably the reason he didn't object when the man slid one strong, tanned arm out from under this dark brown cloak and rested his palm lightly on the agent's hand. At first, his fingers clenched against the counter; then they relaxed as he realized that he was being silly. He knew this man. He wouldn't hurt him. He was nice. Polite.

"I have very important business to transact in PortCity. Surely you can hold the flight for me?"

I'm not supposed to. He opened his mouth, intending to refuse, but something stopped him. *Oh, what the hell. He seems like a nice guy. What harm could it do?*

"Sure. Just let me get on to the gate." He tapped the panel a few times with his free hand.

"There you go, but you still need a ticket to board."

"Would you mind helping me out? I'm a bit strapped for cash. Why don't you charge it to yourself?"

The agent frowned again, not certain this was right. "My account?" The man nodded, his smile charming, his fingers squeezing a little tighter on the agent's hand. *He has such dark eyes. Brown, I think.* He stared at them, unable to look away, feeling as if he were falling into them. From a distance, he heard the man talking.

"You won't have to pay much. Staff members get discounts, remember?"

The agent nodded. "I have points. I won't have to pay for it." He'd been saving the points for an offworld vacation in six months. But that wasn't important anymore.

"Then it's a simple matter, right?"

Yes, now that you mention it. "Very simple." The agent grinned, feeling a great weight lifted from his mind. "Would you like that ticket first class?"

"Why not?" The man smiled back.

··· ——— ···

Chris walked away from the counter and the man who would remember nothing of their encounter without triggering a massive headache. He tapped his panel against the palm of his hand as he strode toward gate access, careful to keep his anger hidden and his face expressionless.

That shouldn't have taken so long. Wouldn't have, normally. For the thousandth time, he cursed both Andraju and his own habit of waiting until he came near the end of his cycle before returning to Oux. But what the hell could he have done? Everything took longer than he'd anticipated and he'd gone ahead, secure in the knowledge that Oux would be waiting for him when he returned to Serron.

Big fucking mistake. He could last a few more days though, and he knew exactly where to go. Mathis Clinic. Andraju had been very forthcoming. He had paralyzed the alien before convincing Andraju with a touch that his eyes had been torn out. The Algaran had been reduced to a blubbering heap on the floor. He told only the truth after that.

He no longer needed the circus anyway. His arrangements were almost complete. Everything had gone according to plan and soon, he and Oux would have much bigger things in front of them than wowing marks with their ESP act.

Much bigger things. Without warning, the tightness of his face gave way to a beautiful smile.

CHAPTER 10

We have found them.
—*Roulon Fleet message to Dak High Command*
"The History of Earth's Discovery" (Year 3 AA)

I

As the sun began to peek over the horizon, the faint glow of early morning rays making PortCity's skyline glimmer gently, a small, thin shape folded itself deeper into the recesses of a doorway. That doorway was located opposite a tall, rectangular structure that took up an entire city block. The figure was watching the structure intently, not moving.

One of the shadows alongside the thin figure in the doorway stretched and twisted. A pale hand came into view. Eyes the lightest gray blurred out of the dimness under a hood. Brown hair fell past broad shoulders, unmoving in the early morning breeze. The man in the black cloak stared across the street at the building.

When the sun's full brilliance flashed across the sky, he spoke in a voice too soft for human ears to hear, and in a language few would understand.

"It's time. Wake her and go with her. Then let Chris do what he must."

The sun's rays spilled over the top of the building, and touched the sidewalk in front of the doorway. The street was clear of traffic and the creature was alone in the entrance.

The man was gone, but his shadows remained, hiding the small shape the rest of the day. The building's transparent doors opened and closed as it watched, black eyes never blinking, taking in every person, every vehicle that came and went.

It did not move as the sun rose higher and the heat increased and tiny, iridescent insects started to buzz lazily around it. One landed on a thin upper arm with a flutter of dart-like wings. A soft sound, like a twig snapping, and it fell, smoking slightly, on a crumpled plastic cup. After that, the bugs fluttered away.

Once, around midday, it moved slightly as an aircar approached, rising up on its haunches a bit. Then, as the driver exited, it settled back again, still as a statue once more.

Waiting.

II

Troi tapped her interface and the small patch near her left temple flashed briefly. Her eyes felt too big for her head and she blinked, trying to relieve the tiredness.

Too much to do, too little time. She studied the displays scattered across her semi-circular desk. The wide, black, semi-circular countertop dominated the small room. Aside from the neat metal cabinets and one or two cupboards that held alternate power sources, the office had no other furniture.

Sweeping her gaze over the holos spinning or scrolling before her, Troi found the one she wanted and flicked a finger at the interface on her desk. The interface patch she wore activated with a brief tone she heard deep in her ear. Troi focused her gaze, blinking as she did so. The holo enlarged, showing a detailed blueprint of a building. With another blink, she zoomed in on the red dot glowing amongst green lines. Under her breath, she recited the necessary shortcode. The dot glowed blue, then green and she knew the computer had been successfully reProgramd. With a tap to her interface and a few more words, she struck the repair off her work order, authorized a signature and dispatched the bill to her client.

One down, several dozen more to go. Troi sighed and cast an eye over one of the scrolling screens to her left. Anton's search had been running there all night, but nothing had turned up yet. The computer would alert her when a match was made, but every time she finished a task, her eyes checked the screen. Reassured nothing had changed, Troi turned back to the primary display in front of her, only to find her mind wandering again.

Why is Anton being so guarded about all this?

It wasn't like Anton to be so vague, especially when his time was so limited. And his new request to search the Dead files had been a shock. Why hadn't he mentioned the possibility that she might be in them before?

He was hoping I wouldn't have to search them, probably. And I think he wanted me to know as little as possible.

Troi smiled humorlessly as the network cube before her unfolded into angular pathways. Code flashed past like gold zip cars. *He's been determined to keep me on the edges of this since the start. The question is, why? He says it's to protect his friend, but this seems personal.*

She spoke a daemon and watched the red flash of code spiral down a pathway. *He's trying to hide something.*

The daemon wrapped itself around a tendril of network code and glowed blue for a moment. It uncoiled and continued its search down twisting paths, past more code, deeper into the network.

But what could it be? We've been friends for almost ten years. What could he think he has to hide from me, of all people? Troi didn't flatter herself that she knew everything about Anton, but in the years since they'd met, she liked to think they'd developed a closeness. Like her, he was too solitary to make friends easily. Too sensitive to be social. Naturally, those same qualities drew them together.

And keep us apart. Troi sighed as the daemon latched on to another suspect. Who was she fooling? She cared more for Anton than she ever imagined she could care for anyone. More than was healthy. There were so many things working against them. His nature, her health, their personalities.

But no one else treats me like I'm a woman and not a…freak.

He's like that with all his friends though. He's an empath. It's in his best interest to make people feel good. If he wanted to be more than friends, why did he pull away from me in the restaurant?

Maybe he was scared. After all, you're terrified at the thought of having a real relationship.

The daemon released the code and captured another tendril. The code on the screen turned violet. At the same time, a quick six-tone melody played in her left ear, like crystal bells being rung.

Troi uttered the shortcode for retrieve and repair and spun her chair to face the display for Anton's search. A blue light pulsed at the corner of the screen. She focused and blinked the prompt to maximum. With another blink she found the highlighted match and pulled the picture into focus. The face of a smiling little girl, probably no more than eight, appeared on the screen. Frowning, she expanded the screen and read the brief bio on the left. Her eyes widened in shock.

"Oh, *fuck!*"

III

The nurse, temporarily alone at her station, almost missed his passage, and only looked up from her daily dosing adjustments in time to see him disappearing through the doors to Intensive Care.

"Excuse me!" she called out. He did not look back, dark hair glimmering in the light before the doors closed behind him. She darted out from behind the desk and went after him.

"Sir," she said as loudly as she dared in the narrow corridor. "Sir, you can't just come in here like this."

The man stopped in front of a room and the door slid open. He stood there for a moment before turning to look at her for the first time. The look on his face surprised her into a brief silence, just long enough for him to ask, "Where is the patient that was in this room?"

She glanced into the suite, saw a stripped bed and early afternoon sunlight through the window throwing a bright glow across the white floor.

"And you are?"

"Jamal Vernon. Major Jamal Vernon," he said in a voice full of impatience. "I don't have time for this."

A memory clicked and she said, "Major Vernon. I'm sorry, but we thought you would call first."

"Did something…happen?" The last word said it all.

"No, Major Vernon, nothing like that." She smiled reassuringly. "He was moved out of Intensive Care this morning. If you'll come with me, I'll take you to his new room."

She went back down the corridor, her shoes clicking on the pale blue floor. Her stiff, cream uniform made a swishing noise as she walked. She glanced back at him as they approached the station. "Are you investigating what happened to him?"

"Yes."

She caught the eye of her co-worker returning from a bathroom break and motioned with her head. The woman nodded and took her place at the desk.

"He had us worried there for quite a while, but he's awake now and even talking a bit. He's as comfortable as can be, all things considered."

The nurse clicked past room after room. In one, faint laughter sounded, fading away as they proceeded.

"Here we are." She stopped before a closed pale green door with small numerals on it. It slid open as she added, "He kept asking for someone named Eryn when he first woke up. Do you know who that is?"

A vein in Vernon's jaw tightened as he looked at the still figure on the small bed, but the nurse did not notice. "His fiancée."

"Is there anyway you could get on to her, let her know what's happened? It might do a lot of good for him to see her."

In a curt voice, he said, "It's taken care of."

"That's good then." She paused, sensing his dismissal. "Remember, he's still very weak. I'd go easy on him."

Vernon nodded again and waited outside until the nurse left. When he entered, he could see the city's skyline through an acutal window, rather than transperiwall. He pulled the only chair in the room up beside the bed and sat in it, never taking his eyes off the partially masked face propped up on the pillows. He reached out a surprisingly gentle hand and gripped long, thin fingers that had been badly lacerated.

The man on the bed stirred, flexing his hand. Dry lips parted with effort.

"Someone…"

"Shhh." Jamal tightened his grip a bit. "Just rest."

The man took a breath heavy with some emotion. "Eryn."

"Yes," Jamal Eryn Vernon said, brushing untidy brown hair back off the healing mask. He leaned forward and touched trembling lips to a cool forehead. "It's me, Flax. I'm here. Everything's going to be just fine."

IV

"Can you believe this guy?" Linkow groused, kicking his foot up on the dashboard. "He puts us off, then doesn't even have the decency to show up on time."

They were waiting in a runner just outside the Quarantine Bay with the air-conditioning on. The late afternoon heat had seeped into the small access area, which was not temperature-controlled. Every so often, Linkow would check the rear view in the heads-up and see a lone figure or spaceport vehicle passing the cavernous doors behind them.

"We told him we were going to be late," Sonja pointed out.

"And if he doesn't show?"

"You still think he won't?"

"The Major hasn't been straight with us from day one. He came in here and started investigating without so much as a 'by the way' and put us off when the questions got a little tough. He hasn't exactly filled me with confidence regarding his trustworthiness."

"Few people meet your exacting standards for trustworthiness," Sonja replied.

Linkow glanced at her. "Fuck you."

"You wish."

Linkow turned his gaze back to the closed access port in front of the runner. The doors rose well beyond the limits of the windshield into the domed ceiling. Smaller doors were cut into the two main doors for easy access. Sunlight could not make it all the way across the tarmac and he watched tiny dust motes dancing in the dimmed glow.

"So who do you think is the patient Vernon went to see?" he asked idly.

Sonja sighed. "Damned if I know. All I know is when I called Mathis after we left here yesterday, they said not only had Jane Doe not seen anyone, no one had been to see her except her doctors."

"Another case he's working on then?"

"Beats me."

Silence descended for a while.

"I can't believe he insisted on us collecting the data in person," Sonja continued. "In this day and age, to have us running around like errand boys."

An aircar turned into the bay and parked a few feet to their right. Linkow watched as the driver got out.

118

"Oh, you have to be shitting me."

Sonja cursed. "You're right. He really is an asshole."

Linkow lowered the window as the man placed his hands on the roof and bent down. The musty smell of the bay, mixed with fuel and the faint scent of aftershave floated in. "Who the hell are you?"

The man nodded at them by way of a greeting, close cropped black curls gleaming, before focusing his blue gaze on Linkow. "You must be Linkow. Major Vernon described you perfectly."

"I'll just bet he did," Sonja said. "And you are?"

"Lieutenant Maridon Hawkes. I'm from HQ and I'm the Major's liaison while he's here."

"He kind of gave us the impression that he walked alone," Linkow said.

Hawkes shrugged. "You and everyone else. In all the time he's been here, today's the first time he's actually asked me to do something in the way of my job description."

"Why am I not surprised?" Sonja muttered with a roll of her eyes as they got out of the car.

"So I take it this means Major Vernon won't be coming," Linkow said.

Hawkes shook his head. "Said he had an important appointment and asked me to give you these."

Linkow took the sealed envelope and popped the tab. Several multicolored data clips were packaged inside.

"That's it?" Sonja asked.

Hawkes nodded. " I received no other instructions, so if you don't mind…"

"Yeah, actually, we do mind," Sonja interrupted. "We were told he'd take us on a tour of the *Meridian*."

"But I wasn't told—"

"Look, Hawkes," Linkow said. "We don't have time to waste. He promised us a look at the crime scene and you're here acting in his stead, which means you're going to accompany us on this tour."

"I don't even have clearance to go in there!"

"Then make your calls, do whatever you have to do," Sonja said, "because we're not leaving here until we get a look inside the *Meridian*."

While Hawkes was on the panel, Linkow contacted Dr. Phillips at the lab and uploaded the data clips. His eyes scanned the information as it went—everything from the log and the crew profiles to the daily meal roster. At least Vernon was as good as his word on that, Linkow thought. He copied everything to his comm panel for reading later and sent another copy to Sonja's unit.

"Got it," Dr. Phillips confirmed. "What do you want on this?"

"Get on to HQ's lab and get their DNA samples. I want you to run what we have on our Jane Doe against what they have from the murder scene, see if you can turn up anything. We're looking for a connection here. Any connection. Especially if any of the DNA at the scene matches DNA evidence collected from Jane Doe."

By the time Sonja came over, trailing Hawkes, the sun had begun to go down and the interior lights had come on. Still, her smile said the wait had been worth it. "We're in."

· · · ━ ━ · · ·

The *Meridian* had the wide fan shape of a fourth generation Trooper patrol ship. A tarnished silver in color, she towered some three stories above them. Darker smudges and rust colored spots spoke of long service in deep space.

Her narrow nose, with the shining bubble of the bridge on it, extended back and up into the main body of the ship. On either side of her, under the slender curves of wings, her gun barrels bristled like menacing black needles. The ramp under the middle of the ship, just before the sweep of her nose, had been extended, as if waiting for them. The ship rested alone in the huge ship bay, looking abandoned and alien.

"Now, I can't tell you much about what the techs have done so far," Hawkes said as they walked up the ramp with him in the lead. "Major Vernon was handling all that and he didn't include me in much of anything."

So what do you do to earn your paycheck? Linkow bit his lip to keep from making the sarcastic comment.

The stench hit him first. A low level rot of blood, death and metal that he could taste in the back of his throat. As they moved through the three decks, around cordoned off areas and spots still marked with body outlines—some with limbs missing—they saw more and more evidence of the carnage that had taken place.

"If you don't mind my saying so," Sonja said finally when they were standing in front of the twisted frame that marked the entrance to the brig, "what the *fuck* happened here? It looks like a damn zoo got loose and tore into everyone."

"We're still trying to piece together what happened," Hawkes replied. "As near as we can tell, it started here and continued right through the ship to the bridge."

"And you think one person did this?" Linkow asked. "Doesn't seem possible."

"No, it doesn't. And it's confusing the hell out of the techs, I can tell you. Still, the DNA evidence doesn't lie."

"But how did the killer get on board?" Sonja asked.

"He didn't," Hawkes replied. "As near as we can tell, he was already on board. There's nothing to indicate that the ship was attacked or boarded by force in any way."

"So you think a crew member did this?" Sonja asked incredulously. "Just lost it and killed everyone?"

Hawkes shrugged. "It happens. But not in this case. Every crew member has been accounted for."

Wait a minute. Linkow pulled his panel out of his pocket and started scrolling through it quickly for the crew manifest.

"Sonja, look at this," he showed her what he had found. She scanned it.

"Seven men and two women?"

Linkow nodded. "You thinking what I'm thinking?"

Sonja nodded, a slight smile on her face. "There are certainly enough men to have done it. And look at their records."

"I noticed that too. Not exactly shining examples of the force except for one. Assault, insubordination. Even the captain's got black marks."

"It's a junk ship," Sonja said. "They toss all the bad ones together and send them where they can't get into trouble—deep, uninhabited space. They would have had enough time to do it, that's for sure."

"Do what?" Hawkes asked as Linkow started going through the crew bios one by one, looking at the pictures.

"Rape her," Sonja said simply. Hawkes looked blank.

"Why would they do that?"

"Well, it's not like we can ask them."

"And that doesn't answer the question of when and where they could have done it," Linkow said, lowering the panel. "We'd have to match the ship's logs with the movements of a girl who can't remember where she was three weeks ago."

"Dead end again." Sonja sighed. "I'm getting tired of those."

"But you *could* ask them."

"What?" Linkow said.

"One of them at least," Hawkes continued. "Why don't you speak to Zorida when he wakes up?"

"Zorida? Who's Zorida?" Sonja asked, her voice sharp.

"The survivor. Didn't Major Vernon tell you we had a survivor, besides the killer, that is?"

Sonja cursed and Linkow said, *"You're fucking kidding me!"*

"Why the hell didn't he say something?" Sonja cried. Hawkes looked alarmed and his pale blue eyes went from one face to the other.

"I think the guy's a friend of Major Vernon's. He seemed really worried about him anyway."

"Oh, hell," Linkow spun on his heel and headed back down the corridor. "The more I hear, the more I want to kill that guy myself. That's who he went to see yesterday, not our Jane Doe."

"But why not tell us about him?"

"He's protecting him from the killer," Linkow replied.

"And maybe a rape charge?"

"I don't know, maybe. But something isn't quite right here. Where does Vernon's killer fit into all this?"

"Personally, I don't give a shit about Vernon's case," Sonja said in a curt voice. "We're not Homicide. He hasn't given us the time of day, so let him find his murderer on his own or take the fall if he kills again."

"Fine by me," Linkow said. "Okay. Jane Doe wasn't aboard as far as we know, so how did she end up in the second runner that went missing from this bay?"

"Maybe she was just an innocent bystander." Sonja stopped talking as Linkow halted suddenly and fumbled at his panel. *Shit. The roster.*

"What is it?"

"I just realized something." Linkow tapped the screen. "There, there it is!"

Sonja grabbed the panel and looked at it. "I don't understand. The meal roster?"

"Look at the rationing."

Sonja scanned the screen again. "Fuck me!"

"Exactly. There were nine crew members, so why did the simulator prepare meals for ten people a day for the last few days before the *Meridian* docked?"

"They had a passenger," Hawkes said slowly. "But that's against regs. No Trooper on legitimate business would come along for a ride without the captain adding him to the crew list. So that leaves a Trooper on illegitimate business, or a civilian. But why would anyone want to go on a deep space mission to the middle of nowhere and back?"

"I've got a better question for you—why did they do their best to hide it?" Linkow said, marching toward the open door at the main entrance again. "And what else—or who else—did they hide?"

Sonja stopped and rounded on Hawkes. "Do you know where Major Vernon is?" she demanded. Hawkes looked uncomfortable.

"Hawkes," Linkow said, "trust me. If you *don't* tell us, I'll—"

"He went to the hospital to see Lieutenant Zorida. He woke up and Major Vernon wanted to interview him."

"Which hospital?" Linkow asked.

"I don't know." Hawkes shrugged half-heartedly. "But I can find out."

"Find out."

V

The sun had begun its downward arc. The light took on a golden quality, hazy in the after-heat of the day just past. In the doorway, the alien crouched, its long arms wrapped around thin ankles. Across the street, the doors of the building stayed busy and flashed open and closed, as it had all day long.

A star appeared in the darkening sky. The light from the setting sun turned pink, then slowly faded away to grey. Darkness fell before the alien focused on an aircar parked out in front of the building. Two shapes moved briefly in the darkness before going inside.

As if responding to a signal, the alien sprang from the doorway and crawled up the side of the building smoothly and quickly, like a shadow cast by something aloft sliding along the transperiwall. Once it reached the roof, it leaped from building to building. No one saw its progress, but its speed held an undeniable urgency.

Its long wait had come to an end.

CHAPTER 11

Emergency transmission. Phoenix Facility under attack. Request immediate assistance. Repeat, Phoenix Facility under attack. Request immediate assistance.
—*Transmission to ME&E Headquarters, from Tec Solutions (origin blocked), February 23rd, 261 A.A.*

I

Anton exited the zip car under the evening glow of an arc light and turned to start down the broad, tree-lined avenue to his small house. Few people he knew owned their homes in a city as starved for real estate as PortCity. The rich lived in compounds, but most citizens lived in apartments and those with good jobs got spacious ones, like Colin's. As a qualified human pathologist with a specialty in alien forensic sciences, he was very sought after. He made enough to be able to afford a house, and he had searched long and hard for a stand-alone property. His house and the lot it stood on was small, but it created enough distance from the neighbors to allow him to tune out the emotions of others almost entirely.

People living in close proximity all around him could over-burden his senses, especially if they were in an emotional state. He could not bear living amongst the constant chatter and unspoken feelings of others. For that reason, he did not invite many back to his sanctuary. Only a handful of friends knew its location. Now, as he walked, deep in thought over the search he would begin tonight for Colin and Lex's alien, he sensed something that surprised him into a sudden halt.

Someone is looking for me. He frowned, then his brow cleared and he relaxed as he caught the identity behind the presence. A cloaked figure stepped from the shadows behind a tree several feet in front of him and he strode toward her quickly.

"Troi. What are you doing here?"

"Sorry to drop in on you like this, but I really had no choice." Anton's eyes narrowed at the timbre of her voice. *Something's wrong. She's anxious.*

Her dark blue eyes met his over the filter veil and the scent of citrus clung around him. "Want to go to our diner?"

"Yes."

"Do you think it's still clean?"

"I'm sure it isn't. I bugged it myself." *And they know how much I hate public places. They won't look for me there.*

"Let's go then."

They fell into step next to each other and Anton became acutely aware that she was holding her emotions in check. He never scanned Troi—never scanned anyone—without permission, but often, surface emotions were impossible to ignore. Not tonight. Tonight, Troi wasn't giving him anything. That disturbed him more than he was willing to admit.

"I tried to get you at the office, but you'd left already and you didn't answer your panel."

"Sorry. I turned it off for a meeting this afternoon."

She glanced at him sideways. "Must have been a busy day for you to forget to check your messages."

"Two rush cases this afternoon. Badly decomposed murder victims. Didn't want the wait to be any longer than it had to be."

"Good old Anton. Always going beyond the call of duty. Do they even notice, do you think?"

"Does it matter?" He shrugged.

They were almost to the diner and he could see that the place was practically deserted. No surprise, given it was the middle of the week.

"This is about her identity, isn't it? You found out who she is."

"Yes," she replied and Anton said nothing more until they were seated in the back of the diner. He ordered coffee while Troi, of course, refused anything. They did not speak until after the coffee had been delivered and the waitress had left, the coffee pot steady in the grip of her tail.

"Do you have it on data clip?" he asked in a low voice, smiling at her to make it seem like they were lovers out for a little private time together. He sipped at the coffee, which tasted slightly metallic from the spoon used to stir in the cream.

"Yes. But before I give it to you, I need to know something."

He placed the coffee cup carefully on the table. "This isn't like you, Troi."

"No, it isn't. But once you see the clip, I'm sure you'll understand why I feel I deserve something in return for what I found. At this point, I'm not sure I haven't already signed my own death warrant."

A brief touch of her fear, cold as a winter draft, drifted over him and Anton closed his eyes. *So it's true then. Lex is a product of the Program. Just like me.* He opened his eyes and glanced around the diner once more. The other two customers and the waitress behind the counter were paying them no attention. He looked at Troi.

"I think I know what you're going to ask, and I'm not sure you really want to hear the answer."

"Yes, I do, Anton." She placed gloved hands on the hard, shiny plastic of the red table and laced her fingers together before looking him right in the eye.

"We've both done an excellent job of not becoming anything more than friends over the years, haven't we?"

The silence held its breath before Anton nodded his head. The hiss of antiseptic sounded in tandem with Troi's own sigh.

"Okay, that was the tough part. Here's the easy part. What is it that you've been hiding from me ever since you asked me to do you this favor?"

Anton felt his breath catch in his throat. *Not that. Don't ask me that, Troi.*

"Troi."

"And don't tell me I'm imagining things, because I'm not. I know you thought I might find something dangerous if my search was successful. I think you were right. So I want you to tell me—what do you think I have on this clip? How do you think it relates to you? Because what you're afraid of is that I would find out something about you. Isn't it?"

Anton looked at the delicate hands resting on the table. *I've never let myself touch them. Not once. And if I tell her what she wants to know, she might never speak to me again. Never see me again.* The thought tightened his chest, but he did not let it stop him from stretching out his right hand and closing it over her gloved fingers. He could not feel her skin, but the glove felt like soft, black fur and below it, he could sense the infinitesimal change as her skin gave slightly beneath his grasp. It was such an intense relief to touch without feeling. He looked in her eyes then, and what reached out to him across the table made his heart ache and rejoice at the same time.

I feel the same way, Troi. However big a mistake it is, I feel the same way.

Her palm turned over, grasped at his. Soon, much too soon, he let go and slid his hand back across the table, wrapping trembling fingers around the coffee cup. *Don't you dare try to hold on to her now. If she still wants to be friends afterward, then maybe.*

"I've never told you much about my past."

"Because it didn't matter," Troi said quickly. "I know *you*. Whatever went before, nothing could change the fact that I lo—like you and care for you. You're my friend, Anton."

"A beautiful thought, Troi." He caught her gaze with his own, spoke succinctly so that she would hear every word. "But everything changes, sooner or later. I just hope you can forgive me. Remember, I was a different person then. Young, sheltered. Stupid."

"Anton," Troi's voice sounded uncertain and her eyes were troubled. "You're scaring me."

"I don't mean to. But to tell you this right, it's important you understand the fault was mine alone. I made the decision."

"What decision?"

"The one that made you the way you are. The one that killed your parents."

Shock caught at him like whiplash. Troi's eyes went wide and her hands twitched on the table. "Anton?"

He held up a hand. "Hear me out before you say anything more."

She stopped talking and waited.

He took a deep breath. Impatience and disbelief swirled below the surface of his senses like a whirlpool trying to suck his thoughts in. *Just say it. Don't try to sugarcoat it. Just say it.*

"You know I'm an orphan. But you don't know that I never really had parents. I wasn't born, Troi. I was birthed out of an artificial womb and raised by scientists, nutritionists and tutors. I was a product of the Program. A privately funded attempt by Mars Exploration and Excavation to make the process of mining and settling new colonies more efficient. I never found out where they got the genetic material, but I doubt it was through legal means.

"They made small batches of us, bred us with the skills to do different tasks. My specialty was analysis. I could take evidence like figures, interviews, holos—anything I was given, and use it to create a probability picture. My job was to assess risk and reward. When to take action, when not to take action, what kind of action to take. That was my job from the time I was nine years old."

"Anton, what you're talking about is illegal. Didn't InGene Inc. get shut down because of those experiments fifty years ago? I mean, people were imprisoned for life. There are laws."

"On Earth and most DiploCore planets. But not on Mars, Troi. Mars was the province of ME&E. For a long time, no one wanted to dig too deeply into what they did there. No one wanted the ore to stop coming. Where would space exploration be without fuel?"

He wanted to look at her, but fear of what he might see kept his gaze on the dark liquid in his cup.

"I was thirteen when I killed your parents. The mining accident in Pretoria sector—it was my job to decide whether there would be any survivors left. For two days, there had been no communication from the way stations and the tunnel collapse happened so far down, the bots couldn't detect life signs. It would be at least a week before the bots got close enough to detect anything, or clear a path to survivors, even on continuous shifts. Then there was the question of whether it would be worth the cost to send rescuers in, especially given the risk of radiation escaping into the rest of the mine. I studied the compiled data and told my supervisor that the probability that there were survivors was almost nil."

Troi made a small, strangled sound and Anton clenched his fingers tighter on the warm plastic mug, pushed away her feelings so he could finish.

"They acted on my advice. We took two weeks to clear the tunnel. By then, most of the survivors were dead, including your father. Some of them had been alive just two days before. It would have been possible to save them if I had recommended a rescue operation instead of a clean-up. Your mother was pulled from the mine with five others. By that time, the radiation had reached them and they all succumbed to their injuries and the exposure. You were just four months in utero, but the doctors were able to take you. Of course, your immune system had already been irreparably damaged by then.

I don't think your mother even knew she was pregnant."

Twenty-two people dead. A mass murderer at the age of thirteen. They were just numbers until then. Not people. Oh, Troi.

"I'm sorry," he said forcing himself to look at her. Her gaze speared him like a butterfly on a pin. Pain, shock, anger, disgust—everything he'd expected. Everything he deserved. "I made a horrible choice and people died because of it. After that, I wouldn't work." He dropped his gaze again, sipped at his now lukewarm coffee.

"There had been other problems. With the kids I mean. Many of us didn't survive past our teen years, and those that did died young. But the few of us that had lived up to our potential and been put to work using our talents in the real world had never been as wrong as I was. After my…mistake, there was a shake up at ME&E. Nobody high up wanted a repeat of the InGene Inc scandal. It would have destroyed ME&E and taken most of Earth's economy with it.

"So they decided to discontinue the Program, shove the whole thing under the mat. The few of us that survived and passed their threat evaluation were mind-wiped and released."

"Just like that?" Troi's voice sounded strange, distant. Anton forced himself to focus on the question and nothing else.

"Just like that. I don't know why they let us go. Why they didn't just lock us up somewhere." *And every day I live in fear of them coming back for me. I've looked over my shoulder every moment since I came to in an alley, years ago.*

"But they wiped you. How come you remember all this?"

"I don't know." He shrugged. "I guess being an empath had something to do with it. Whatever the reason, my memory came back, bit by bit. I hid that, just in case they were watching me for any sign that I remembered so they could come back for me. And I never told anyone about the Program. Until you."

"What about the others? How many were there?"

"About a dozen. But I couldn't find them. I've been looking, but they've all disappeared. I guess they all started new lives as well."

"But you found me, didn't you? You tracked me down."

Anton steeled himself and met her gaze. "Yes. I wasn't spying. I just wanted to make sure you were all right."

"But I wasn't all right."

"No." He paused, his throat aching. "No, you weren't."

"And the woman—you thought that she might have been part of your Program."

Anton nodded. "Some time after my batch—the second generation, there were four in all—they briefly experimented with a few children at another company's request. Tec Solutions, it was called. I learned later that Tec might have been a front for part of the military, but I didn't know which branch. I never found out what happened to the subjects after the initial trials. They were there one day and then just gone the next. ME&E never did any more of them and I found out later that all the research they did, all the formulas, the gene sequencing, went to Tec Solutions with the children. A few months later, the company closed up shop and the records just disappeared."

Silence descended, heavy with hurt and uncertainty.

"You think I hate you, don't you?" she asked suddenly.

Her thoughts were too confused for clarity. Emotions came and went like half-glimpsed ghosts, as so often happened when someone was terribly upset. "Do you?"

She looked away from him, her gloved hands curling around each other tightly. "I don't know how I feel. My best friend just told me he killed my parents and made me a freak. And he lied to me about it for years. How do you think I feel?"

An emotion thrust out at him, sharp as a blade to his heart. "I don't have to think."

"That's right." For the first time, the bitterness in her voice was undeniable. "You're an empath. You already know how I feel."

She reached into the folds of her cloak and withdrew a transparent data clip which she tossed onto the table. "You might want to take a look at that."

Anton knew he could say nothing at the moment that wouldn't make things worse, so he took the clip and loaded it into his panel. He brought up first a picture of a little girl and then a short bio. He scanned it briefly, and his gaze flew to meet Troi's.

"This is impossible. She's dead."

"But she's not. And that means either the news reports were inaccurate, or…"

"Or they were doctored," Anton finished and his face lost all expression. "There can be no doubt about this?"

"None. Ironic isn't it? After everything you've told me." And the casual tone of her voice cut him more than the pain he sensed she was holding back. A thought occurred to him.

"Troi—she's at the Clinic." He caught her gaze. "The Mathis Clinic."

"It would probably be a good idea to call your friend," was all she said.

II

"Are you ready?"

Lex spun away from the holoshow in front of her. "Off," she said and the commercial faded away. Ranie stood waiting in the doorway, a black jacket thrown over her blouse and her panel tapping against her leg. She surveyed Lex's jeans and the sleeveless green shirt that showed off slender, muscled arms.

"So the clothes fit okay?"

Lex nodded, looking down at the white adjustable sneakers she wore. "Fine, thanks."

"Well, I guess we can get on with it."

"Isn't Colin coming?" *Damn. I wasn't going to say anything.* "I haven't seen him today."

"He's been in surgery all morning and has another scheduled for this evening. He should be out later tonight. By then, I'm hoping you'll be settled at the shelter. He can visit you there later, if you want."

"Oh."

Ranie jerked her head a little. "We'd better be on our way."

Lex stepped out into the corridor, feeling a bit guilty as she did so. Leaving her room, in plain clothes no less, felt wrong, like she was breaking the rules.

After a short ride in a lift and a trip through a busy waiting room, Lex found herself standing on the sidewalk outside. She paused just beyond the double doors and enjoyed the feel of the wind against her face, the way it tugged at her loose hair. The night was warm and the air smelled of the city. Dirt and plastisteel and people, tarmac and ozone. Lex looked around at the dark looming buildings, the narrow street with its floating arc lights and a short distance away, the glow of zip rails arcing upward. There was a slumberous energy to it all, like a beast stretching itself before the evening hunt.

None of this feels familiar. I don't think I've been here before.

"Feels good to be outside, huh?"

"Yes." Lex turned to face Ranie. "It does."

Ranie's battered black runner was parked half a block away and as they approached, Lex heard a beep and the doors on the runner slid up.

"You just leave it parked here like this? Aren't you afraid someone will steal it?" Lex asked as Ranie tossed her panel into the small backseat and they got in. The display in front of them blinked and Ranie slammed a hand down on it. The lights came on and she poked the button for manual control.

"Hell, no. Who in their right mind would steal this heap of junk?" Ranie grinned and swung the runner out from the curb.

The trip didn't take long, but it did take them through the city proper. Lex stared at everything around her, the startling array of beings walking, running, undulating, hopping, floating or rolling along the sidewalks. Here and there, languid shapes leaned in doorways or against walls. Huddled bodies lay in sheltered corners.

Neon and laser signs flashed off buildings, windows and bots. Holos shifted past too fast to make sense of them. Arc lights shone down on creatures every color of the rainbow and in some areas left narrow alleys between multicolored buildings dark and threatening, like open maws. Lex felt a chill go through her as she remembered her own alley. Air cars and runners flashed past, and once they went by a zip rail just as the car lifted off, rejoined the rail and sped away. Lex couldn't look away. It was all so fascinating, and yet so intimidating. Why did she feel so out of place?

The Kentwood shelter was sandwiched between an apartment complex and an office. Across the street, low, domed structures shone dark in the light of several bright arc lights, like giant black pearls. The shelter itself was a square, solid looking building, made of something gray, non-reflective and thicker than plastisteel. Three stories high, it stood between the rose colored trapezium of the apartment complex and the modern gold prism of the office. Here, the streets appeared cleaner and Lex could see no one loitering nearby. Ignoring the no parking sign, Ranie pulled up directly in front of the steps that led up to the closed, opaque glass doors.

"A friend of mine runs this place," Ranie said as she went around the front of the runner to join Lex where she stood waiting on the sidewalk. "Marla Kentwood. You'll have an admission interview with her before we look at your room."

"She hasn't agreed to let me in?" Lex asked as they started to climb the stairs together. Shadows made dark recesses on either side of the high stone banisters.

"Sure you're in. But Marla has to meet with you, ask a few questions. It's about getting an idea of who you are and the best way to help you."

Too bad I have no idea who I am. "You make it sound like I'm going to be here for a while."

Ranie paused three steps from the landing. "Of course, the sooner you're able to leave, the happier we'll all be. But we can't fool ourselves. Your recovery could take a few days or a few months, there's no way to tell. Until then, you might as well be comfortable, right?"

Comfortable. With a bunch of strangers. Fellow victims, if you will. Somehow, I doubt it.

But Lex pushed away the sarcasm. "Sure." Her quick smile felt insincere on her face.

Out of the corner of her right eye, she saw something shift. A small green blur went up the stairs, past Ranie's right side. Ranie's head lolled back and her legs started to fold. Without thinking, Lex stretched her arms out and caught the woman before she could hit the stairs. She looked up, tossing her hair out of her eyes—and froze.

Oux's gaze met hers as it lowered its arm, the finger it had used on Ranie still extended. It stood on the step just below the landing. The alien seemed smaller out in the open, under harsh arc lights.

"What are you doing here?" She glanced down at the woman in her arms. Ranie's eyes were closed, her chest rose and fell in the wake of slow, regular breathing. "What did you do to her?"

"Sleep now. Not hurt." The voice sounded higher than it had before, reedy rather than hollow. And a lot more substantial. Lex straightened and swung Ranie up into her arms, feeling the weight but not nearly as much as she had expected. *Then again, nothing's going as expected. What the hell is going on?*

"Oux?"

"Come."

She paused, looked around her to see if anyone had spotted the strange scene taking place on the stairs. She saw no one.

"Come with Oux. Now."

Definitely, something had changed. "You're talking a lot better," she said.

Oux said nothing, only looked at her.

"I can't leave Ranie like this."

"Come with Oux."

Even though its tone had not changed, something about the way the alien spoke made Lex go very still.

"Why?"

The pause that followed only seemed long. "Time."

"For what? Time for what?"

"Truth."

Lex breathed out. She didn't have to ask what it meant. *If you're fucking with me.*

Oux fluttered a hand downward. "No. Not...do that."

"Why now, Oux? Why did you leave me like that?"

The alien hopped down and folded dry, cool fingers against her left wrist. "Oux feel change. Hurt One must come or not know truth."

"Change? What's changed?"

Oux's fingers slid away, but its eyes never left her face. They glittered like the night sky.

"Angry One—here."

III

The taxi driver straightened up against his air car, putting down his panel and the latest news briefs as a tall man strode out of the terminal doors and headed toward him. A cloak rested over one of the man's muscular arms and bright red hair shone like a beacon against the collar of a tight, dark blue shirt.

"Taxi?" he inquired, hoping he would prefer a live driver to a talking bot. Fares were getting harder and harder to find these days and his second job barely paid the rent. The red-headed man stopped and gave him a considering look before smiling.

"Do you know where Mathis Clinic is?"

"Sure do. Hop in," the driver replied.

That was when the fare did an uncharacteristic thing. Holding his hand out, he said, "Name's Chris. Pleased to meet you."

Probably just got in from the South. Would explain the cloak. The driver took the proffered hand. "Nice to meet you too," he said, before he realized he really meant it. *Nice guy. Polite too.*

"You know," the man continued without letting go, "It's my first time in PortCity and I was wondering. Could I ask you a favor? Just a small one?"

The driver smiled, feeling generous. "Well, if it's just a small one, why not?"

··· ▬ ▬ ▬ ···

The taxi pulled up across the street from the Clinic. "This is it," the driver said.

Without taking his hand from the man's shoulder, Chris leaned forward and surveyed the building in front of him. He opened himself up, letting the essence inside him fan out, searching for a matching signature like ghostly fingers tapping at closed doors.

He did not sense Oux. Not in the Clinic and not anywhere in the vicinity. A low sound of disgust escaped him and the driver flinched as if hit, no doubt feeling Chris's anger through their connection. Yet he dared not let go of the man. Normally, he would have been able to maintain control without frequent touching, but not now. In a few hours, he wouldn't be able to exert any control at all.

Then I'll be up the spacelanes without a hyperdrive. Damn that fucking Andraju. If they took Oux to the Troopers or to Customs and Immigration…

The possibilities didn't bear thinking about. Needless to say, all his grand plans would collapse in an instant without the alien. *I turn my back for a fucking minute.*

At that moment, he sensed something faint but undeniable. Like the smell of a woman's perfume the morning after, it lingered, teasing his memory before drifting away.

Oux.

"Start the car," he ordered the driver. With a soft gush of air, the vehicle rose in readiness.

"Turn around and go back."

The man did as he commanded and when they had driven almost five blocks, Chris said, "Here. Turn right here."

They made a right turn onto a narrow alley and the feel of Oux grew stronger, pulled at him slightly like a string tied to his finger.

"Yes," he murmured, pleased. "It came this way. Keep going. Take another right at the end of the street."

I'm coming, Oux. I'm coming.

135

IV

Oux waited as Lex placed Ranie in the car. She shut the door on her, and looked in at her peaceful face lolling against the headrest.

I don't think I'll see her again. Lex shuddered, unsure where the thought had come from. She looked up at the shelter, at the warm, orange light emanating from the arcs, and turned away, swallowing a strange tightness in her throat. Oux looked at her, motionless.

"Okay. What now?" she asked, her voice tense.

Oux turned and started off down the street, its spindly legs moving with a fluidness she had never seen. *Is it just me, or is it walking straighter somehow?*

She followed, feeling as if her world had come to a halt. She did not know what was coming next, could not fathom where Oux would take her, but emotions twisted her stomach. Anticipation— and trepidation.

They walked for a short while under gold and white street lights, passing cars every now and then, but no people. Oux moved swiftly in and out of shadow, sometimes running along the dark side of a building when a vehicle flashed past. At those moments, she wondered if she were seeing right; wondered if the alien wasn't running *on* the side of the building. But then it would emerge into the light and she would have to concentrate on keeping up with its brutal pace.

Lex spotted the building a block before they got to it. Her body tingled as she saw the big structure sitting just back from a semi-circular driveway. She didn't have to be told it was their destination. Something in her already knew. When they reached the holo sign that proclaimed the building, "PortCity Mercy Hospital", she stopped and looked at the alien, standing silently at her side.

"Why are we here? What's in there?"

It raised a small hand and wrapped its fingers around hers. "Truth," it said, before tugging her on.

She wasn't sure how, but the alien walked her up the driveway, past white clad figures unloading patients unto floating gurneys and into the lobby, without anyone looking at them once. They slipped past doctors on rounds, nurses at stations, patients walking halls, visitors sitting with the strain of waiting on their faces. A few turned their way, but to Lex, it was as if they weren't really seeing her and Oux. As if they were looking through them instead.

They took the stairs to the fifth floor. Oux clung to her hand like a lost child, never looking at her. Lex could feel it trying to comfort her, but she didn't understand why.

They passed another station where a single nurse sat before turning down a pale green corridor. Near the end, Oux stopped before a door and it opened, even though Lex was sure they were still outside the sensor range. Oux pulled her into the room until the door closed behind her and then let go of her hand. Lex took a step toward the sleeping figure on the bed.

The man had a healing mask over the left side of his face. Patches dotted his bare arms and peeped out from under the neckline of his hospital gown. He lay with his face to the right, as if looking out the room's window. She could not make out his features. His body bore the gauntness of a long illness and his brown hair seemed in need of a combing. Still, for some inexplicable reason, she began to tremble. On the bed, the man moved his head and mumbled something.

"I don't understand. Why did you bring me here? Am I supposed to know him? Does he know me?"

The alien gestured toward the bed. "Touch."

She stared.

It repeated the gesture. "Touch. See."

Lex took a step forward and moved the only chair in the room out of her way. "Are you sure?" she asked, shocked by how small—how frightened—her voice sounded, even to her ears.

Oux made a slight nod. It grasped its own hands to show her how.

Lex turned back to the bed and breathed deeply. She extended her hand and took the hot, slightly moist fingers in her own. She stood there, holding the man's hand, waiting for what, she did not know. A moment passed. Two. She looked at Oux. It had drawn closer to her and she started to ask it if she had done something wrong.

On the bed, the man turned his head.

At that moment, Oux reached out and grabbed her lower arm.

And throbbing sang along her nerves, like a horrible, grating symphony. She felt light. Afloat and confused. Until her head hit something, hard, and she rolled into a wall. Dazed now, her body numb, it took a while for her to process what had happened. Her eyes would not open. They felt as if they had been glued shut.

I've landed. Something threw me.

But even that didn't seem important. What did seem important— what was desperately important—was that she find the spray.

What spray? Where the hell am I?

But she knew where she was. Or rather, who she was. And a cold feeling started to trickle into her stomach. She could not move, could not feel any part of herself and, damn it, she only wanted to go to sleep. Just for a little while.

Find the spray or you'll die here.

Die, why die?

The chair. The captain's chair.

Her eyes opened and with blurry sight, she could just see a metal wall in front of her. Something dark made a streak against it. Dirty streak. Who dirtied it? It dawned on her, with calm indifference, that she was looking at her own blood. She did not move, lay between life and something darker for what seemed like eternity. Until a sound crept into her consciousness. A sound pinched at the edges of her awareness, pulled at her mind.

Tap, tap, tap. Tap...tap...tap. Tap, tap, tap.

Her chest felt like ice water had been poured down her throat. The sound came from her left and in front of her. Fear swept through her, taking all reason with it. She forced herself to raise her head a bit, to turn to her left. Toward a dark shape that cast a darker shadow. Her gaze moved upward.

And she saw. For the first time, she saw.

Time ground to a halt. In that second of seeing, memory hit her like a savage white light, burning out the shadows in her mind, rooting up forgotten events, casting its unforgiving glare everywhere.

And she remembered. She remembered everything.

No. Please. No.

Pain crushed her, obliterating all thoughts but one.

Andor.

Too much. It was too much. She cried out, tried to pull away, to shift back—

—and let go of the arm she held on to. With a high, breathless, despairing cry, she stumbled backward, tripping over the chair. Oux dropped her arm and she brought up trembling fingers to cover her mouth. She dropped to one knee and retched repeatedly. Nothing came up but spittle and afterward, a bitter, sour taste, like chewed green leaves, remained in her mouth.

The whole time, she could not stop thinking—could not stop remembering. *Orgala. Rhiannon. That bastard Ru-ad. And the ship.*

When she stopped gagging, she knew only minutes had passed since she'd first grabbed hold of—

Michael

—the man's arm, but in her mind, it seemed like hours. Unsteady, she wiped at her mouth and rose to her feet, only to realize that—

Michael

—the man's eyes were open and looking at her. She stared, unable to look away from the raw emotion in that gaze. The unmitigated terror. His chest heaved, as if he were trying to draw air and not finding it. His dark brown eyes were wide in his thin face.

A coldness filled her. A numbness she recognized and tried to fight. She drew closer to the bed and watched as *Michael* tracked her movements with his eyes, watched as his fingers twisted the sheets. She looked down on him, clenching her hands into fists.

"You know, don't you?" she whispered, and a terrible, soft whimper left his lips. "You were there. You remember what happened. Don't you, *Michael*?"

The cords in his neck stood out and his head dug back into the pillow as his eyes rolled up in his head. Somewhere above them, a computer chimed.

"Code Blue, Room 327, patient in cardiac arrest. Code blue, room 327—"

"What the fuck?" a voice said behind her.

She hadn't heard the door open. She sensed Oux turning next to her, noted the shock and the anger in the male voice. She did not think, she simply reacted.

She leaned forward and swept a leg back at the voice. Her foot smashed into something soft and she heard a strangled cry. There was a small splash and the rich smell of coffee permeated the room.

She followed the motion through, dropping her leg as she came around. Lex watched as the man flew across the room, out the door and against the wall. He bounced off onto the floor, his outstretched hand half in the doorway. Her shoe had left a mark on his throat. *Oh, god, no. Not again.* Beyond him, she could hear the sounds of people approaching—realized that the computer had not stopped sounding the alarm. She looked across at the alien.

"Oux?"

It bounded toward the window. One blurred motion and Oux was gone, leaving warm night air to wash into the room.

She ran out the door, kneeled next to the unconscious man and checked his pulse. *He's alive.* Relief flooded her. She looked up. A few feet from her, the end of the corridor loomed like an open doorway.

Two figures stepped into that space. A man and a woman. The woman was dark-haired, unfamiliar, but she recognized the man. *The trooper that interviewed me.* She saw the look of recognition that crossed his face too. It occurred to her how she must appear, bending over a body like that. *And the thing of it is, they're right.*

Beyond them, she could hear people approaching. *Code Blue. I can't be here when Security gets involved.* She got to her feet in one movement and ran straight at them, her gaze steady on—*Linkow. That was his name.* They read her intention and both reached for their guns even as they drew closer together to try and cut her off. Linkow shouted something and she swerved to her left, darted behind the woman and jabbed at her neck as she went.

The woman dropped like a stone and Lex stopped, swiveled her weight and brought her left leg up at the gun the Trooper had pulled free of his holster. The lasgun fell and then Lex's foot caught him under the chin. Part of her marveled at her reflexes, her balance. The other part just used both, coldly confident. His head rocked back and a thin trickle of blood escaped his nose as he stumbled into the wall. Lex heard the lasgun skitter away into a corner. She grabbed his shirt and slammed his head back against the wall. She had let go of him and run around the corner before he finished his slide to the floor.

She almost collided with an orderly—"Hey!"—just had time to sidestep him and leap over the floating crash cart. She kept going, ignoring the first scream. Darting past the startled nurse at her station, Lex leaped through the door to the stairs as it opened automatically. *Almost out of here.* She held on to the railing and catapulted herself down the stairwell, jumping from landing to landing with an eerie grace. *I have to get back to Colin. Have to explain.* She burst out of the door at the bottom of the stairs—and skidded to a stop.

A man stood a few feet from her, a redhead with dark eyes. His blue shirt was immaculate even though his boots were worn. His gaze met hers for a heartbeat.

I know you. Even as she thought it, she shook her head from side to side, as if in denial. A strange tension sped through her. In her head, a voice rose—*yes, yes, yes.*

"Chris," she breathed, the name a strange, yet familiar taste on her tongue.

"Hello," he said with a smile that did not reach his eyes. "In a hurry to leave? But I've come such a long way."

With a speed that surprised even her, he crossed the few feet between them and grabbed her arm. There was a lingering touch, *inside* her head, as if something slippery grasped at her mind. Revulsion made her gag. All conscious thought fled, replaced by pure instinct.

She threw up her arm, twisted out of his grasp and punched him, the impact shivering up to her shoulder, but not hurting, not hurting at all. He dropped her arm, grabbing his face as blood welled from his mouth. She started to run past him, but he surprised her again, stepping in front of her, his eyes narrowed.

She threw another punch and this time, he grabbed her fist and back-handed her across her face. The slap stung and her eyes watered, but instinctively her right leg aimed itself at his crotch. Again, his hand was there, and he grabbed her ankle, trying to toss her back and off balance.

Lex went with his movement, ripping her hand free with a sharp pain as she back-flipped and landed in a crouch, hair falling forward over her face for a second. She saw his feet move as he came at her and she leaned to the right, sweeping her left leg out in front of her. Her ankle crashed into his shoes and she hooked her foot and pulled.

Off balance, he fell on his ass. Lex launched herself to his right, but he grabbed her leg. She dropped low and kicked at his face. There was a satisfying smack as her shoe made contact with his forehead. His head snapped back and he let go of her. She kicked him one more time then rolled to her right.

Breathing hard now, Lex thrust up from the floor and ran through the parked runners and cars, past an idling taxi, looking for the exit.

V

"Doctor?"

Colin slid his hands into the sanitizer and looked over at the virtual receptionist. "Yes?"

"Anton Slake has been trying to contact you all evening. He asked if you could call him as soon as you were out of surgery."

Damn. He must have found something. "Thanks."

"You're welcome." The woman disappeared.

Colin closed his eyes as the sanitizer dried his hands, feeling the exhaustion of a six-hour surgery settling over him. But he could not rest. Anton wouldn't have called without a very good reason and he had left his comm panel in his office. He pulled his hands free of the slits, releasing a fresh apple scent into the air.

As he left the washroom, his mind wandered to Ranie and Lex. She should be settled into her new home by now. He made a mental note to call Ranie and find out how things had gone. He would not be able to see either of them tonight, but maybe, if things worked out, he would go to see Lex later that week.

It will be the first time I won't be seeing her as my patient. I wonder how she'll think of me.

As a friend if you know what's good for you. Nothing more. Not now.

But maybe, when she's better…

"Lights," he said as he stepped into the office. And froze as his office lit up, illuminating the shape standing in front of his activated transperiwall. He recognized her at once. Her back was to him and she wore street clothes, but her dark hair and the line of her body were familiar.

"Lex?" he said, surprised. She did not turn, did not acknowledge his answer. On his desk, the flashing of his comm panel told him he had messages waiting.

"Are you okay? I thought you went to the shelter with Ranie." He took a few steps that brought him to the desk. "What are you doing here in the dark?"

"Admiring your city," she said, and her voice sounded—different.

"Lex, is something wrong?"

"I haven't seen a city in a while, you know," she continued, as if he hadn't said anything. "Not since I was little. There are no cities like this in the desert. That's why I felt so strange here. So out of place. I truly don't belong. Not anymore."

Holy shit! "Lex, has your memory returned?"

"Stop calling me that," she said, her voice sharp as she turned her head to the side. "It's not my name."

He paused, realizing for the first time how tense she seemed. Her hands hung straight down at her sides and her fists were tightly clenched. He walked around the desk slowly, so that he was on her right. She did not look at him.

"You've remembered everything then?"

The laugh that escaped her was both soft and bitter and he saw a muscle tic in her jaw. "Everything, yes. And you know what they say. Be careful what you wish for, you just might get it." Her breath caught for a moment, as if in the wake of a sharp pain. When she spoke again, for the first time, she sounded her age. "I had just turned eighteen when they took me. My birthday was three nights earlier. I was still a virgin when they raped me."

Shocked, Colin could only look at her. *Oh, God. How could they do that? What kind of beasts could do that?* He wanted to go to her, hold her and tell her that she was safe now, but something stopped him. Something in the way she held herself.

"God. I'm so sorry."

"I know you mean well, Colin, but it's my fault. I shouldn't have trusted anyone. People like me can't afford that. But I was stupid. I forgot. I *wanted* to forget." She paused. "You won't understand. You don't know who I am. *What* I am."

He said softly, "So tell me."

The expression on her face when she turned to him grabbed at his chest like a fist. Her calmness was terrible to look at, difficult to comprehend.

"My name," she said, in a voice that never wavered, "is Shalon Conway. I am the daughter of Jason and Falon Conway and heir to Conway Enterprises. Gilene Conway is my aunt—and the woman who murdered my parents."

INTERLUDE

Study the past, if you would divine the future.
— *Confucius*

Excerpt from the Confidential Report on the Phoenix Facility Incident as presented to a meeting of the Board of Directors of ME&E, April 4th 261 A.A.

The revolt was carefully planned. The soldiers were in communication with their counterparts offworld, and they were stockpiling weapons in the desert just outside the training grounds, under the very noses of Tec Solutions' personnel. Several mercenary ships broke service from a nearby colony and arrived at the Phoenix Facility within hours of the start of the revolt. Tec's people never had a chance.

Negotiations at this juncture may be pointless. As near as we can tell, there is no one from Tec left alive at the Phoenix Facility. The Orgalian subjects have killed anyone foolish enough to land, and only activating the self-destruct options have kept our spacecraft out of their hands. Offworld Groups have severed all ties with Tec Solutions. Their employers are desperate to keep the services of the soldiers and won't assist us in capturing them. Due to the present war, all deep space patrols and warships must be accounted for. Our contacts in the military cannot break ranks to carry out cleanup operations.

Which is exactly what the Orgalian subjects may have intended. Given the nature of their planning, I think it is safe to assume they knew ME&E would be in no position to help Tec before the damage was done. The soldiers have retained most of the Facility and its equipment, and it's possible that with the knowledge gained by the subjects who assisted the Facility's former staff, they might find a way to reverse the procreation failsafe.

To protect the integrity of the genetic material used to create the subjects, and to ensure that experimentation would continue under our full control, most of the subjects were rendered infertile. Only those with genetic traits we wished to encourage were allowed to procreate. This meant the subjects relied on us for their very existence, and could not increase their numbers without our assistance.

We believed the number of subjects allowed to go offworld would keep the population on Orgala from expanding past our capacity to contain them, should they ever try to gain independence. It was also believed that those who were sent offworld had been carefully vetted and indoctrinated into the Program's main aim of producing superior soldiers, totally loyal to Tec Solutions. Their devotion to the mission had been tested many times, and they expressed nothing but gratefulness for the opportunity to serve offworld, which would allow a certain amount of freedom as a consequence. Even if this did not prove true, we did not believe the genetic subjects on Orgala and those offworld would ever work together, or find a way to remain in communication without our knowledge. We were wrong. And now, should they use the resources left at the Facilities to figure out how to reverse the infertility we engineered into two-thirds of the population, it will be impossible to control them. Certainly, with the help of the offworld Groups that have returned to Orgala, soldiers of their abilities and numbers would decimate our Security forces if we tried.

All indications are there's nothing to be gained by involving ourselves further. Tec Solutions had a tenuous relationship with us at best. They entered into this with InGene's blessings, and we honored our agreement with them and Tec well beyond the original contract due to our own investment in the Program.

Since the InGene scandal only ended five years ago and the Program was discontinued, we would open ourselves up to worse legal proceedings by drawing attention to Orgala now. If we destroy all evidence of our involvement with Tec Solutions and Orgala, we should be able to avoid future liability. Best case scenario: the soldiers die out under the twin burdens of infertility and casualties inflicted offworld, and become the cause of their own downfall.

Worst case: they survive and become a recognized colony. Even then, any repatriation due to them could only be paid by Tec, which is now defunct.

In other words, gentlemen, let's leave well enough alone. Tec Solutions was not our problem before this, and we certainly can't afford to make the company's mess our problem now.

PART TWO

Excerpt from "A Short History of the Planet Orgala and the city of Rhiannon" by Ru-ad Whelan, Chief Advisor to the First Commander and Co-founder of the city of Rhiannon

Tec Solutions and their parent company, Conway Enterprises, had always underestimated our loyalty to each other. They never suspected that one of the effects of their cruel indoctrination techniques and forced copulations would be to unify all Orgalians in our hatred toward them. Early on, we learned that it would be best to comply with all that was demanded of us until we were in a position to be sure that any action we took would result in the freedom of all.

We developed a version of ancient Latin and used it carefully and sparingly to communicate our plans and thoughts secretly, whether we were trapped in the Facility's constant experiments, or released offworld into service as mercenaries. The idea of revolt was born soon after and eventually it just became a matter of time...

...We were able to continue receiving necessary shipments of food and equipment from offworld mercenaries the same way we had before. The supplies were collected by our people at outposts throughout the galaxy, and then brought to Orgala using ships piloted by our own people so that our location remained secret. We were also able to continue all business arrangements set up by Tec Solutions. With the war in full swing, and most colonies well outside the protective embrace of the Troopers and left to fend for themselves, our soldiers were the difference between life and death for many. We threatened to withdraw our forces permanently if the colonies sided with Tec

Solutions and reneged on their contracts. If they accepted us under our own terms, we would provide longer contracts, which we called Apprenticeships, for a much lower price. Under those new terms, the colonists were more than willing to sever ties with Tec Solutions, and negotiate contracts with us instead.

What Cu-don and I did not know was that our greatest threat would not come from outside. The possibility of Conway Enterprises discovering our genetic makeup and claiming us by legal right had always been a concern. Hence, we were careful to keep our society and our city, Rhiannon, secret, hoping that in time we would be able to increase our number and become a people instead of an elite army. However, in the end, it was internal divisions that did the most damage.

Once we had won our freedom, a few groups of soldiers felt they should be able to follow their own path offworld and demanded their own ships to leave Orgala as soon as our victory was assured. They had been scarred by their time under the control of the doctors and felt that having a command structure of any kind was a return to being stripped of their freedom, even if it was under First Commander Cu-don, who had won their freedom for them. They had no plan aside from leaving Orgala—no understanding that the ships we had were limited and could not simply be turned over to those who had no purpose for them that served Orgala as a whole. These renegade soldiers—who we came to call Outsiders—would not understand that their insistence on leaving Orgala on their own terms would only endanger all Orgalians, should offworlders discover their origins. Under Group Leader Ta-el, they retained control of the Facility, and the key to reversing our genetic infertility lies within the databases. Thankfully, they have no knowledge of Rhiannon and believe we hold only the two Outposts abandoned by our former masters.

I did not take the decision to make war on the Outsiders lightly, but I believe I made the right choice for our future. Either the Outsiders will join us in a united front and work for the good of all Orgalians under the leadership of the Assembly, or we will force them to relinquish the Facility. We have no choice if we are to survive.

CHAPTER 12

The Three Principal Laws of Rhiannon:
3) Lex Talionis: Those that attempt to enslave or destroy us must be shown no mercy.
2) No Orgalian may take the life of another unless under the law of Vendetta.
1) Every Orgalian life is valuable. No one shall be left behind on the field of battle.

— The Laws of Rhiannon

I

Whiteway Sector
The planet Orgala
Two months earlier

Shalon strode down the twisting bedrock passageway, her feet so light in scuffed, dusty boots, they were silent on the loose shale that littered the floor. Ahead of her, the tunnel forked, an apparent rockfall blocking the left entrance. She turned sideways, slid carefully through a small opening in the blockage, feeling the soreness in her aching body and willing herself to move past it. Her ribs still hurt from an unceremonious slide into a tunnel. *Rest later. Ru-ad first.* Once she emerged, Shalon kept going down the tunnel, hunched over now. Her shoulders almost touched the walls. Cool air, thick with dust, whispered past her as she walked.

Around her, the rough dirt walls changed and began to show the sparkle of jape quartz that winked blue and green in the light of the white lumidiscs stuck onto the ceiling. In the shifting earth tones of the rock, the chips made a beautiful display, but Shalon did not allow herself the time to admire them today. She focused instead on putting one throbbing foot in front of the other.

The tunnel widened and the ceiling rose enough so that she could walk upright. She passed caves that had been hollowed out of the rock on both sides of the tunnel. A few were empty. Others held crates and packages of food and equipment, stacked in neat rows for easy retrieval. A slight breeze blew past her, lifting her loose, dusty hair, unwashed and uncombed after three days in the desert. Her hips felt light without the accustomed weight of her holster and guns. She still wore her filthy scout suit. Its light armor was in need of a thorough cleaning. Ru-ad could take offense at her appearance, but she figured he should be willing to forgive her once he heard the news about Andor.

And if he still takes offense, the hell with him. I've got no time for his protocol crap today. Not after the battle I went through to rescue Andor. Not after the way Ru-ad used him.

The passageway widened enough so that two people could walk abreast. Ahead, she could hear a faint voice, rising and falling in the unmistakable rhythm of a monologue. She rounded a small bend to the right and saw a brightly lit cave, the source of the voice. The cool wind she'd felt before emanated from the open doorway of the temperature-controlled chamber.

Ru-ad's tall, thin figure stood just beyond the entranceway, gesturing with careful, controlled movements. His lean arms were bared by the sleeveless brown vest he wore over close-fitting, durable pants, designed to avoid getting caught on rocks and jagged edges. In a rough semi-circle before him, a half-dozen children—boys and girls—were seated lotus position, listening in intent silence. They looked far too serious for their ages, which ranged from about three to nine. Dust streaked a few faces from their passage through the tunnels while being instructed by Ru-ad.

On a gleaming table to Ru-ad's right, a holoprojector stood on a tripod next to four VR learning helmets. The helmets lay like scattered black gems, and had obviously just been used by the children and put aside. Ru-ad was speaking in the bastardized Latin that Orgalians used in the battlefield when they wished to keep their conversations from others. No doubt to test the children's knowledge.

"...is Lex Talionis—the law of revenge. A system of justice practiced widely during the Middle Ages on Old Earth, it works on the eye for an eye, tooth for a tooth principle. Remember it, children. It formed the basis for what we do here today."

Shalon paused in the doorway. She did not wait long. The children all swung around as Ru-ad looked up. She cast her eyes downward, the customary gesture of respect, before meeting his gaze.

"Chief Advisor, I regret the interruption but I have news."

Ru-ad nodded, the expression in his cat-yellow eyes distant. "Children, reflect on what we've discussed. There will be a quiz tomorrow."

Together, Shalon and Ru-ad stepped into the rock passage and walked far enough away so that their voices would not carry. As soon as they were out of earshot, he murmured in Latin, "You've come straight from the battlefield, Vi-Commander?"

"Please, Ru-ad," she replied in Universal, her voice soft, but firm. "We're away from the kids. You don't need to be formal."

Ru-ad switched languages effortlessly. "You're angry with me?"

Shalon stopped walking and faced him. He clasped his hands behind his back, annoyance flitting over his face as he took in her dusty clothing. His aristocratic nose tilted upward slightly in disapproval. A kernel of anger began to build in her, but thoughts, darker and more subtle than her own, filled her head as Andor spoke to her through their mind link.

Be calm—and fair. The fault was mine as well. Exhaustion tinged his words.

You need to rest. Stay out of this.

I'll be fine. The healers are tending to me as we speak. Just remember. We both planned it.

But it was his idea, wasn't it?

Silence. She probed after him, searching for confirmation in his memories, but Andor had blocked her out or fallen asleep, she wasn't sure which.

Shalon forced herself to let go of her anger. Andor was right. Only logic and an even temper would see her past Ru-ad's icy veneer.

"You think it's my fault Andor was captured." Ru-ad made it a statement, not a question.

"I think it's damn lucky he wasn't killed. Or anyone else for that matter."

"Then he's unharmed?" And although his tone had not changed, Shalon knew him well enough to hear the concern behind his question. *You love him like a son, but if you have to, you won't hesitate to send him into harm's way. I don't know how you do it, Ru-ad, and I don't want to.*

"He will be. He's in bad shape, but he'll pull through, with rest."

"Is that your opinion or the healer's?" he inquired in a mild voice.

"Both," she shot back and decided she'd had enough.

"He's in the healing chamber. You can visit him there if you like. I'm going to get cleaned up and I'll meet with you and the Assembly for the debriefing this evening."

"Perhaps you should meet with us now," he suggested. She cocked an eyebrow at him.

"Why? It's not like I'll forget the details."

"There are other considerations."

"Which will be dealt with in a manner appropriate to their priority," she interrupted. "Right now, the only thing requiring immediate attention is Andor. Need I remind you that with my Sub-Commander injured, I'm in charge? Or do you wish to challenge my right to make such decisions before the Assembly?"

Brave words, Shalon, considering they could demote you or have you exiled for what you've done. She pushed the thought away, refusing to give in to the nervous uncertainty that lay under it.

Ru-ad paused before answering. "No."

"We're agreed then. Four hours from now in the Assembly Hall. That should give you enough time to finish your history lesson. Just don't forget to include the part about me." She stalked off without looking back.

··· — — — ···

Shalon stepped through her front door and placed the holster she had retrieved from her Attack Leader on the small stone table near the entrance. Her slender lasguns clattered noisily against each other. No other holster lay on the table and she realized that her foster father, Ku Olang, must not be home.

"Ha-Ka, I'm back," she called out, loosening the tight collar of her suit. She touched the tiny, rectangular panel on the inside of the left sleeve of her suit. A hiss sounded and the small buttons disappeared beneath their retractable cover as the suit powered down. In front of her, three shallow stone steps descended to a semi-circular living area.

Two sofas, their ornate frames carved by Ku himself from rare wood, had been placed on either side of a table fashioned from sparkling blue-green quartz. The metal top of the table was polished to a shine that reflected the large, flat lumidisc in the domed ceiling high above. The dark green cushions on the chairs had been woven from the same recycled plant fibers as the large, decorative wall panels. Ha-Ka had made them all herself many years before. The turquoise ocean waves moving toward a distant shore rippled in the slight breeze from the air regulators built into the walls and ceilings of every residence in Rhiannon.

To Shalon's left, a rock staircase led to a ledge with a stone railing. On her right, an archway led to the compact kitchen. She could smell something smoky and meaty cooking and her stomach clenched. Her last meal had been more than a day ago.

At that moment, Ha-Ka Pravet appeared at the stone railing. There was a question in her foster mother's slanted amber eyes and Shalon answered it with a slight nod of her head. Ha-Ka let out a pent-up breath. She came down the stairs quickly, bowing her head when she reached Shalon.

"Vi-Commander," she said in a low voice, smooth as velvet. "I am grateful that you have returned to this house safely, your mission successful."

"I am grateful, foster mother, that I return to find you safe as well." Shalon completed the ritual gratitude greeting and hugged her mother. Ha-Ka hugged back, her dark hair smelling of desert flowers from her work in the Greeneries. It was a display of emotion that would have shamed any other Orgalian, but Ha-Ka had always been different. Had always understood Shalon's needs.

She was really worried about me this time.

Of course she was. I dropped everything when Andor called me and just took off. That close to the Facility, with comm silence in effect, how could she be sure I hadn't been captured or killed?

A bittersweet feeling tightened Shalon's chest. She loved the desert, loved the feeling of freedom and vastness under the sky after the caves of Rhiannon. But every time she made it back, wonderful as it felt to come home, she remembered her first family, dead now for almost ten years.

Remembered the homecomings she would never have again.

"When did you get the news?" Shalon asked against Ha-Ka's hair, which was short and cut like a boy's.

"A few hours after you failed to relieve the Group at Outpost Two. They called in and a check revealed that only Andor and your Group were unaccounted for. Ru-ad told us that Andor was out on a solo recon and we put two and two together."

"I'm sorry I worried you all, but there was no time."

Ha-Ka leaned back and shook her head. "It's all right. But if it hadn't been for the mind-link you two share..." She sighed. "Was Andor hurt? Did you lose any of your Group?"

"I lost no one, but Andor was tortured before we got there and shot during our escape."

Ha-Ka searched her face, her hands light on Shalon's shoulders. "He will be okay?"

"In a few weeks. For now, he needs rest."

Ha-Ka made an amused sound. "As if that will ever happen."

Shalon stepped out of the embrace and started down the stairs. "He may not have a choice." In her mind's eye, she saw Andor's pale face, blood welling from the deep slash on his left cheek as she slung his arm around her shoulders and urged him to his feet.

"He almost died this time." She tried to distract herself with unfastening the seal down the middle of her chest. Ha-Ka moved in front of her.

"What you mean, Shalon, is that *you* almost lost *him*."

Shalon sighed and lowered her arms. "I'm that obvious?"

"No." Ha-Ka shrugged, her face serene and mischievous at the same time. "You're many things, daughter, but you've never been obvious. A bit arrogant, yes. Too brave for your own good, yes. A pain in the butt, definitely. But obvious? I think not."

Despite herself, Shalon gave her a rare smile. "I'm too tired to argue. And I have an Assembly meeting in four hours."

Ha-Ka frowned, a thin, vertical line creasing her smooth forehead. "You should rest."

Shalon waved a hand in a dismissive gesture. "It doesn't matter. You know how well I sleep most nights."

"I know you'll sleep better with Andor here," Ha-Ka said quietly. Shalon nodded absently and stood for a moment, thinking.

"Ha-Ka, do you think he—?"

"Feels the same way about you?" She shrugged. "He's as hard to read as you are. And I think you know him better than I do."

Shalon sighed. "Yes. Yes I do." *I don't really need anyone to tell me what I already know.*

So what are you going to do about it?

Nothing for now. It's too soon. But later, when he's healed, we will talk.

"Four hours." Ha-Ka put her hands on her hips. "Well, let's get you cleaned up and put some food into you before you offend the Advisors." She steered Shalon toward the steps that led to the balcony.

"Did that already. I delivered the news to Ru-ad in person half-an-hour ago. Really, Ha-Ka, I don't know how Ku can stand to be in the same room with him."

"Because he's not a man to be taken lightly. He did, after all, help Cu-don found Rhiannon. They were InGene's most senior and trusted trainers before the rebellion, and fought offworld several times. His strategies are part of the reason we still grow and thrive while the Outsiders struggle to keep the Facility going."

"You're trying to tell me something I've heard before, Ha-Ka."

"Only because you don't really hear it, daughter," Ha-Ka chided as they walked to Shalon's bedroom. "Be careful how you treat Ru-ad. He's Chief Advisor, after all. As smart as you are, he is also smart—and experienced. And he holds Andor's ear. Do you really want to offend your Sub-Commander's mentor?"

"Only when he's being unbearable," Shalon replied.

"No wonder you have trouble keeping hold of that tongue then," Ha-Ka said with a wink before following her daughter into her room.

II

Shadows slipped across and around the screen that surrounded the hospital bed. Soft murmurs could be heard as healers tended to other patients. One tall shadow swept over Andor's face as he slept, and as if he felt its passage, his eyes opened and he blinked. A few minutes passed before he turned his head. "Chief Advisor?"

"Sub-Commander." Ru-ad replied. "Welcome back."

Andor tried to sit up, failed and fell back on the pillow with a slight grimace. The synthskin bandage on his cheek made a pale, curved slash from his dark hairline to his angular jaw. His left arm had been bandaged up to the elbow, while the fingers of his right hand were splinted. "I'm surprised to find you here."

"Where else would I be?"

Andor merely looked at him. Ru-ad smiled, a thin movement. "I have an Assembly meeting in a couple of hours."

"Ah." Andor nodded a little. "You want to debrief me."

"I only have one question. And you know what it is."

Andor lay back and stared at the lumidisc high in the domed rock ceiling. "You were right. The Outsiders have deduced that Outposts One and Two are not our primary bases. They have halted their operations while they consider what this means. But they do not know of Rhiannon, or that we live underground."

"Still, it will only be a matter of time now." Ru-ad leaned back in his hard, metal chair.

"I agree." Andor tried to flex the fingers of his left hand and winced. "We must find a way to end this conflict, and soon."

"I have a way. But the Assembly might be reluctant to try it."

"I suspected as much when you asked me to go out on this mission."

Ru-ad remained silent for a moment. "I'm sorry for my part in your capture."

Andor shrugged. "All of us take risks every day. I've been lucky for a long time."

"And you continue to be lucky."

Andor glanced at him. "You mean Shalon."

Ru-ad did not answer.

"You know she's the reason I went alone. I'm the only other person in Rhiannon who doesn't need a comm to call for help. It is a good thing I had that option."

"Unfortunately, she must have some idea of what you were doing now."

"You weren't planning to hide it for much longer."

"Yes, but I wished no one to know before I spoke to Cu-don." Ru-ad paused. "You're sure she knew nothing before you were captured?"

Andor's jaw tightened. "We don't do that to each other. We have blocks, you know that. She didn't pry."

"You're sure?"

"I'm sure." Andor closed his eyes. "You have something more

you want to say?"

"Yes." Ru-ad leaned forward a little. "She is ten years your junior, Andor, and too young for you. If it wasn't for the genetic accident that is the mind-link between you two, you would see that."

"I'm perfectly aware of the difference in our ages," Andor replied, his voice icy. "But I notice it did not bother you when she was eleven and you accepted her into her first Group. She's been an Orgalian most of her life. It is not unusual for us to marry at her age. She's as mature as any of us. She's had to be."

"You cannot possibly hope to have a relationship with her."

Andor opened his eyes but did not look at Ru-ad. "Why? Because you do not think of her as Orgalian?"

"She *isn't* an Orgalian," Ru-ad said, then paused and took a deep breath. "You are being stubborn simply to irritate me. You know what I say is true."

Andor ignored him, choosing to remain silent.

"I only want you to be careful. Shalon is the youngest Vi-Commander we've ever had. There are those that would see her take the post of Commander some day."

"What are you trying to say, Ru-ad?" Andor's voice sounded calm and disinterested.

"I'm saying that you have worked long and hard to become Commander. Your daring rescue, right out from under the noses of the Outsiders, is the stuff of which leaders are made. The Council will find that hard to ignore."

Andor finally met Ru-ad's gaze, his golden eyes expressionless. "I suppose it is an insignificant detail that should I be appointed Commander, you will be standing right behind me as my Chief Advisor and mentor?"

"I have never denied my own reasons for supporting you, but you know what I do goes far deeper than that. As a Council member and Chief Advisor to First Commander Cu-don, I have already attained the highest post I can hope for.

"I have done this for you, Andor. All of it. You understand power. And you will not hesitate to use it for the good of Rhiannon, whatever the cost. We need that if we are to succeed as a society. But Shalon is a Conway. She has power in her veins as well. And if you do not control her, she will take what is rightfully yours."

Silence fell for a while, still like the air before a storm.

"No one controls Shalon," Andor said, enunciating each word

with care. "And no one controls me. I am not your son, Ru-ad. My father is long dead. You would do well to remember that."

Ru-ad met his unwavering gaze for long minutes. Shadows came and went on the white screen, like dark ghosts. "Of course, Andor."

"And Ru-ad. I would be very disappointed if the Assembly finds Shalon at fault in any of this."

Andor turned his head away and Ru-ad rose from his chair, aware he had been dismissed.

"Rest well, Sub-Commander," he said, before parting the screen and walking away.

III

"Shalon."

She paused before the door to the Assembly Hall and sent out a tendril of thought, a seeking finger in the wind. *"You're awake."*

"I wanted to let you know—the Assembly will find you without fault in this."

"Well, the possibility exists, but you know how Ru-ad feels about me. I'm not Orgalian after all. I'm the little girl who fell into your lap ten years ago and turned Rhiannon upside down."

"You're no Outsider. Your life has been spent in service to Rhiannon. You are not a traitor like the rebels at the Facility." His thoughts resonated in her head like a plucked string. *"I've spoken to Ru-ad. The Assembly knows my wishes."*

"Thank you." Shalon smiled to herself, broadcasting the expression to Andor. *"But the first round of questioning didn't exactly inspire my confidence."*

"They're always tough. You know that." And then, because he could see into her deepest fears, he added, *"You will not lose your command."*

"No one's irreplaceable here."

"And no one's stupid. You are the best Vi-Commander we've had in years. Your Sub-Commander would have no other."

The emotion behind his words washed over Shalon and made her flesh goosebump. She wanted to luxuriate in that small moment of truth between them, that all-too-brief second that acknowledged how he really felt about her, but she didn't have the time.

"I must go. I'll see you afterward."

"There is no need."

"Just try to keep me away." Clouding her mind to shut out his protests, she grasped the large brass handle and pushed one half of the huge metal doors open.

There were larger caves than the Assembly Hall, but none higher. The bedrock that formed the ceiling of the Hall was obscured by shifting shadows. Lumidiscs placed at regular intervals along the curved chamber walls illuminated the lower hall without casting light into the upper reaches.

Four steps in front of her led down to a perfect circle that had been cut into the clean-swept floor. In the middle of that circle stood a slender lectern carved from the blue-green brilliance of jape quartz. A stone table, polished to a dark shine, curved around the half of the circle in front of the lectern. A small jape brazier in the exact center of the table wafted creeping white curls of smoke, and the sweet, nutty musk of lichen that grew in the deepest part of Rhiannon.

Seated around the table were three men and three women, all dressed in sand colored robes with the hoods thrown back. All but one of them had short hair. Their strikingly similar golden eyes regarded Shalon calmly as she walked down the steps. Shalon caught the quick, kind smile of the middle aged man with the salt and pepper hair in the last stone chair to the right. The smile was gone as fast as it came, his thin face smoothing over before anyone else could see. *Thank you, Ku,* she thought, grateful for his support.

Shalon descended the steps, picking up the skirts of her robe as she went. It was blue and layered to keep the transparent cloth from revealing too much. Wearing it made her feel like she wore swaddling cloths, but an Assembly audience demanded more than her scout suit. Ha-Ka had even forced her to braid her hair into one smooth plait.

When Shalon reached the lectern, she placed both hands on either side of the top. A soft tone sounded, indicating the recording device had been activated.

Shalon bowed her head before meeting the eyes of the woman seated at the center of the table, pointedly ignoring Ru-ad, who was on her right. The First Commander's bald scalp was so tanned, it seemed cut from cured wood. A tiny scar bisected her upper lip near the left corner. Her cheeks were gaunt, but her eyes were bright with purpose and strength. The aura of power she emanated dwarfed even Ru-ad's impressive presence.

"Shalon Conway, daughter of our hearts and minds, we welcome you into our presence once more." Her voice, a firm contralto, filled the room and the kindness in her tone was unmistakable.

Shalon stood stunned. *She spoke before me. She greeted me first, as she would a superior. But she has no superior. A mistake. It must be a mistake.* She found her tongue.

"Cu-don, mother of my soul, you honor me. Your regard gives me great joy, but you grant me far more than I deserve."

"It is the duty and the privilege of this Assembly to decide what honors Orgalians deserve. In your case, we would be remiss if we failed to greet you as the hero you are." Cu-don, First Commander and the Liberator of the Orgalians of Rhiannon, raised her eyebrows in an ironic gesture. "Or do you propose to tell your Commander and this Assembly how you should be treated?"

Shalon cast her gaze down, glad of the chance to hide her consternation. "I would do no such thing."

"Then, as First Commander, it is my duty to inform you of our decision."

Shalon squared her shoulders, aware the news could not be bad if Commander Cu-don addressed her like this, but still not quite ready to believe the best.

"Vi-Commander Shalon Conway, you stand accused of the gravest of crimes among true Orgalians. You abandoned your duties and your post without authorization and engaged in battle against the Outsiders without support. In so doing, you risked your life and the lives of those under your command.

"However, your actions were precipitated by the certain knowledge that your superior was in need of support and you were unable to inform Command of your plans due to your proximity to Outsider listening devices. You performed the impossible by successfully infiltrating the Facility and extracting my Sub-Commander before he was killed or forced to reveal Rhiannon's existence. Your Group returned with no casualties while the Outsiders lost at least six men. I have also been reliably informed—" and here she glanced at Ru-ad, "—that your actions ensured important information vital to our security was safely delivered to our Chief Advisor.

"In view of these mitigating circumstances, the Assembly finds you without fault in this matter and further congratulates you for your courage under fire and your exceptional execution of strategy in the battlefield. You have upheld the highest tenets of Orgalian law—to leave no one behind and to hold every life as dear as your own. In short, Vi-Commander, you have made us proud."

Shalon's heart raced. *She's proud of me. The Liberator's proud of me.*

"Thank you, Commander, but I only did what any of us would have done." Out of the corner of her eye, she saw the ghost of a smile cross her foster father's stern face.

"We would have tried, yes. But I doubt we would have succeeded with only a dozen fighters to aid us. In gratitude for the safe return of our Sub-Commander and our Vi-Commander, the Assembly has decreed a feast day, one month from today on the occasion of your eighteenth birthday. All of Rhiannon, except those on active duty, will be allowed to participate, and by then my Sub-Commander should be recovered enough to partake in the festivities."

Oh, shit. I knew there had to be a drawback. "Commander, I'm overwhelmed by your generosity, but I'm not exactly one for public celebrations."

"Then I suggest you use the time between now and then to get used to the idea," Cu-don replied in a dry voice, but there was a hint of a smile in her eyes. "In addition, as a reward, you will be off active duty for a week."

Shalon stifled a groan. "A whole week?"

"And if I see you near a practice chamber, I will strip you of your rank, is that understood?" Cu-don asked.

"Understood." *What the hell will I do with myself for a whole week?*

"If you're wondering what to do with all that time, might I suggest rest and recuperation from your own injuries."

"Of course, Commander," Shalon replied with another deferential inclination of her head, chafing inside at the thought of the long torturous hours to come.

"You are dismissed."

Shalon stepped from behind the lectern, and turned on her heel. *At least I'm not going to be demoted.* She climbed the stairs at a dignified pace and exited without a backward glance.

As soon as she was outside, she called to Andor, only to come up against the shifting mind-murk of a block. She frowned to herself and pushed against it, trying to get his attention. A stray thought leaked out. *Not now.* She realized he had someone with him.

Oh, no you don't. I'm coming to see you now, you cheat. You won't get rid of me that way.

163

Raking her fingers though her hair to pull her braid loose, she started down the twisting corridors to the healers' chambers. Here, the passages were wider, the lumidiscs more plentiful and there were many junctions with a great deal of traffic. Even a few tunnelers rolled by. The city's residential area began here and open caves gave way to closed metal portals that led to small homes.

As she walked, she passed more than one person who nodded and murmured, "Vi-Commander," before moving on. Once, a Group headed out to duty snapped a salute to her and she acknowledged it before they jogged past, heads held high, wearing sand-colored scout suits already dusted for better camouflage. She looked after them longingly.

Twenty minutes later, she arrived at the white portal that led to the healers' chambers. She stepped across the threshold and almost bumped into someone coming out.

"Niala!"

Niala Quemar bowed before smiling at her, a wide, genuine expression of pleasure that disappeared before some passerby could see it. "Vi-Commander. Praise be that you have returned safely."

"Praise be that old friends greet me on my return." Shalon smiled back. Niala looked impeccable as usual, and the absence of armor signaled she had come from her home. She wore light, golden robes that set off her eyes, and straight black hair brushed her chin. A sweet scent, like crushed modo petals, surrounded her. Shalon felt a slight pang of envy as Niala grasped her shoulders in a soldier's greeting.

She never looks bad and never screws up. She's a great fighter, a clever strategist and insanely beautiful. And she's not even aware of how perfect she is. What I wouldn't give to be that self-assured.

Especially around Andor.

"I heard of your exploits. Our Vi-Commander has become a legend in her own time." Niala's eyes betrayed her mirth. "You must tell me how Andor Calleden felt about being lugged around by his protégé."

"He had no choice in the matter," Shalon replied. "I wasn't about to let him die. You've seen him?"

"Just leaving. He told me the Assembly was meeting with you. It went well?"

"Better and worse than expected."

Niala's expression turned quizzical.

"Better in that I'm still Vi-Commander. Worse, in that there will be a party to celebrate it next month."

Niala laughed. "So you will finally celebrate your birthday. Oh, how you must be looking forward to that."

"Your amusement warms my heart," Shalon said in a wry voice. "I'm glad someone will be enjoying the prospect of my birthday celebration."

"Oh, Shalon, you must accept it with good grace."

She's right, of course. It's an honor.

Don't give me that, Andor. If you were in my position, you'd be just as pleased about it as I am.

Niala let go of her arms. "He's talking to you, isn't he?"

Shalon nodded. "Trying to get me to be happy about the feast."

"Hypocrite." Niala grinned. "I have to go. I have a practice session with some novices in an hour."

"Stop by when you're done. Ha-Ka would love to see you."

She watched Niala leave, then made her way between the neatly laid out beds. Two archways were in front of her and she took the left one. Here, a smaller, less crowded chamber had been sectioned by white screens, five in all. She could see the shadows of healers moving behind three of the screens. Musty, minty herbs tainted the air. Shalon went to the farthest screen on her right, pulled the plastic aside and stepped in.

Andor rested against his pillows, a ghost of a smile on his face. A white sheet had been pulled up to his waist and she noted the splints and bandages as she sat in the chair next to the bed.

You look—nice. It went well. He shifted in her mind, a collage of amusement.

Don't start with the clothes, okay. I'm annoyed enough as it is.

They're giving you the recognition you deserve.

I'm not the one who almost got killed.

"No," he agreed, "you're the one who risked her life for mine."

"You did the same for me ten years ago. I'm just returning the favor." Shalon propped her chin on her fists. "So, I'm on leave for a whole week. Any idea what I should do?"

"None."

"Well, I was thinking that maybe I would spend it keeping you company until they let you out of here."

His smile disappeared. "Shalon, you don't have to do that."

"I want to," she replied.

"Shalon."

"I know what you're going to say," she said quietly. "Don't bother. You won't change my mind."

Andor plucked at the sheet on his legs. "You're very stubborn, you know."

"You must be rubbing off on me." She took one hand out from under her chin and grasped the fingers of his bandaged hand. For a moment, he let her hold him, then he gently extricated his hand from her grip. She stifled the sense of loss she felt as he drew away.

"You shouldn't."

"Don't, Andor," she said and threw him a pleading glance. "I know what they—what Ru-ad thinks. I don't care. And I know you don't. So why discuss it?"

"Because Ru-ad has a point. This isn't fair to you."

"I'll worry about what's fair to me," she said.

He sighed. "Go home, Shalon."

"Make me."

For a wordless, chest tightening moment neither of them moved. In a corner of her mind, far from his reach, she thought, *He's so tired, and he won't admit it. Even to himself.*

"I doubt I was this stubborn when I was your age."

"No, you were probably worse." She raised an eyebrow at him. "I'm not going away."

She could feel his reluctance to give in to his body's needs, but in the end, he settled back on the bed.

"I don't want you wasting your time sitting here."

"I'll leave when you're asleep," she promised.

Shalon watched as he relaxed, eyelids fluttering. *So quick and so easy. I almost envy you.* When she was sure he was no longer awake, she reached out a hand and touched the bandage on his cheek with gentle fingers. *You never let me touch you, do you? Always afraid of what might happen. What someone might think.*

She drew her hand back. *Well, that's going to change, Andor. I'm not going to let you call the shots anymore. Whether you like it or not.*

IV

"Lights."

Lumidiscs illuminated a tiny stone chamber. The room Ru-ad stood in was a niche hallowed into the rock just off his bedroom.

It lay hidden behind a stone door carved to fit flush in the wall. Only two things were in the room. A vidphone mounted on a tripod and a curved plastic chair that faced the vidphone.

Ru-ad sat in that chair now and said to the phone, "Capture uplink."

A deep tone sounded. "Uplink captured. Secure line engaged. Awaiting instructions."

"Tu-dan Melik, planet Serron."

A few minutes later, a man with a narrow face and dirty blond hair caught in a ponytail appeared. The background had been obscured by a green screen for privacy. Tu-dan dipped his head before meeting Ru-ad's amber gaze with his own.

"Chief Advisor. I had not expected to hear from you again so soon." His voice sounded hoarse, as though he had a sore throat. The scar across his narrow neck, however, proclaimed his true ailment.

"Things move at a pace that demands swift action," Ru-ad replied. "I am forced to call upon you in a manner I hoped would not be necessary."

"In what way might I serve my Chief Advisor?"

"The contact you found for me three months ago. I want you to initiate talks."

Tu-dan was so surprised it showed. "Chief Advisor, are you sure?"

"Do not question me, mercenary," Ru-ad said, his voice sharp. Tu-dan bowed so that his head almost disappeared from the screen.

"Of course. Forgive me, Chief Advisor."

"Make the arrangements for a pick-up. Be careful and discreet. Do you understand?"

Tu-dan nodded. "You wish me to contact someone of a certain—character."

"Precisely. It may take some time, but once you are successful, tell that person further negotiations can be carried out only by your superior and contact me again. I will give you the time and place for our conference call."

"It will be done, Chief Advisor."

"Yes, Tu-dan. In your capable hands, I have no doubt that it will be."

CHAPTER 13

You are right to be proud of your selection.
There is no greater honor than Apprenticeship.
It is the chance to give back to the community that gave you
life and purpose.
—*Ru-ad Whelan, Final Address to Apprentices (290 A.A.)*

I

Andor lowered the lance to the ground and leaned upon it, his chest heaving. Sweat rolled down his face, dampening his short, dark hair, and the strong column of his neck. It stained his cream-colored sleeveless vest in patches across his back, chest and armpits, and arrowed down to where the vest met the waistband of his pants. He threw his head back for a moment, breathing in through his bared teeth. The scar that slashed down his face twisted, pink and livid.

Around the large circular room, rack upon rack of weapons and light armor stood against the walls. The sandy floor had been marked off in several different areas for specific types of training. At the far end of the room, directly across from the entrance, a line of targets waited for firing practice. Andor rested opposite one of several sand filled bags that hung from the ceiling at regular intervals. A small tear in the bag leaked golden grains onto the floor and he watched the miniscule waterfall for a while.

Without warning, his breath stilled. For a space of a few heartbeats, he did not move. Then, he spun on his heel, bringing the lance up in a sweeping motion.

In one fluid movement, Shalon took a step back and grabbed the end of the thin, black pole. It shuddered to a halt. She let go with a quizzical smile.

"You're jumpy tonight. Didn't you hear me come in?"

Andor tossed his lance at a rack. The attractor pulled it into an open space where it clung with an audible click.

"No," he admitted. "I was tired—distracted. I had a few things on my mind."

Shalon glanced around, her eyes lingering on the damaged bag. "Relieving your frustrations, I see. No sparring partner?"

Andor shook his head. "It's late. I sent him home."

She opened the seal on the collar of her scout suit to just below her neck. Grains of sand fell from her fingers and disappeared against the sand colored weave. The tiny control pad on the inside of her left sleeve glinted when she dropped her hand from her neck.

"Did it occur to you that going home might be a good idea?"

"I'm back on active duty in three days. I need the practice. Why are you here?"

"Just got in from O2. Emergency relief call. One of Rakin's Group got side-swiped by a sandwraith."

"Trying to avoid tomorrow?" He half-smiled at her.

"Definitely. But O2 was quiet and Cu-don was ahead of me. She sent To-maq with polite orders to get my ass back here and rested for the festivities tomorrow." She studied his face, frowned. "You're hurt."

"Hurt?"

Shalon drew closer and touched him just behind his right ear. When she showed him her fingers, the tips shone red in the harsh light.

"Must have happened earlier," he said.

She started to reach for the rectangular first aid kit on her left hip.

"No." He grabbed her hand as she flipped up the cover on the pack. She stilled and looked up at him. He shook his head. "I'm fine. It's just a scratch."

He started to let go but she held on. A frown marked a line across his brow.

"Don't," she said. "Don't brush me off."

"I'm not."

"You are. You always do."

He pulled against her hold and she released him, the gesture a self-conscious one. "Shalon, that's not true."

"Oh, you let me have a token contact here and there, but never anything more. Anything that matters." Frustrated, she dropped her hand from her first aid kit and squeezed it into a fist against her thigh. "Damn it, Andor. You know what I'm talking about. You *know*."

He said softly, "And you understand why. We can't let ourselves be ruled by our feelings."

She pounced on his words, a glint in her eyes. "Then you admit you *have* feelings for me?"

Andor sighed. "Of course I do. You're my Vi-Commander. We share a mind-link. How could I not?"

"I wasn't talking about that and you know it," she grated out.

"Shalon, this isn't the time. Ru-ad needs to talk to you."

She folded her arms defensively. "What the hell does Ru-ad have to do with this?"

"More than you know. I can't explain."

"Try anyway."

"Shalon, it's not my place. It's important that you talk with Ru-ad first."

"And if I do? What then?"

He held her gaze with his own. "Then we'll talk."

She said nothing at first. "Just so you know, I intend to hold you to that, Andor." Without another word, she stepped around him and stalked off toward the door.

Andor did not turn to watch her go.

II

Shalon pulled herself out of the small access hole to stand next to Ru-ad on the sand-blasted rock ledge.

"You wished to see me, Chief Advisor?"

Around them, the desert stretched away into the night like a black sea. The sand dunes made undulating shapes under the night sky, which was pinpointed with cold, bright stars. Two moons hung low overhead, one full, the other in its first quarter. A pinkish cast covered their pock marked surfaces.

"Indeed, Vi-Commander. How did you find me?"

Above their heads, a natural shelf protected the niche from easy view. Ru-ad's dark robe brushed against her leg, caught in a light wind that smelled of dust and carrion. The gritty air blew cold against her face, but the scout suit's sensors adapted to the temperature change, switching off the cooling effect of the temperature-controlled lining and activating the heat instead.

"Ku mentioned you might be up here."

Shalon sat down, dangling her boots over the edge of the mesa. The drop was at least seventy feet, and jagged rocks stood up like teeth. "Need a little peace and quiet to strategize?" She tried to keep her voice respectful, but knew as soon as the words were out of her mouth that he could not miss her meaning. This time, he chose to ignore it.

"It is conducive to thinking up here, yes. I believe you come here yourself."

"Sometimes," she admitted. She looked west where there was a faint glow far in the distance, so pale it might have been an illusion. It came from Outpost Two, ever watchful against Outsider attack. If the rough tower formations of the mesa had not blocked her view, she could have looked left and seen a similar glow from Outpost One. Instead, she saw a tiny winged form in the distance, a faint shadow against the lighter sky. Then, a much larger shadow rose up from the dunes below. A blunt, triangular thing, shaped like the hood of a snake. It blotted out the smaller shadow and when it fell to the desert again, the sky was empty.

The sandwraiths are rising. Rain's coming.

"Andor said you needed to speak with me."

Ru-ad drew his arms around himself, folding his robes closer. She could not see his face, but it did not matter. Like all Orgalians, Ru-ad Whelan had never been one for outward emotion. That had been bred out of them during long years of confinement and training under ever watchful cameras and tutors.

"I received word today that Rath Nulen was killed in a Madinah raid."

Oh, God. Niala's twin brother. The last of her family. Shalon closed her eyes for a moment, remembering the quiet, serious man that had been her first Attack Leader.

"Have you told Group Leader Quemar?"

"She has been informed. His body will be returned to us in the next drop. The raid was unsuccessful so our contract is intact, but we are short a mercenary, and a Group Leader at that."

"You wish my advice on who should be sent as a replacement?" she asked, mentally beginning to run through which of her Attack Leaders was deserving of promotion and of age to be apprenticed offworld.

"No." In the dark, she could see his cat eyes as the starshine reflected off them. "I ask you to consider taking his place."

Shalon struggled to keep the shock off her face.

"Ru-ad, we had this conversation before. You felt it would be too dangerous for me to leave Orgala. That Gilene might find me, or worse, realize that InGene's Program had not been discontinued. I was to be exempt from the mercenary apprenticeship. You made it a condition of my inclusion into Rhiannon."

"I know, but frankly, I did not expect you to survive your ordeal. Nor did I expect you to become the warrior you are now. You are more than capable of keeping yourself hidden from the Conways."

His gaze turned toward the desert. "There are not so many of us that we can afford to have our clients question our ability to meet their demands. I cannot emphasize enough how important it is that we continue to provide our services without problems."

You don't have to. Orgala's history had been drummed into her as a child. The fight for freedom from Tec Solutions. And the divisions that had torn a young society apart after victory had been won. Then, five years after the civil war began, a ship crashed into the desert the Orgalians called Desolation.

And that was me, she thought, steeling herself against the pain of her memories. Of her father's death at the hands of the Outsiders. And the part her aunt had played in that. *Now Ru-ad's asking me to leave home so that I can keep it safe, keep it going. It's something every Orgalian dreams of—to be asked to serve offworld.*

But...what about those I'll be leaving behind? She reached out to Andor, but the block he had erected in the practice room remained firmly in place. *Damn it, Andor. I can't make this decision without you.*

Ru-ad continued. "This contract with the Vreek colony is one of our most profitable. If we do not adhere to the conditions, we could lose a very important client."

Somewhere in the distance, something made a dry, hacking cough that trailed off into silence.

"Your First Commander and I have a schedule. Despite her condition, she ensured that we kept to it. There are roughly four thousand of us now. If all goes well, in ten years, the Outsiders will have been destroyed or forced to join Rhiannon. We will number enough to live openly.

"But for now, our clients must not know we are having problems reproducing. Without access to the labs, it will be years yet before our technicians find the problem with our reproductive abilities and solve it."

Another delicate pause. "Cu-don will not long be with us. The cancer has returned and our most aggressive treatments are having only limited success. We will need a new First Commander and, most likely, a new Sub-Commander. She has indicated an interest in seeing you take her post someday. However, the Assembly has never elected an un-apprenticed Orgalian to either post. Am I wrong in assuming that you one day plan to hold both positions?"

Shalon gritted her teeth against a flippant answer. *Just making sure the fly is well and truly caught in your web, Ru-ad?*

"You are not wrong," she answered, her tone flat. "But an apprenticeship lasts at least two years. Who's to say that I won't be eclipsed by some energetic Group Leader before then?"

"You have my word that the Assembly will be sure to consider you upon your return. After your exploits last month, you are not likely to be forgotten or overshadowed."

Shalon cringed inside at the reference to Andor's rescue. *I just want to move past that damn day, and everyone keeps bringing it up.* She swung her left leg in a small arc, back and forth, feeling her boot knock sand and fragments from the mesa's side.

"Let's say I agree to this. How soon would I have to leave?"

"We would leave together for the pick-up in two days, at the latest."

Shalon bit her lower lip. "So soon?"

Ru-ad nodded. "Vreek was concerned about the likelihood of repeat attacks from the Madinah. The ship is already on its way and the rendezvous is three days from here. You see why I had to discuss this with you as soon as you returned."

He met her gaze. "I'm sorry, but I must have an answer by tomorrow night. I hope that will be enough time for you to think it over, as I suspect you wish to do."

Shalon pushed herself to her feet. A tiny piece of the mesa crumbled away onto the rocks below and she heard the pebbles striking like marbles.

It did not surprise her that Ru-ad would take her to the

rendezvous, even if the prospect of his company did not fill her with joy. Only high ranking officers and Assembly members were entrusted with the location of the pickup and Ru-ad, as the oldest Orgalian and Chief Advisor, was not as necessary in every day situations as the military officers.

This is too soon—too unexpected. But then again, apprenticeships are always sudden. And if Cu-don is really considering having me take Andor's place, it makes sense.

"How much of this has to do with the fact that you want me away from your protégé?" she asked, her tone casual.

"I'm not sure I understand you."

"Well, it's awfully convenient that you have an opening for me offworld just as Andor and I are—

(getting closer)

—in contention for the same post, don't you think?"

Ru-ad faced her, and the breeze picked up a little, flinging his robe against the mesa with a hollow flapping sound. "I am aware that we do not always see eye to eye. However, I think even you must agree that I would not, and could not, arrange a Madinah attack to kill one of my best mercenaries, simply to pull you out of the running for First Commander."

"True enough," Shalon conceded. "And I apologize, Chief Advisor, if I offended you."

He inclined his head, a polite acceptance of her statement. "Then you will consider my proposal?"

Shalon stared out across the desert at the glow of the Outpost. Remembered the horror of her mother's sightless eyes staring up at her from the deck grille of their space yacht—of seeing her father's half burned body stretched out on blackened sand.

Remembered the first time she returned from a teaching tour in Desolation and felt the relief and sense of peace that accompanied her homecoming.

The look on Andor's face as he said, *then we'll talk.*

"I'll consider it," she answered.

··· ——— ···

Later, at home, sleep did not come. She did not try to speak to Andor, determined that he should contact her first. *I'm not the one shutting anyone out.*

That left her with very little to do—and not enough peace of mind to rest. After tossing on her small bed for hours, she gave up. She kicked off the scratchy sheets, allowing cool air to caress arms and legs bared by her thin white undershirt and shorts. Rising, she sat at the small table next to her bed and keyed the interface on her ancient comm panel, a relic rescued from her father's space yacht. Behind her, the rough, unadorned walls of her tiny room curved over her head. The sand blasted smoothness of the bare floor was cold beneath her bare feet.

She shifted through news from the outside world—a hobby of hers. Nothing had changed in the week since her last check. The Madinah were rampaging through Plain Sector, causing an outcry at the most recent gathering of the DiploCore. Marulen plague had forced the closure of the second largest spaceport on the Roulon home world, affecting trade between Earth and their closest allies. Conway Enterprises had announced plans to launch a new starship line and Gilene Conway had opened a new wing of a children's hospital. By proxy, of course. She looked at the downloaded images of a cousin so unimportant his name did not even grace the caption. Instead, the line, "Conway Enterprises opens new wing at Mercy Infants, Planet Serron", scrolled past under the picture.

Anger burned in her—banked coals that had been waiting for the moment when they would be stirred to life again. *That heartless bitch.* She tried hard not to think about what Gilene had taken from her. The callous way she had killed Shalon's parents and orphaned her. The two friends whose bodies she had left behind on her long trek through Desolation.

Now emperors and presidents, governments and corporations pay court to her, tabloids report her every move, ordinary citizens treat her like the royalty Earth no longer has. The woman with more blood on her hands than Desolation has sand.

But she didn't get me. She didn't count on my mother seeing her death coming. On her saving my life at the cost of her own.

She severed the news connection and stared at her reflection on the blank, gray screen. *Lex Talionis. It's my code now. My people's code. The law that drove our revolution. I spent my life seeking justice for father's death at the hands of the Outsiders—and I didn't do the same for mother. I let the woman behind it all go free.*

But I didn't have a choice. I was so young. How could I fight a woman with the power of worlds behind her and only my death in the way of her plans? What could I have done against the curse of my mother's bloodline?

The fingers of her left hand drummed against the transparent interface, once, twice. *But Ru-ad may be right. I'm older now, and maybe the time for safety has passed. Maybe I need to take the law to Gilene Conway.*

Shalon touched the panel, drew a finger around the reflection of her eyes, so different from Andor's. It would mean a great deal of risk. She might expose Orgala or get herself killed going up against a woman with Gilene's resources. But there might also be ways to outsmart Gilene, or to hurt her the way Shalon had been hurt. Ways she would not find if she stayed on Orgala.

Ru-ad would never approve of that. Ha-Ka and Ku would never let me go.

And none of them have to know.

They don't deserve to be lied to.

And mother didn't deserve to die. No matter what, Gilene can't be absolved of her part in that.

Shalon rose to her feet, padded across the floor toward the screened off niche on the other side of the bed that served as her wardrobe. She had to find something to wear tomorrow that Ha-Ka would approve of.

Orgala is my family now, but I can't forget my first. I can't forget my mother's mission, no matter how much I want to. Maybe that's Ru-ad's part in this. To get me back on track. And if that's the case—she shoved aside the screen and started scanning the small selection of clothes—*perhaps leaving is something I should have done a long time ago.*

III

The Gathering Hall stood off the main thoroughfare of Rhiannon and had been finished two years after Cu-don first led her party of Orgalians into the maze of natural caves she'd found deep in Desolation. The biggest cave in Rhiannon, its vast space sparkled in the light from many lumidiscs reflecting off the veins of jape quartz that threaded their way through the walls. Here, the floor had been tiled in ceramic, painstakingly painted by hand in swirling patterns of green and blue. Two huge panels, done in abstract designs, hung from the ceiling opposite the massive steel doors. Behind the panels, two doors opened on man-made tunnels; exits that led to the vehicle junction a small distance away.

In front of the panels was a small plastisteel stage. Six chairs waited in gleaming silence behind a slender jape podium. Twirling dancers packed the floor all the way to the wide steps that rose up to the entrance. To the right of the stage, a holoband played their ethereal instruments, the wall a flickering presence behind them. Two little girls kept putting their hands through the illusion.

Opposite the band, tables covered with thin, white tablecloths had been drawn together. They overflowed with food and drink, a rare break from the careful rationing that Rhiannon enforced to ensure the equal distribution of resources. The scent of roasted meat and fruity wine rose to mingle with the sound of laughter and conversation.

Shalon stood near a table loaded with roasted bana, a fat, blind lizard that lived in the deep caves of Rhiannon and fed off the microorganisms that lived in the waters of the deepest grottos. The meat smelled spicy with precious herbs. The breads were still warm and she had not eaten since that morning, but Shalon was not hungry. She sipped the lavender wine in her fluted glass, rolling the tart taste around on her tongue. Her eyes remained steady on the door as she resisted the urge to tug at the weight of her layered gray skirts again. She was unaccustomed to wearing more than her smooth armor and the fabric felt like it was dragging at her legs. The beads that decorated the armholes of her silver vest scratched her arms.

Her hand rose to the smooth chignon Ha-Ka had made of her hair. The single piece of translucent quartz that Ha-Ka had fashioned into a hairpin was smooth and cool against her fingers. Shalon wanted to tug the pin free and lessen the unaccustomed ache of tightly pulled hair. Even as she thought it, Ha-Ka, who was serving preserved fruit two tables down, caught sight of her. She frowned and mouthed, "Don't you dare," before turning back to the man in front of her and ladling more fruit onto his full plate.

Shalon sighed and dropped her hand. At least she looked okay, she told herself. Andor would be surprised. She never wore skirts. *And I want him surprised. I want him off balance. I need him to see me the way I see him, or I need him to tell me he doesn't. Either way, I'm not leaving Orgala without finding out what he wants.*

Ku swung past her, his arms around a thin woman with black hair caught in a bouncing braid. He smiled as he passed, letting her know he was proud of the way she had handled Cu-don's introduction.

He should be proud. I've never felt so exposed in my life. I didn't think she would make me stand up there in front of everyone like that. And I certainly didn't expect her to make me open the festivities by dancing with Ku.

But in a secret part of herself, she knew what really bothered her was when she looked out over the sea of faces, the one face she'd wanted to see hadn't been there. Determined not to feel for him, she had taken herself to the table, where she could easily keep one eye on the door. A half-hour and several refused invitations to dance later, she started to wonder if he was even coming.

Then the unmistakable, dark velvet touch of him filled her senses—and she saw him standing in the doorway of the Hall. He did not look at her at first, stopping instead to converse with one of the two guards. He wore a suit she had not seen before, in a rich, brown material that sparkled gold highlights. The high collared tunic fitted smoothly against his chest, no buttons or seals in sight. The pants gripped his muscular legs above his polished combat boots. His scar twisted up the side of his face, pale against his tan skin.

Shalon's gaze had been so focused, it wasn't until something moved just behind him that she realized he wasn't alone. Niala draped a graceful hand over Andor's right arm. Resplendent in flowing white robes, she nodded a greeting as he turned to her. After a few words, they separated, and Niala went down the steps alone. She caught Shalon's eye, and started toward her, but Ru-ad swept into her path, his cream colored robes of state brushing the floor. Niala gave Shalon an apologetic look before greeting Ru-ad with a respectful bow of the head.

On the stairs, Andor's gaze finally found Shalon. Her heart beating harder than usual in her chest, she raised her glass to him in a casual salute. He came down the stairs and Shalon kept her mind blank as he gave Ru-ad a wide berth and headed straight for her. She placed her glass on the table and when she looked up, he was in front of her, his golden eyes as veiled as his feelings.

"Sub-Commander." She inclined her head. "You're looking well."

"As are you, Vi-Commander." His gaze swept over her. "Happy birthday. You look quite…different tonight."

Different? That's the best you can come up with? "Thank you. It's Ha-Ka's fault. She was determined to make me look the part of an Assemblyman's daughter for a change."

"I should have guessed."

"You missed the spectacle of me being lauded by our First Commander." She gestured out into the moving, dipping crowd, where a bald head was surrounded by many others.

"I would not call that a spectacle. I would call that an honor."

Over Andor's shoulder, she caught sight of Ru-ad and Niala approaching. "Your mentor is coming, probably to separate us."

"You never ascribe good intentions to his actions, do you?" Andor said before sipping at his glass.

"I'm not given to delusion."

"Not discussing strategy, I hope?" Niala inquired looking from Shalon to Andor. Shalon waved a dismissive hand.

"On the contrary, we are deep into the spirit of the festivities." Shalon inclined her head at Ru-ad. He returned the gesture. She turned back to Niala.

"I was so sorry to hear about Rath."

Niala's pleasant expression faltered for a brief, telling moment. "Thank you. He fought well, I am told. It was a good way to die."

"The grieving ceremony will be soon?"

"A week from now. I want to weave his shroud myself." She smiled as she regained her poise. "But this is not the time for such discussions. It is your night, Vi-Commander. Happy birthday."

"I could not have said it better," Ru-ad agreed. "Happy birthday, Shalon. Forgive me, though. I'm afraid some Assemblymen would like to speak with you, Andor."

"What a surprise," Shalon murmured.

"Just don't forget, I have the first two dances," Niala said, wagging a finger at Andor. Shalon paused in the act of raising her glass to her lips and her eyes met his. He glanced away from her and focused on Niala.

"Of course not. Such a pleasurable duty is easily remembered."

He strode off, Ru-ad beside him and Shalon turned to the table, her hand tight on the glass. *A pleasurable duty. He didn't ask me, didn't notice what I wore except that it was different, but dancing with Niala is a pleasurable duty.*

Come on, Shalon, you know it's important that the two of you don't act inappropriately in front of others.

Shalon relaxed her grip. *Fuck it. The way I feel is not inappropriate. It's just the way I feel. And I won't let him ignore me.*

"Niala," Shalon said, forcing her voice to sound natural. "I'm sorry, but I'm tired of all this attention. I think I'll go outside for a moment."

Niala looked concerned. "Are you feeling okay?"

"No," Shalon placed her glass down next to a basket of bread. "I think I just need to get away from the formality of it all for a while. I'll be back."

She glanced over to where Andor towered above the small knot of cream colored robes around him. Then she walked past the sea of multicolored robes weaving across the dance floor. Past the guards and out into the wide tunnel that led to the vehicle junction. A row of blunt nosed tunnelers were parked near the entrance to the Gathering Hall for community use, the tinted plastisteel roof and metal treads dull beneath a light veneer of dust. She climbed into the front of a two-seater and powered it up. With a deft touch to the panel, she swung it out of the line and down the long tunnel toward the Greeneries.

··· — — — ···

Shalon stepped through the doors of the greenhouse and closed them carefully behind her. The damp coolness of the air caressed her bare arms, and she could feel the unaccustomed give of grass beneath her flat shoes. Above her, artificial sunlight gleamed down from the raised greenhouse ceiling. Established deep in Rhiannon, above one of several water tables, the Greeneries was an even more important secret than Rhiannon. The source of most of what Rhiannon needed to survive. And the Outsiders—who existed on rationing from the much smaller hydroponic and meat labs in the Facility—had no idea it existed.

Shalon moved away from the entrance to the wineries on her left and started down one of several winding paths that cut through the middle of a dark green paradise. Trees, broad-leafed and tall, shrubs short with dart-like foliage, flowers bright with life and surprising color, dimmed the light to a shadow-filled presence. Shalon strolled through a small cavern that abutted the larger caves in which the attendants grew everything from food to the rare berries for Orgalian wine. The air smelled of soil and grass. Water from a recent sprinkling dripped around her, dampening the hem of her skirt.

There were no attendants in any part of the Greeneries this evening because they were all at the feast, and Shalon sighed with the pleasure of being free of duties and alone for a change. She pulled the hairpin from her hair and shook it loose. Dropping the pin on one of several benches scattered through the gardens, she wandered the paths at random, letting her mind drift and her hands slide across the slick, cool leaves.

Waiting.

Some time later, she bent over to look into the glistening heart of a bead of water hanging from a leaf, studying the hues and the dance of light it projected. Then she straightened up and spread her arms wide as she closed her eyes. She breathed deep, feeling the air fill her lungs.

"You are beautiful."

She opened her eyes, twisted to her right. A tall shape stood on the path, almost hidden by the overhang of leaves. She didn't have to see his face to know who it was—didn't bother to dwell on how silently he'd crept up on her.

So you followed me after all. A fierce glee burned through her.

"You say that to all the girls." Her smile felt as flippant as her voice.

"Don't say that. You know it is not true."

"You deny there are other girls?" Her smile grew wider as she caught the discomfort coming off him. *You deserve it, damn you.*

"I don't tell them they are beautiful."

"Why not?" She turned to him and took a step in his direction. The air whispered past her, like an echo of her movement. "Aren't they pretty enough for you?"

"Nothing is beautiful for me. Except you."

His words made the blood rush through her and to cover her surprise at his candidness, she crossed her arms. The light material of her vest scratched her skin. "You're lying. I know one other thing that's beautiful to you."

He said nothing as she drew closer, close enough to make out the indistinct lines beneath dim, tree-filtered light and shifting shadows. *If we're going to talk it out, then let's talk it out. All of it.*

"Power. I think...I know, it is much more beautiful to you than I am."

He remained still, as if he'd stopped breathing. She couldn't sense his thoughts, but his feelings were muddy, confused—a whirling enigma. She came to a stop, determined not to move closer. *Come to me. If you want to. If you want me.*

"You are...different today. Why do you say these things to me?"

"You know why."

Recklessly, she dropped her block, let him into the corner where she had hidden her feelings and her desires for so long. Her mind expanded as she took a breath and felt the cool life of the forest easing through her, like liquid. Felt the freedom of breathing out.

"No." His refusal was soft, unconvincing.

"Coward," she taunted, feeling power over him for the first time. Something he had never directed toward her before whipped out at her. It took her a moment to realize what it was. *He wants me. And he can't hide it.* She luxuriated in this truth; savored it like someone would savor a fine wine.

Calm and sure of herself as never before, she smiled and raised her arms, ran her fingers through her hair. She threw her head back, closing her eyes as she did so. She could feel him looking at her. Felt her vest stretch tight across her breasts.

"Not cowardice. Self-preservation."

His voice sounded strained—and very close. Her eyes opened as his arms slid around her, cool and unbreakable as metal bands. Before she could focus on his features, his head dipped. His lips were soft against hers, the pressure of them firm, insistent. Shalon's head fell back as he pressed her mouth open. He tasted of wine and heat. Her blood sang with his touch. Her arms circled his neck and pulled him closer. He felt hard against her through the silky texture of his suit.

Finally.

His tongue brushed the inside of her lip, and she felt the touch to the soles of her feet.

Mine. Whatever happens, whatever they say, you're mine. You always will be.

Andor's hand moved in her hair, stroking, grasping. And then he pulled away. She reached after him, but his hands slid forward, gripped her upper arms as he held her from him.

"We cannot do this," he said, his voice a fierce whisper.

"Why not?" she said, ignoring the tremor of emotion in her own voice.

"Because you're leaving," he said simply. "You know it, and I know it."

CHAPTER 14

Once, our names were determined by our batch codes.
This new generation will be the first free to name themselves.
Free to decide their fate.
They are more independent than we could ever understand.
Let us rejoice in that.
—*Ku Olang, Address to the Assembly (295 A.A.)*

I

She concentrated on the rough, welcome feel of his callused fingers against the skin of her arms. "I haven't made any decisions."

"You have," he said. "You showed me your mind."

She looked at him, at the face he always kept so calm. *But he can't hide from me. Not from me.* "Nothing's written in stone, Andor. That's why I wanted to talk to you."

"I know." He let go of her. "I meant what I said. You want to go and you will. It's what should happen."

Shalon forced herself not to scream. "So Ru-ad got to you."

He looked skyward for a brief moment. "You know it's the best thing to do. We need distance."

"Distance?" Shalon couldn't believe what she was hearing. "When has that ever worked? Did it work when you left on your apprenticeship? Surely you remember what it was like before we figured out how to mind block? What it was like for an eight year old to be connected to everything you did for the next two years?"

"I've forgotten nothing, Shalon," he said, his tone curt.

183

She ignored the interruption, too angry to stop. "Everything, Andor. The fighting, the killing. The women. You think it was easy for a child to experience sex when she hadn't even gone through puberty yet?"

He jerked slightly, as if he'd been slapped, and folded his arms across his chest. "You forget the nightmares. *Your* nightmares. Your pain and fears. I felt a responsibility to try to help you then and I still feel it now. We have to put things into perspective."

Shalon laughed, the sound short and bitter. "Perspective?"

"Yes," he continued, relentless in his determination. "We cannot forget what this connection really is. A high concentration of Conway DNA in my genetic mix. A phenomenon that has happened four times in your own family, if only between twins. A mistake that our scientists could barely pinpoint, much less figure out how to control. It is an accident, Shalon. A coincidence."

"A coincidence?" Shalon spat out. "You sound like Ru-ad. Trying to rationalize anything that doesn't fit into your grand plan."

"Because of your mother? Because of what you have to do?"

"Yes, damn it! You did not save me by accident. I should never have been able to reach out to you with my mind the day I crashed here. We're not twins, we had no knowledge of each other before that day. No idea how to control a mind-link. But I *saw* you. I called you. You think that was a coincidence?"

"What does it matter?" He shrugged. "It changes nothing. You have simply proven my point. If you believe what you say, and I know you do, then you have no choice but to leave. You cannot finish what your grandmother started by staying here."

Shalon took a few steps away from him, trying to keep her anger from lashing out at him even as she sensed Andor trying to control his. Water dripped into the silence.

"And what if I decide not to finish it?" she asked. "What if I want to stay here instead?"

"You wouldn't do that."

"Why not? I *can* do it, you know." A star shaped flower nodded at her from the low branches of the tree, its speckled tangerine shape bright against the green leaves. She focused on it, using its beauty to calm herself.

"If I choose, I don't have to go through with any of it. All the pain, all the sacrifice. It won't be my problem anymore."

"You would betray the sacrifices that have already been made?

The pain you've already been through? Where is the logic in that?"

"Logic has nothing to do with it." Shalon faced him, letting him see her frustration. Her determination. Her need.

"Shalon." His voice sounded calm, but the utter stillness of his body conveyed another emotion. "Don't do something—say something you cannot hold to."

"It wasn't a coincidence, Andor," she continued, her voice low. "You saved me for a reason. Maybe it had nothing to do with me, and everything to do with us."

"There is no reason for us to share anything beyond this mind-link. You are young yet. When you leave, there will be other worlds. Other men. Why tie yourself here when you know my ambitions and have your own?"

"Perhaps because you've been bred to one ambition all your life, you can't understand how I could have more than one." Shalon took a step toward him. "Well, I do, Andor. And you know how determined I can be when it comes to what I want."

"I did not come here for this."

"I did," she replied, taking another step. "You and Ru-ad need to understand a few things. I won't be ignored and I won't lie to myself, or let you do the same. What we share is not just about DNA and synapses. If Ru-ad wants to believe that, let him. But not you, Andor."

She stood in front of him, so close, she could feel his body heat. "Not you."

"Don't."

"Tell me I'm wrong. Go ahead. Tell me we don't share the same passion for our people. The need to be out there, in the desert, protecting them. The same vision of what this place could be, one day. Try to convince me that we aren't two halves of the same whole."

Andor did not move or speak.

"I thought so. So why tell me I'm too young and try to make everything fit into Ru-ad's plans when you know it can't? You're fighting something you don't need to."

She raised her arm, traced a finger along the scar on his face, the skin warm and waxy under her touch. "But then again, I'm not the one you're trying to protect, am I?"

Andor's hand closed around her wrist, but his eyes never left hers. "This is not just about us, Shalon. Do you realize what you're doing?"

Shalon smiled, unaware how the simple act transformed her face. "I'm saying I don't want anyone else. I only want you."

The words had barely left her lips when Andor's arm went around her waist and drew her against him. Her head fitted in the hollow of his shoulder and Shalon breathed in the warm scent of him, feeling as if she had come home. He released her hand and she let her arms slide around to stroke the soft fuzz of his hair. His lips touched her neck and Shalon shivered at the moist, airy caress. When he spoke, his voice was a low vibration against her skin.

"Tell me to stop."

She said nothing, her throat tight.

His arm tightened around her, and his other hand tunneled through her hair, tugging gently so that she leaned back. His tongue touched her neck just before he drew the skin between his lips. Shalon gasped, an electric feeling lancing through her from the place his lips touched to the pit of her stomach. She turned her head, searching for him—then his mouth was on hers, open and urgent.

Her mind was a chaotic jumble of thoughts and impressions and Shalon did not try to understand which came from her and which came from Andor. She didn't realize they'd moved until she bumped into a tree behind her. The contact jarred their lips apart before he brought his hands up to cup her face and slanted his lips across hers again. The rough bark grated against her bare shoulders, but the cool shadows of the overhanging leaves were a welcome embrace. The tree's knotted roots stood far apart, leaving more than enough room for two people to stand against its trunk.

Shalon's vest felt heavy against her breasts as he leaned into her. Her arms fell away from his back, searching for the seal to his shirt and at the same time, his hands left her face. Shalon felt his touch against her breasts before Andor's fingers brushed the seal under her arm and the vest gaped open.

She sighed as his lips slid over her collarbone. Cool air tightened her nipple before his mouth covered it, his tongue rough and slick. Her head fell back against the tree's trunk as she held Andor to her. The intense feelings that rose within her crowded out thought and speech. Her eyes slid shut and she made a sound between a moan and a gasp and hooked her leg over his, pulling him against her.

At some point, he turned her away from the tree and lowered her to the ground. Shalon reached up and unfastened his tunic, her finger flicking over his small nipple. Fascinated, she watched as he shivered, gasped as she felt the sensations from her touch fill his mind and hers. Her skirts were a crushed bundle under her hips.

Grass dampened her hair and brushed her cheeks with water like tears. Shalon did not care. As Andor tensed over her, she raised her arms and drew him down into a breathless kiss. His smooth chest against her breasts felt warm and solid.

They were kissing in a slow, teasing movement when she sensed a shift and a mind block drew between them like curtains over a window. Frowning against his neck, she tried to hold him to her, but he pulled away. His breathing harsh, he held himself above her, his bare arms like cables on either side of her.

"Did I do something wrong?" she asked.

He closed his eyes. "No."

She drew a finger down his right arm, watched as the flesh quivered beneath her touch. The block slipped and sensation filled her. In the blink of an eye, he moved away, shifting to her left so that he half lay, half leaned against a tree root. Surprised, she rose on one arm and twisted to face him.

"What?"

His gaze drifted over her, and she did not miss the expression in them. She sat up, refusing to cover herself.

"Tell me."

"We—I have to stop."

Shalon groaned. *Goddamn it, Andor.* "We're back to that."

"We never left it."

"Ru-ad can send someone else."

"No, he cannot. He should not. And you know it."

She struck a fist against the grass in one fierce, emphatic movement. "You won't let me take anything with me, will you?"

"I won't let us do something we might both regret. You know how important it is for you to be focused when you get to the colony."

You stubborn bastard. Shalon rose to her feet and turned away from him, determined not to let him shame her into a further display of emotion. But her gaze fell on the tunic she'd tossed aside, and fingers trembled as she started to pull her vest closed.

Andor's arms came around her and he tugged her back against him. His hands brushed her fingers aside so that his palms lay, warm and heavy, over her flat stomach. She stiffened and started to pull away, but he stilled her by tightening his embrace. Shalon felt his breath stir her hair as he pressed his lips to her temple.

Don't fight me.

You son-of-a bitch.

I know. But I'm right. Things are too complicated for this. We can't afford to lose that contract.

Defeated, she let her head fall back against his chest. His hands tensed on her stomach.

You must go now.

Must I? It was silly, pointless, but she thought it anyway, desperate for another answer. *Isn't there another way? Something else that can be done?*

No. No other way. You must go.

But I don't want to.

Don't be afraid. You can do it. You won't always be alone.

I'm not afraid. I don't want to leave you.

Silence.

We can't always have what we want.

Does that mean you don't want me to leave either?

Again, the silence.

Does it?

His lips brushed across her cheek, cool and light.

It doesn't matter. It's too late now. You have to go back. To entertain the thought of anything else is a waste of time.

With skillful, gentle fingers, he drew her vest closed and fastened it. When he finished, he turned her in his arms and looked at her wordlessly, one last time, before he let go and stepped back. Too hurt to show it, and feeling hollow inside, Shalon bent and picked up the tunic. She held the shirt out to him, but when he reached for it, she did not release it immediately.

"Understand this. I'm not going to change my mind. I will go, but there won't be anyone else. Not for me."

She let go of his shirt. "I'm going to come back for you, Andor. And when I do, I won't let anything—not even Ru-ad—stand in my way."

He shook his head, a stiff gesture. "I wish you would not do that. I can't give you want you want."

"You're what I—"

A bass tone sounded above them. "Alert. Alert. Please proceed to your designated Group rendezvous. Alert. Alert. Please proceed to your designated Group rendezvous."

In the time it took for the words to sink in, the mood shattered, broken as surely as glass on the floor between them. An alert meant that someone, somewhere, had come under attack.

Shalon ran for the entrance, grass slippery beneath her flat-soled shoes. She could hear Andor following, the rustling as he put his tunic on, then he was beside her.

How did you come?

I walked.

We'll take my tunneler to go back.

When Shalon swung the tunneler into the junction ten minutes later, a murmuring crowd was still streaming out of the Hall. Shalon caught sight of smaller Groups gathering together as she stepped out of the tunneler.

A novice, who appeared to be twelve or thirteen, gathered the few children to him with curt instructions. An Attack Leader stood near the Hall's entrance supervising a change of guards, the lasguns on her hips glinting as she moved. A Group Leader organized his soldiers with quick, short orders and gestured toward the line of vehicles. Still more people scattered through the five tunnels that branched off from the junction, some moving at a run, headed for their posts.

Two Assembly members swept into a waiting tunneler and started toward the tunnel which Shalon and Andor had just left. They pulled up as Andor disembarked from Shalon's vehicle and the driver gave a respectful nod. "We are headed to the nearest strategy room. Will you join us?"

"I will confer with Cu-don in the Assembly Hall before going to the surface," Andor replied.

The Assemblyman drove off as Shalon faced Andor over the dusty top of the tunneler. *I'm going to the barracks to gather my Group. You'll contact me there with whatever information you learn.*

Andor did not waste time acknowledging her. He set off down the main tunnel to their right without looking back. Shalon turned toward the Group Leader organizing his soldiers near the Hall entrance. He had commandeered several tunnelers so that he could make all possible speed for the barracks. Intending to get a lift, she had not taken more than a few steps before a hand closed around her left arm. Surprised by the physical contact, she looked up into Ru-ad's calm eyes.

"Vi-Commander. I've been searching for you." He released her arm with a self-conscious gesture, aware that he had violated her personal space without permission.

"I left the celebration to get some air," Shalon replied, trying to keep the requisite politeness in her tone. He was the last person she wanted to see.

"I'm sorry, but I need your answer. Will you be leaving for the Vreek colony?"

Shalon did not bother to keep the annoyance out of her tone. "Chief Advisor, in case you didn't notice, we're under attack. My Sub-Commander needs me."

"I understand your impatience to be gone, but it is imperative that I have my answer now."

Shalon's eyes narrowed and she lifted her chin. "Very well. I will leave to take Group Leader Nulen's place as soon as I return from the surface."

"You cannot go to battle, Vi-Commander," Ru-ad said, his voice calm. "We are due to leave Rhiannon in four hours. You will miss your drop."

"I will not leave Andor to this!"

"He has capable hands besides yours, and I have no doubt the counterattack will succeed, even without you. It is a matter of numbers, after all."

Shalon's brow furrowed. "You know what is happening?"

"I escorted Cu-don to the Assembly Hall for a last review of the reports before she retired for the night. The distress calls came while we were there. The Outsiders have attacked both Outposts simultaneously. Our people need reinforcements if they are to repel the advance."

Shalon shook her head. "Ru-ad, I belong with my Group."

"You belong where you are most needed and that is the Vreek colony, not here. I have already spoken to Cu-don. She agreed with me that you should leave as soon as possible. You're relieved of your duties here the moment you decide to depart."

Shalon looked around her, torn between the need to join her Group and the disturbing realization that Ru-ad was right. She could not participate in a battle when, in a matter of hours, she would be required to leave on her apprenticeship. She opened her mind.

Andor.

Yes.

Ru-ad insists I can't be part of the reinforcements. He wants me to leave for the rendezvous tonight.

Then you can't go to the Outposts. I have Group Leaders Rakin and Quemar. Their assistance will be adequate.

Andor—

We discussed this. You know my wishes.

Shalon could sense him distancing her. Already, he had become caught up in the preparations for the counterassault. She could not continue to distract him from his job.

To Ru-ad, she said, "I have to speak to Ha-Ka and Ku before I leave."

He inclined his head. "Naturally. I will meet you at the second northwest exit in four hours. Pack rations for three days. We will be on foot."

It made sense. With the weather changing and the sandwraiths coming out to feed, vehicles would not be a good idea. The vibrations would be enough to wake sandwraiths for miles around from their stupor. "Fine," she said. "I'll see you there."

II

Shalon ran a finger up the seal of her scout suit, closing it to her throat. She was putting rations into her pack when she spotted her father entering the empty barracks through its arched, doorless portal. His boot heels were muffled on the sandy floor, but the sound still carried down row upon row of lockers and benches.

Shalon propped her left leg up on the knee-high bench in front of her and pressed a finger to the fingerprint analyzer on the inside of her boot heel. A handle popped out of the back of her boot. Shalon pulled the small, serrated blade free and it glinted blue-gray in the light as she checked the edge. Ku stopped at her side as she slid the knife back into the sheath.

"Vi-Commander."

She lowered her leg and bowed. "Advisor. I looked for you in the strategy rooms."

Ku sat on the bench, his hands arranging his robes into neat folds out of long habit. "I went to the surface for two hours. Cu-don and Ru-ad had matters to attend to and could not oversee the departure."

His thin face was calm under the salt and pepper of his prematurely graying hair.

"Ha-Ka was rostered for emergency duty this month. She has gone to O1."

Shalon felt her heart sink. She did not doubt that her foster mother would survive the battle, but it meant she wouldn't be able to tell her goodbye before she left Rhiannon. She pulled her holster free of her locker and closed the door.

"I didn't realize that. I hoped to speak to both of you."

"I will have to do, I'm afraid." He focused his gaze on the row of gleaming metal lockers in front of him. "Ru-ad told me of your decision."

Shalon shoved her bag and holster aside and sat next to him. "I'm sorry, Ku. I didn't tell you before because I wasn't sure what I wanted to do."

"I understand, Shalon." Ku glanced sideways at her. "And I approve."

She gave him a wry smile. "I thought you might. It is a great honor to be chosen to represent our people offworld."

"That is not why I approve. I think it is right that you leave. You were never meant to stay here, Shalon. Your destiny is larger than Orgala. You cannot be true to yourself if you remain in Rhiannon."

"Perhaps. But I'm betraying part of me by leaving. I should be out there, in the desert."

"In the end, you serve Orgala best offworld. You will find out now what awaits you out there—where you were meant to be all along."

"Is that what you think? That I wasn't meant to be here?"

She glanced down in surprise as Ku's long fingers grasped and held hers. "Do not believe that I want to lose my only daughter." His smile could not obscure the seriousness in his eyes.

"Part of me would have been overjoyed if you chose to stay in Rhiannon. You would have been the finest Commander our people have ever seen—and I, the proudest father in all Orgala. But there are those who would say that Andor deserves the post more. It is good that you leave and allow them no room to manipulate the Assembly to their ends."

"I'm not so sure I'm doing that. I'm positive I've made Ru-ad very happy."

"He thinks to slip Andor in while you are gone so his position as First Commander would be secure. It is a good ploy, as long as Cu-don passes on before you return."

"You don't think she will?" Shalon asked, surprised.

"I cannot say for sure, but she has a great deal of life in her yet.

I can tell you these things now that you go to Vreek. At the moment, the Assembly is divided over the choices for her successor should she pass on."

He squeezed her fingers. "We are a harsh people, I'm afraid. We try to settle into the mores of civility, but leadership means too much to us to leave it to chance. We work for the good of all, but we will die for what we believe. And each of us makes our own decision on what matters deserve our life. Had you stayed, your friends might have become foes and I do not think you want this."

Shalon frowned and bit her lip. "Ku, I know Ru-ad has made his opinions clear, but is the situation really so bad?"

"Not so much that I have to fear for you yet. Still, we are long term planners and it can take as little as one person to change the course of our history. Cu-don and Ru-ad have proven that. I would rather you be away while we are still—becoming. After what you have been through, you do not deserve to be caught up in our schemes and plans."

Moved by the vulnerability Ku had allowed her to see, Shalon leaned forward and kissed his cheek. Her heart soared when he didn't pull away. "Thank you, Ku. For all you've done for me and for keeping me safe. I only survived because of you and Ha-Ka. I'll miss you. Until I return, my heart is here, with you."

"And someone else, Ha-Ka tells me."

She released his hand. "With many of my friends, yes."

"I meant Andor, as you well know. You both hide it well, but your connection with him runs deep."

"I'm not so sure he knows that."

"Shalon, understand him. He is Orgalian and a leader. He cannot indulge his feelings, no matter how strong they might be. He has never been free to do as he would like."

Ku rose from the bench. "Give him time. Ambition passes and when it does, be there for him. Ha-Ka was for me."

"Things were different for you two."

"We loved each other. How is that different? You are a good choice for him, Shalon. You are both fertile and you care greatly for each other. Sooner or later, everyone must accept that. Even Ru-ad."

"Let's hope so."

Shalon stood, slung her holster around her hips and fastened it. The weight of the lasguns felt good against her thighs, like a piece of favorite clothing.

"Be safe, daughter, and may your long journey end in joy."

She acknowledged his departure blessing with a deep incline of her head. "Be safe, Ku, and may we meet again in health and happiness."

"Do you wish me to come with you to the exit?" Ku asked as Shalon shouldered her pack.

"No. It's better if I go alone. When I arrive at Vreek, I will send a message."

Shalon brushed past him without looking back, not because she didn't want to, but because she knew the tears in her eyes would shame her. Much the same way the tears in Ku's eyes would shame him.

III

"You are sure they will be on time?" Ru-ad asked.

"I'm sure," Tu-dan replied. "I received word from them when they entered Whiteway Sector. They will be at the rendezvous point on time."

"I have a message for the captain. Tell him that I will approach first and give him something he will need in order to complete his task. He must have everything in place by then."

"It will be done, Chief Advisor. Is there anything else?"

"Yes. But I must ask you, mercenary—are there doubts in you over what you do now?"

Tu-dan never hesitated. "I have no doubts, Chief Advisor. You do what is necessary for the good of our people. I see that. I have always seen that."

Ru-ad nodded, satisfied. "Very well. Your part in this will end once you have ensured there are no more loose ends. Am I understood?"

"Perfectly, Chief Advisor. I believe I have the means to accomplish this without any trouble."

"Very good. Contact me when it is done and I will make the arrangements for your reward. An early return to Rhiannon, wasn't that your request?"

Tu-dan bowed his head, gratitude in every line of his body. "It was. Thank you, Chief Advisor."

IV

Shalon stood in the observation niche where she and Ru-ad had spoken just the night before and waited for the sun to come up. The sky was lightening to a dark gray, the stars receding in the encroaching daylight. The moons had long since set. In the distance below her, near the Outposts, the sand moved in fitful waves, despite the lack of a breeze. Shalon recognized the movement as two separate, camouflaged relief forces, each several Groups strong, moving at top speed for Outpost Two.

She crouched down, balancing herself on the balls of her feet, thinking but not thinking. She allowed her body to feel the force of the earth beneath her feet. The air against her skin. And the tug of another mind below her and to the west.

Shalon.

Andor, there were sandwraiths near O2 last night. Watch out for burropacs. They might be resting there and they'll draw the sandwraiths for sure.

I will.

We really should get those sounders working. They would eliminate a lot of the guesswork during the rainy season.

The techs are doing their best. We have done well without them.

Yes, but we could do better and move faster if we didn't have to watch every step, or slow to look for signs of hibernation.

I agree, but until the technology works, we will have to rely on ourselves. As we always have.

Shalon shrugged to herself, conceding the argument. *By the time I get back, I hope you'll have finished.*

Let's hope. He paused. *You should be leaving soon.*

Yes.

She could feel he was not at rest. His thoughts were strong, but the undercurrent spoke of his observations and movements. Of markers set and passed and a tally of dangers to be avoided or overcome. In Desolation, the tally never quite came to an end. The desert had many ways to take lives. Shalon tried to think of something to say that would not bring up all the emotion of the evening past, but it was no use. In the end one thought came to her. A traditional battle blessing.

Good luck, Andor, but may you never need it.

Good luck to you, Shalon. And after a long pause. *Be careful out there with Ru-ad.*

Oh please. We can handle the desert, rainy season or not.
Just…be careful.

She smiled a bittersweet smile, aware that even now, Andor could not acknowledge how he felt. Still, he had said a great deal more in those few words—and in his actions in the gardens—than he ever had before. Ku had warned her to be patient and although that wouldn't be easy for her, she could see the wisdom in his words.

For the first time, she felt that it would all work out. They could never be out of touch. This goodbye would only be for a short while. The day would come when she would return older and experienced, and there would be no more excuses. Nothing separating them anymore.

She went back down the access ladder. After a pause to don her small pack and settle her holster straps more firmly, she set off through the obscure and twisting tunnels of Rhiannon's back roads. She went at a comfortable jog; a pace all Orgalians learned at a very early age that could be kept up for some time without exhausting the runner.

Half an hour had passed when she drew up beside Ru-ad at the base of a metal ladder that led to a hole above them. The tunnel they stood in was smaller than most and deserted. The sky through the grate had lightened to a pale gray. Shalon could feel the day approaching on still air not yet blasted by the sun to a furnace's heat. Her blood raced in anticipation as she nodded a greeting to Ru-ad. He returned the greeting, his own pack riding high on his shoulders and his holster low on his hips. He wore a scout suit, his body trim as a young man's beneath its skin-tight lines.

"You have said your goodbyes?"

"Yes." Shalon reached into the neck of her suit and unzipped the lining. Ru-ad mirrored her actions as she tugged out her hood and settled it over her loose hair. Shalon had already treated her eyes with drops to protect against the sand blindness. She watched now as Ru-ad took a vial from his pack and did the same.

"Ready?" she asked. He nodded.

"Let's go," she said and started up the ladder.

CHAPTER 15

Betrayal is a matter of perspective.
— *Madinah Warrior's Code*

I

Shalon and Ru-ad kept up a swift pace. Conditioning made it possible for them to keep moving for hours at a time. Dust puffed up into their hot faces, but their scout suits kept their bodies cool. The air smelled of baking sand and left a salty taste in their mouths.

They moved north-east, toward an uneven line of jagged peaks. The reddish-brown rocks shimmered in the waves of heat that rose from the sands and looked closer than they were. Above them, the sky was a washed out blue without a cloud in sight. The too-brief rainy season would not begin for weeks yet.

Here and there, a few grassy plants clung to the shifting sands, drooping in their isolation. Twice, birds soared above them in the sky, too high against the sun to see, casting skinny shadows on the desert floor. Sand grits, tiny bright pink biting flies, buzzed around them every so often. The repellent Ru-ad and Shalon wore kept their exposed hands and faces safe from the insects. The grits flitted away, frustrated.

Their steps light and sure, the two of them made no noise as they ran. Alert to their surroundings, they kept one eye on the sky and the other on the sands. Nothing stirred. Most of Desolation's denizens were night creatures and avoided the scorching daylight as much as possible.

Ru-ad and Shalon did not speak to each other for most of the day. They fell into the trained, silent teamwork Orgalians had perfected for travel through Desolation. Shalon covered their tracks as much as possible, and Ru-ad stayed a few steps ahead, to scout for danger.

When the sky above them began to pearl and spiral into the pinks and corals of sunset, Shalon looked behind them and spotted something. She stopped and, conscious of her actions, Ru-ad paused as well. Shalon pointed at the tiny dark smudge that rested on the horizon behind them and a little to the south-west.

"How soon do you think before we have to use the goggles and filters?" he asked.

"Depends on the wind. A day. Maybe two if it keeps blowing away from us all day today."

"Then you should be in no trouble."

"And you?" Shalon glanced at his sharp profile.

"There is a shelter at the rendezvous. I can ride it out there if need be."

They kept running even after night fell, dark and all-enveloping as a cloak. This part of the desert had no quicksand or falsewater to watch for. They were reasonably safe going by the moonlight. The temperature dropped and Shalon could feel the air against her cheek like the first jarring touch of ice. The number of insects increased after dusk, creating a constant annoying drone. Now and then, the call or bark of some far-off creature would rend the air, but not often. In this season, most animals kept the noise to a minimum to avoid disturbing lurking sandwraiths, especially since many of the sand-dwellers migrated during this time of year.

They made camp some five hours after nightfall. Shalon dropped to the ground in the shelter of a dune and Ru-ad followed her. Together, they hollowed out beds in the sand. After munching on dried bana meat and bread, Ru-ad took the first watch and Shalon curled onto her side. Warm in her suit, with her pack under her head, she threw her arm up across her face to guard against sand, insects and the cold. Her other hand lay over her chest, holding one of her guns. She fell into an immediate, light doze. Deep sleep was a rare, wonderful thing which, for the most part, had eluded her since childhood. When Ru-ad touched her shoulder hours later, she sat up as if she had never lain down.

As Ru-ad dozed, Shalon kept watch under the cold stars.

Her gun lay across her lap and her finger rested against the trigger. In a far corner of her mind, she could feel Andor, as she had all day long. A small, permanent presence that carried the familiar cold-heat of battle. She kept herself separate from long experience, knowing that to talk to him now might mean distraction and a quick death. It didn't bode well that the battle had lasted so long. But she couldn't worry about that now.

In the morning, the smudge on the horizon was darker but no closer than the day before. They had breakfast and were off before the sun came up properly. The desert in the morning was something Shalon never grew tired of. She enjoyed the pure, physical exaltation of being on the move. She felt a small pang of regret that she would not see it again for so long. There would be new places, though, with new sunrises. She had not been offworld since her eighth birthday.

It was mid-morning when they ran into the herd of burropacs.

They were halfway across a flat that was several miles wide when Ru-ad halted abruptly. Shalon did the same and gazed around her, searching for whatever had caused Ru-ad to stop. Ahead of her, the land rose gently toward low, undulating hills. Behind and around her, the flat stretched away into the distance. Not a breath of air stirred the sand and nothing but thin wisps of clouds shifted overhead. Still, Shalon could feel a wrongness to the day. As if something approached.

She felt the vibration in her feet first. A faint tremble that traveled up her shins. *Burropacs.* Ahead of her, Ru-ad stood frozen, one foot positioned just behind the other.

The first burropac broke the surface in the ten feet between Shalon and Ru-ad. The sand dimpled, then became a depression. The depression humped, like a tiny hill, and the top if it began to break apart into rivulets of cascading sand. The hill grew larger as the sand flowed faster. One gray, paddle-like foot appeared, black claws glinting as they grabbed for purchase. With a heave and the soft hiss of falling sand, the creature pulled free of its nesting place and stood, its blind head weaving from side to side.

The burropac stood as tall as Shalon's knee and its body was covered in overlapping scales, each the size of a hand. Four stubby legs ended in flattened paws divided into three large, clawed toes. The legs supported a round body with a short neck and a head that looked too small for it. As Shalon watched, the animal cleared the blow hole in the top of its round head, shooting a small stream of sand into the air with a sharp sound. It shook out two shell-like ears that had been flattened against its skull.

Raising its snout, it opened small jaws filled with sharp needle-like teeth as if yawning. The smell of the carrion burropacs fed on rushed out. The animal moved slowly, a good sign. Burropacs, once they had eaten, were calm and deliberate and posed no threat to anything unless provoked. However, they did not travel alone and until the herd had come and gone, it would not be a good idea to spook any of them.

The burropac began to refill the large depression behind it with powerful movements of its back legs. At the same time, tiny hills appeared all around Ru-ad and Shalon, humping and breaking as if the sands were bubbling. By the time the herd stood revealed, Shalon had counted a little under three dozen, eight of them calves. Snub-nosed females nuzzled clumsy babies, flat black tongues rasping over tiny heads.

Shalon found herself between two young adults and their first ambling steps took them away from her. Ru-ad was not so lucky. A mother and her calf had nested right next to his left leg. As the female cleaned the calf, the baby stumbled on unsteady legs into Ru-ad. He shifted his weight, moving his right leg further back in an attempt to steady himself. Sand hissed.

The burropac between Shalon and Ru-ad swung its head around. Burropacs had a barely decent sense of smell, but their hearing was excellent. Dust puffed from its back, and there was a sound like the rattling of knives as every scale on the animal's body stood on end. Sharp edges, free of sand, were clearly visible in arc after arc of bristling scales. A single scale above the creature's head and between its ears bent forward, as if seeking something. Then it bent back and started to beat rhythmically against the scale behind it. Shalon knew the sound well. It was a warning to predators—and a call to arms.

Tap, tap, tap. Tap…tap…tap. Tap, tap, tap. Tap…tap…tap.

The deadly, grating sound of hundreds of scales rising at the same time filled the air. The herd remained silent as the lead animal turned toward Ru-ad. Its head jabbed forward and Shalon heard a soft sound, almost a click. The scale that had been bent forward slashed through the air and imbedded itself into the sand at the back of Ru-ad's foot. It quivered there, the visible tapered end of it greasy with a thin, white liquid. Stillness fell, tense with waiting. Sand grits buzzed around her hooded head. Shalon let her breath go shallow in her throat. *Don't move. Just don't move.*

LEX TALIONIS

The lead animal turned side on and Shalon could see the small, seeping slit where the scale had been. In a few months, another scale would grow back to replace the lost one. At that moment, the burropac launched another scale. It cut through the air and the edge of it grazed the back of Ru-ad's boot as it slashed into the sand, throwing up a tiny line of dust.

To the Chief Advisor's credit, he never moved a muscle. His arms hung relaxed at his sides as he waited. Careful to keep herself loose as well, in case she had to move suddenly, Shalon stared at the back of Ru-ad's head, willing him to stay immobile. If they antagonized the herd and had to fight, it was unlikely they would get clear of hundreds of scales.

A long ten minutes later, the lead burropac nosed the ground. The first arc of scales, near its head, collapsed. A minute later, the rest fell into place. One by one, the herd followed suit. The lead animal began to move off in careful, mincing steps, its body swaying from side to side. The burropac lowed, the sound a deep vibration Shalon could feel beneath her feet. The herd pulled in a little closer, calves and their mothers near the center. With the soft sounds of shifting sand and the occasional rattle of scales, the herd moved past them.

Shalon watched their slow progress. Burropacs had fascinated her from the moment she realized that a herd, working together, could bring down a full grown sandwraith if threatened. Moving at top speed, they could launch their lethal scales while the sandwraith was in mid leap, if need be.

She had good reason to hate sandwraiths. Ten years before, while she tried to survive in the desert after the crash, an encounter with one had almost killed her. It had been just a baby, barely ten feet from wing-tip to wing-tip, and yet she had been lucky to survive their meeting. She had been wounded so deeply, she'd carried a scar for some time, before her body's exceptional healing abilities erased it as if it had never been.

She felt a certain kinship with the herd. They were wanderers, peaceful until provoked, like her. They protected family units the way her own people did. They would live out their lives under the desert sky, feeding off the carcasses of others and bothering no one, if they could. But when they had to fight to protect their own, they did not hesitate to do so.

Once the herd had passed, Ru-ad went down on one knee and checked his boot. Shalon joined him and she noticed the deep groove the scale had carved into the back of Ru-ad's shoe heel.

"Will it hold?"

"Yes." He stood and without another word, continued running as if nothing had happened. Shalon threw one glance at the swaying gray bodies diminishing into the distance before she followed him.

Some time later that day, Shalon realized that Andor's thoughts no longer spoke of battle. The fighting had come to an end. Without having to think about it, she knew that things had gone the way of the Orgalians. Relieved, she sent Andor a mental congratulation. He did not respond, but she knew he'd felt her.

The line of peaks they were headed toward gleamed like fire before night fell and swallowed them in darkness. In the south-west, the smudge of the sandstorm remained like a dirty thumbprint on the sky. They might make it to the rendezvous before the storm came, but only just.

Shalon took first watch and passed it to Ru-ad after an uneventful lookout. She lay down, as Ru-ad shifted back onto the sand, his gun gripped loosely in his lap.

After tomorrow, a whole new life begins for me. I'd like to see you try to control me then, Ru-ad. Shalon thought of revenge and Gilene Conway and smiled to herself in the dark.

II

Ru-ad felt Shalon's eyes on him but did not look at her. He could only imagine the thoughts going through her mind. Thoughts, no doubt, of freedom, ambition—perhaps even Andor.

She had no idea that if things went as planned, she would be dead by the time he returned to Rhiannon.

He did not look forward to the prospect of her death. Shalon was the best Vi-Commander he'd seen since Andor, and her skills as a warrior were remarkable. But if she ever attained a post on the Assembly, Ru-ad knew she would be a thorn in his side. Her unrelenting curiosity and deep distrust of his methods would make her question his plans. If he ever hoped to get rid of the Outsiders, he could not allow her to stand in his way. He needed to have Andor's full support on the Assembly when the time came for more ruthless measures.

More importantly, she had become Andor's weak spot. His protégé was not yet aware of how dangerous his regard for Shalon could become, but Ru-ad knew that once Rhiannon had been successfully established, their leader had to be capable of forcing his way onto the galactic scene and lobbying for Orgala's place among the DiploCore Worlds. Andor's biggest obstacle would be the Conways. When they realized the Orgalians' origins, they would do everything in their power to bring such a potentially disruptive—and valuable—force to heel. The last thing Andor needed then would be the distraction of a relationship—and the vulnerability it represented. The Conways, particularly Gilene Conway, were as ruthless as Ru-ad, and they would stop at nothing to achieve their goals.

He had tried to make Andor see this. In a part of the caves far from the main thoroughfares, before Shalon's birthday celebration, Ru-ad confronted Andor with the need for Shalon to be removed. Her links to the Conways would make her vulnerable to them when the Orgalians revealed themselves, he told the Sub-Commander. When they realized that Shalon still lived and held a position of power in Rhiannon, there was no telling what they would do. Or how they would try to use her.

To that end, he had dispatched Tu-dan to watch the Conway family years ago, to ensure that their attention did not sway toward the mercenaries offworld. The Orgalians knew that the death of Shalon's parents had been orchestrated by Gilene Conway. Tu-dan had discovered that someone high up at Conway Enterprises was discreetly inquiring about Shalon's missing body. And over at Conway Securities and Services, a subsidiary that provided armed protection to companies and colonies, officials had begun to investigate the origins of the Orgalian mercenaries, alarmed by their negative effect on Conway profit margins.

As yet, Tu-dan did not have the identities of the searchers, or anything linking the two, but given time and the Conways' resources, it meant Shalon could not be allowed to stay on Orgala any longer. She knew Rhiannon's location. It would be too much of a risk to let her go back to the outside world with the knowledge she possessed about their origins and capabilities.

"Shalon has become a liability," he told Andor as they stood in one of the tunnels. "If you care nothing for your ambitions, remember your obligations to Rhiannon and all Orgalians."

"I remember them quite well," Andor replied. "I have no wish to arrange the loss of my Vi-Commander, who is as loyal an Orgalian as you and I."

"Nor do I, but we have no choice. Events demand that we remove our weaknesses before they are exploited. Rath Nulen's death has provided us with an opportunity we should utilize."

Andor remained silent for long moments and it was then that Ru-ad realized just how much sway Shalon already had over him. Still, Andor hesitated, which meant he knew the truth of Ru-ad's logic.

"How do you plan to get rid of her?" Andor asked finally. "She is a hero to her people and her death would draw a great deal of attention. Should she die on your trek through Desolation, how would you defend your inability to protect her? She is more than a competent soldier, and you were once Sub-Commander. It is inconceivable that you could not repel an attack, or that you would somehow accidentally cause her death. Everyone is aware of your reservations about her. You would be removed from the Assembly long before suspicion became a certainty."

"Suspicion will not fall on me," Ru-ad countered. "I have made arrangements. I could not surprise her in the desert however carefully I planned. She does not trust me, and will be on her guard the entire time she is with me. No, it is best that she leave Orgala alive, and fail to arrive at Vreek. What I need from you is your assurance that when the time comes, you will confirm her loss to the rest of Rhiannon. You could tell them she went rogue once she arrived offworld, choosing to go after the Conways for what they did to her family. They will believe whatever circumstances you present to them regarding her disappearance because of the mind-link you both share. I will take care of things offworld."

"That would mean Vreek would still be without a Group Leader."

"A situation I could easily rectify. Believe me, I hoped it would not come to this, but your future—the future of all Orgalians—is too important to risk. We made a pact when you were younger. I would do all in my power to place you in charge if you allowed me to do what was necessary to protect Rhiannon. I remind you of that now. We are more than comrades. Do not let Shalon come between us and our goals."

Andor let out his breath slowly. "I must think on it a little longer."

"Then we will lose our opportunity. If she consents to go to Vreek tonight, it is my place to take her to the rendezvous.

I must know your answer now."

"As you wish." Andor turned to him, his lips a set line. "It is a good idea to distance her from Rhiannon. She should not stay here any longer, that much is obvious. But Vreek needs her. Let her take over Group Leader Nulen's position. Within a few weeks, I will tell you of my final decision. If she dies on the frontline on Vreek, the result will be the same. I'm sure you can arrange for her to be in the worst of the fighting when she arrives."

It was not the response Ru-ad wanted, but it was the one he expected. It made two things very clear. Andor was too involved with the Terran outsider to be trusted to proceed on his own instincts. However, he had not left his relationship with Ru-ad, or his obligations, behind. He simply needed help to let them come into play. Because he knew that in the end Andor would stand with him, Ru-ad decided to take Andor's assent as his final answer.

"Very well," he said. "She will no doubt come to you tonight when she returns from the Outpost. Send her to me and I will speak to her."

Waiting was not something Ru-ad did when it was clear what action should be taken. Andor might outrank him in military concerns, but Ru-ad held sway over him in political matters for a reason. Informing Andor of his plan had been a calculated risk. If Andor did not want Shalon dead, he would have said so, or turned him in to Cu-don and the Assembly for plotting against another officer. He had done neither of those things, proof enough that he was uncharacteristically divided over the issue. He would leave Andor the temporary illusion of a nobler death for Shalon and spare him from having to betray his own Vi-Commander. What he had said to Andor was true. He could not possibly surprise Shalon and kill her himself—even now, he could feel her eyes on him as she supposedly slept. But he needed to cast suspicion away from himself, and he could not do that if the security vids at the landing site's hut showed him never arriving—or arriving without Shalon— and no actual landing by a ship.

Tu-dan had found a ship that could go into deep space on short notice without raising concerns. It bothered Ru-ad that Troopers would know the location of Orgala. The Assembly had approved the use of mercenaries who were not Orgalians recently, due to the limited number of ships available because of the Madinah's constant attacks on the colonies they were hired to protect. He had gotten

Tu-dan's ship approved by falsifying the information to make it look like one of the discreet underworld transports they had used before. The Whiteway Sector was only partially mapped due to its position on the edge of the known galaxy, far away from more habitable and settled planets, or important defense outposts for the Troopers. That made Orgala difficult to find. Which was the very reason Tec Solutions had chosen it for the location of their secret Facility. The transports the Assembly approved had been vetted by the Apprentices offworld, and were happy to take the money and keep their mouths shut in exchange for steady, profitable business. But they were not killers; just private transporters with a smuggling business on the side. He could not use them for his plans. He had to use Tu-dan's Troopers. No Group would agree to be part of a plan to murder a Vi-Commander, and a ship could not be commandeered without a Group's involvement and the Assembly's knowledge. And then there was the matter of the small window of time he had to act within.

Tu-dan had to watch the Conways, and could not accompany the ship to Orgala. Still, all would eventually work in their favor. Upon the foreign crew's return, Tu-dan would have the element of surprise. Once he was finished, Ru-ad's hands would be clean and all loose ends tied up by Tu-dan on Serron, and by his officers offworld.

Ru-ad tugged open the backpack on the sand next to him. After a brief search, he pulled out a strip of cured meat from the food packet atop another cloth package. The cloth was wrapped around several bottles of Orgalian wine, to keep them from clinking or breaking. Brewed once a year from special berries grown in the Greeneries, the wine was incredibly potent—and rare. Until a few weeks before, only Orgalians and their offworld soldiers had known of it.

Next to it was a metal canister even more important than the wine. It was a hard-won chemical made in small quantities by their techs for battle against the Outsiders. It was only experimental, and far from perfected, but if things worked out and larger quantities could be manufactured, it would one day come in very handy in his future strategies.

And if his plan worked, as he knew it must, tomorrow would be one of those days.

III

During the night, the wind changed direction, and the smudge on the horizon became more than a threat. All that day, they ran before the approaching storm. Around them, sand danced like spirits or spun in tiny whirlwinds before the increasing wind. The air was heavier and grittier than before. Behind them, the cloud obscured the horizon and when Shalon looked hard enough, she could see the slow shifting within its mass.

They did not stop to eat that day, choosing instead to keep moving while they drank. Shalon bit down on thin meat strips as she scrambled up the side of a dune. Tiredness pressed down on her from a night spent resting with one eye always on Ru-ad, making her muscles ache more than usual.

Ru-ad kept checking the time on the panel of his suit as he went, until Shalon inquired if they were late.

"Not if we keep moving," he replied.

Late that afternoon, they reached the butte and mesa formation, its rocks red like Martian dust. They paused long enough to drink water, settle filters over their noses and pull goggles over their eyes. Once they had synchronized their comm links, they began the climb up the side of the center formation. Small handholds, impossible to see unless someone knew where to look for them, had been carved into the dry, sharp stone. Dust flung by a gusty wind pounded against the rock and rebounded into Shalon's face, stinging her exposed cheeks and forehead. She could hear her own breathing now that she had pulled the hood forward, over her ears.

They could not afford to be caught at the top of the formation when the storm hit. The wind would blow them right off the edge onto the plateau below. She climbed with no regard for the harsh way her breath came from her throat, or the slow fires of pain building along limbs that had been working without rest.

When she arrived at the top of the formation, the setting sun cast a strange, mellow light over the scene from a sky touched with pinks, yellows, and something darker. Shalon knelt on the ground, feeling jagged points trying to push past the armor of her suit. As Ru-ad pulled himself over the top behind her, she looked down at the plateau, some seventy feet below. A white plastisteel hut stood near the rocks. Next to it, four or five tunnelers had been anchored to the rock wall and the ground by thin silver cables. The sand

207

several hundred meters in front of the hut had been burnt black in a huge circle from years of spaceship landings, and glittered in places where it had crystallized. Dust blew across the plateau in sheets, driven by the wind.

"Ru-ad," Shalon said, her voice turning on the comm link in her helmet. "How are they going to find us in this?"

"There's a beacon in the hut. And I'll guide them in."

They both turned as one and swung down the side of the mesa. The rocks made a small overhang, and Shalon ducked under it, grabbing onto a handhold and pulling herself against the mesa. She scrambled down to make room for Ru-ad and raised her head to watch his progress.

As Ru-ad swung under the overhang, the sandstorm swept down on them. The air pressed in on Shalon, heavy and gritty, slamming her chest into the wall. The sunlight disappeared, like a snuffed out candle. Everything turned into shifting shadows of black and gray. Wind howled against her back, too loud to speak over, even inside her suit. Sand and rock fragments hit her goggles with loud clicking sounds. The temperature began to drop.

Her hands were scoured and bruised by the blasts of air, but she held on. She could just make out a dark form and a foot right above her. Satisfied he was still with her, Shalon began to work her way down.

IV

More than an hour later, two forms fell into the musty darkness of the hut, wind sweeping sand in behind them. The entire hut shuddered against the power of the storm, but the heat-resistant, reinforced plastisteel held, and the door slid shut. The wind died from a painful shrieking to a loud moaning. Ru-ad sat up and pulled the filter free of his sand-grimed face.

"Lights," he said, and the lumidiscs cast a soft white glow over the room. Crates stood against the back wall, covered with dusty gray tarpaulins. A metal table and four chairs were grouped to the right, next to a closed door. On her left was a console, the top smooth, black crystal. Ru-ad went to it and palmed it on. Blue light edged its surface. He keyed in the necessary codes and an orange light started to pulse in the top right hand corner. Seconds later, a white light next to it began to pulse in the same rhythm.

Shalon pulled off her goggles and hood, and sand fell to the floor in a soft whisper. She tugged at her filter.

"Did we make it on time?"

Ru-ad nodded. "They should be here shortly."

Ru-ad walked over to the crates and raised a corner of the tarpaulin. He pulled out two bright orange glowing rods the length of his arm and a roll of ultrathin cable that glittered.

"I'm going to guide them in and run a lead cable from the hut to the ship. I'll come back for you."

"Be careful," Shalon replied, sitting on a chair.

Ru-ad settled his filter back over his nose and mouth and ducked out of the hut, into the howling dark of full night. The Outsiders knew supplies came in from offworld several times a year, and they were constantly searching for the landing site. To keep it hidden, only a low-range, high intensity homing beacon—too weak to be picked up by the Facility's security scans, but easily detected if the approaching ship was using the correct, pre-arranged frequency—was used to help guide in the spaceships.

Landings were done only at night, with the ships coming in low behind a mountain range on the far side of the planet that kept them from popping up on the Facility's screens. The terrain had been left unaltered to better camouflage it, but that meant no lights illuminated the landing site, to prevent any possibility of an Outsider noticing the artificial glow on the horizon at night. It also meant the ships had to be guided in by hand, with two other low frequency beacons that would ping the ship's instruments with a precise location.

After the door closed behind him, shutting off the light from inside, the cable gleamed in his hand. The light it cast even made it possible to see where he was about to place his feet. Gusts of wind beating against him like fists, he felt with one hand to the left of the door. His fingers touched the metal frame, which was shaking with the power of the wind. With deft fingers, he stuck the end of the magnetic cable with the circular retractor at the base to the doorframe, and the other end to the holster around his waist. Fighting for every step, he started to move forward, toward the edge of the landing field.

He'd almost made it, when he heard a regular keening sound over the scream of the wind. He looked up and saw the brief flash of light from the breaking thrusters high above him through the shifting curtains of sand. Ru-ad flicked the buttons on the torches. Golden lasers cut through the darkness. Raising the devices above his head, he started to wave them in a repeated pattern. The thrusters fired again, and the ship began to descend.

Ru-ad started forward once the ship had landed. A short while later, a small square of illumination appeared ahead of him. A figure moved in the doorway, dark on pale. He went toward it, unsteady in the wind and sand.

Ru-ad found the ramp by accidentally walking into it. At the top, he bent and attached the magnetic end of the glimmering cable on his belt to the side of the ship. Then he stepped inside. Behind him, the airlock closed, blocking out the sound of the wind as if it had never been. There was a man waiting in the airlock. The entryway could just hold them both.

The man opposite him had his arms folded. A gold insignia, attached to the navy blue Trooper uniform, glinted on his chest. His face was tanned and creased like leather and pale gray eyes studied Ru-ad without expression. His nose, hooked like a slag bird's beak, was the most prominent thing about him, along with his silver-gray hair. A faint scent—sweet and powdery—hung around him. Ru-ad removed his filter and raised his goggles.

"Captain Marchand," Ru-ad said in Universal.

The man gave him a slow nod. "You're Ru-ad Whelan?"

Ru-ad pulled his bag off his shoulder. "I do not have a lot of time, Captain. She'll get suspicious if I take too long to return."

Marchand watched as Ru-ad removed a small metal cylinder from his bag. It had a dull finish and a spray nozzle. Ru-ad held it out to him and the Captain took it, frowning at it.

"It feels cold. Light. What is it?"

"A spray that will help incapacitate her. It will knock her unconscious and it has a paralytic effect as well, but I caution you— do not let your men breathe it in. It could kill someone with the wrong genetic profile who hasn't been through conditioning."

Marchand's lips twisted into a humorless grin. "You're really determined to get rid of this girl, aren't you?"

"Captain, do not make the mistake of thinking you've been assigned an easy task. Without this spray, you will have no chance of capturing her. As soon as she realizes you are not Orgalians, she will not hesitate to make her escape. Most, if not all of you, would die."

"A girl of eighteen? You must be kidding."

"Believe me, I am not. Be careful how you use the spray. Its effect will diminish over time as her body builds up a resistance to it. That is why it is important that as soon as she is incapacitated, you kill her and retrieve the suit she's wearing."

Marchand's bushy gray eyebrows went up. "Why the suit?"

"She will not let you remove it if she's alive. Do as you will with the body, but the suit will be proof that you have met the terms of our contract. Understood?"

"Understood. And our second payment?"

Ru-ad reached into his bag and pulled out the golden bottles of Orgalian wine. Marchand's eyes gleamed as he shoved the cylinder into his pocket and accepted the half dozen bottles.

"Tu-dan will pay you the rest of your money when you present him with her suit upon your arrival at Serron."

"Sure," Marchand replied. "Whatever you say."

Ru-ad shouldered his bag. "Remember, Captain, have things in place by the time she gets here. I will not be boarding again and she will be cautious. Attentive."

"Don't you worry about us," Marchand said. "You just get her here. We'll take care of the rest."

V

Shalon looked up as the door opened and a blast of wind and Ru-ad came in. "It's time?"

Ru-ad nodded. "Get your things."

Shalon stood, backpack in hand. *Offworld. I'm going offworld.* Her stomach felt tight, but it was not an unfamiliar or disturbing emotion. More like the butterflies she sometimes had before a battle.

"I will come with you to the ship and leave you at the ramp."

"You don't have to do that," Shalon said, surprised.

"Andor made me promise I would see you off. I do not think he would excuse me, even in light of this bad weather."

Touched despite herself, Shalon nodded her concession.

"We will not be able to talk out there, so I'll say this now. Goodbye, Shalon. Make us proud."

"I will," she replied, marveling at how normal her voice sounded around the lump in her throat.

Outside, the air blew icy cold. The storm's ferocity had settled into a steady pattern of howling, blasting wind and small lulls, when it seemed almost possible to hear something besides the scream of air and sand. Then the wind would rush back in, erasing that tiny reprieve as if it had never been. Shalon walked with her left hand always on the glowing lead wire. She knew Ru-ad followed, but the storm made her feel isolated.

Five minutes later, she saw a square of light appear in front of her. Her foot hit the ramp and she placed one boot on it and turned. Ru-ad stood right behind her, a dark shape beside the glowing wire. She raised one hand in a salute for the last time. Then she crossed into the airlock.

One minute, the wind had her in its harsh grip. The next, she could hear its howling, but stood free of its power in brilliant light. Ahead of her, an open inner airlock led to an empty gray metal corridor. Sand scudded along the floor into the ship.

Behind her, the outer airlock closed and silence descended, deafening after the storm. Shalon pulled off her goggles and threw back her hood. She tugged the filter off her face and dropped it into her backpack.

"Hello," she called. "Anyone here?"

No answer came back. She started across the small space to the inner airlock.

With shocking suddenness, it irised closed.

Shalon stopped dead, her skin prickling inside her warm suit. *What the hell?*

A soft hissing sound began, and she caught a whiff of something chemical and tart. It coated the back of her throat like oil. Shalon held her breath. She recognized the scent and knew the filter would be useless against it. A quick glance around showed her that there were no control panels for the doors within the entryway.

Oh, my God. A set up. He set me up.

She dropped the bag. Before it hit the floor, she had launched a kick at the outer airlock. A dull boom sounded, but the airlock held. Holding her breath, Shalon continued to lash out. After the third kick, a small dent appeared, but the booming vibrations that hurt her ears told her the airlock had not been breached.

And still, the hissing continued.

Shalon spun and threw herself at the other airlock. The need for air burned in her chest as she pounded fists and feet against the metal door. She dented it in several places before she caught sight of something that glittered in the upper right-hand corner above the inner airlock. She focused and realized the glint came from a camera lens as small as a coin.

The bastards are watching. Anger and shame burned through her. *Not that it matters. He won. That bastard Ru-ad lied to me and I fell for it.*

She dug her fingernails into her palms, defeated and conscious of how alone she was now. Helplessness flowed through her.

Ha-Ka. I never said goodbye.

The need to breathe clawed at her throat. She unclenched her hands.

Andor, she thought, broadcasting everything that had happened with a power she knew would stop him in his tracks. And then, at last, she took a single breath.

She was unconscious before she hit the floor.

CHAPTER 16

Let us remember that whatever our age, whatever way we choose
to serve, we are all warriors.
No enemy can overcome us so long as we fight together to the end.
— *First Commander Cu-don, Final Address to Apprentices (297 A.A.)*

I

"Small for a soldier, isn't she?" Matka said, staring at the image of the woman on his console as she took off her goggles. He pushed his blond hair back from his pale blue eyes as Marchand bent over his shoulder.

"Doesn't matter," Marchand replied, his thick gray brows drawn together as he waited to make sure his trap had worked. "If Tu-dan's anything to go by, these people can't be judged by their size. I don't know what the fuck they are or why they're on this god-forsaken rock I've never even heard of, and I don't care. All I know is, we're getting paid to get rid of her."

"We can't kill her."

Marchand turned to see Michael Zorida entering the bridge, Raydell trailing behind him. Raydell met Marchand's gaze and rolled her eyes at Zorida as she folded her arms and leaned against the captain's chair. Tall for a woman, with muscular arms hidden by the dark green recreation jumpsuit she wore, she had an air of perpetual nervous energy around her. Her hair, which she kept short as a man's, was dyed a blinding shade of red and her eyes had been modified to match.

214

"Are you all crazy?" Zorida said, jabbing his finger at the air for emphasis. "If you think I'm going to be part of this—"

"If you think you have a choice, you're the one who's crazy," Marchand said, his voice low and menacing. "We are all in this together, whether you like it or not. Now shut the fuck up before I leave your ass on this damn planet."

The lieutenant's mouth opened and closed, like a fish. "You can't do that."

"Oh, yeah?" Raydell said, leaning away from the chair. "Space is a dangerous place. Lots of people go on tour, have little accidents. Sometimes, we can't even retrieve the bodies."

Zorida looked from her to the captain, the expression on his face shifting from anger to shock. "Captain Marchand—"

"Matka," Marchand said over his shoulder as he folded his arms. "Close the airlocks."

"Aye, Captain."

"Ganesh."

A tone sounded from the console and a male voice answered. "Captain?"

"Push the button on that remote and get the fuck away from the vents. I'll tell you when she's down."

"Right."

"As for you, Zorida, you'll be happy to know we have no intention of killing her."

"You don't?"

"Hell, no," Raydell said with a half smile as she looked at the captain. "He told us to do what we wanted with the body, right? Well, there are lots of uses for a human female back on Serron. Lots of uses. Some of them might even make us a little money."

The lieutenant was speechless at first. "How the hell can you do this? What kind of Troopers are you?"

"The kind that's going to retire on something more than a sorry excuse for a pension," Marchand replied, his voice sharp and bitter.

"Fuck. Look at this," Matka called, awe in his voice. The others gathered around the console and watched as the girl attacked the closed airlock door, her movements so fast, they blurred a little on the console screen.

"How long has she been holding her breath now?" Marchand asked.

"Going on two minutes. She's fucking amazing. She's even dented the damn airlock."

"Well, the old man wasn't lying after all. We're going to be rich, boys and girls."

"We're putting her in the brig?" Raydell asked.

"Yeah. Take Zorida with you when you go and use the mag cuffs. The grav cuffs are broken."

"Money and a few bottles of wine," Zorida said, striking his hand against a console, his tone full of disgust. "That's what a girl's life is worth to you?"

"Damn right," Marchand shot back. He strode over to the gleaming metal captain's chair and sat.

"What you have to do right now is decide where you stand. We wouldn't have had this problem with your predecessor, but unfortunately, he got laid up with the plague and you got assigned to us. Thank god you're on weapons, and not navigation, like Matka and Raydell. That's why I told Raydell here to only tell you what was happening when you asked why we were landing on a planet. Now we're going to find out if you really know something about being part of a crew, or if it's all about the damn rule book with you.

"So, Zorida. What's your life back home worth to you? Raydell told you about the pay-off, but it seems that's not good enough for you. Well, it's going to have to be. Because you can either join us and end this tour a rich man, or you can stay right here and die in this storm and nothing changes for the little lady. Your choice."

"Three minutes," Matka said. "I think she saw us."

"Your choice, Zorida, so make it quick. I want to get off this hellhole."

In front of him, Matka said, "You know, she's kinda pretty."

Raydell nodded as she stared into the furious green eyes of the girl on the screen. "She sure is." And a slow grin parted her thin lips.

II

Gray mist swirled and ebbed. Parted to reveal a deck grille flowing past beneath. Searing light above. Her body swayed from side to side. Snatches of far-away speech drifted over her.

"...heavier than she looks..."

"…watch her head…"

The air grew cold. A clicking sound began. Her teeth chattering.

"…a blanket…"

"…fuck that. This isn't a hotel…"

"…at least leave her boots…"

"…check them…"

The last voice bothered her, grated on her ears. She tried to reach out. To end it. Her arm felt strange, detached. It hit something with a numbing force and bounced back to lie on her stomach.

"Fuck! My nose!"

"…accident…"

"…She hit me in the eye! Bitch!"

Something solid hit her cheek. She slipped away into the gray.

Woke to a hard surface beneath her. Rings of ice around her wrists. She tried to fight. Tried to move her body. Her muscles were weighted with lead. Her eyes stayed closed though she fought to open them. Only her lips had life. She whispered, "Aida. Aida Me."

No one answered. Tired beyond thought, she let the mist take her again—

··· ▬ ▬ ▬ ···

—and awakened to silence and darkness. She lay still for long moments. Forced open her eyes. White spots danced against shadows. Her head throbbed in a steady beat that matched her heart. Memory flooded back.

Ru-ad. The ship.

Shalon grimaced as she lifted her head and looked down at herself. She lay on a bunk suspended from a metal wall. Her hands wore metal wrist bands. One seemed to be stuck to the metal frame of the bunk, the other to the wall. Two more bands attached to the bottom of the bunk circled her ankles and kept her legs together. Mag cuffs, she realized and dropped her head back onto the thin mattress. There was something wrong about what she'd seen, but her mind was too foggy to think clearly.

At least I'm still alive.

Weak and dizzy, she twisted her head to take in her surroundings. There wasn't a lot to see. The small cell featured the bunk, a commode to her left, near her head, and a sealed metal airlock. Tarnish dulled the shine of the walls and the commode and the air smelled of aged perspiration. Tired, she let her eyes drift shut.

The sound of the bolts in the airlock releasing caused her to open them again. Shalon watched as a man stepped into the room. He stood staring at her after the airlock closed behind him, and she had time to take in his neatly trimmed dark brown hair and eyes, his spotless blue uniform and the guarded expression on his face. A sweet powdery smell came from him; the obligatory scent spacers wore to ensure body odor didn't make working in close confines uncomfortable.

Shalon cleared her throat. "You're a Trooper."

The man nodded. "I'm Acting Lieutenant Michael Zorida. Do you remember your name?"

"I'm Vi-Commander Shalon—" she almost added her last name, but thought better of it, "—Olang."

"Do you know where you are?"

"On a ship. You took me from Orgala." Her jaw tightened. "Ru-ad set me up."

Michael took a couple of steps toward her bunk. "How are you feeling?"

"How do you think I feel?"

He avoided her eyes. "Are you hungry?"

"How long has it been since I passed out?"

He sighed. "You're making this difficult."

"For the bastards that have me cuffed in a cell, damn right I am. How long has it been?"

"Almost two days."

A wave of dizziness passed through her and she turned her head to her left, trying not to retch. She saw her shoulder out of the corner of her eye and realized what had struck her as wrong a few minutes before. She wore a green spacesuit now instead of her scout suit. *Ru-ad, you bastard. What else have you told them?* "What do you want from me?"

"I'm sorry. I didn't want this to happen, but there's nothing I can do about it."

His voice sounded muffled. She looked up at him and saw that he held a white filter over his nose and mouth. A metal canister shone in his outstretched right hand.

Clearing her mind as best as she could, Shalon called to Andor, but there was no answer. Her thought had gone nowhere—as if her mind was too weak to broadcast it very far. "Please," she said. "If you don't want to do this, don't. Help me get out of here. I don't know what Ru-ad told you—"

"It doesn't matter. It's out of my hands," he said, and depressed the nozzle trigger.

··· — — — ···

"She begs really pretty, doesn't she?" Marchand said, taking the canister from Zorida after he'd returned to the bridge.

The Lieutenant looked at him with disgust. "You were watching us."

"Of course," Matka said, swiveling his seat to face the captain's chair. "It's for your own good after all, look what she did to Raydell's face by accident."

"What's the point? What do you think I could do against all of you?"

"Nothing, Zorida," Marchand said, reaching down to flip open a compartment in the base of his chair. He shoved the canister into the small space and pressed the lock closed.

"You had it right the first time. It's out of your hands."

III

Ru-ad strode down the twisting corridors he had left Rhiannon by seven days before, his hood thrown back to reveal his dusty face. His sandy backpack swung from his right hand. Musty, salty air caressed his warm cheeks. The slight frown on his face reflected how deep in thought he was. So when Andor stepped in his path from a tunnel opening on his right, Ru-ad barely halted in time to avoid running into him.

"Sub-Commander." Ru-ad started to greet him but noticed that Andor was wearing his scout suit. When their eyes met, the words in his throat died before they were spoken.

"Explain yourself." Andor's voice sounded frigid as the desert night air.

"Is that really necessary?"

"You went against my express wishes."

"Only because they were not the best solution. It is my place to make strategy decisions for the good of Rhiannon, Andor."

"It's not your place to lie to me."

219

"You were being unreasonable. Your suggestion would have wasted valuable time."

"Wasted time?" Andor took a step toward Ru-ad, his body taut. "You have no idea what you have done."

Ru-ad let his breath hiss out. "You speak nonsense. I know exactly what I have done. I made the decision you should have made. I did what was necessary. You blinded yourself to the truth and I refused to let that put Rhiannon in jeopardy."

"Shalon was no threat!"

"You can still say that? After everything we discussed? Her family caused all of this! We would never have been used, exiled, or forced to claw our way through this world if Gilene Conway had not decided to create us. Her own personal guinea pigs. And you think her niece is one of us? She is the very flesh and blood of the family who treated us as little more than convenient slaves. I would never have submitted to her inclusion on the Assembly!"

He stopped, chest heaving, conscious his voice had begun to echo down the tunnels. Disturbed by his loss of composure, he brought himself under control. "The biggest threat to any person is the one who knows him best. Accepting Shalon would have meant turning over the society I have worked so hard to build to those I wrested it from in the first place. I could not let that happen, whatever the cost. Sooner or later, you will see that I was correct. But if you did not agree with me, then why agree to get rid of her?"

"Because," Andor replied, his voice harsh and unsteady, "I was stalling."

Ru-ad frowned as he searched Andor's face. "Stalling? Why?"

"For time. Time to figure out what to do about you."

The bag in Ru-ad's hand fell to the floor with a muffled thump and the sound of shale sliding against shale. His hand went to the holster on his waist.

"Do not try it," Andor said without moving his gaze from Ru-ad's face. "You are not as fast as you once were."

Ru-ad paused. "You cannot mean to kill me. All I have ever done is try to help you achieve your destiny."

"And what did Shalon ever do to you?" Andor slammed his right fist against the tunnel wall and dust and particles fell in a small shower. "She was never a Conway. Not the way you think. She is more than a collection of genes and family traits. There are things you do not know about her. Things that are bigger than your selfish concerns.

And you may have ended all that. Generations of preparation and hope, down the drain because you could not let go of your hate."

"I did this for all of us."

"You did this for yourself," Andor said, his voice sharp as a cutting edge. "You could not handle the idea of losing control of Rhiannon before you had shaped it into your own image. You thought to control me, use me to turn the Assembly to your own ends. But you did not teach me to follow orders, Ru-ad. Things might have been better for you if you had."

Ru-ad drew in his breath. "No. I could not have read you so wrong."

"I didn't think you would betray me either, or lie to me. But when you came to me about Shalon, I realized I had underestimated your hate and your determination. For years I did my best to stay away from Shalon, to draw your attention away from us and keep her out of your scheming. When you told me your plans, I knew I had failed. If you could plan such an end for her, then the Ru-ad I thought I knew never existed.

"I didn't want to hurt either of you. I tried to dissuade you and when that did not work, I tried to stall for time, to get Shalon away until I could find a resolution to this that would not put her at risk or betray my pact with you. I thought I could save you both. It was my one mistake, and because of it, I may have cost Shalon her life. I should have realized I could not trust you when it came to her. But I have always trusted you and it is a hard habit to break." Andor lowered his fist from the wall. "Why couldn't you let it go?"

Ru-ad sighed. "I could ask you the same. Don't you see? Even now, she has managed to do what I tried to prevent. She has driven a rift between us, made you weak and unable to see past your emotions. I knew when she arrived she would be trouble, but I never imagined she would destroy the work of my life."

"That is all I am to you? Work?" Andor shook his head incredulously. "You had me fooled for so long. You do not love or care about anything but power and control. You never have. But you taught me well and served Rhiannon all your life. For that, I owe you the chance to present your case to the Assembly so that they may decide your punishment. It is more consideration than you showed her."

Behind him, from the shadows that concealed another entrance, Cu-don appeared. Her pale robe swished against the floor and the lasgun in her steady, outstretched right hand shone gray-blue.

"Chief Advisor Ru-ad Whelan. I hereby strip you of your post and command you to stand trial before the Assembly for the attempted murder of Vi-Commander Shalon Conway."

Ru-ad looked quickly from Cu-don to Andor. "Attempted?"

"I cannot be certain. Our link is weakened somehow, but I still sense something. I don't think she is dead."

Andor reached out a hand and removed Ru-ad's lasgun in one deft movement. "Before your trial, you will tell me what you have done, and who helped you. If I cannot rescue her, I will avenge her death."

Ru-ad did not move as Andor stripped him of his knives and holster while Cu-don kept her gun trained on him. When Andor stood before him again, he said, "It is seldom that I find myself bested at my own game. The pupil has learned well from the teacher. I should have listened to my own advice. The biggest threat to any person is the one who knows him best."

Andor clenched his fist around the weapons he held. "I never would have betrayed you, Ru-ad. But you left me no choice."

"I know that now," Ru-ad replied and incredibly, a proud smile flitted across his face. "Whatever you do, she will no longer be in your way. I have succeeded, however much it cost me. Remember that, Andor. My last lesson to you. Choose your path and walk it to the bitter end. Regrets are for the indecisive and the weak-minded. They are costly things for leaders of men."

Andor removed a pair of grav cuffs from one of the packs on his waist as Cu-don moved to stand to his right.

"I am sorry for this," she said. "When Andor came to me, I did not believe him at first. Murdering a Vi-Commander is not something I thought you capable of."

"Really?" Ru-ad said mildly, "I would have thought you knew me better than that."

"So did I, Ru-ad. So did I."

IV

Time passed in a blur of events and sleep. Shalon woke twice more to find herself alone, and fell asleep again almost immediately. The next time she awakened, she was stronger and alert. Forcing herself to focus, she counted off seconds in her head. An hour passed before the door opened and Michael Zorida came through it. He balanced a tray on his right hand with a cup and a small bowl of something warm, yellow and spongy looking. Her stomach clawed with hunger at the sight of it.

Michael sat on the bed and balanced the tray on his knees. "Hey. Are you okay?"

"Do me a favor," Shalon said. "Don't try to act like you care."

His gaze slid away from hers. "I thought you might be hungry." He waited, as if expecting her to answer, but she said nothing. He dipped the spoon into the bowl and started feeding her. Shalon did not resist. The food tasted warm and seemed to be some sort of sweet porridge. She stared into Michael's face as he ferried the spoon to and from her mouth, determined to make him look at her, to see her as a person, but he refused to meet her eyes. She tried to reach Andor again, but got nothing but a vague sense of his presence.

When she finished drinking the water in the cup, he laid her head back onto the mattress, placed the tray aside and pulled a filter out of one of his pockets. She watched as he pressed it over his mouth.

"You know how dangerous that stuff is? It's been known to kill unmodified humans and filters don't do much against it."

He did not reply. Instead, he reached into the same pocket and tugged out the canister.

She laughed softly to herself. "Why am I even telling you that? If you drop dead, all the better for me, right?"

He finally met her gaze, and the desperation in his eyes silenced her. He leaned forward so that his body hung over her head.

"It's better if you sleep. The less anyone has to come in here, the better for you. The others…they're not like me." His voice was very low through the filter, so low, she could barely hear it.

"If you want to protect me, undo these cuffs. I can protect myself once I'm free," she whispered back.

"I can't," he said, "they're watching and listening all the time."

"It doesn't matter. You can release me before they have a chance to do anything."

"I don't have the key. They don't trust me with it."

"Then get it."

Michael made a slight negative movement of his head. "Marchand has it on him all the time. I can't get to him and you can't fight them all."

"I'm a soldier. You'd be surprised what I can do. Especially if you help me."

He searched her eyes. "You say that now, but you can barely stay awake, can you?"

"If you stopped dosing me with that stuff it would help."

He paused, torn for a moment. "They'd know. And if they suspect I'm helping you, they'll let someone else look after you. Believe me. You don't want that."

"Michael," she said, and he started at her first use of his name, "if you don't help me, I'm dead anyway."

"No. They're not going to kill you." He held out the canister. "But if I help you, I'm not so sure they won't kill me."

Realization dawned and she looked at him with contempt. "You're a coward, you know that?"

If he answered, she never heard it.

$\cdots \, \text{---} \, \cdots$

She woke to a dull headache and a foggy mind, but did not feel as she usually did. As if days had passed. She was flexing her numb hands in her cuffs and trying to move her body a little when the airlock opened. She looked up expecting Michael, but instead, someone new came in. This man was shorter and blonde, with bright blue eyes filled with malicious humor. Something about him made the hairs on the back of her neck stand up.

"Who are you?"

"A friend of Michael's." He grinned.

"Where is Michael?" The way he looked at her made her feel dirty.

He walked over to her bunk. "He's busy. He asked me to check in on you if you woke up."

Sure he did. "Well you checked. You can go now."

He laughed. "You got balls, girl." He sat on the bed and looked her over from head to toe.

She remained silent, sensing trouble and clenching her fist as she tested her bonds. They remained firm. "What do you want?"

"A little peek, is all," he said with a grin and an arch of his eyebrow. "Just a little practice. Where you're going, you'll need the experience. You don't mind, right? Raise your hand if you mind."

She spat at him. The smile on his face froze. He wiped off the mess and with the same hand, slapped her twice across the cheek. The sting of his blows hurt less than her helplessness.

When she looked at him again, fury twisted his face.

"Don't fuck with me, bitch. I will make you regret it," he said in a low, savage voice.

"If you're such a big man, why don't you release me and then try to take a peek?"

He tugged a finger down the seal along the front of her suit. "Because I don't have to do anything you want." He pulled back the material to expose her bare breasts. "You have to do what I want."

Humiliated, she tried not to flinch as he clamped a rough hand over her left breast, pinching the nipple cruelly. He slid his other hand down her flat stomach and below her waist.

She tried to keep her legs pressed together, but she was still too weak. He forced his hand between her thighs, straining her legs and her ankles where they were clamped together in the manacles. His finger pushed into her, cold and flexing, like a worm. It hurt and it was all she could do to keep from gagging. Her heart pounded in her chest. Her hand grabbed and twisted the slightly grainy material of the cheap sheets between her fingers. *You son-of-a-bitch. I will make you pay for that. Count on it.*

"Nice and tight." He smiled at her. "We're going to have some good times together soon. Real soon."

V

"She woke up after just eighteen hours this time," Raydell said to Marchand as they walked down the corridor to the bridge. Her nose was no longer swollen but her left eye still had a yellowing bruise around it. "The old man was right. The spray is getting less effective."

"It will last till we get to Serron in three days. That's all we need." Marchand said.

"There's also the little matter of Matka and Ganesh. They've been making visits to the brig recently, whenever Zorida's not around."

Marchand paused outside the bridge and shrugged. "Boys will be boys as the ancient saying goes. The Factors I'm dealing with won't care if the merchandise is a little used. They might test it themselves, actually. A little harmless fun is good for the men after all this time on tour."

"That's not the problem." Raydell folded her arms across her chest. "I think the rest of the crew might be upset about being left out."

Marchand considered the statement. "Well, you have a point." He palmed the bridge open. "Even with her drugged, it might be hard for one person to hold her down. I trust you'll see to it that everyone gets the news and plays nice with each other."

Raydell smiled, the bruise on her face pulling tight with the action. "With pleasure."

VI

"You have to help me."

Michael said nothing. He tried to feed her another spoonful of food and Shalon twisted her head away.

"You have to eat."

"Do you know what they've been doing to me when you aren't here?" she whispered, hate burning through her as she thought of a finger pushing inside her. "Do you? Do you have any idea how that feels?"

"I..."

"For God's sake, what kind of Troopers are you? You're supposed to uphold the law, not break it. Don't let them —"

The airlock opened and they both twisted their heads toward the portal. Two women entered; one a red head with eyes to match, and a fading black eye, the other, a woman with skin dark as night and proud cheek bones that jutted past the fall of her copper-colored braids. Behind them was the man she had come to know as Matka. For the first time, fear curdled her stomach.

"Well, fancy meeting you here," the red-head said joining Michael by the bed. The cell could just hold all four of them, and the cloying smell of their perfumes coated Shalon's throat.

"What are you all doing here, Raydell?"

"Taking a well-earned break," Matka said. "Captain's orders."

"Leave her alone," Michael said, putting aside the tray on the bed and standing.

"Make us," the dark-skinned woman laughed. Her lyrical accent was unfamiliar, and her gaze left Shalon ice cold.

I will not let them take me like this. She tensed herself, trying to ready her body for the assault, but weakness still flooded her limbs. She was in no shape to resist three determined people. And they knew it. She could see it in their eyes. Fear fluttered in her chest like a tiny caged bird, but she smothered it with anger.

"For fuck's sake," Michael said savagely, "she's just a kid."

"Is she now? That's not what I heard," the dark woman said.

Matka walked around to the top of the bunk and bent over her face. "What do you say, honey? Want to have some fun with us?"

"Fuck you," Shalon said distinctly, her heart pounding.

Raydell laughed. "What did I tell you, Swanson. Feisty." And the look she threw the woman left Shalon in no doubt as to their relationship. Raydell glanced back at Shalon and raised a finger to tap at her bruised eye. "Remember this? Payback's a bitch, huh?"

"Yes." Swanson pushed at the tray and sat on the edge of the bunk. She ran a hand over Shalon's chest, flicking a finger at her nipple. "I think I'd like to hear her scream a little."

Never. I'll never scream. "You won't make me scream," Shalon said, her voice as hard as she could make it.

"So brave." Matka slid a hand under her chin and jerked her face upward so that he could press a hard kiss to her lips. His mouth was closed, his lips cold and moist. It was like being kissed by a fish. Shalon's right hand strained against her cuff as he leaned away and smiled at her.

Out of the corner of her eye, Shalon saw Michael try to grab at Matka. Raydell got in his way, and the next thing she knew, there was a scuffle, a thud and a crash as the tray fell to the floor. Something sharp poked at her thigh. She heard the tray clatter under the bed. The bowl and cup spun and rolled around each other like dance partners before slowing to a stop.

"Stay the fuck out of our way, Zorida, unless you want to participate," Raydell said.

Matka looked across at Swanson. "Get her legs free."

The bunk shook a little as Swanson got on it. Shalon didn't see what she did, but she felt fingers graze her ankle and her legs became lighter. Feeling desperately slow, she swung her left leg up. Relief coursed through her as she made contact with Swanson's jaw and a satisfying pain jolted up to her hip. She heard a thud even as she got her foot under her, twisted and swung out with her right leg, making contact with the meaty part of Raydell's thigh.

The woman cried out and cursed.

A hand grabbed at her neck in a choking vise, fingers squeezing the air out of her. Matka hit her in the face, his fist landing so hard her cheek went numb, then tingly. Shalon gasped as something sharp pressed against her neck; a slight sting, and the warmth of blood trickled down her throat.

"Listen, bitch, I can hurt you in ways that will make you wish for death."

Then do it, you son-of-a-bitch. Kill me if you want. It would be better than this. His grip tightened on her throat, the short nails piercing painful crescents into her. Her lungs were on fire with the need for oxygen and dark spots developed in her vision. From far away, she felt someone ripping at her clothing, hands scratching her legs as they held her down. Cold air kissed her body and made her nipples tighten.

"Oh, no you don't, Zorida. You're staying here and watching. We're all in this together."

"The hell I will." His voice sounded congested, as though he spoke though his nose.

"The fuck you won't," Matka said and released her neck. Shalon gasped, struggling for air even as a hand clawed between her legs. She bucked, but the hands holding her were firm and unforgiving. A thumb rubbed against her, calluses painful on the tender dry flesh within. Shame and anger flooded her in a confusing tide.

Raydell and Swanson kept trying to force her legs wider apart. The muscles in Shalon's thighs strained and cramped as she fought them. She managed to twist her pelvis, dislodging the thumb, but the effort made the weakness in her limbs worse. Her right ankle hit the wall with a jolt of pain. Swanson grinned her triumph and licked her lips in a slow parody.

"You bitch," Shalon managed to rasp out. "You won't get away with this. You should have killed me when you had the chance."

Raydell laughed as Matka crawled onto the bed. "But then," he said, smiling full into her face as he knelt between her legs, "you would have missed all the fun."

He grabbed her hips, lifted, and shoved into her. Pain tore at Shalon's insides and she stifled a scream. When he pulled back and tried to enter her again, she dug her hips into the bed to get away from him. Her teeth bit into her lip as she strained and twisted her hips, trying to throw him off.

He leaned forward, using his torso to hold her down. The coarse hairs on his stomach prickled her sensitive skin and the revolting sweet smell of him washed over her. Shalon jerked her head up and butted his forehead. Pain blossomed behind her eyes. Matka cried out and leaned back on his knees, sliding out of her. She snapped her teeth at him, narrowly missing his throat. The skin on her wrists pulled taut against her bonds and the hands on her ankles squeezed tight.

"Zorida," Raydell cried out. "Hold her down so I can put the cuffs back on!"

Shalon twisted her head to look at Michael as he stood up from the floor. Blood ran from his nose in a thin stream. His gaze met hers. *Please, please help me.* He looked directly at her, his expression agonized. Finally he said, "Fuck you, Raydell."

"Michael!" Raydell yanked something from her belt and handed it to Matka. Shalon heard a small snick and then he was holding the blade he had used earlier and must have given to Raydell for safekeeping. Long as the distance from his wrist to his middle finger, the silver edge of the knife glinted wickedly in the light. "Either you hold her down, or Matka will put this into her eye. Or anywhere else it hurts."

Michael stared at Shalon, but despite the coldness coiling in her stomach, she gasped out, "Don't. Help me or let them kill me."

"Who said anything about killing you?" Swanson asked, her voice languid. "Come on, Zorida. It's no big deal. It's not like she'll ever have the chance to tell anyone who cares."

Michael said nothing. He looked from Swanson to Shalon one more time and then he backed away, toward the airlock.

"Where the hell are you going?" Matka bellowed.

Michael looked at him, rage narrowing his brown eyes. "You can knife me in the back if you like, but I'm not standing by another second. I'm done with this, and I'm done with you. All of you." He turned to the airlock and when he broke the sensor barrier, it opened to reveal a tall, gray haired man. Michael did not spare him a glance. He shoved past him and Shalon heard his boots echoing down the corridor.

You left me to this? You walked out on me? You fucking coward! You bastard! More exhausted than she'd ever been in her life, Shalon turned her rage on Matka. "Get off me, you fucking pig, or I will shred your throat."

The gray haired man made an amused sound as he entered the room. "The view from the bridge made it look like you were in a tight spot, Matka. Maybe you should take a break."

Matka looked annoyed and frustrated at the same time. One hand held the knife, the other hovered uncertainly around his privates. "Captain Marchand—"

"Captain's prerogative, Matka," Marchand said, his voice genial. Matka hesitated just a second longer before he climbed off the bunk. Shalon's skin quivered away from where his knee touched the inside of her thigh. As he pulled his clothes together, Marchand walked over to Shalon and smiled down at her.

"Hello there. You're being very difficult at the moment, aren't you?"

Shalon did not say anything. Her chest heaved as she glared at him, hate and unshed tears of pain making her vision waver. His frank appraising gaze made her feel exposed, hollowed out. Trapped.

"Release her handcuffs."

"Sir?" Raydell sounded shocked.

"Release the cuffs. I want to turn her over. Hold her head, Matka."

Her skin goose-bumped as she realized what he meant. Matka grabbed her head and pressed the blade under her chin. Raydell and Swanson worked at her cuffs. The moment Shalon heard the click, she started to raise her torso, but Marchand appeared over her. His fist smashed into her face, flattening her lips against her teeth. She tasted the salt on his skin just before blood from her split lip flooded her mouth with the taste of copper.

Shalon's head seemed to come loose from her shoulders. Flashes of light danced in her vision. Her hands were brought together and cuffed in front of her, roughly. The skin on one of her wrists split open on the cuff and the metal dug into her flesh, sliding against the blood with a tugging, cutting ache. A knife grazed her throat, and then it was gone and there was a momentary weightless feeling. Her head slammed against the wall suddenly. As the left side of her face landed on the mattress, blood began to trickle down the back of her neck.

Despite the pain and the disconnected feeling in her mind, she tried to struggle, but a hand clamped down on her neck from behind, forcing her cheek back against the coarse grain of the sheet. Something jabbed into her ribcage as her legs were pulled apart and the cuffs placed back on. Bile and terror rose within her.

"Move aside," came the captain's voice.

A soft contact blossomed in Shalon's mind. Faint as the touch of a butterfly's wings. *Shalon. It's me. What's happening? Where are you? Andor.*

She lifted her head, trying to pull away. A fist crashed into the back of her neck and the touch of Andor's mind faded. She was alone. Completely alone.

"Behave now." A hand gripped her throat, pressing down on either side of her esophagus. Far away, she heard someone say, "We're not done with you yet. Not by a long shot."

This isn't happening to me. The need for air in her lungs began to fade.

I'm not here, she thought, imaging that she was out of her body, floating above herself. *This isn't my body. They're not hurting me. They can't hurt me.* But even as the world around her fell away, the pain jabbed at her clouded mind, insisting on its reality.

Go somewhere. Somewhere I'm safe. Somewhere she could block it all out and let go. Where she could be in control and the real her would remain untouched. She knew where she wanted to be. All she had to do was let go. She just had to let—

CHAPTER 17

If an Orgalian should be found to have willfully caused the death
of another, there is no place in Rhiannon for this person, and they
may be Exiled. If the original crime is judged to be severe, a death
sentence may be delivered in only one circumstance. The Assembly
may choose to allow the family of the wronged person to carry out
Lex Talionis under the rite of Vendetta.
However, all wrongs must be addressed by one contest between
two citizens in a manner to be decided by the accused, and the
survivor will be held innocent of any charges. Should the accused
survive, he must be aware that Vendetta cannot be imposed twice.
If another Orgalian is willfully killed by either combatant in future,
a sentence of Exile will be carried out.
—*The Laws of Rhiannon: Vendetta*

I

"Ru-ad Whelan, know that Rhiannon, through the Assembly, has
voted your fate," Cu-don said, staring stone-faced at the former Chief
Advisor. He stood behind the jape lectern in the center of the Assembly
Hall. His hands were cuffed behind him, his posture relaxed as if he
were not awaiting his own sentencing. On the steps before the doors
to the Hall, two motionless guards kept an eye on him.

"You and your co-conspirators have been judged guilty of
treason and the attempted murder of Vi-Commander Shalon
Conway. You have violated our laws and caused the loss of several
Group Leaders, who were your accomplices. You would have

232

been executed for treason along with your collaborators offworld, but your actions against Vi-Commander Conway require a more appropriate sentence."

Cu-don glanced at Andor, who now occupied Ru-ad's place at her right hand. "Our first vote could not bring back a decision for the harshest penalty—exile into Desolation without weapons or food. However, after deliberation, another sentence was decided upon. It is my duty to inform you that the right of vendetta has been requested."

Ru-ad's eyes narrowed and he looked at Andor. However, it was not Andor who stood to speak the ritual words. At the other end of the table, his face impassive, Ku rose to his feet.

"Ru-ad Whelan, I, Ku Olang, as foster father to Shalon Conway, challenge you to the rite of vendetta. Should you accept, I propose that we meet with the weapons of your choice in the Gathering Hall tomorrow, so that all of Rhiannon may bear witness."

Silence descended on the chamber as he took his seat again. The white curls of smoke from the jape brazier, smelling of nuts and earth, made curious reaching shapes in the quiet, like mournful ghosts.

"Are you willing to consider this option?" Cu-don asked.

Ru-ad raised his chin a notch. "I will need time to make my decision."

"You have one hour." Cu-don signaled to the guards and they moved forward as one to collect the former Advisor. As soon as the doors closed behind them, three members of the Assembly rose, murmuring amongst themselves and throwing surreptitious looks at Andor and Ku. Once they were gone, Andor stood, his chair sliding back into the stone walls with a resounding clatter.

"You can't do this, Ku."

"It is my right," Ku replied.

"Vendetta is to the death. He is a better fighter than you."

"No, he *was* a better fighter than me. He will not be so tomorrow."

"You can't be sure of that."

Ku placed his arms on the table in front of him and folded his hands together. "She is my only daughter, Andor."

Andor glared at Cu-don. "This is your doing."

"No. Ku came to me and I presented the choice to Rhiannon. The vote was unanimous. Vendetta is preferred to exile and Ku has a right to exercise it."

"And what if he fails, have you considered that?" Andor asked in a hard voice. "If Ru-ad survives, he will be cleared of all charges and allowed to remain in Rhiannon as an ordinary citizen. He will not have paid for his crimes and Rhiannon will lose two Assembly members instead of one."

"But if I succeed, then he pays the true price of his actions." Ku settled back into his chair. "I'm lucky I survived this long, Andor. If I die, there are others, like you, who can take my place. I cannot let him live when he betrayed, and may have killed, my only daughter. I will not let him disappear into the desert. It is too uncertain an end for what he did. I will not risk an Outsider finding and saving him so they can gain information from him. I will not trust that his treacherous soul could not find his way across Desolation to the Facility. From his point of view, Desolation is almost certain death. He will accept my vendetta and trust his superior skills to save his life. And when he does, I will kill him."

"It is too dangerous." Andor shook his head. "I can't let you do this."

Cu-don placed a hand over one of Andor's fists. "You feel it is your place to exact revenge."

Andor straightened and Cu-don allowed her hand to slide off him. "I am faster, stronger. I could best him and ensure that Shalon is avenged." He glanced across at Ku. "She is your daughter, but she means something to me as well."

"Despite that, it was your actions that enabled Ru-ad's plans to succeed as they have." Ku's voice did not carry the inflection of accusation. It did not need to.

"I am aware of that, believe me. And it is exactly why you should consider letting me take your place. Allow me this chance to—"

"Make up for it?" Cu-don sighed. "Andor, nothing you do now can change what went before. I think Ku would agree with me on this."

"You must know," Ku added, "that he would not accept vendetta if you are the challenger. He knows as well as you do that you would win the fight. Why would he take such a chance? But if the offer came from me—"

At that instant, Andor frowned and took a step back. He raised his hands to his head, a grimace contorting his face. Cu-don swiveled in her seat and Ku stood, alarmed.

"Andor, what is it?" she asked. His eyes narrowed in pain.

"Shalon. She's…she's…" He caught his breath, holding his side as if he had been wounded. "I lost her."

Ku advanced to stand next to Cu-don, tension in every line of his body. "Then get her back."

"I can't. Not here. There's something in the way of our connection." Andor took a deep breath and met Ku's gaze. "She's being hurt. There was a lot of pain and she lost consciousness. I have to go in after her."

"What does that mean?" Cu-don asked, her forehead wrinkling.

"It means that I will have to go to sleep. Fast."

"Then do it. Do whatever it takes." Ku's calm words belied the look in his eyes.

··· — — — ···

Andor sat on a bed in the healing chamber, watching as the healer affixed a dosing patch to his arm. The scent of crushed green leaves and oil filled the air as the patch was smoothed over his arm. Behind the woman—whose dark hair had been braided close to the skull—a white screen rippled. A shadow moved across the cloth before the screen parted and Ha-Ka Pravet appeared. Her long hair had been pulled back in a tight bun. Her scout suit carried the black scorch marks of lasers and a strip of synthskin covered one cheek. Nevertheless, she looked every inch the wife of an Assemblyman.

"Ha-Ka. You've returned." Andor lowered his arm as the Healer finished.

"I was relieved of duty. Ku told me some of what has happened." She glanced at the healer. "Are you done?"

The woman nodded. "But he will be asleep shortly. It is not advised that you remain. I must stay to monitor him."

"I will only be a moment. Leave us, please."

As soon as the cloth fell behind the healer's retreating back, Ha-Ka took a step forward and whispered in a vicious tone, "How could you have lied to us this way?"

"I thought I was doing what was best for all concerned."

"By harboring Ru-ad while he planned murder? You expect me to believe that?" Her lips twisted scornfully. "I told her to be careful of Ru-ad. I never thought to warn her against you as well."

Andor took her right hand and pressed it to his forehead in the deepest gesture of repentance an Orgalian could make. It was a display of emotion and physical contact that only the most sincere intentions permitted. "I did not plan this. I failed Shalon, I failed you. Most of all, I failed myself."

Ha-Ka tore her hand from his. "You ask too much too soon. Until my daughter is returned and Ku forces Ru-ad to pay the price for his actions, I cannot forgive you." She reached out a bruised, dirty hand and placed it on his head, tugging on the short hairs slightly so that Andor tilted his gaze upward.

"I do understand, Andor," she said, "but you must understand as well. There is no room in my heart for your pain."

Andor tried to nod and began to lean to his right instead. Ha-Ka let go of his hair and caught him under the arm with one hand. With the other she thrust the screen aside. "Healer!"

The woman returned at once and together, she and Ha-Ka helped Andor onto the bed. As Ha-Ka lowered his head onto the pillow, Andor whispered, "I am truly sorry."

"Then find her. Bring her back," she replied, her voice sharp and fragile as shale.

Focusing his thoughts on Shalon, he turned his consciousness inward and thrust his essence outward. He let his eyes close…

II

…and opened them to the dim foliage of the Greeneries. Water dripped a comforting rhythm around him and with the vague certainty of dreams, he knew the air against his skin blew hot and cold, even if he could not feel the sensation.

It made a terrible sort of sense that Shalon would escape here, where they had been together so many times before.

He moved forward, not bothering to call out, knowing that he would find her. The trees were larger in her mind, wilder and closer together. His boots crushed grass that grew to his ankles. He walked for what felt like minutes and hours at the same time, pushing branches and shrubs out of his way. The undergrowth thinned. The grass beneath his feet became shorter, sparser.

Without warning, he found he had reached the end of the path. Before him, the forest had been replaced by the pale, endless sands of Desolation. A setting sun turned the sky into breathtaking pastel shades and warmed the sand to an ivory glow.

Shalon stood a few feet away, on the line of demarcation between the forest and the desert, with her back to him. The dress she had worn on her birthday shone pewter in the sunlight, and the skirts billowed out behind her in the wind coming off the desert. At her feet, to her left, a burropac rested. Its head lay on its front legs, while its back legs were folded beneath it. At his approach, two scales on top of its blind head rose to a vertical position and one began to tap against the other in a staccato rhythm.

Andor stopped. He was not afraid of the burropac, but he was cautioned by its presence. Something had changed in Shalon's mind. When she was younger and prone to nightmares, he had often taken her to the Greeneries in her dreams, to ease her mind away from the terrible memories of her journey across the desert. To find her in the Greeneries and the desert at the same time indicated a disturbing parallel in Shalon's mind. And she'd never had a burropac with her before.

He shielded his feelings behind a block. It was essential that he not let his own thoughts bleed into her mind before he understood what had happened to her.

"Shalon."

The burropac stopped its tapping. An instant elapsed and the scales on its head lowered.

"Shalon, it's me, Andor."

Nothing moved except her skirt, and then the wind died as well.

"Please. Talk to me."

He saw her head come up a bit and tilt to the right.

"Andor?"

Relieved, he took a step forward. "Yes."

She waved a hand at the desert. "You're just in time for the sunset." Her voice sounded strange—lifeless. Andor could hear a warning in his mind clear as the burropac's tapping.

"Why are you here?"

"I'm waiting."

"For what?"

"For it to be over."

"For what to be over, Shalon?"

She bowed her head. "I don't want to think about it. I just want to look at the sunset."

He took two more steps so that he stood within touching distance of her, and the burropac's scales leapt to attention again. *Tap, tap, tap. Tap…tap…tap. Tap, tap, tap. Tap…tap…tap.*

"Shalon, look at me."

She turned, her skirts brushing against the burropac and causing sand to slide off its scales. The expression on her face was calm and empty.

"Shalon, what has happened to you? Why are we here?"

A frown flitted across her face. Beside her, the burropac got to its feet, still tapping. "I don't know. Does it matter?"

Aware he was on the right track, Andor pressed her. "Yes, it matters. Think hard. Why are you here?" He reached for her right arm, seeing the burropac swing around to face them out of the corner of his eye.

His fingers touched her arm and sensations, emotions and pictures poured into his mind. He squeezed convulsively and cried out as he went down on both knees. He knew she had fallen with him, but barely heard her tortured cry over the turmoil in his mind. Pain, terror and shame filled him and someone was ramming into him, violating him.

"I think she passed out."

"A good fuck will do that to you."

"No. Something's wrong."

He came back to himself with horrible suddenness, putting a hand down on the sand to keep from tipping over. Above them, the sun disappeared, replaced by an inky sky, void of stars or moons. Shalon knelt across from him, rocking herself back and forth. Her head was bowed, the dark fall of her hair hiding her face. Beside her, the burropac stood motionless, its scales still raised.

The truth of what was happening to her ached in his chest. He stretched out a hand. "Shalon."

"No!" She flung up her arm, knocking his hand away. Dust puffed up from the desert as she scrambled back from him, still not looking at him. "Don't touch me!"

He paused, torn by her pain and the need to help her escape it. "I only want to help you."

She drew her legs up and wrapped her arms around her shins, hiding her face behind her knees. He moved forward, wanting to go fast, careful to go slow. "You don't have to hide from me."

"You don't understand," she whispered. "You have no idea."

He stopped on his knees in front of her, fighting the urge to pull her into his arms. "Tell me."

"They…they…" She raised her head and the tormented look on her face was like a blade to his stomach. She looked right through him, as if he wasn't there. "I should have fought harder.

I should have forced them to kill me."

"No," he said, his voice low and fierce. "This is not your fault. Don't say it. Don't even think it."

"I had to get away." Her voice sounded like a shadow of itself. "I couldn't stay there. I'm more of a coward than I thought."

"You are no coward. You are Shalon Conway, Vi-Commander of the forces of Rhiannon and you will survive this."

"I don't think so. My head. I couldn't breathe. I think I'm dying, Andor." Beside her, the burropac knelt again, facing her this time.

"You are not dying. It's not your time. And I won't let you."

"It's okay," she continued as if not hearing him, her eyes still fixated on a point somewhere beyond him. "I'm not sure I mind anymore. I'm tired of fighting. Tired of carrying all my secrets."

"Then don't think about the past or the future. Think about freeing yourself. You have to escape."

"I can't. I'm alone. I'm not strong enough." She let go of her knees and leaned her head into her hands.

"You are not alone." Andor heard the tremor in his voice and did not care. He had caused this. All of this. He would get her out. No matter what it took. "Let me help you."

She shook her head and moisture shimmered in her eyes. For the first time, she looked directly at him. "I can feel myself slipping away."

"Then fight. Hold on. Do not give up."

Tears slipped down her cheeks, but she said nothing.

"This is not like you," he said, frustrated. "You don't think like this. I won't let you start now."

Shalon shook her head. "I'm not who I was."

"You fool yourself. They didn't take your courage. They couldn't. You are who you always were, and you aren't meant to die here. We both know that. Shalon, we wouldn't be here if you did not want to *live*."

He grabbed hold of both her arms. Again, her consciousness came rushing through, but he was prepared for it and he shielded himself while he gathered his strength and his mind. Shalon groaned and tried to pull away, but he held on. What he was going to do would either work, or kill them both, but it was a chance he had to take. He had no choice.

"I'm going to drop my barriers—all my barriers—and you have to do the same."

She shook her head and Andor felt an astonishing weakness within her. "Andor, no."

"Shalon." He shook her, desperate to make her understand, aware that time was not on his side. "We have to do this. There's no other way. You must survive. I will give you my strength and you'll use it to free yourself."

"I could kill you," she said, her voice full of anguish. "If it doesn't work, and you're still connected to me when I die, you don't know what could happen."

"I don't care." He searched her eyes, trying to make her understand. "I will not stand by and do nothing. I've done that too many times before. Don't make me force you to drop your blocks. It will tire us both and we need our strength."

He could see the struggle in her, the desire to somehow refuse him, but in the end, she could not fight him. Around them, the landscape wavered, like a passing hand disturbing water. Darkness cloaked everything except Shalon, Andor and the burropac. "I don't want to hurt you," she murmured, her eyes closing as she leaned into him. Her hands slid around him and he gathered her into his arms, feeling her pain battering at his mind like a hostile stranger at a door. And beyond that, there was a sensation as though a pit had opened beneath his feet and he was falling into it.

"I can't lose you," he whispered and closed his eyes just before he dropped his barriers. A moment later, she did the same.

Next to them, all of the burropac's scales suddenly stood at attention. Sheet lightning rippled across the black sky. Andor's fingers clenched on the slippery material of her vest and he felt Shalon's arm muscles trembling with the effort of holding on to his waist.

"I can't," she ground out suddenly.

Andor's grasp tightened and he pressed his lips against her hair. "You must."

"You're too—"

"—much," he finished in a tight voice. "I feel—"

"—weak. Too weak," she whispered.

"No. Fight. Fight. Let your anger."

"Take you." Her fingers dug into his back. "You're angry."

"Yes," he hissed.

"Because. I'm hurt. Because. Ru-ad." A moan escaped her. Above them the lightening ripped jagged lines in the sky and faded to leave glowing cracks. "Ru-ad lied."

"Yes."

Her fingers pressed harder, drawing blood through a wound he did not feel. Shalon began to shake in his arms. "You lied to me."

He had no choice. He couldn't deny it. And perhaps—perhaps he could turn it around. Help her. "I lied to you."

"You did not tell me and he did this to me." Her voice had become hard, almost unrecognizable.

"Yes." He pushed her away from him, caught her chin in his hands so that she had to look at him. Pain and relief over what he had done flooded though him. For the first time, anger made her face come alive. "I let this happen. It's my fault."

She hit him, her fists landing blows that should have been painful. "You fucking bastard!"

"I betrayed you," he told her. "Get angry. Get angry with Ru-ad, and me. With the men that did this to you. Claim your rage."

She snarled at him and their minds connected in a swirl of angry red and black, bloodlust and darkness, that played across the ruined sky above them.

"Take my anger and yours," he whispered, feeling her emotions—and his—swell in him like a tidal wave racing to shore. "Use it. Use it!"

"No!" she gritted out. "I can't control it."

"Don't try. Go back. *And take me with you.*"

Beside them, the burropac filled the air with the sound of its call to arms.

"No."

"Yes."

"No."

Then, in a single voice, "Yes."

··· ——— ···

They blinked, lashes fluttering like wings. Swanson bent into their line of sight.

"Hey, Matka. I think our girl's back."

"Great. She's just in time for the encore. Ganesh should be here soon."

"Welcome back," Swanson murmured. "We thought we'd lost you there for a second. Couldn't tear yourself away, huh?"

Behind her, the door opened and Ganesh entered the cell. He smiled as he surveyed the scene in front of him, his hazel eyes narrowing as they fell on Shalon's naked, battered body.

"Captain said there's a hell of a party going on. Have I missed all the good parts?"

"Nah." Swanson grinned. "We've barely begun."

Behind her, on the bed, they closed their eyes again. Their hands, trapped and cuffed under them, were freed for a few seconds as they were jerked from behind. Unnoticed, they grabbed at the spoon that had been stabbing into their side. Pulling it under their torso, they folded their hands closed and lay quiet once again.

III

"Ru-ad Whelan, you have agreed to the request for vendetta made by Assemblyman Ku Olang. You will be taken to the Gathering Hall in two hours to make the selection of the weapons."

Cu-don motioned to the guards and they stepped forward to stand next to Ru-ad. "Take him to the holding chamber and make sure he is not left alone."

After Ru-ad left the Assembly Hall, Cu-don drew alongside Ku as the Assembly filed out of the chamber. "Has there been any word on Andor's condition?"

"He is still in a coma. There is no reason why he should still be asleep. The sedative was removed yesterday. The healers do not know what went wrong, but they say he is stable. Ha-Ka will stay with him until he wakes."

Cu-don looked surprised. "She does not wish to be at the Hall to support you?"

"No."

"She is afraid you will lose?"

Ku pulled on the doors. "She is afraid I will win."

IV

Michael tried not to wince as he sat on the bed next to Shalon's motionless body. The air smelled of blood, mingled with the sweet musk of deodorant. No one had bothered to cover Shalon when they finished with her the day before. Bruises made blue-black blotches on her skin. Whole handprints had left their mark on her legs and arms. Cuts and lacerations marked out a map of pain on her body. Her face was turned toward him and he could clearly see her split lip, bloodied nose and black eye. She did not move as he touched a hand to the back of her head, where matted hair clumped together.

"Those bastards," he choked out, sick to his stomach.

She moved, twisting her head away so that she stared at the wall. "Leave." Her whispered voice sounded hoarse, raw, but the depth of contempt and hate in it struck at Michael like a shard of ice. Guilt made him pull his hand back.

"Shalon?"

"Don't come back here. Don't ever come back here, because if we get the chance, we will kill you."

We? There was a ring of warning, of conviction, in her voice that stopped him cold. That and the fact that her voice had changed. Become…unfamiliar, for an instant. He paused, torn between the sudden need to get away from the taint he could smell and feel around him, and the fact that she needed help.

"I can't leave you like this."

"Take your fucking platitudes and go."

He rose from the bed, feeling every inch the coward she had called him. A hot tide of shame flooded him. "I'm sorry."

She never replied.

V

The Gathering Hall had been filled to capacity and the doors remained open so that those outside might see in. The tables from the banquet had long since been cleared away. In their place stood row upon row of Orgalians, male and female, young and old, healer to soldier. They stood around an oval that had been drawn on the tiled floor in red paint. Inside that oval stood Ku and Ru-ad, both stripped down to their leather pants, each holding two curved knives the length of their forearms. They waited on opposite ends of the oval, faces impassive as those around them.

Behind Ku, on the stage, Cu-don stood in front of the weapons rack from which the knives had been chosen. Two Assembly members waited on either side of her. She stepped up to the lectern and gripped the edges.

"Citizens of Rhiannon, we are gathered in the wake of a tragedy. One of our number has been condemned for the callous murder of another. He faces his judgment now in vendetta. No good can come of this, for today, we lose a fellow Orgalian. Together we survive, divided we fall. But justice will be given or denied in this fighting ring, and as citizens, we must see this done so that none may dispute the truth of it. We stand together in victory. We must also stand together in tragedy. This is what it means to be Orgalian."

"This is what it means to be Orgalian," a thousand voices echoed.

"Do you bear witness to this and agree to abide by the result of vendetta?"

"We do."

"Then I say, the time for tears has passed and the time for justice has arrived."

··· — — — ···

Long after Michael left, they heard the door to the cell open.

"Hey, little girl. How you feeling?" Swanson's voice asked, cloying and fake as artificial sweetener.

They lay still as a rock, holding their breath, eyes closed.

"She sleeping or something?" The voice was male. One of the new ones. Arthurton. He was the one who, along with Raydell, had — *Stop. Don't think about it. Think about revenge. Lex Talionis.*

"Don't know. She was talking to Michael earlier and she ran him off. She hasn't moved since. Captain said we should check on her."

The voices came from directly above. A hand poked at their ribs.

"Hey, sleeping beauty. Wake up."

Anger churned within, a kaleidoscope of emotion, straining to get out. And behind it all, forcing it to a head, the inhuman calm of battle readiness. *Lex Talionis. It is time.*

"She's not breathing." Concern now, a little fright in Arthurton's voice.

"She can hold her breath really long. She's probably just faking."

A hand tugged their hair, pulling at the spot where the scalp had split open. But the pain was very far away now and easy to ignore. *Leave it to me. I will free us.*

"Hey, stop fooling around and wake up."

A pause, filled only with the sound of two people breathing. The cold metal of the spoon burned against the inside of their left arm.

"Shit, Swanson, she's really not breathing. What if we killed her?"

"We didn't kill her, all right?"

"Well she looks fucking dead to me!"

"Who the fuck asked you?" Hands slapped at their face and body. "Wake up, bitch. Wake the fuck up!"

"Oh, shit. She's cold as ice. We weren't supposed to kill her, Swanson. Just sell her and collect the money. I'm not a murderer, for fuck's sake!"

"No, just a rapist. Goddamn idiot." But the undercurrent of worry in her voice was unmistakable.

"Marchand is going to be so pissed."

"She's not dead till Fayn says so. Go get him. Maybe if it hasn't been too long, he can revive her."

"You said she hasn't moved since Michael left."

"Would you forget that? Go get Fayn and I'll start CPR. Move it!"

Boots clumped away and the door closed. Hands worked on the leg cuffs. They waited, limp as possible, as the leg cuffs were pulled off. Swanson flipped them over onto their back and tilted their head up, muttering to herself about how it was great, just fucking great that this had to happen now. The handcuffs released and they let their hands fall to their sides, hiding the spoon against their thigh. *There are cameras. They must have no reaction time. We have to wait for the door.*

Slick lips that tasted of coffee covered their mouth, forcing air into them. Hands pressed hard on their chest. "Come on, bitch. Don't die and take my money with you."

··· — — — ···

The door to the cell slid open. "We don't know," Arthurton was saying, "we just found her like this."

Over them, they felt Swanson bending down, her fingers pinching their nose shut. In that instant, they opened their eyes. The look on her face changed to one of shock and realization. They smiled.

Then grabbed Swanson's waist and jammed the handle of the spoon into her stomach.

CHAPTER 18

No more tears now. I will think upon revenge.
— *Mary Stuart, Queen of Scots*

I

Ru-ad and Ku circled each other in the quiet that descended after the Assemblywoman's pronouncement. Their bare feet whispered across the gritty floor. Along the outer edge of the blades they held, jagged teeth bent back toward the hilt. The sharp cutting edge glinted under the lumidiscs. Guns were not allowed in vendetta, since a wild shot might hurt the spectators. Instead, Ru-ad had chosen his favorite weapon, the shriek blades.

Ku, of course, had never been good with the shrieks.

Without warning, Ku charged at Ru-ad, one blade low and thrusting forward. Ru-ad sidestepped, turned and slashed at Ku's head and torso. He missed and their blades met with a ringing clang. His blows turned aside, Ru-ad stepped back, settling into a defensive crouch. Ku tracked him, the blades in his hand twirling to disguise his next movement. Ru-ad noted that with raised eyebrows.

"I have been practicing," Ku said and lunged at Ru-ad with his blade, pushing it forward—

· · · — — — · · ·

—and up. The spoon sank in. A knife through butter. Swanson made a choking sound. Blood slimed their hands. They brought up

246

a leg and pushed hard, ignoring a vague soreness. She fell sideways, to the floor.

They rose to their knees and slid down to the bed's end. There, on the floor. The green jumpsuit and their boots.

They heard a gasp. Saw Arthurton turning, trying to escape. An old, wide-eyed man behind him, black bag in his hand. Doctor. *The boots.*

Leaned down and grabbed them. Pressed their thumbs to the inside curves along the instep. The fingerprint ID locks clicked. Two knives ejected from the heels. They grabbed the hard, smooth rubber handles as the boots fell. The first knife hit Arthurton between the shoulder blades. He screamed and landed on his stomach, just short of the door. A dark stain blossomed on his jacket.

The doorway is empty. Where is the doctor? Machinery clicked. The airlock started to close. They leapt to the floor, bare feet slippery in a puddle. Arthurton screamed. "No!" He stretched out his hand and his wrist fell across the frame. The door stopped closing, began pulling back.

They scanned the ceiling quickly. Two cameras winked from corners. They scooped up the cup and bowl and threw. Shattered lenses rained onto the floor. Three strides and they reached Arthurton. Bent down, ripped the knife out and plunged it into his spine. His screech was inhuman. Grim satisfaction and horror warred within them. *This is wrong.*

No. This is what they deserve.

Swanson lay on the floor, gasping. Her reddened hands slipped on the spoon. She had almost pulled it out. Thick, dark blood came with it.

They reached her side. She tried to fight them off, but they pushed her fingers away. Looked into her eyes. Grasped the spoon. And shoved down slowly. Her cry of pain trailed off. Arthurton whimpered. Tried to pull himself over the threshold.

Rage burned, sweeping reason before it. *You shall pay for what you have done. You shall pay and pay and pay.*

They raised the knife. Brought it down and across—

··· — — — ···

—with a deft flick of the wrist. A crimson line welled from the slash. Ku glanced down at the shallow cut on his lean abdomen. Ru-ad used the moment to thrust again, but Ku blocked the blow with one knife, and dragged the other across the top of his opponent's left hand. Blood spattered like rubies on the tiled floor. Ru-ad pulled back and cut at the Assemblyman's still outstretched arm. Ku's blade clashed against his, blocking the blow. Metal screamed as they wrenched the knives apart. Ru-ad brought his left leg up and kicked at Ku, catching him on the right thigh. With a grunt, he staggered backward, lost his balance and went down on one knee. Ru-ad pushed his advantage, rushing in low with flashing blades, just as Ku rolled to his right and thrust his leg out, into Ru-ad's path.

Without pausing, the Chief Advisor leapt nimbly over the leg and spun around. Ku was already on his feet and their shrieks met in a blistering series of thrusts and parries. Ru-ad found himself forced to fall back. The tang of perspiration tainted the air. Glistening beads of it covered Ku's chest as he raised his arm to bring his shriek down on Ru-ad's exposed shoulder. He did not see the blade that suddenly reversed its direction and sank into his stomach. Ku's breath rushed out on a pained gasp. Ru-ad followed the shriek, pushing in for the kill, but Ku brought his left elbow up and crashed it into the side of Ru-ad's neck. He fell, losing his grip on the knife.

Blood trickled down Ku's torso as he clutched his fingers around the shriek's bronze hilt. Ru-ad leapt to his feet, his second blade firmly clenched in his left hand. His chest rose and fell with his harsh breathing as he murmured, "You're making this worse than it has to be. You know you're going to—"

··· ▬▬▬ ···

—*die*. They stood slowly. *Just die, you bitch.* Warm blood was dripping off them. Leaking sluggishly from Swanson's slit throat. She gagged, grabbing at her neck. They had purposefully missed the important arteries. Her death would not be quick.

Shouting outside. Boots thudding down the corridor. Behind them, Arthurton begged for mercy. *You will have mercy. The same mercy you showed to her.* They turned just in time.

The door was closing.

They're using the override.

They grasped Arthurton around the waist and shoved him forward, into the path of closing portal.

"Oh, fuck, Ramirez, *help me!*"

"*Arthurton!*"

They picked up the dented metal cup and bowl. Darkness slipped down as they broke the overhead lights. Not that it mattered. They could still see. The door continued to close. Arthurton's cries turned to gasps. They grabbed their weapons and waited until the door slowed. Threw the cup and bowl one last time at the corridor lights. Now there was only gray light from the corridor's end.

"Bridge! It's Ramirez. Stop the door! Stop the fucking door, captain!"

They tugged the knife in Arthurton's back free as the door closed on him. There was a muffled sound, like twigs snapping in a blanket. His ribs giving way. The door halted. Arthurton's body kept twitching. They glimpsed movement through the gap in the doorway over Arthurton's head. Ramirez raised the gun in his left hand.

They dove to their right. Something blue flashed past their shoulder as they rolled against the corner. There was a smell of cooking metal. The lasers had hit the wall. Metal pattered to the floor as the bulkhead melted. Three tones sounded.

"Warning, warning, weapons fire on Deck Three. Hull damage on Deck Three. All hands to battle stations. Repeat, all hands to battle stations. This is not a simulation."

"You bitch! I'll kill you! I swear, I'll kill you!"

"Initiating sealant dispersal now." A hissing sound, then a waxy odor.

They leaped over Arthurton's body. Straightened up next to the opening. Thrust the knife through at head level. Viscous fluid covered their fingers as the knife went through Ramirez's eye. They jammed the other knife into Arthurton's side and grabbed Ramirez's gun. Slack fingers released it. They jerked the knife out of Ramirez's eye. Outside, the body thudded to the floor. Boot heels drummed and stopped.

The gun was warm. Smooth to the touch. They aimed at Swanson and pulled the trigger.

Nothing happened.

They checked the side of the grip and saw a small, transparent oval. *ID locked. Only the crew can use it.* They stalked over to the bunk and grabbed the jumpsuit on the floor, tossing the gun aside. It—

··· ━ ━ ···

—clattered across the floor. Ru-ad's foot stopped its progress. The Chief Advisor picked the knife up. His eyes never left his opponent. Blood seeped from the wound in Ku's side and Ru-ad realized that it was not as deep as he had hoped. Ku's face looked strained, but didn't betray pain in any other way. Instead, he settled into a defensive stance and said, "This is your time to face what you've done."

We'll see, Ru-ad thought. He had struck the first blow. The wound would weaken Ku. If he could keep the momentum going, keep Ku off balance, he would ensure his survival. One of them had to die, and he would not let it be him.

They circled each other slowly, Ru-ad looking for the opening through which to attack. Before long, his careful observation paid off. With all the speed of his genetically fine-tuned reflexes, Ku leaped into the air and aimed a kick at Ru-ad's head. The Chief Advisor spun away from the blow like a dancer, coming to a stop just as Ku landed on his right. Before Ku could move, Ru-ad launched a powerful kick at him. The blow caught him on his jaw. He fell hard, rolling to the perimeter of the ring and leaving a trail of blood. Spectators pulled back from him, boots shuffling on the sand.

Ru-ad waited for him to rise. Better to let Ku expend his energy attacking, while Ru-ad chose his moment to act. It would be easy to manipulate him into making a mistake then. One mistake was all Ru-ad needed.

Ku rolled onto his back and jack-knifed off the floor. Ru-ad saw the flash as Ku got to his feet and dove away from it. *He camouflaged his movement well.* The knife ripped past him. A teenaged boy, tall as a southern mesa, reached out a steady hand and caught it by the handle. The boy met his eyes, nodded respectfully, and threw the knife back to Ku.

He has learned a few tricks after all, Ru-ad thought before banishing all such thoughts from his head. For now, he had one focus, one mission. To—

··· — — — ···

—*Kill. They must die. All of them. It's the only way to escape. The gun is a waste of time, but I have the knives.* The thought filled them with purpose. And a terrible joy.

Tinny voices outside, in the corridor. *The intercom.*

"...you fire? Ramirez! Did you fire a laser? Answer me, you idiot!"

So the lasers were a mistake. This must be his personal gun. They are not supposed to use such weapons on board. Good. Very good. They stopped sealing the jumpsuit. Bloodied fingers slipping over their crimson-streaked breasts.

Boot-falls. Heavy, insistent—far off, but coming closer.

LEX TALIONIS

Three people. Men.

They ran to the door. Put the other knife between their teeth. Grasped the edge of the airlock and pulled. Metal groaned. Muscles in their arms strained and ached. A finger slipped; the nail broke, blood seeping out from the nail bed. Still they pulled. With a groan, the airlock moved. The edge beneath their hands bent back. A depression formed in the airlock's center. There was a massive, teeth-grating screech. And it lurched back three more inches.

The boots sounded very close now.

They kicked Arthurton out of the way and slid through the opening into the corridor. The air was frigid here. But the smell was the same. Their *smell. But we are out.*

Metal gray walls, narrow hallway, low ceilings. Two ways to go. One opening to their left. The other way, straight ahead, before the corridor curved right. The sounds came from the left.

Now to finish it.

They moved to the left exit. Stood against the wall. Time slowed to a crawl.

They smelled him first. The iron scent of fear. A hand appeared. Snake tattoo on the back, blunt-nosed gun grasped in the fingers. They grabbed the arm. Brought a knife down on the wrist. The sharp blade severed cleanly. Blood spurted. Lashed their face with warm, accusing threads. They yanked forward. A blond man appeared, mouth just opening to cry out. *Matka.*

"A good fuck will do that to you."

Fury consumed them. They clamped a hand over his mouth and tugged him against them like a lover. Looking into half-crazed blue eyes, they brought the knife up—and slid it home below his chin. Blood spurted. Pattered on the floor.

She told you she would shred your throat, remember? They jerked the knife up, twisting as it went. Fingers pushing into the soft tissue, and beyond. Matka's body began a death dance. Their hands, chest, were a slick red. Blood ran from his nose and mouth. Only the whites of his eyes showed. Finally, his body stilled. *He died too quick. Too easily.*

Movement. Over his shoulder. Someone rolled to the corridor's center.

They shifted fully behind Matka's body. There was a loud pop and Matka's body jerked.

"Fuck! Matka!"

Projectile weapons. Probably with special ammunition to prevent hull breech. They will only be deadly at close range. This is what they are supposed to have. Not the lasers. Two more pops. Two more shuddering impacts.

They peered over Matka's shoulder. A man got to his knees, his gun raised. *Ganesh.* They pulled Matka's body against them, removed the other knife from their mouth.

"He's dead already. You can stop shooting him now."

Ganesh fired. They hid behind the body again. Waited for a pause in the popping. When it came, they dropped the body and threw the unblooded knife. It thudded home, into his heart. He froze, caught in an eternal moment. Then he keeled over sideways, against the wall. They took a step over Matka's body.

Two down. But where is the third?

Instinct warned them. They ducked right. Felt the air from a bullet whispering past. There was a scraping sound directly behind them. Fiery sensation erupted in their lower back. Something hit them in their ribs, hard. Pain blossomed. They turned and a solid object slammed into their face, spreading numbness.

They dropped to their right knee. A blow to their shoulder tilted them sideways. Something cracked and pain splintered through them. They gasped, trying to breathe. Reached behind them with their right hand. Felt a familiar handle in their lower back. *Stabbed. With our knife.* Looked up into manic gray eyes. *Marchand. We've been careless.*

"Poetic justice, you cunt. For what you've done to my crew," he hissed, and started to pull the trigger.

You should have just shot me.

Their right hand reached up. Caught his wrist. Broke it with a sharp twist. The gun fell to the grille.

"Aaarggh! *Shit!*"

They tugged him forward, ignoring the grinding pain in their shoulder. Pulled the knife from their back and slit his throat open. Crimson gouts of liquid arced high. Slapped against the floor.

He tipped to his left. Storm-cloud gray eyes filled with anger, pain. But he did not die immediately. Weak fingers reached for the gun. They hit it away, against the wall. Movement awakened a thousand places of pain. But it felt light—vague. A thin gauze wrapping them tight.

"Your crew meant nothing. Not after what they did to her."

They kicked him over on his back. Raised the knife, slashed at his torso. Slashed again.

And heard a shuffling behind them. Down the corridor.

Skidding around on their knees, they got behind and pulled him into a standing position. The newcomer swallowed, unsteady hand holding another gun.

"Michael," they spat. "We warned you not to come back."

He stared with terrified dark eyes. "You…you…"

"We killed them. Yes. Now, it's your turn."

They threw Marchand's body at him. It hit Michael full in the chest and bowled him over. The gun landed against the wall. Discharged a bullet that ricocheted harmlessly in the corridor.

Stop.

They leaped forward, over Ganesh's body. Reached down and flung Marchand aside. Kicked the gun away. Michael lay there, stunned and groaning, eyes fluttering. *You left her to them. You didn't even try to help.*

No. Jagged pain slashed through their head.

She fell to her knees. Hands pressed to her temples. *Not him. Leave him.*

Michael had regained consciousness. He started to scramble away from her. His shoes rang on the grille. Loud as thunder.

He deserves to die. Like the rest. They grabbed at his leg. Reached behind them and located the knife in Ganesh's chest. Yanking it free, they slashed at Michael's leg. His bellow rebounded off the low ceiling.

"*Stop!*" Chest heaving, she ground her teeth. Forced her fingers to release the knife. Slammed her hand down on the floor. The grilles clashed against each other, buckling under the stress. "Listen to me!"

Let me finish it.

"We will finish it," she agreed. She looked deep into Michael's eyes. Could not fight the hollow satisfaction that filled her when she saw his terror. *He understands. He knows I'm not the woman he captured.* "But there are other things to consider. Important things."

Garbled words fell from Michael's lips. He pushed away from her on his elbows. Raw flesh, like uncooked meat, showed through the tears in his uniform pants. *He's getting away.* Anger burned through her, threatening to overtake her mind again. She closed her eyes. Slammed her right fist against the wall. Again and again, she slammed out a familiar rhythm. Used it to anchor her mind and body. Closed her eyes, threw back her head, howled her pain, anger and defiance.

Let him go. She opened her eyes to see Michael crawling out of sight, around the curve. Heard his labored breathing and almost tasted the salt of his tears. Feeling her control slipping, she pushed her thoughts through as hard as she could. *We can't fly this ship. We'll need him alive, later.*

Understanding. *Later then. We will deal with him later.*

They picked up the knife. Went over to Marchand's body. Stared around them. Not enough blood. Not nearly enough. They had to suffer in life and death.

Kneeling, they began to slash. Tear. Rip. Once, the knife snagged on bone and they paused, forced to—

··· —— —— ···

—tear it loose. As Ru-ad tugged, Ku back-flipped, catching Ru-ad under the chin with his toe. The Chief Advisor fell backward, his jaw numbed by the blow. He got his hands under him—knives scraping on the floor and nicking his palms—and turned the fall into a somersault. He landed a little off-balance, picking up the knives as he did so. Ku was already rushing toward him. He dropped onto his back and kicked his legs into Ku's torso.

Ku flew backward and hit the ground with a thud that vibrated the floor under Ru-ad. The Assemblyman grunted in pain. Ru-ad rolled to his feet and tossed the knife at Ku's chest in a smooth, quick action. It struck the tile where Ku had been moments before and skittered away. Someone in the crowd threw the knife back at Ru-ad and he caught it high overhead. Ku rose to his feet. Dust marred his face and the streaks of blood on his stomach. The wound was seeping more now, Ru-ad noted.

Ku attacked with a series of standing kicks that forced Ru-ad to duck, weave and parry with his arms. But the Chief Advisor knew Ku Olang was tiring. Just as he had planned. His muscles screamed pain at him, and he ached from a thousand tiny cuts and gashes. Still, Ku was in worse shape and had begun to slow. Ru-ad found it easier and easier to avoid his blows.

Not much longer now before—

··· —— —— ···

—*it all comes to an end. There can't be that many of them left.*

She could not remember all that had happened. Things blurred together. Sometimes she was in control, with him. Other times, he took over. Awareness—often weak—occurred only a few times after the escape from the cell.

In a corridor, with a vent above. The smell of fear coming from it unmistakable. But she took control, without him. Tapped out her warning. *Not yet. Not yet.* And they moved on. To a medical room. Where they slammed equipment into glistening consoles. Chased a screaming doctor under a table. He died there. Blue in the lips and choking. She made them leave him alone. He deserved death, nothing else. He did not hurt. Had not helped.

Then a corridor, dismembering a gurgling form. Rooms where she found oblivion in destruction. Outside a door. The fear-smell strong from behind it. They ripped the lock off. Angry. Wanting to taste revenge. Mad with bloodlust. Lost focus when they heard— *Someone running. Light steps—not a man.*

Raydell.

Grayed out. Returned to find themselves holding her neck. Slammed her against a wall. Held her inches above the floor. Stared into her red, red eyes. Savored the sound of her choking.

Her vision blurred out—

··· ▬▬▬ ···

—came back to see Michael airborne. Watched him slam into a console and roll against the far wall, in front of the captain's chair. They began to tap the knife. Skipping it from console to console. Relishing what was to come. He stared, his mouth open—

··· ▬▬▬ ···

—in a silent scream. Ku grabbed at his arm, the shriek blade falling from his left hand. Blood poured from a deep gash along the inside of his arm. Ru-ad took the opportunity to chop a hand across his throat. The Assemblyman fell to his knees, landing heavily on his injured arm.

Exhausted, unaware of how long it had been since the fight had begun, Ru-ad knew only one thing. *This is it. This is what I've been waiting for. I have him.*

He booted the second knife out of Ku's hand and with his foot, shoved him down onto the tiled floor. Dust puffed into the air as Ku's head hit the tile with an audible crack.

Ru-ad kicked him over onto his back and bent over him. He raised the shriek. The knife edge—

··· — — — ···

—caught the light briefly. Liquid mercury flowing along a line. They pointed it toward Michael.

Wait. Pain slammed behind their eyes. They moaned, holding their head. *You've hurt him enough.*

No. It can never be enough.

It must be.

Heard Michael moving, crawling across the floor, toward them.

Anything more will kill him and strand us here.

Sounds of fumbling. Metal grating on metal.

She opened her eyes. Went across to where Michael lay at the base of the captain's chair, one hand scrabbling at it. His breathing was shallow, pained. She knelt over him. Saw herself reflected in the horror of his gaze.

"Hello again, Michael."

"Please. Don't kill me."

She shook her head, resentment rising in her. "I begged too. Do you remember? And what did you do?"

She saw the muscles in his arms tense. "I'm sorry. I'm so sorry."

"That won't help you now. I can't hold him back for long. And I don't want to."

Too late, she glimpsed the compartment. A cubbyhole at the base of the chair. Too late, she saw his hand and the canister in it. The mist, tasting of oily bitterness, coated her throat. Weakness gripped her by the neck. Collapsed her against the captain's chair.

No...

··· — — — ···

"...No," Ku whispered, looking up at Ru-ad. Blood flowed down the side of his face from a split scalp.

"Goodbye, Ku," Ru-ad said and brought the knife down.

Ku deflected the blow, twisted his wrist around Ru-ad's, and with the flat of his palm, drove his opponent's blade deep into Ru-ad's stomach.

Ru-ad froze, an icy sensation spreading across his belly. Ku smiled at him, his teeth pink with blood.

LEX TALIONIS

"You lose." He forced the knife up until it hit bone.

There was a terrible splitting, and grinding pain. Ru-ad fell backward, leaving the knife in Ku's hand. Warmth filled his lap and spread under him. Something within him pulled free, unspooling like cable from a roll. He looked down and his intestines glistening in his lap like fat, gray, red-streaked snakes.

No. This can't. Can't be—

· · · — — — · · ·

—happening. Unable to stop him, she watched as Michael rolled away from her. Dragged himself across to a console. Blood glistened in his wake, a dark snail's trail. She felt her consciousness slipping, fought to hold on to it. *Please no. Not this. Don't let him trap me here.*

"Don't do this," she whispered. But he did not hear. He pulled himself upright. His hands moved over panels that answered with soft tones. He laid his right hand flat against a console, said something she did not catch. And slid bonelessly—

· · · — — — · · ·

—to the floor. He lay there, his skin warm in his own blood, his body cold inside, the life ebbing out of him. The strange, sickening touch of air caressing the cavity of his torso.

He heard a sigh go through the crowd, like the wind passing through the cracks of a mesa. Ku's face appeared above his. Blood from his head wound fell onto Ru-ad's cheek. Drops of sun-warmed rain. The expression on the Assemblyman's face was void of pity or mercy. He was calm as the desert after a sandstorm.

"You die as you deserve to. Gutted like the animal you are. I have my vengeance. Enjoy your hell."

Ru-ad's vision narrowed, darkness creeping in from the right. The pain rose, a crescendo before the end of a movement. *But it doesn't matter. Because you still lose. You...*

"...lose," he whispered.

"What?"

Ru-ad grimaced, unable to see Ku's face now. His limbs were going numb, one by one.

"You cannot save her. It is over."

"Yes," Ku's voice held no emotion. "It is over. For you."

One by one, the voices fell away. Until there was nothing left—

··· ▬ ▬ ▬ ···

—at all. No feeling in her body. No connection to her limbs. She was detached from everything. Unable to find the strength or will to lift her head.

"Acknowledging," a voice said. "Acting Lieutenant Michael Flax Zorida. Emergency protocol 972AB initiated. Distress beacon and auto pilot activated. Course and speed reset for nearest facility. Bradley Spaceport, planet Serron. Time to arrival: nine hours."

If they find us here. The solid metal against her shoulder started to feel soft. Pillowy.

She slid backward. Stared into an oblivion dark as midnight. Struggled.

Andor!

I'm here. I won't leave you till you're safe.

She was wrapped in a soft embrace. *Don't be afraid. I'm with you.* Comforted, exhausted, she drifted into a deep sleep.

··· ▬ ▬ ▬ ···

Wake.

She opened her eyes. Took a deep breath. Coughed. Rolled over on her side. The floor was ice-cold. The air smelled musty—ripe somehow. The silence hurt her ears. Her body ached like a broken tooth.

What?

Caught a glimpse of a shape on the floor, to her right. In front of the main console, below the blank viewing screen. *Michael.* Memory clicked into place.

"Docking completed," a disembodied voice said. *The computer. We're in the bridge. We've landed.*

She pushed to her feet. Grabbed at a console to steady herself. Saw that her hands were red as paint. Revolted, she looked away to the closed airlock on their left. *Landed where?*

"Releasing outer seal."

We can't be found here. We have to move.

I can't. Tired.

You have to. I'll help.

Where are we going?

Where Michael hid before. Air vent. I will cover our tracks. They will not find us there.

What if they can help us? Maybe they will understand.

No. A picture formed in her mind. A flayed body, lying on its side. It did not look human. She suppressed a shudder.

They won't understand. They're Troopers. They'll protect their own. As I must protect you. Come. You'll rest while we hide. We'll move when it's safe.

"Atmospheric adjustments complete. Airlock open. Awaiting further instructions from boarding crew."

They peeled gummy hands off the console. Stumbled toward the exit.

··· — — — ···

She woke again after they left the vent. A man was collecting samples as they crawled out. *An investigator or detective.* He did not hear them drop down behind him. They hit him hard, with the edge of their palm. Found their way through the ship by following the tracks left by others in the endless splashes of blood. They stopped just once, to change their jumpsuit with painful slowness at the storage closet.

When they found the outer airlock, they waited for a while, making sure there was no one nearby. A runner gleamed silvery blue under the hanger lights, near the ship's ramp. The walk to it took forever, and the hairs on their head stood up all the way. As though a million eyes were on them.

She collapsed into the runner, tired and relieved.

"Destination?" a soothing male voice questioned.

"I want to leave the spaceport," she murmured, curling up on the front seat. "Help me leave the spaceport."

"Please give a specific destination."

They opened their eyes briefly. "Spaceport exit."

The runner set off, its motion lulling her to sleep.

··· — — — ···

"...wake up!"

She stirred. Mumbled.

"Lady, wake up! Damn! Who did this to you?"

Men. Dead now. All dead.

"Shit. I'd better go get help. Listen, I'm going to call this in to Security. Can you hear me? I'm going to move you over so I can call Security."

No. No Security. We can't let that happen.

She sat up. Surprised, he stared at her. A short, fat man with thinning black hair. "Lady?"

She hit him hard, in the neck, with the flat of her palm. Too hard. She heard something snap, and he fell back against the seat.

Oh God. What have I done?

No time for this. We can't stop now. I'm getting weaker.

They kicked the body out of the runner. It hit the tarmac with a loud thud. His runner was outside the spaceport. Beyond it, vehicles moved over dark tarmac. Shapes shifted in the distance. Spires of light rose into the sky.

"Vehicle, take us away from here."

"Destination."

"Away from the Spaceport."

"Does the passenger mean to go into the city?"

"Yes, yes. Please." Her head fell forward onto the dashboard. *I need a doctor.* "Take me where I can get help."

··· — — — ···

The runner was in a dimly lit street when she came to. *Stop. We've stopped.* No other thoughts came back to her. *Andor?* Silence.

"Why — why have we stopped?" she rasped.

"We are inside the city. The vehicle now requires a more specific destination."

She barely heard the answer. Opening the door, she fell out onto the road. It was hard to move now. Hard to even breathe. The road was quiet. Monoliths surrounded her, taller than mesas and shaped like blocks. The air blowing against her skin smelled of strange things. *But it is wind. We're off the ship, Andor.*

She limped around to the front of the vehicle, holding on to the hood.

Andor? Are you there?

But there was no answer.

Unable to think, her vision blurry and not knowing what to do, she started walking.

When she tripped and fell, she decided to just lay there for a while. Her ankle hurt too much to move anyway. The dampness of the ground against her cheek was a cool, comforting hand.

Memories ran through her head. Bloody memories. She did not want to think.

I'll just rest. Just lay here and rest.

... — — — ...

She slept. Dreamed. Went in search of somewhere she did not find.

A hand tugged at her, and she woke again. But that place was cold, ugly and full of suffering, and she slipped from it almost as soon as she entered.

That was when she found her way back to the garden. And him.

II

While an unidentified girl lay unconscious in Mathis Clinc, Tu-dan Malik strode along the carpeted hallway of a Galaxy class passenger freighter. His heavy grav boots, worn in case of the unlikely event of gravity loss, made muffled thumps against the plush purple fabric. On his right, special floor to ceiling walls relayed adjusted pictures from the ship's sensors. Stars spread out along the slightly curved hallway—diamonds on a jeweler's black velvet, glimpsed between ornate golden pillars.

Behind Tu-dan was the crowded, sparkling dining room of the Conway Enterprises Ship *Liberty*. He'd stayed long enough to ensure that Gilene Conway would not be attending dinner, then left for his room. Gilene Conway kept a schedule that even he found taxing sometimes. He had maybe three hours before she rose to take her daily exercise on the observation deck.

He pulled at his long sleeves as he walked, looking forward to reaching his room and removing the v-necked jacket and dhoti he wore. The yellow and green gold-dusted suit was necessary to blend into the high society munificence that followed Gilene everywhere, but it chafed him to be so conspicuous. His primary training had been in the art of assassination. Staying in the background was second nature to him.

As he made the final turn to the E deck living quarters, his comm panel sounded. He pulled the slender bejeweled device from one of his many pockets, and his eyebrows rose as he glanced at the code.

Orgala? An official call? He had been expecting to hear from Ru-ad, not his handlers in Rhiannon. He didn't look forward to that conversation. Ru-ad would not be pleased to find that he had failed to make contact with the *Meridian.* He would be even more displeased to find out why. "Transmit."

To his surprise, Ru-ad appeared on the screen. The connection was fuzzy this time, since the call had been made on his official link. *Why is he using the official code?*

"Chief Advisor."

"Tu-dan," Ru-ad said.

A line formed between his brows. Ru-ad almost never called him by his chosen name.

"If you are receiving this message, it means that I have not been able to enter the stop-code on the virus I implanted into our main comm server. I couldn't be sure all would go well here, since I couldn't be sure of Andor. If you are receiving this, I have most likely been found out, betrayed or killed."

Tu-dan leaned against the gold-painted metal bulkheads. His breath escaped in a harsh gasp from between his teeth. *My father, betrayed and probably killed. Because of Shalon. And maybe Andor too.* The image on the screen continued.

"The virus has three functions. Once I do not prevent its activation with twice weekly stop-code inputs, it will launch itself. Its first function will be to beam this message to you via every space link we possessed. Its second will be to erase all data on your whereabouts, recall codes and past mission locations from the comm servers. The third will be to cause a temporary shutdown of the communication system while erasing itself."

Tu-dan stared ahead unseeingly. "I can never return to Rhiannon."

"It should give you enough time to sever all connections with our mercenaries offworld and disappear, even if they have forced me to disclose your involvement. Within two days, you must transfer funds out of First InterGalactic Bank, where I have created an account for you. The account keys have been transmitted to your panel with this message. The money should enable you to live comfortably—and carry out the last mission I will ask of you."

As the image on the panel paused for emphasis, Tu-dan raised a clenched fist and rested it against the bulkhead. *Betrayed. Most likely by the man he regarded as a son. More of a son than me.* A bitter chuckle escaped him. *And yet, some part of you expected it. Planned for it.*

What a mind you had. What a mind Rhiannon has lost.

"Finish what we started, Tu-dan. Meet with the ship, dispose of the crew, ensure that Shalon is dead. If this is not taken care of, all of this will have been for nothing. I do not fear betrayal, trial or death. I fear only that what I intended will not be achieved. If you accept this mission, you will not be able to return to Orgala. I know this will be a hard choice for you, but I am sure you understand the importance of securing Orgala's future, whatever the cost. I know once you accept this mission, you will walk your path to the end." Ru-ad's smile was thin.

"Remember me well, Tu-dan. Remember that I sacrificed all for Orgala and help me make it worth the price."

Ru-ad's image winked out. Tu-dan gripped the panel in his hand so tight, a few crystals fell from it. *I can never go home again. Never. Even if I don't finish this, they will know I was involved with Ru-ad's plans. And I have no doubt he considered all of that when he maneuvered me into this position.*

But he could not have foreseen the Trooper ship being quarantined when it arrived on Serron, forcing me to leave with Gilene's entourage before I could find out what happened to the crew. And if my sources are right, then the Vi-Commander most likely freed herself and killed the crew.

The panel beeped, indicating a message waited for him. *The account keys.* He looked out at the vast silence of space. *All your careful planning and she still escaped. But I finish what I start, and there's nothing left for me to go home to anyway. So I will find her and end this. For you. I owe you that much, father.*

"Display," he said. He would not be able to return to Serron for almost a month. Until then, he had a search to begin. And he knew exactly who could help him with it.

III

It seemed she sat with his head in her lap forever. His tanned cheeks rested against the gray satin of her skirts. His face was turned up toward her as she stroked his short, dark hair, which was soft as a baby's.

Next to her, a burropac skeleton lay scattered, smashed like ancient pottery. It did not bother her. Nothing bothered her anymore.

He did not open his eyes and she knew that he was caught between life and death. Her life and his death. They had fought a battle and won. But now he lacked the strength to go on.

And she did not want to be without him.

So she sat and waited and knew they were both slipping away.

Until she sensed movement behind her.

A figure stood there. Small and slender, it watched from the bushes. Unable to see it, she nevertheless felt a change in the atmosphere. A kind of—dynamism.

It's not your time.

A crease formed between her eyes. Not my time?

No.

She considered this statement. I'm supposed to survive? To go on?

Yes. You know this.

But how do you know this?

Because we know you. The touch of your mind. Our creator gave this to us on our awakening. We have waited to find you. Have searched for you so long. Now we have found you. And this is not your time.

She looked down at the sleeping form in her lap. I'm dying.

Yes.

I don't want to leave him. I'm tired of losing people.

You won't lose him unless you choose to.

It was an odd statement, one she didn't understand. The small shape was closer now. Do you promise?

We promise.

A thin hand stretched toward her. Ask. Say the words.

What words?

You know them already. Ask and we will do it.

She stared at the hand. Looked down at the statute-still body of her lover. Ask.

She turned, grasped a hand dry as a branch and soft as cotton. Help us, *she said.* Help me.

And sat up.

And opened her eyes.

PART THREE

AFTER

Poor wandering one,
Though thou hath surely strayed,
Take heart of grace,
Thy steps retrace,
Poor wandering one.
—*W.S. Gilbert*

CHAPTER 19

They will believe the truth shall set them free.
They will be wrong.
Sometimes, there is no stronger cage.
—*Wisdom: The Fifth of the Seven Holies*
Ancient Dak Scripture

I

Shalon bowed her head against the warm, convex surface of the transperiwall in Colin's office. Memories flowed and twisted through her head. Some murky as stones glimpsed in dark water, others flashing clear as a mountain spring on a sunlit day. From the last words her mother spoke to her, to the realization that Andor had lied about Ru-ad—everything she had ever experienced filled her head, jostling for primacy.

Everything. Including the touch of grasping hands and the ache at the very core of her being. She shut her eyes, breathed out, trying to push past it and focus on the present. But it was hard. So hard. *The funny thing is, I thought I was handling it before. That I would be over it soon.*

The transperiwall vibrated against her skin. She rolled her forehead against the slick surface and looked across at Colin. A line of incomprehension marred his brow, and she saw the questions in his eyes, the unconscious denial. *Oh, Colin. Despite your high ideals, all you've saved is a doomed murderer who can never tell you the whole truth about herself.*

269

"Ain't life a bitch?" she said.

"You're sure about this?"

"I'm sure," Shalon replied, leaning back and folding her arms across her chest. "Believe me, there's nothing I would like better than to be wrong."

"But you—died. I remembered the news broadcasts because you were the same age as Conor. It was all everyone talked about for months. Jason and Falon Conway's space yacht crashing with no survivors. The funeral was a public day of mourning. They holovised it. I saw your casket."

"Empty. Gilene knew better than to let anyone know there were survivors. She assumed she could dispose of me before anyone found me. She was wrong, of course."

And someday soon, I'll make her pay.

Like you made them pay? By letting Andor take vengeance for you? By copping out?

Andor. She clenched her teeth at the thought and forced herself to focus on the present. "You want proof? Think back to your own examination of me when I first came in. The eternity symbol on my chromosome. I'll tell you a secret only Conways know. The symbol is a trademark of our personal science Program, and a marker that every Conway carries. A foolproof way to identify us. But it's not something anyone outside of my family is aware of. That's why you couldn't tie the symbol to a genetics company. And since I've been dead for ten years, my file was deleted from the few public databases and archives that maintained my identity."

"My God." Colin turned away from her and sat on the desk. She saw the skin on his knuckles stretch tight as he gripped the edge of the table. "You're telling the truth, aren't you? You really are Shalon Conway."

"Yes. And I'm telling the truth about Gilene too."

Colin's gaze, blue as the Earth sky, flew to meet hers. He shook his head. "No. She's a great woman. A philanthropist. I wouldn't even have this clinic without her."

"She's a ruthless bitch who killed my parents in order to regain her position at Conway Enterprises." *A callous monster who used my people to further her own goals.*

The same way you used Andor to further yours?

No. That was different.

Sure, keep telling yourself that.

"You have no idea what she's capable of. She has one face for the public, another in private. My own father..." Her voice broke as she remembered their last dinner together as a family. Sitting in the main dining room on their space yacht, mellow light reflecting off crystal ware and plush carpeting.

"I can't believe Gil would be conspiring against me."

"My father didn't believe she was a threat either," she continued. "He paid for it with his life."

Colin ran his hands over his face and through his hair. She had hit him with a lot all at once and she knew it. *But if he thinks he's confused, he should try being me.*

"If all of this is true, where have you been for the last ten years? What happened to you?"

Too much. And if I could tell you any of it, I still wouldn't.

Because then he would know what a murderous coward you are. A coward who let herself be tainted by those animals.

Shalon's body prickled with the urge to get away from her thoughts. The touch-memories on her skin made her long to shed it. "I hid," she said. "I can't tell you where. But I found a new home. New parents. They rescued me. Raised me. Until I was tricked into leaving them and captured."

"By Gilene?"

Shalon shrugged, glanced at the night sky outside. *In a way, it was her. She started the chain of events that ruined my life. Twice.* "I don't think so, but it's not impossible. Either way, it doesn't matter now."

"Of course it matters." Colin sounded shocked as he stood. "These people who took you, they raped you didn't they? We have to tell the Troopers."

"They're already dead, Colin." She held his gaze, her stomach hollow with the knowledge of what she was about to tell him. "I killed them. All of them." *With a little help that no one on Serron would believe anyway.*

Help. Nice name for murder by proxy. You're getting really good at this denial thing.

"You what?" His voice was quiet, unbelieving. She would have to make him understand. He deserved the truth. *And you might need his help. If he doesn't call the Troopers on you by the time you're finished. Which is what you deserve, after all.*

No, I don't deserve that. I don't deserve to die, or to feel this pain, so why don't you just SHUT UP?

She took a deep breath before she spoke. "Colin, the men I killed, the men who raped me, were Troopers. And I may have killed several more at a hospital tonight."

"Shalon."

"*Just listen.*" *Because you have no idea how hard this is to say.* "I didn't mean for tonight to happen. I was with Oux—the alien— and it was helping me remember. Things got out of hand. It was a mistake, a terrible accident. But I didn't make a mistake when it came to those bastards who raped me. I wanted them dead."

She stopped, a shiver running through her as she remembered the heavy sound of a headless body being dragged over clanging grilles. "If I had to do it all over, I'd kill them again. It was the only way to escape."

Shalon tugged at the hem of her t-shirt, twisting it over her index finger.

"I want you to know the truth about that because there are things— things about me that I can't tell you. Issues even more important than who runs Conway Enterprises. And to deal with them, I have to remain hidden from Gilene Conway. I can't be found by the Troopers or they'll execute me for what I've done. And Gilene doesn't like loose ends. If she catches up to me, I won't be the only one in danger."

Shalon blew air through her teeth and moved to stand right in front of Colin. "I came here to tell you this—and to ask you not to give me up to the Troopers when they come looking. Because they will come looking. I killed their own—twice. They won't let that go."

Colin said slowly, "You're saying you think Gilene will use the Troopers to get to you?"

Shalon nodded. "You see why I can't trust them? Why I have to get away from here instead of trying to clear my name? They think I'm a cold-blooded murderer and they'll shoot first and ask questions later. I am...dangerous, Colin, and I've killed people. But I would never hurt you or anyone else except in self-defense. Please believe that." *Because after what I did on the ship, I'm having trouble believing it myself.*

That wasn't just me.

It might as well have been for all I did to stop it. And that's the truth.

"Do you believe me, Colin?"

He ran his hands through his hair again, tossing his head back for a moment. "I don't know what to believe at the moment, Le— Shalon."

"I'm not lying to you, Colin."

"Look." He heaved a sigh. "I'm just not sure how to deal with any of it. You're asking me to go against my ethics, my sense of civic duty."

"Colin," Shalon said, twisting the hem of her shirt in her clenched fist. "A crew of Troopers raped me repeatedly and beat me almost to death. Forgive me if the words 'civic duty' makes me want to punch a wall right now."

Shalon saw the tension in his frame. Part of her understood the turmoil he was going through and felt guilty for putting him on the spot. The other part hated him for not taking her side immediately. *If you really understood what they did to me, you wouldn't be standing here on your soapbox, trying to make a decision.*

That's not fair. He's been nothing but kind to you.

Sure. When you were Lex. Now, you're Shalon Conway. How much of his hesitation has to do with the law—and how much has to do with the fear of losing his grant from Conway Enterprises if anyone finds out he helped me?

"Colin, you can't tell anyone who I am. If Gilene thinks anyone knows I'm alive, they will be in danger."

Behind her, she heard the door hiss open. Conscious it might be one of the hospital staff, she dropped her head and turned away so that her face could not be clearly seen. "Well, what do you know. There she is."

The silky voice stiffened her spine like a blow. Shalon spun around.

Oux stood in the doorway. Holding one of its hands, like a father leading an errant child, was the red-headed man named Chris.

II

"Officer Linkow."

He stirred, pain pressing down on him with cruel hands. It was hard to breathe.

"Officer Linkow, can you hear me?"

Of course I can.

"Can you hear me?"

He groaned and swallowed past the cotton ball feel in his throat. *Why the hell can't I breathe through my nose?* "You're fucking yelling in my ear. Of course I can hear you," he rasped.

Blinking, he realized he was lying flat on his back. Without thinking, he started to sit up. The throbbing in his head exploded into a mind-numbing surge that funneled down his spine to every other part of his body. "Ahhh, *shit.*"

Hands eased him back down. He raised his arm, touched a damp bump behind his skull and drew away fingers tipped with blood.

"You might want to hold off on sitting up." The voice was female, deep and professional.

"No kidding." He touched a nose that felt twice its size. The speaker bent over him, blocking the sun-bright light from the pale ceiling. She had a tanned, serious face with eyes black as space and hair the same shade of brown as Sonja's.

A hand. Chopping down on his partner's neck with unbelievable swiftness.

"Sonja," he said, recollections surfacing in his mind like a rush of bubbles in water. "Where is she? Is she okay?"

The woman looked blank. "Sonja?"

"My partner. She was in the hospital with me."

The doctor's expression relaxed into understanding. "Officer Helene. She'll be okay. She's being treated for minor injuries."

Linkow forced himself to sit up and hang his legs over the side of the bed, gritting his teeth. He was in a small treatment room with shiny bots of varying sizes lined up against the far wall. The sliding door on his right was closed.

"Officer, I need you to stay still. Your head wound needs to be closed."

"Fuck that," Linkow said. *That bitch is not going to get away while I lie here.* "There's a Trooper out in the corridor. Get him in here."

She looked surprised. "How did you know that?"

"Because he has to take a statement as soon as I'm conscious. Show him in, okay?"

Her lips pulled tight. "Officer Linkow, I don't know if you've noticed, but you're under my care."

"Then treat me while he asks the questions. I have information that could lead to a suspect's capture. Don't make me charge you with obstruction."

Her eyes narrowed, but without another word, she spun on her heel and went to the door. Linkow touched his head again and blew air through his nostrils as pain lanced down his neck. *Fuck, that hurts. But that's okay, because I have her now. I fucking have her now.*

III

"You," Shalon gritted through her teeth. Chris—

(why the hell do I know your name when I've never seen you before today?)

—shut the door behind him.

"You know this man?" Colin asked, incredulous.

"In a manner of speaking." He took a step forward. "Remember me?"

"I should be asking you that." She jerked her chin at the faint bruise on his forehead.

He touched his hand to it, and a slight grimace twisted his lips. "You fight a lot better than I expected."

Really. Well, get ready to have your expectations exceeded again. Shalon tensed herself, calculating the distance to him once she leapt over the table. She started to lean into the action—and found herself unable to move.

What the...? She could feel herself, feel her muscles straining under her skin, but her body simply refused to obey.

In front of her, Oux let go of Chris' hand.

<<Stop. Not Angry One. Not threat.>>

She recognized the touch of Oux's mind. The flavor of urgency in its thoughts.

"What are you doing to me?" she asked, anger and a frisson of fear tightening her chest.

Chris clapped his hands once, twice. "Oux, you tricky bugger. You haven't told her anything have you?"

Oux swiveled and regarded Chris with a blank stare. Chris cocked his head at it in a challenging manner.

What the hell is going on here? "Oux, what is he talking about? What haven't you told me?"

Oux turned back to Shalon. *<<Stop fight. No need.>>* Its shoulders made a tiny, elegant shift. *<<No time. Angry One wake soon. No time.>>*

No time. The thought echoed inside her and Shalon shuddered in confusion, her mouth dry. Because the thought was not her own. And it had come to her in a melody of voices.

"Oux."

In a single bound, the creature settled itself in a half-crouch on the desk in front of her.

<<Am here. With you.>> It pointed one stalk-like finger at her chest and something in Shalon yearned toward the contact. *<<With you.>>*

Oh. My. God. Her eyes widened as she looked into smooth black orbs, shiny and expressionless as stones. "You infected me?"

"Infected you?" Colin's voice sounded sharp, worried and she could not turn her head to look at him. "Infected you with what?"

"With itself," Chris cut in. "The Oux healed her at some point, didn't he?" His brief smile was strangely mirthless.

"Who are you?" Colin demanded.

"I'm the guy that son-of-a-bitch Algaran stole Oux from. They call me Chris." He sat on the desk behind Oux and folded his arms, his dark blue shirt pulling tight across his shoulders.

"You must be the doctor. Mayfeld. Oux told me how you fought to keep our girl here alive until it could get to her. You did a hell of a job. It wants you to know it's in your debt." He sounded disinterested, his dark eyes were cold and focused. Shalon longed to smash his jaw in.

<<*No. Stop. Listen. Proud One not bad.*>>

"Says who? He tried to kill me at the hospital," Shalon said through her teeth.

Chris waved a finger from side to side. "Actually, *you* tried to kill *me*. I was just trying to get you to stop running long enough to hear what I had to say. But apparently you're not big on talking."

"He attacked you at the hospital?" Shalon could sense Colin looking from her to Chris and back again.

"Colin, not now," she said, her voice sharper than she intended. Her head had begun to hurt. *So what do you have to say for yourself, Oux? Why are you here?*

Oux folded and refolded long fingers. <<*Help. Save Hurt One.*>>

"From the Angry One?"

<<*Yes. He will hurt/kill. Oux keep Hurt One safe.*>>

"But where is the Angry One? Who is he? And what does this—Chris—have to do with keeping me safe?"

"I'm the guy that's going to get you away from the bad guys. I'm your ticket to your real destination." Chris got up and put his hands down on the desk, palms gripping the edge. "The Oux says it will talk through me from now on. It doesn't want to hurt you again."

"You know what it's saying?"

"Sure. I'm not sensing your thoughts and feelings too well at the moment, but we're all connected now that the Oux's changed you. Pretty soon, we'll be one big happy family."

The silk in his voice grated on her ears. Remembering the alien feel of him in her mind at the hospital, Shalon fought down her revulsion. "Is this true, Oux?"

It opened its mouth and a single syllable escaped. *"Yes."*

"Okay." *This is crazy, but what the hell. I lost my mind a long time ago.* "Talk. I'm listening."

Just like that, her muscles released, and she took a stumbling step forward, catching herself against the desk with an outstretched hand.

"The Oux says you don't really understand what it is, and it doesn't have time to explain everything now. But it wants you to know that you can trust it—and me. It's been looking for you for a long time. Ever since I met it actually."

"And when was that?" She couldn't put her finger on it, but something about Chris made her want to get the hell away from him. *He's a user. And he's dangerous.*

"Years ago." Chris shrugged. "Doesn't matter. What's important is the Oux agreed to come with me only because it knew I would cross paths with you some day. As much as it hurts me to be a means to an end, I went along with it."

Sure, at no benefit to yourself? I find that unlikely.

"You're saying the Oux predicted your meeting?" Colin scoffed. "That's ridiculous."

Chris ignored him. "How did it find you when you needed it most, Shalon? How did it heal you just by touching you? The Oux can do many things."

The skin on her arms prickled at his use of her name. "Why do you call it 'the Oux'? It's just Oux, isn't it?"

"Oux means vessel in its language. It doesn't have a name. Just a function. That function has always revolved around finding what it called the Hurt One. And now that it's found you, it wants you to leave here, with us. It says you hurt the Angry One at the hospital. Bad. He's still there. But he will wake and when he does, he will come after you."

Leave. With us. Please. The thoughts in her head were urgent, cajoling. Unwelcome. She shook free of the harmony of more voices than she could count.

"It's talking to you, isn't it?" Chris asked. "The rest of them. Of it."

Shalon bit her lip, allowing the pain to focus her thoughts. "What's inside me?"

"A gift. That's all you need to know for now. Oux says people are coming for you and if they catch you, everything you've been through, all you've survived, will have been for nothing."

All for nothing. Save yourself.

And smooth as velvet. *Shalon, please. Go now.*

Oh, God. That mind. That touch. She put out an unsteady hand and the Oux caught her palm in its grasp. Shalon looked at the delicate green face with its huge eyes. *Andor.*

<<*In you. Caught/trapped. In you.*>>

Its skin was dry and soft as she fought to bring herself under control. Her fingers closed tight on its small hand. *All this time. All this time.*

<<*Safe. Promised Hurt One. Not lose him.*>>

Shalon pulled her hand from its grasp. She stepped back, chest rising and falling rapidly as she looked within herself, trying to find him again. Trying to catch the thread of his passage in her thoughts. But he was gone. All she found was the tumbling urgency of the *others.*

Chris watched her, dark brown eyes intent. "Shalon? You with us?"

Stop using my name. You don't know me.

Oux stood up on the desk. <<*Okay if Hurt One come/go with Oux. Oux keep promise.*>>

Shalon hesitated only a moment longer. "Yes," she answered. "I'm with you. But when we're safe again, you have to tell me everything. Everything, you understand?"

"*I* don't understand." Colin cut in. Shalon started. She had forgotten he was even in the room. His blue eyes were worried, his face drawn tight with tension.

"Colin. I have to do this."

"You can't be serious. How can you go with them? You don't know what this Oux really is. You don't know where they're taking you. The only thing you know about this guy is that he attacked you."

Chris shrugged. "Again, I wasn't the one who started it."

Shalon threw him a venomous glance. "This is my business. Stay out of it." Chris's lips tightened, but he said nothing more.

She turned back to Colin. *How can I make you understand that this feels right? That Oux makes me feel safe. That I believe what it says.*

She searched his gaze, reading the concern there. And in a split second of understanding, reading the deeper reason behind it. *Oh no. Oh, Colin.* "I'm sorry. I have to do this."

He grasped her shoulders in his hands and she remembered the tingle of his palms against her skin just days before, in the examination room. Somehow, despite that memory, his touch now made her feel violated. Defiled. She shook his hands off and moved out of his reach. She saw the stricken expression that crossed his face. *Shalon, you silly girl. He's not one of them. He won't hurt you.* But she couldn't shake the feeling of disgust that enveloped her.

"You don't have to do this. Let me help. I can hide you, take you somewhere they wouldn't find you."

"No," Shalon shook her head, unconsciously rubbing her hands against her arms. "You can't. You're the first person they'll come to. If they find out you helped me, you'd lose everything. The clinic. Your life. Ranie."

Her deliberate strike hit home. He flinched a little and looked away.

"I'll be okay, Colin. I'm sure of that. If Oux wanted me dead, I would have been dead already. I can't let you get any more involved in this. You've done enough." *If I stay, I'll only end up hurting you.*

"You don't need to protect me. I can handle myself."

"Not where she's going," Chris said. "You wouldn't last two minutes."

Colin rounded on him, and Shalon knew it was mostly relief at having someone to lash out at. "If you hurt her, if you get her killed, I swear I will come looking for you."

Chris raised his eyebrows. "Tough words." He rounded the desk in a sudden smooth movement. "Problem is, I've heard them from people a lot scarier than you." He reached toward Colin—and stopped. Shalon saw the veins in his neck stand out. Satisfaction uncoiled within her.

"Oux," Chris said through his teeth.

The small creature picked its way along the cluttered desk and settled next to him. "Be-have," it intoned.

"Fine," Chris replied. Then he was pulling back and rubbing at his wrist as though someone had gripped it hard. He eyed the Oux. "Don't fucking do that to me again, okay?"

Oux did not reply. It leapt down from the desk and stood at Colin's feet. "Safe," it said, waving a hand at Shalon and then at itself. "Safe."

Colin looked at Shalon over its head and she could see he still wanted to argue. But the escalating urgency thrumming through her body made her cut across him.

"I'll be all right. Just please—"

"I won't tell them anything." His voice was firm. The look in his eyes unmistakable. *I don't deserve you, Colin.*

"Thank you," she said. "For everything."

Colin nodded. "Ranie?"

"I left her at the shelter, in the car outside. She'll be fine. Tell her—tell her, thank you. And that I'm sorry."

"You could tell her yourself, someday."

Shalon shook her head. "I wouldn't count on it."

"Oh." Colin took a breath and stuck his hands in his pockets. "Okay. Well."

"Fucking hell," Chris broke in. "Can we move this along?"

He's right. Damn him. She tore her gaze from Colin and went to the door, pausing as it slid open. "Don't forget to wipe the holorecords."

Colin looked surprised. He'd forgotten about the hospital's security network.

Chris sighed. "Already done. How do you think the Oux and I got in here unnoticed?"

The Oux bounded past her, and Chris went out after it.

Shalon faced Colin again. He stood next to his desk, his hands in his pockets and emotions she didn't want to acknowledge written in stark lines on his face. He looked younger than his years and so very lonely. Lonely as she felt inside. As she had always felt. Before Andor. The thought of him pierced through her, a swift, unforgiving pain.

*Don't waste it on me, Colin. I can't return it. Not now—*she remembered a finger pushing into her—*maybe not ever.*

"Shalon," was all Colin said.

She shook her head in mute denial and walked away before she could give in to the urge to stay with the one person she had grown to trust. *The one person I know gives a damn about me on this world. This fucked-up world that I'm stuck in now.*

Her heart felt tight as she half-walked, half-ran down empty back corridors behind Chris, smelling the orange of disinfectant over the staleness of ancient coffee. Pale yellow walls with closed numbered doors blended into white ones. She thought of pale sands under freezing dark skies and longed for home with an intensity that made her eyes sting. *Not now. Probably never again.*

Shalon caught up to Chris as he entered a turbo-lift and said, "Ground floor." The lift went down with a fast sliding motion that made her stomach turn over. She leaned against the hard, fake wood walls. The Oux watched her from the corner near the door, its hands wrapped around its ribs, and Shalon could feel the concern coming off it.

Don't you worry about me. I'm a murderer. Tough as a Madinah warrior. Just ask the Troopers. Looking for a way to escape her thoughts, she asked Chris, "Why doesn't it hurt you when it talks to you in your head?"

"Let's just say there's a lot more of Oux in me, than there is in you. You're getting kind of crowded from what I heard."

Asshole.

The turbolift opened onto a hallway with a pair of gray double doors directly opposite. The Oux crossed the corridor and pushed them open. Shalon found herself in a bustling cafeteria with row upon row of bright blue bucket seats and low plastic tables. Long lines queued at the food dispensers. Constant chatter among doctors, waiting relatives, and security staff made a low rumble in the room. The place smelled of cheese and fried meat. Two conical cleaning bots operated at opposite ends of the room, working industriously at the white tiled floor.

No one turned to look at them as Oux headed straight across the room toward a small red door. It slid open as they approached and the alien disappeared from view. Shalon stepped out behind Chris and found herself in a narrow, low-ceilinged tunnel that appeared to be an access point for maintenance staff. They walked along it, twisting and turning past storage closets, power outlets and exposed junction boxes. At the tunnel's end, another portal slid open. They emerged into a dark, slick alley that smelled of old chemicals and new garbage.

"I have an air car a few blocks from here," Chris said. Automatic garbage collection units loomed around them like sentinels. "Once we get to it, we'll head straight to the spaceport. I have someone waiting to take us offworld."

"Where are we going?" Shalon asked. They turned onto the street. She could hear an urgent wailing on the air, a familiar sound. The noise drew closer and Chris and the Oux, still bounding ahead, increased their stride.

"Troopers," he clarified in one short word as she looked at him. They reached a bright yellow air car with the word "Taxi" glittering above it, just as the first blue and white police runner came sliding around the corner behind them. Its urgent wail filled the space around Shalon. She got into the front passenger side of the car, while the Oux jumped in through the back window.

"You drive a taxi?" she asked Chris over more rising wails. Chris smiled at her in the purple tinted light of the dashboard.

"I borrowed one for the occasion. Better to hide in plain sight."

The seat restraints were still settling into place over them when he pulled away from the curb, executed a turn that made Shalon's stomach push against one side of her body—and slammed on the brakes. "Shit!"

A blurred black shape filled the windscreen with frightening speed. There was an endless, waiting moment as the runner's detection system beeped frantically, activating too late. Then a shuddering, grinding impact. Shalon's head slammed back against the headrest as the taxi was driven sideways onto the curb, and scraped to a metal-screeching halt against the side of a building.

CHAPTER 20

There is no shame in retreat, if that retreat leads to a stronger attack
at another time.
—*Madinah Warrior Code*

I

Troi watched as Anton slid his panel back into his pocket, a frown
creasing the space between his brows.

"Still no luck?"

"Colin's not answering his panel. Must still be in surgery."

They were half a block away from her home, shoes clicking
on the deserted night street. Around them, domed transperiwall
buildings threw back the glow of floating arc lights like the tinted
visors of helmets. A slender tree shook broad leaves down on them
in the wake of a sudden gust of wind that carried the scent of rain.
In times past, it would have been a nice stroll and she would have
enjoyed the chance to be alone with him for a few minutes. Now,
she knew only that she wanted time to herself.

*He lied to me. I thought I knew him better than anyone else. Now, I just
don't know if I know him at all.*

He had insisted on accompanying her back to her apartment after
the diner. Troi saw it for what it was; an attempt to do something for
her, however small. A way to show her he still cared. *I wish it were
that simple, Anton. I wish I could just forget what you did and remember
what you've meant to me. But I'm not half as forgiving as I thought.*

"You have to get over there. Warn him. If Shalon Conway's still alive, then someone in that family has been lying to the public. And that person probably doesn't want to get caught in that lie."

"Yes." Anton glanced at her. "After I get you home safe."

"I'll be fine."

"Maybe. The Conways have extraordinary power and resources."

"They can't have back-tracked me." She stopped in front of her building, and pulled out her keycard. "I'm good at what I do, Anton." She slid the tiny chip into the waist high slot on the glimmering wall. A door opened, spilling warm golden light onto the sidewalk.

"So are they." He didn't ask to come up and she didn't try to dissuade him. *You want to ease your conscience, fine. Do what you must. Then for god's sake, leave me alone.*

Out of the corner of her eye, she glimpsed Anton flinch behind her as she started up the narrow, curving stairs that dominated her foyer. Then he grabbed the rail and followed her. For a moment, her heart hurt for the pain her emotions must have caused him. Then her own pain and disappointment robbed her of any sympathy. *My pain and your pain. It's twice as bad for you right now. And I think that's how it should be.*

Her bot was standing in her office when she walked in to check on her systems, her long skirts swishing on the carpet. It was facing her screens, motionless.

"Asja?"

The bot turned its head. "You are home." Its silver eyes shifted to look at the large shape filling the doorway behind her. "Dr. Slake. How good to see you again."

"Asja," Anton replied. Troi joined Asja at the center of her semi-circular workstation, casting an eye over the flickering screens. "What are you doing in here?"

"I thought I detected an alarm." Asja waved a hand at the screens and the flashing images ran up its metal arm like colored quicksilver. "It would appear that I am wrong. All is normal."

Troi frowned and took her seat in a rustle of skirts and veil. Affixing a tiny patch to her temple, she tapped fingers against the transparent interface and started checking her systems and security features.

"Troi?" Anton drew up next to her as Asja withdrew to the door. "Something wrong?"

"I don't know yet." *I just feel like something's not right.* A voice spoke up in her head, level and logical.

Asja is a bot. They can't hear something that isn't there. They haven't got the imagination. Why would it be in here, just staring at the screen?

The alarm systems were undisturbed. The modules she had left in progress were fine. No cyber attacks, bugs, recording Programs or interruptions had been registered. Everything remained completely within the parameters designed for them.

She shrugged and looked up at Anton. "Everything's as it should be."

"In other words, perfect?" Anton inquired, his tone neutral.

Troi nodded. "Perfect." Their gazes locked while Troi's breathing sped up and her brain raced.

Just staring at the screen. As if it was in resting mode. As if it wasn't operational.

And why didn't it know I'd come home? It's connected to the house and the security system. Why didn't it know we'd come in?

Finally, Anton said, "I'll make the arrangements."

"How much time do I have?" Troi rose to her feet, heart fluttering in her chest like a trapped butterfly. *They found me. Somehow, they found me. Shit. Shit!*

"Could be days, could be hours." Anton went to the door. "Delete everything you can and don't take more than a small bag. I want you out of here within the hour and I'll send you a message to meet me at Bradley when it's safe."

"What about Asja?"

"I'll take care of Asja."

"Anton." He turned in the doorway, the look on his determined face quizzical. *Isn't it just like you to protect me, even when you know exactly how I feel about you at the moment?*

Maybe I do still know you.

"What if I'm wrong?" she asked. "What if I'm panicking for nothing?"

"Troi," Anton said, his deep voice firm. "You know as well as I do that you've never panicked in your entire life."

Then he was gone, and she heard his shoes thumping down her stairs.

I've been an idiot. He's trying to protect me. He's always tried to protect me.

But he lied to me.

And I've reacted just the way he feared. She sat down slowly.

I can't forget what he did.

But no one's asking me to. He was only a child, though. What would I have done?

Her fingers flew over the interface as she blinked her way through multiple screens and uttered short-code commands. *What would I have done?*

II

"Fuck!" Chris groaned and leaned forward in the driver's seat, feeling the back of his head. Deep red hair, pulled loose from his hair-tie by the impact, wisped across his cheek. He glanced across at Shalon. "You okay?"

She nodded, feeling a sharp ache in her neck and nausea swirling in her stomach at the action. Somewhere, strident hissing told a tale of escaping gas and there was the pungent smell of something burning. A purple dashboard light had started a rhythmic flickering. Shalon twisted around and sighed with relief when she saw the Oux kneeling on the seat behind her, unharmed.

Chris stabbed at the dashboard with stiff, quick fingers. "What?" Shalon asked.

"Trying to cut the computer off. It's obligated to report any vehicular accidents to the nearest precinct unless I cancel the instruction."

Damn it! The last thing we need is the Troopers coming to us. Movement through the driver's side window made Shalon look up. The black runner that had hit them rested at an odd angle in the street, its nose slightly dented. The driver's side door stood up like an extended wing and she watched as a man got out. When he crossed in front of the runner's lights, she gripped Chris's arm with sudden, urgent fingers. He glanced at her, then out the car window. Behind them, Shalon sensed rather than saw the Oux slide onto the floor and out of sight.

"Oh, fuck."

The man paused in the street and Shalon heard more sirens coming closer. "Are you okay in there?"

"Yeah!" Chris shouted back. "We're okay. Just a bit shaken up."

"Stop talking to him," Shalon hissed. "Don't you see the uniform?"

"If I don't answer him, he'll think something's wrong," Chris muttered.

"I'm sorry, I didn't see you," the man continued, drawing closer, light shining off hair dark as the runner. "Guess I took the corner faster than I thought." He paused, and Shalon saw a frown cross his face and his blue eyes squinted at her.

"You know it's against city ordinances for taxis to carry fares in the front seat."

"She's my girlfriend," Chris explained, moving a little to block Shalon from view with his shoulder. "I was giving her a lift home."

"Oh." The man came up to the window and bent down. "Well, you still shouldn't—"

Shalon saw the moment when recognition crossed his face. *He knows who I am.* Fear made her heart leap as the Trooper said, "Shit!" and reached for his weapon.

Chris grabbed his head and pulled it against the car, slamming it into the door post. He punched the Trooper once and tossed him back. He hit the pavement with a sound like a giant hand slapping the ground.

Chris shoved the door open and Oux slipped past him before Shalon had a chance to absorb what had happened. Chris made a sharp gesture at her.

"Come on! We're taking his car." He stepped over the Trooper's body and ran to the runner.

Shalon slid over the seat and out onto the pavement. The Trooper's eyes were slits, his body sprawled half on the pavement, half in the street. Something in the way his neck was angled made her bend down, heart in her throat, and place her fingers against his neck. *Please have a pulse. Please.* But as she watched, a dark puddle started to spread behind the man's head.

"Shalon!" Chris was staring at her across the top of the runner. "Move it!"

Numb with shock, tired in ways she could not begin to express, she went to him.

Chris started the car and tapped his fingers over the interface as it moved down the street, heading back to the hospital. "Damn car already reported the accident. The Troopers will be here any moment."

"Chris, I couldn't find a pulse."

"So now you're a doctor."

"He's dead."

"For fuck's sake!" He slapped his hand against the dashboard. Outside her window, the Mathis Clinic slipped by, washed by strobing blue and white lights from runners parked in the street. "I did what I had to do. I hit him—once. That's all."

But you hit almost as hard as I do.

"You killed him," she said, her voice hard.

"I got us out of there," he shot back, pushing his hair off his face. "And you're the last person who should be pointing fingers."

Sick with guilt, Shalon stared out the windscreen without seeing.

"You're not much better than dead weight right now," Chris said. He pulled his hair loose from a small blue hair-tie and started to gather it into a neat ponytail. "So if I were you, I'd keep my mouth shut and follow instructions." He picked the hair-tie out of his lap and fastened it with practiced fingers. "We need to focus on getting off Serron, not whether some damn Trooper hit his head too hard or not. Because if they catch you, *you* will be dead. So remember that. I saved your neck tonight. While you stood by and did fuck all."

Shalon looked down at her hands, feeling layers of dirt and grime that she could not see lying heavy on them. *My fault. All of this—my fault.*

<<*Accident. Proud One not intend.*>>

Shalon ignored Oux, guilt smothering her in an unforgiving embrace.

III

"You're sure she didn't come here?" The Trooper's skeptical expression said he didn't believe a word Colin had told him over the last half-hour.

Believe whatever you like. "I'm telling you officer, if she came here, she didn't make it to my office." Colin smiled politely and leaned back against his desk, hoping the nonchalant gesture would mask the tension strumming through him. "You're welcome to take a look at our security logs if that will help."

The Trooper slid his panel into his breast pocket. "I think we'll have to do just that, Dr. Mayfeld."

"The security office is down the hall to your right. I'm sure you can find it on your own."

The officer—Hansom or Honsu, he couldn't remember which— kept looking at him with that stare all officers perfect. The one that caused perpetrators to give themselves away, that made guilty consciences turn ordinary gestures into incriminating ones. *But this isn't about me. You people hurt Shalon in ways I can't imagine. And I'll be damned if I betray her to you now.*

"Doctor, you realize that if you've lied to me about any of this, you'll be an accomplice in several murders. The law takes a very dim view of harboring killers."

"Well, then it's a good thing that I'm telling the truth," Colin replied. Behind Hansom/Honsu, another Trooper appeared and close on his heels, her braid coming loose over her shoulder, was a tired looking Ranie. Her smile, when she saw him, was both relieved and troubled, and it took Colin just two strides to make it to her and fold her into his arms.

My my, aren't we the loving boyfriend. Too bad you don't have the guts to tell her what happened. Guilt made his fingers draw her closer.

"Oh my," she said against his shoulder. "I guess I should fall asleep in cars more often."

He heard the officers behind him conversing in low voices as he pulled back to look at her.

"Lex is gone."

"I know. I fainted just outside the shelter—exhaustion I guess— and apparently she put me in my runner and left. Is that why all the officers are here? I tried to get you on your comm panel, but you weren't answering."

"Surgery." He stroked her hair back from her face. "They think she might have come here to see me and they want to arrest her."

Ranie frowned, blue eyes concerned. "For what?"

"It's a long story." Behind him he made out two words "Hawkes" and "dead", and then the officers left, boot heels thumping down the corridor.

"A long story?"

"I'll tell you everything later."

"Why not talk about it now? Colin, is something wrong?"

Everything's wrong. But I can't tell you the truth without making you an accomplice, and that I will never do.

"It's okay." He smiled. *I just need a little time to come up with a suitable lie.* "This is not the place to talk. Give me a few minutes to wrap up here and we'll go home. I'll tell you everything there, I promise."

IV

Linkow threw himself into his office chair and winced as the contact jarred his head.

"Careful," Sonja told him, seating herself gingerly behind the desk opposite him. She rubbed a hand across the back of her neck and he caught a glimpse of the flesh-colored bandage wrapped around her sprained wrist. "Don't want to shake something loose again."

Linkow blew air through his teeth and leaned back, trying to ignore the constant rumble of noise around them and the strong smell of coffee that made his empty stomach roil with nausea. "I'd like to shake something loose all right. Hawkes's skull, for example. Too bad somebody already beat me to it." He ran a finger over the slippery plastic of the thin strip across his nose. He was lucky it hadn't been broken. *She hits hard, that girl.*

Sonja started digging through her drawer. "You didn't expect him to wait until we were patched up."

"I would have left with him as soon as I knew you were okay. Five minutes was all I needed. Five fucking minutes."

"Yeah, well." She tossed a packet of gum on her desk and closed her drawer with a touch. "He paid for it, didn't he? Now we have another dead Trooper and we're back to square one. Looking for a woman with no name."

He shook his head as she offered him gum and watched as she unwrapped a strip. "I wanted to get her myself, you know?"

"We had our chance." Sonja popped the gum in her mouth and Linkow caught the strong, spicy scent of cinnamon as she chewed. "She kicked our asses but good. Is it any wonder Hawkes thought he could do better on his own?"

"Well, he was wrong. And now he's dead." Linkow turned to his desk panel and tapped the interface to bring up the screen. He started scrolling through the latest reports, looking for any mention of their fugitive.

"We were all wrong. About a lot of things." Sonja sighed. "Looks like the doctor is our only lead now."

"Says here he doesn't know where she went. Says he sent her to a shelter and she disappeared en route."

"Bullshit. He's protecting her."

"I think so too, but the security logs at the hospital back him up."

"Logs can be altered. He's the owner. I'm sure he has the necessary codes to get it done."

"But why protect a murderer?"

"Come on, Linkow." Sonja leaned back in her chair and he was struck by the dark circles under her eyes. *Shouldn't be surprised. We've been awake half the night and long past our shift's end. Not that anyone cares.*

"You know as well as I do that girl was raped by the Troopers on that ship. She was their passenger. God knows where they picked her up. Either way, after what happened at the hospital, I'd be willing to bet that she's the killer Major Vernon's been looking for."

Linkow shook his head as he scanned the reports, knowing she was right and not wanting to admit it. "She's barely eighteen. How could she have done all that by herself?"

"Maybe she didn't. Maybe she had help. Another passenger. But she took care of everyone at the hospital pretty easily. And it looks like she killed Hawkes too. In the end, it doesn't matter. What matters is Dr. Mayfeld would find it very easy to take her side after all she's been through."

"She's a killer, Sonja. It's our job to find her. We've got to make him talk."

Sonja shrugged as she un-wrapped another piece of gum. "I wouldn't bet my pension on making that happen. We've got nothing on him and he's got every reason to stay quiet. We could try to make trouble for him, but with the sponsors he's got, it would probably backfire."

A heading caught Linkow's eye and he tapped the screen up. "Goddammit. You won't believe this."

"Try me." Sonja popped the last of her gum into her mouth.

"That Trooper at the hospital, Michael Zorida? He just died. The Major's still in surgery. They're repairing the damage to his spinal cord. The bitch broke his neck."

"Great. Our only witness bites the dust. Now we'll never know what really happened on that ship. What else could go wrong?"

Linkow's comm panel beeped. "Incoming call. Lieutenant Ian St. Germaine for Lieutenant Marakesh Linkow."

"There's your answer right there." Linkow sighed. "Transmit."

The inter-departmental liaison's ruddy face filled the screen. "Hey, Linkow, got some good news and some bad news. Which do you want first?"

"Whichever, I don't give a fuck at the moment."

"Got back the requests for transfers you and Helene put in. Hers has been denied, yours has been approved. Looks like you're finally headed for the One-One."

You're fucking kidding me. Linkow looked at Sonja and saw that her grin matched his. He started to chuckle the same time she started to laugh.

On the screen, Ian frowned. "Hey, what's so—" Linkow tapped the interface off and laughed so hard and so long, he gave himself a headache. He was still doubled over with tears in his eyes when Sonja started to taper off.

"Of all the fucking luck." Helene wiped at her eyes.

Linkow straightened up, his shoulders shaking with brief spasms. "This is probably the worst day I've had in a long time."

Sonja smiled and ruffled her short hair. "Me too. But it looks like you're finally on your way out of here. That's good, right?"

Linkow shrugged. "You know, I was never that big a fan of the One-One and if you're not coming with me—"

"Linkow, don't be a shit. They'll never give us a transfer to the same precinct." She crumpled her gum wrappers in her hand.

"Even so, I think I'll hang around a few months longer. Just till we find this girl."

"A few more months of you?" She tossed the wrappers at him and he ducked. "Don't do me any favors. I'd probably get more dates without your ugly puss to scare them off."

He grinned at her, and for the first time in a long time, it was not a cynical gesture, but a real expression of amusement.

"Hey," he said softly. "We cracked this case. Despite everything, we did find out who raped her."

"We did, didn't we?" Sonja gestured around her. "Too bad the only people who will ever know are you, me, and the walls. If we ever filed a report about what we think happened on that ship, we'd be out of a pension faster than a Conway starship up the Whiteway lanes."

"You got that right."

Sonja keyed her interface and sighed. "I've got six more cases from the cold files here. You?"

"Same. What do they think we are? Fucking robots."

"Nah. They don't think we have that much imagination." She stabbed at the interface. "Fuck this. I'm going home."

Linkow rose to his feet. "I'm with you on that, partner." He stretched as Sonja stood. "You want to commiserate over an alcoholic beverage or two?"

Sonja froze and lifted her eyebrows. "You want to be *social*? You really *did* get hit over the head today, didn't you?"

"Bitch," he said, and grinned.

CHAPTER 21

The thing that makes you exceptional, if you are at all,
is inevitably that which must also make you lonely.
—*Lorraine Hansberry*
20th Century Terran Playwright and Writer

I

Anton spotted Troi before she spotted him. She came in through one of the tiny side doors at the entrance to Bradley's main terminal and stood in a sea of people like a statue draped for an unveiling in her black hooded cloak and veil. Nervous fingers curled around the handle of the small pink overnight bag she held, and she shifted her grip constantly. Fear and uncertainty came off her in waves, swamping all the other emotions swirling around him.

He knew how much it tore her apart to accept his help. The help of the man who had lied to her and betrayed her trust, and was now about to take her away from everything she had ever known.

It was always going to be dangerous. Especially if Lex turned out to be one of the company's experiments and they found out someone was snooping. But I let her get deep into it anyway. I let her go looking, knowing full well what could happen.

So now I have to make things right.

When he pushed his way through the crowd to stand next to her, the relief that washed over him was a balm to his senses. *There's still hope as long as she can forget she hates me sometimes.*

"Your flight's in five minutes." He took her bag and settled a hand in the small of her back. Using his bulk to crest the waves of passersby, he moved them across the pale yellow floor to the back of the building, where numerous gates winked flight numbers at them. "I got you a connecting ticket to Pontrachain under the police department's company account. Once there you'll find two tickets waiting for you in the name of Ashley Tranton to two different destinations. Choose one. When you arrive, buy yourself a new ticket in a new name. Then don't use it. Just dump it and take the rails to somewhere else."

"Anton..."

"Troi, we don't have much time, so just listen." He made himself not look at her, not wanting to acknowledge the sudden flood of contradicting feelings, his and hers, that made his nerves sing. *This is not the time for that. Just get her safe.*

"Don't trust or speak to anyone. Don't accept any help from anyone. Keep yourself as isolated as possible. Anyone who comes into contact with you could hide a tracker on you. Don't try to contact me for at least six months. Find somewhere you would never go— somewhere you hate—and go there. Stay away from computers, it's the one thing they know about you. Try to use the networks as little as possible. They can track you through everything from your groceries to your comm panel. Use these IDs to get away. Then get new ones." He pressed her new ID chips into her hand, the smooth fabric of her gloves raising an ache in his chest. "Never, ever use your real name again."

"What about you?" she said in a low voice as a gate with a smiling attendant loomed closer.

"I'll be fine. Even if they connect me to you, I have some experience at dropping out of sight. The important thing is that you don't get found. I've taken steps toward that."

"Steps? What kind of steps?"

"The house is gone, Troi," he said simply. "There was a fire tonight. Asja was destroyed trying to save you. Luckily, no other buildings were damaged. The sprinkler systems kicked in and the fire department arrived in time."

"You did all that, on your own? How?"

"I work in a morgue, Troi. I know a thing or two about crimes. Bodies lie around unclaimed every day. I'll be doing your autopsy tomorrow morning before I take my flight. Rest assured, Troi Marcus is dead."

They stopped in front of the gate and the attendant took Troi's ticket and ID and checked them with a smile. Seconds later, she nodded and waved Troi through. Anton looked down into the huge blue eyes that stared at him with a mixture of emotions as confused as his own.

"I'm sorry for all this. I will miss you."

He waited for her to go past the barrier and into the small corridor beyond, but instead she gripped his arm and stood on her toes until her lips were next to his ear.

"You were just a child, Anton. Just a child being used by people who should have known better. It was the lying that got to me."

His skin felt heated as her fingers squeezed his arm. "My life isn't over. You didn't ruin it. I'm not leaving behind anything I couldn't stand to lose." She pulled back to look into his eyes again. "*I'm not leaving anything behind.*"

Anton's head spun with the implications of what she had said.

"When it's over, we'll talk. Okay?" She took her bag from him.

"Yes." He nodded, swallowing. *She can forgive me. Somehow, she's found the strength to consider forgiving me.* "Troi."

She waited, and the smile behind her veil reached out to him. It gave him the courage to say what he felt for the first time in his life.

"Wait for me. I will find you. Whatever it takes. Unless. Unless that's not what you want."

Her hand reached out to touch his for one electric instant. "There's nothing I want more. Just don't make me wait too long. I think we've wasted enough time as it is."

He watched as she walked through the security gate, leaving him with the scent of oranges and the feel of her brief touch on his arm.

Thank you, Troi. Thank you.

··· ▬▬ ···

The man with only a number for a name watched from the tinted interior of a runner as the burly figure of the pathologist appeared in the entrance to the spaceport.

"That's him," he said to the tall, muscular man next to him that everyone called Boll.

"You're sure?"

"He's an empath, so it was difficult to get in without triggering his abilities, but I got the gist of his thinking. Trust me, he knew her and he's protecting her. He doesn't know where she's going, but the connection between them—let's just say it wouldn't take much to get him to go after her."

Boll laughed, an alien sound that made the other start and look around with wide eyes. "What's so funny?"

"I'm pretty sure I've seen him before, a long time ago. If what you say is true, we should hold off on picking him up."

"Mr. Threadstone said we should do whatever it took to find Troi Marcus."

"Mr. Threadstone had no idea someone like this Slake was involved with his pet experiment in waiting. Besides, you just said he doesn't know where she is, so what's the rush?"

"The rush is, I want to keep my job at Conway Enterprises and I do that by following orders."

"I know." Boll sighed. "I've worked with enough of you drones. But the reason *I'm* here is because I think, and right now I think Mr. Threadstone would be very interested to know that an empath of Dr. Slake's talents is involved with the Marcus woman."

"So this Slake is special?"

"By himself, not at all." Boll grinned, a white slash in the shadows as down the street, Anton Slake reached the sidewalk and hailed a runner. "But given what Mr. Threadstone has in mind for the woman, he could be special. Very special indeed."

II

Shalon had her legs drawn up on her bunk, looking out the tiny portal at the busy spaceport outside, when the door to her small cabin opened. She didn't bother to turn, knowing instinctively that it was Chris—feeling it through that inexorable connection that existed between them. There was one chair in the cabin opposite the bed and Chris turned it around so that when he sat down, his arms rested on the back of the chair.

"We leave soon. Once we make the jump, we should be at Pirates Rock in two days. We can lay low there until the furor dies down."

"It will never die down," Shalon replied, still not looking at him. "I killed Troopers, and so did you. They'll do whatever it takes to find us."

"They'll fail. I've gotten pretty good at flying below the scanners.

They won't find us."

She turned to look at him, so many questions on her lips she didn't know where to begin. In the end, she said, "Why?" She waved her hand at the ship around them. "Why?"

"Would you believe I'm just helping a damsel in distress?" His smile was charming—and dug into her like a knife.

"I want a straight answer."

His laugh was soft and mocking. "You're in the wrong part of town for that."

"Tell me."

Chris shrugged. "You're supposed to help."

"Help what?"

"Help me get what we need most to disappear. Money."

"Money?" Shalon frowned. "All I've got is the clothes on my back."

"But you're a Conway," Chris said, his voice low and insinuating. "Isn't that right?"

Shalon's heart skipped a beat. She sat up and swung her legs over the side of the bunk. "Why do you care who I am?"

"Because the Conways have more money than God. You have unfinished business with them. And I have a plan that benefits us both."

Shalon's chin lifted a little. "I have no interest in being your pawn."

"Good, because I'm not looking for a pawn. I'm looking for a partner."

"A partner for what?"

"Crime." Chris' smile was feral. "How would you like to get rich quick, and hit the Conways where it hurts, at the same time?"

Shalon folded her arms. "I don't trust you. I don't like you. What makes you think I'd ever work with you?"

He tapped his skull. "I'm in your head. I feel what you feel. When I say the word Conway, you want to smash something. That's all I need. That and your genetic profile."

I didn't even feel you in there. Stung he had been able to read her without her permission, she reached out to him with her mind. He shook his head at her. "You're out of practice. You'll have to get a lot stronger before you can read me the same way."

She pointed an angry finger at him. "You stay out of my head, or I swear—"

"What? You'll make me go a few rounds in a parking garage somewhere? Or you'll lay me out like all the Troopers you killed?" His lips curved in amusement. "You may be a soldier, but you just got out of the hospital, and I've been with Oux for ten years now. Try me. You might as well know, though, I can't promise I'll hold back like I did before."

Shalon let her disgust show on her face. "Is that supposed to be a threat?"

His face went blank, but his eyes were furious. "It's a warning. Don't fuck with me, I won't fuck with you. There's no reason to be at each other's throats, girl. We both want the same thing. We can help each other get it."

"And what is it you think I want?"

"That's easy. Revenge." He tapped his head again. "Don't bother to deny it."

"I'm supposed to believe you want revenge against the Conways?" She shook her head. "What did they do to you?"

"Everything the devil could think of." Chris grabbed the side of the chair back, his knuckles white. "You think you're the only one they've made suffer? Take a number. The Conways are rotten to the core. And Gilene is the worst of a bad lot. My reasons are my own, but I'm just as motivated as you are. Never doubt that."

He's telling the truth. But there's so much about him I don't know and can't trust. "What's your plan?"

"Oh no," Chris said. "You want details, you have to commit. You're either in or out."

Shalon made a dismissive gesture. "How do I know what I'm committing to if I don't have the details? I've been out of that family for ten years. A lot would have changed. How do you know I can deliver?"

"I spent the last four years researching the Conways. I know all there is to know about all 243 of you and most of all, I know where the accessible ones can be found. The cousins and nieces and nephews that live off the interest of the interest of the interest. A few weeks ago, I made contact with a man that could get me into the inner circle of one of those cousins."

He raised his arms in a "what can you do?" gesture. "Of course, I didn't think the Oux would find you while I was away, putting things in place. He's very good at predicting long range events, but not so much in the short-term."

The bunk beneath Shalon shuddered and outside the spaceport began to move backward. "I still don't see what this has to do with me."

"When I get into that inner circle, I'll need a Conway to get past their security measures. That's where you come in."

"I'm not a thief."

"Neither am I. But I'm willing to learn."

If you're not a thief, I'm a Dak courtesan. "And if I refuse?"

"You're not going to get very far without money, Shalon. And if you want the revenge the Oux says you want, you're going to need a lot of it. Admit it. You don't have the time or the connections to go it on your own."

Shalon looked up at him sharply, but his face was void of any suggestion of mockery. *It's crazy. But the irony of bringing Gilene down with her own money…*

"They're too careful. It won't work."

"Ah, but no one's ever attempted anything like this before. They won't see it coming."

The door to Shalon's cabin slid open and the Oux leapt into the room and onto the bed in one bound. Shalon jumped, startled. The alien curled its arms around its knees as Chris said, "Shit. Don't you ever knock?"

Shalon tucked herself into the corner where the bunk met the wall. "And you," she asked the Oux. "What do you get out of this?"

Chris hesitated. "It says you already know. It says the man in black sent it to help you, just like he promised."

Shalon's short nails dug into her palms. *The man in black. Oh, sweet hell. I'd forgotten. How could I have forgotten?* The memory of a golden summer day, and the sight of her mother turning to laugh at something her father said as they started up the ramp to their space yacht. A glimpse, over her mother's shoulder, of a tall pale man, dressed all in black standing in the airlock. Time slowing as she saw the way his long, brown hair blew back over broad shoulders, the way his eyes, gray and clear as glass, looked at her mother with such love. Such sadness. The look in them when he slowly turned his head to stare at her.

And disappeared before her eyes, fading away like a morning fog in the sunlight.

My benefactor. My curse. The creature that put my grandmother on this crazy path to save the universe. Anger scorched a trail along her nerves. *The bastard that took my family away.*

"That thing?" she said, bitterness curdling her tone. "What do you have to do with him, Oux?"

Chris sat up straight in the chair, as though someone had pulled him up by his hair. Shalon watched as he turned to stare at her slowly—and her skin crawled at the vacant look in his eyes. The voice that came next belonged to Chris, and yet seemed as alien as Oux.

"We are his creation. We are the vessel for his power. We are an organic machine. A being of destiny. We will serve you. Then, we shall move on."

"What the fuck does that mean?" Shalon's voice cut the air, but Chris continued to stare at her without answering. She tried another tack.

"So you do this for the Messenger? For the man in black?"

"And ourselves. You were the key. We laid hands on you and unlocked the code of our survival. You have given us our lives again. In return, we have given you and your children that which you need to save yourselves and your race. That which he has commanded us to pass on to you."

Code. My DNA. It's altered my DNA. And I've altered—whatever the hell it is that makes up an organic machine. The thought disturbed her. *What the hell have you done to me?*

Chris's eyes rolled up in his head and he fell forward over the chair's metal back. His arms slid to his sides, swaying slightly. Beneath Shalon, the ship shuddered again. *This is too much. I'm too confused, too tired. Too damn angry for all this cryptic shit.*

"Oux, this change you've made, what does it mean for you?"

<<*Oux, grow. Change. Become.*>>

"What does it mean for me?"

<<*Same. Slower.*>>

Slower. But what will I change into?

The Oux had no answer, only an obsidian stare.

There's time enough to get that information out of it. But for now...for now I need to deal with what I've been putting off since the hospital.

<<*No. Too soon.*>>

"I decide when it's too soon," Shalon said sharply. "Not you."

<<*Think. Be sure.*>>

Trembling inside, her entire being focused on Oux's eyes, she saw her own lips move in them as she asked, "Can you do it? Can you help me?"

<<*Hurt One. Stop. Think.*>>

301

"Can you do it?"

"Yes," it moaned.

Shalon held out her hand. "Then do it."

<<*Too soon.*>>

"Do it!"

With a slow, reluctant movement, the alien took her hand.

III

White curtains billowed above Andor's head. He blinked and stared at them, fascinated by the way they moved. Bellying and drifting, bellying and drifting. They were endless. Eternal.

Pale light shone through like a sun's corona. The fragrance of nuts and smoke filled the air. The silence held its breath. He turned his head to the left.

Shalon stood by his bedside, looking down at him, white curtains swaying behind her.

He breathed out, feeling strength returning to his body.

You're safe, he thought and watched as she inclined her head. The scout suit she wore was pristine, brand new.

Yes.

I'm glad.

She clasped her hands behind her back. *Are you?*

Her thought lashed out at him, a slap in the face. His breath hitched at the unexpected onslaught. *You're still angry.*

How perceptive of you. Her face looked smooth as a mask; her eyes glittered.

The ship. Of course. *I'm sorry. I know you wanted to do it yourself, but you were growing so weak. I did what I had to do to save your strength for later.*

You mean you did what you wanted to. Shalon's smile tasted bitter as gall in his head. *How does it feel to have eased your conscience at my expense?*

No. He tried to lift his arm toward her and found he couldn't move. *I lost control but—*

Don't bother, Andor. I know.

Confusion slipped between the spaces in his thoughts. *Know what?*

You opened yourself to me, remember? I saw everything. Including the meeting between you and Ru-ad.

Around him, the curtains stopped moving, still as the waiting air.

Do you remember that, Andor? Or have you blanked it out, like I did, for a time? Shalon tilted her head, watching him as though he was some rare species of bug. *Did you manage to forget that infinite minute when you thought how easy it would be to go along with him? How easy it would be to just let me die. How all those feelings you didn't want—all those problems you'd never expected—would be dealt with in one stroke.*

Shalon, I tried to stop him.

You gave him a false sense of security. And look at what he did with it. Her lip curled. *Ru-ad believed in what he was doing. He had an excuse. You betrayed me. It might as well have been you raping me on that ship.*

He squeezed his eyes shut, trying to ignore the pain that swept through him. Hers—and his. *Shalon.* He looked up at her. *I made a horrible mistake.*

I know. It will be your last. With me anyway.

Don't do something you will—

Regret? Her gaze roamed over his face as if memorizing it. Her sadness flooded him—and her determination.

You have no conception of what they did to me, or your useless platitudes would stick in your throat. Just know this. Never speak to me again. Stay out of my head.

Shalon. He tried to touch her, desperate to hold on to her. His arm would not move. *Don't do this.*

You're dead to me, Andor. She straightened and her gaze went to the opposite side of the bed. *Do you hear me? I'll never forgive you for this. Never.*

Without warning, in the space between one breath and the next, she was gone.

Shalon! Andor thought, the word echoing in his head, a shout in an empty room.

His eyes opened and he saw white curtains stretched above his head. Still as clouds caught on old-fashioned photographs.

"Shalon," he whispered.

"Andor?" The soft voice had come from his left. He turned his head, hoping against hope.

Niala stood there, joyous realization spreading across her face. She grabbed his hand where it lay on the bed and squeezed it, allowing a rare smile to grace her features.

"You're awake. You're finally awake. Ha-Ka, Ku and I had almost given up hope."

He closed his eyes, searching for the connection that had always kept him and Shalon together. The pull of her personality. Her warmth and vibrancy.

But there was nothing. *Awake. I'm awake and alone.*

"She's gone," he murmured and heard the concern in Niala's voice when she spoke.

"What? Who's gone, Andor? What's the matter?"

But there was nothing he could say to give voice to his loss. Nothing at all.

IV

Shalon sat up, gasping for breath. One of her hands clawed at the wall next to her bunk. The other remained caught in an immovable hold.

"For fuck's sake, take it easy, girl. I'm not going to hurt you."

Chris sat on the bunk next to her, his hand on her wrist, restraining her. Behind him, the Oux watched, crouched down as if to protect itself.

You felt it, didn't you? Every last bit of it. Desolation spread through her, her mind was empty and scoured. Andor was gone, and now she was truly alone. Alone with her memories and a body so sullied, it barely felt like hers sometimes.

She tugged her hand from his, rubbing at the place he had touched. Chris raised his hands in the air, palms toward her as if surrendering. She flushed.

"Don't ever touch me without my permission."

Chris shrugged. "I was just doing my bit to keep you from hurting yourself. Next time, I'll let you claw your eyes out. No problem."

She ignored him and met the Oux's gaze. "You're sure he's in his own body now?"

"He's sure," Chris replied. "For all the good it will do the bastard."

She glared at him, but Chris waved a hand. "I'm not eavesdropping. I'm connected to Oux, remember? He showed me the guy in the black coat. I get that I'm just part of a greater plan that involves getting you to safety, but that means fuck all to me. I signed on for my own reasons and Oux understood that. If you want to stay hidden, you're going to have to forget your boyfriend and start thinking about saving your own skin."

"It's none of your business, so I'd appreciate it if you shut up about him. " Shalon said, her voice stiff as her spine as she drew away from him, into the corner where the two walls met. Chris folded his arms.

"Whatever. I could give a shit. There's only one thing I care about and you know what that is."

Sure. You want me to do your bidding. And I don't want anything but to be left alone.

She looked out the portal that would soon be empty of ships and filled with endless, star-sprinkled space. *I want to be out there on my own. No rules, no people to worry about. Just me and the darkness.*

She did not look at him. "So we're going to be at this Pirates Rock place in two days. What's it like there?"

"Hell." Chris replied. "But it's a hell I understand. Stick with me and you'll be fine."

No, I won't.

<<Not so. Hurt One heal.>>

Shalon looked at Oux and shook her head. "You have no idea what you're talking about."

<<Heal. Some day.>>

"You want to heal me?" Shalon said. "Then get whatever you put in me out of me."

<<Help heal faster.>>

"I don't want anything else inside me, and I certainly don't want *him* in my head whenever he likes. I have enough to deal with on my own. Get the fuck *out*."

There was no mistaking what she meant. Chris rose silently and left the room. Oux remained still for a long time, then placed a hand on her bare palm. A rush of warmth tingled Shalon's fingers and she glimpsed a faded, yellow aura around her fingers before the Oux drew back.

<<Done.>>

"Good," Shalon said. Then she lowered her face into her hands to hide tears that had sprung from her shattered heart.

V

Major Jamal Vernon heard the door to his hospital suite open, but he didn't turn his head to see who had come in. He continued to stare at the azure sky through the old fashioned glass window as clouds drifted past.

In a voice like nails scratched across metal, he said, "I told you I didn't want anything, nurse."

"And I'm sure she understood you the first time around."

He swung his head around so fast, he made himself nauseous. An impeccably dressed man stood next to his bed. His blond hair was cut in a fashionable short style, and his eyes were yellow. He smiled at Jamal as if he were meeting an old and dear friend. It was a smile that did not quite reach his eyes.

"Hello, Major Vernon."

Jamal frowned and forced words from his throat, still sore from the repairs made to his crushed larynx. "Who—?"

"You'd better save your voice. Don't want to ruin all that work the doctors did." The man sat in the conform chair that faced his bed. "I heard about your loss. I'm very sorry."

Flax. Jamal clenched his fist on the sheets, oblivious to the pain the action woke, his thoughts chaotic. "Who the hell are you?"

"You see, we have something in common, Major Vernon, only you don't realize it."

"I—"

"Your voice, Major Vernon. Please. Let me do the talking." He steepled his hands under his chin and leaned forward in his chair. His red suit glimmered like rubies.

"You don't know this, but the woman that put you in that bed, the same woman that killed your fiancé and your liaison, Maridon Hawkes, also killed my father."

My God. He knows who she is. The man read the look on his face and inclined his head.

"Yes, Major Vernon, I know her. But that information, such as it is, will come at a cost."

Jamal croaked out. "Obstruction."

"Major, do not waste your time with threats. The law cannot touch me, any more than you can, lying there in that bed. However, I do have a proposition for you, one that should benefit us both. Will you hear it?"

Jamal fought with himself, with the urge to flick the sensor on the end of his finger and summon the nurse. But in his mind's eye, he saw Michael seizing on the bed and the woman standing over him and rage swelled inside him. He knew what he had to do. He nodded.

"You're as sensible as your Lieutenant Hawkes was. He was a great help to me and due to his unfortunate death I find that I must replace him now. I need someone on the inside. He did it for the money, of course, but you—you would never be so crass, would you? I can tell you're a man of moral fiber. A rare thing."

Maridon, a snitch. I should have known. He was always underfoot.

The man lowered his hands to grip the soft arms of the chair. "But I digress. I can give you information about this woman. Who she is, what she's like, anything that I know that could help you find her, but on several conditions." He met Jamal's gaze with a steady amber one. "First, you will never question me on how I know this woman. Second, any information I give you cannot be traced back to me. You cannot use it in your reports or in any way that could lead your fellow officers to question the source of your information. Our relationship must remain between us. Last, when you do find her—you must kill her."

The man leaned forward, his face set in stone. "That is the most important and non-negotiable condition. She killed my father and ripped me away from all I know. I want no trials, no incarcerations, only her death. I don't care how you do it, but if you agree, I guarantee I will do everything in my power to deliver her to you. Is it a deal?"

To have a chance to catch her. To take her life with my own hands. Jamal shivered, curling his fingers against his side. Anger coursed through him and goosebumped his skin. *You don't know what you're offering me. You have no idea.*

"I never killed before," he rasped.

"Then the woman that took your lover is a good place to start, don't you think? Or didn't Mr. Zorida mean that much to you?"

You could never know what he meant to me. You could never understand.

"I'm sick."

"But you won't be for long, Major Vernon. You'll heal, be reinstated." The man gave him another brief, heartless smile. "I think you'll find that I'm quite patient."

"If I refuse?"

"We part company, here and now. No harm done. But," he shrugged, "I'll get someone else to do it for me. Think about it,

Major Vernon. Your chance for revenge is what I'm offering you and in the process, you'll be taking a killer off the streets. It's a win for everyone."

He's using me to do his dirty work. As an officer, I shouldn't even be listening to him.

Yet I am. Because he's right. He's absolutely right. If I don't take his offer, how am I going to find her? There are no leads, and her trail is weeks cold. This way, I have help, information—and carte blanche to do what I really want to.

"I do things my way?" he asked.

"Major, I don't care how you do it, as long as it's done."

Jamal didn't speak for a few minutes, struggling with the last remnants of his ethics. Ethics that had done nothing to save Michael in the end.

The man started to rise. "Perhaps I underestimated your need for justice."

"No." Jamal met the stranger's gaze, feeling a strange calm settle over him. He had made his decision. There would be no going back. The anger that had burned bright in him every day since he awakened to find Michael gone became banked, sizzling embers.

The man studied him, then sat down. "I'm glad you feel that way." He extended his hand. "You may call me Tu-dan."

Jamal hesitated for a second, and then grasped Tu-dan's strong fingers in his own.

CHAPTER 22

When you have faults, do not fear to abandon them.
—*Confucius*

I

We're not done with you yet. Not by a long shot.

Shalon shot upright, a cry locked in the back of her throat. Her heart thrummed in her chest, each beat painful. Despite the darkness of her bedroom, she saw the Oux blinking at her from the chair opposite her bed.

I'm not on the ship. I'm in the hotel. It was just another nightmare, that's all.

She swallowed, running damp hands over her sweaty face. The coolness of the room could not ease the fever-like heat that pulsed beneath her skin.

I'm so tired of these damn dreams.

She hadn't had nightmares this intense since her parents died. Then, thanks to her perfect memory, the dreams had been just as vivid, just as intense.

But I had Andor. He helped me through it. Kept me sane.

That was before he betrayed me.

Shalon lay down on her pillow again, tossing the thin cotton sheets away and allowing cool air to waft over her bare legs.

Is that what he did, though? Ru-ad was like a father to him. Is it so wrong that he tried to find a way to save him from making a mistake?

R. S. A. GARCIA

He could have stopped Ru-ad. He could have told me what Ru-ad was planning. She flipped over on her side and ground her fist into the mattress. She was tired. Tired of the self-pity. Tired of trying to figure out what she could have done differently. In one half of her mind, she never got on the ship, had instead stayed with Andor, content to live her life and leave Gilene Conway to hers.

But I had to have revenge. And I knew the only way to get it was to leave Orgala. I had to satisfy the need to see that woman suffer. Twice now, I let her ruin my life.

Shalon lay on her stomach, grinding her face into the pillow, trying not to think. But it didn't work. Because she knew it wasn't just Gilene who had ruined her life.

I got myself into this. Ru-ad played me and Andor like the naïve fools we were. I was too busy planning revenge to see past his motives. If I had thought past my old anger, just once, I would have seen through him. If I had just listened to Andor and held off, Ru-ad would never have felt threatened enough to try to kill me in the first place.

Shalon lifted her face from the pillow, her lips trembling. *And what happened on the ship—that wasn't all Andor. I wanted revenge, and I took it. I let him use me to kill. I was in control enough to save Michael when it mattered. What happened wasn't Andor's fault. Or Gilene's. Or Ru-ad's. It was mine. I brought this on myself.*

She heard Oux coming toward her, but she couldn't move, couldn't breathe.

I'm Shalon Conway, daughter of Jason and Falon Conway, heir to Conway Enterprises. And I've wasted my life yearning for petty things and pretending I'm normal, when I'm not.

Oux's hand caught hold of her arm, a comforting heaviness.

I have to remember that I'm alone in this world. Andor, Ku, Ha-Ka— they were good to me, but they blinded me. Made me weak. I have to make my own way. My mother saved my life for something much bigger than revenge. I can't afford to ignore that any longer.

Shalon sat up and Oux's arm fell away from her. She swung her legs over the side of her bed, breathing hard in the wake of her speeding heartbeat.

I can't waste time being scared in this room anymore. I have to learn to keep going. I have to learn to survive outside Orgala. Because if I don't, someday, when the man in black calls on me, I won't be ready. And that can't happen. My parents' death can't be in vain.

She threw her head back, staring at the ceiling. The Oux hopped up on the bed next to her and she looked at him, wiping the sudden blurriness out of her eyes as she did so.

"I've been a fool, haven't I? I blamed him for all of it when I was part of it too."

The Oux didn't reply, its large eyes somehow sympathetic. Shalon put her head in her hands.

"All those people. I killed them. I gave in to the anger and the pain and just let myself go. I let myself lose control. I don't ever want that to happen again. But the worst part—" she barked a laugh, "—the worst part is I understand what Andor did and I can't forgive him. Because he should have known better. Just like me."

She dragged her hands through her hair.

"So what do I do now? What do I do? Because I have to get back on track. I have to take back what's mine. I have to be ready for what's coming."

Shalon sighed and glanced at the alien. "Any suggestions?"

Oux fluttered its fingers. "Is. Is."

Shalon frowned for a while, then her brow cleared and a bitter smile spread over her face. "Of course. Is."

··· — — — ···

Chris woke the instant the door to his room opened. His hand was under the pillow, grasping the butt of his lasgun before he realized who had entered.

"Shalon?"

She remained in the doorway, light from the sitting room backlighting her dark shape, the Oux crouched at her feet. He sat up, his hand still under the pillow, just in case.

"Light," she said and he blinked in the sudden illumination, scrubbing his free hand across sleep blurred eyes.

"What do you want?"

"I need you to understand something." She said and he saw the determined look in her green eyes. *Well, what do you know. She's finally ready to talk.*

"I don't care about why you're going after the Conways. I don't even care where you've been or what you've done. But I'm not doing this just for a few credits. I want something more from you."

He let go of the gun and tossed his sheets aside. "You took so long to come to me, I had just about decided to leave you here.

What makes you think you're in a position to ask for anything?"

"You're the one who came asking," she said. "So I'm naming my price."

He laughed as he got to his feet. "We have a price now? I guess that whole not trusting me didn't last long."

"Don't be ridiculous. I don't trust you. But you can give me things I need."

He folded his arms across his bare chest. "Like what?"

"Control. Knowledge." She moved to stand in front of him, graceful and languid as a cat. The expression on her face unsettled him, made him wary. *What the hell is she up to?*

"I think you know how to land on your feet, no matter what. I want you to teach me everything you know about surviving in this world. You can do that, can't you?"

"Sure I can. If I want to."

She seemed to understand. "If I agree to help you, then you'll want to? Is that it?"

"Give the girl a thousand credits."

"Don't call me that." Her lips were a thin line. "Do we have a deal?"

He let her sweat for a few minutes. "We have a deal."

"One more thing. The Oux will need a name."

"It's got a name."

"That's not a name, that's a function. He's a lot more than just a battery for you. Besides, he's changing. Growing up, maybe. He will need to start over. Just like the rest of us." Chris barely caught the last few words, whispered under her breath as they were.

"Why does this even matter?"

She said harshly, "Because he's part of this, and he's not a pet. You need to respect that. You've had him in a circus, for god's sake. If we do this, you can't use him like that anymore. Oux will decide on a name. When he does, you should use it."

All this passion. Where's it coming from, I wonder? He folded his arms. "Fine. When *it* decides. The circus days are over anyway. We'll be moving up in the world."

She turned to leave.

"What made you change your mind?"

"Do you really care?"

"Once I get the ball rolling, we won't be able to back out. I won't risk my life if you can't go all the way."

"Chris," she said softly, "if there's one thing I've learned I can do, it's make a decision and stick with it. All the way. I keep my promises."

"That doesn't answer my question."

He saw her shoulders shift as she folded her arms. "Every action has consequences. Gilene Conway has managed to avoid any for years now. I'd be lying if I didn't say that part of me wants my face to be the last thing she sees, but revenge won't help anything. She's been running my father's company, twisting his legacy to her own ends for ten years. I can't imagine how many lives she's destroyed. How many people she's killed, broken. That's not what my father would have wanted." She paused and said in a voice so low, he almost missed it, "Or my mother."

"So you're going to set things right, is that it?" He didn't bother to hide the sarcasm in his voice.

"Yes. I'll do whatever it takes to make sure that Gilene Conway won't be able to do to anyone else what she did to me."

"Please. You think you're better than me? That you have some sort of higher ideal? It's still revenge."

"It's called justice," she answered, her voice soft. "And it is very different from revenge."

"Well, whatever you call it, you just be sure it doesn't get in my fucking way."

"Funny." She looked back at him, and the expression on her face was harder than a Madinah's exoskeleton. "I was just about to tell you the same thing."

Chris studied her as she walked away. *Well, well, little girl. Maybe you were worth saving after all. You've got balls. Where you're going, you're going to need them.*

There is no Pattern without the Weaver.
There is no Weaver without the Will.
—*Message of the Will*
Book of the Seven Holies
Ancient Dak Scripture

CHAPTER 23

People in prophecies rarely have happy endings.
—*Dak proverb*

PortCity
Three years later

Colin tossed his jacket across the chair by his front door and stood scrubbing his hands across his face, trying to work warmth back into his skin.

"Good evening, Colin." The soothing voice of his new housekeeper Program filled the living area. "It's nice to have you home again."

Two days of non-stop lectures and surgeries. Trust me, you're not as happy as I am. Which, he reminded himself, was a silly thought. Habitat Programs, after all, were not capable of emotions.

"It's nice to be home, Beatrice." Colin rolled his head on his neck in an attempt to relieve the tense muscles there. "Any messages?"

"One, from Ranie. She arrived safely at Pontrachain and will call you tomorrow."

Hope she remembers to take some time off from the conference circuit to visit the beaches. Colin walked toward the archway directly in front of him. Colored beads that made a silvery sound when they were touched hung on thin strands and obscured the opening to the kitchen. Next to that archway, the door to his bedroom was ajar and he could see his neatly made bed beyond.

317

The tinted windows to his right let in a view of a misty city, obscured and fractured by a million diamonds rolling down the transperiwall in a ceaseless pattern. He hardly glanced at the view, which had lost its beauty for him after a long drive in the rain.

"I warmed a dinner for you in the dispenser. Chicken Alfredo. The latest newsholos are ready for playback and there's hot water for your shower."

Colin paused. *A hot shower.* He changed direction and headed for the door to his bedroom instead. "Playback please. Audio only."

The breathy, excited voice of a male news anchor chased him as he stripped off his white wrap shirt and dark trousers and stepped into the shower.

"Our top stories of the hour. Earth officials, prompted by lobbying from Conway Enterprises and other corporations, have voted to grant New Mars special admittance into the Terran Federation of Nation-States. Janus Corp has announced plans for a new starship line, and confusion here on Serron as customers of First Intergalactic Bank experience closed doors and a downed comm site all afternoon today. Details in five minutes."

During the pause, Colin soaped his blond hair, trimmed and highlighted at Ranie's insistence just before she left. "I'm not leaving you to go to those lectures looking like a hobo," she'd said. So he'd submitted to his barber's ministrations despite his ambivalence. They'd agreed to end their relationship and remain friends over two years ago, but she still looked out for him. Sometimes he felt guilty, knowing it was his fault they'd broken up, his confused feelings that had been the last straw. Other times, with Anton having moved away from Serron to take up a post on a deep-space colony, he was just glad he still had a good friend around.

"To the news. New Mars has attained inclusion into the 172 member Terran Federation of Nation-States."

The voice came to an abrupt halt as a tone sounded.

"Colin, I'm sorry to interrupt, but there are two people downstairs asking to see you."

He switched off the water, a slight frown marring his brow. "They didn't identify themselves?"

"No, and they are blocking my identity scan."

What the hell? Well, even if they don't have ID chips, they can't block the cameras. Colin stepped out of the shower and grabbed at the towel on the rack. Rubbing at his hair and looking into the mirror, he said, "Show me. Head view only."

A colored wash of pixels coalesced over the reflective surface. The accompanying audio was faint and tinny. Rain filled the room with the sound of white noise, and the tarmac behind the cloaked figures glistened. The holocam showed two bent heads. The water-soaked, dark brown material of the hoods that hid the visitors from view looked like oil ran off it. The figures stood so close together, their heads would have touched if one had not been at least a foot shorter than the other.

Colin settled his towel around his damp neck, curious, but not worried. Not yet. "Beatrice, keep the precinct link on standby, just in case."

"Of course, Colin. Already done."

To the holoimage, he said, "Can I help you?"

The shorter figure looked up.

Colin's fingers tightened around the ends of the wet towel as he stared into green eyes fringed with dripping lashes. The rest of the face was unfamiliar. Pale when it should have been tan, the cheekbones too high, the lips a bit too full. But those eyes.

"My God," he whispered. *It can't be. Not after all this time.*

Her voice came through the speakers, calm, far off—and unmistakable. "I need to see you, Colin."

He dragged the towel from around his neck, twisted it around his right fist. *It's her. It really is Shalon.* And just like that, his balanced world came off its fulcrum and fell away from him. Questions filled his head and his lips tried to shape them, but no sound came out. A thought crossed his mind—he would need to put some clothes on.

"It's me, Colin. Are you going to let me in?"

There was a tone in her voice he could not place. He gave his head a little shake, trying to dislodge the confusion. "Yes. Come on up. I mean, Beatrice, let them in."

He hurried into the bedroom as the front door to the apartment complex opened behind him with a loud click.

"It is not advisable that you allow strangers into the complex given their ability to block my scans."

Colin pulled a clean shirt out of a drawer and touched it closed. "She's not a stranger."

"I do not have her identity on file."

"I knew her before I downloaded the habitat Program.

Beatrice, I'd like you to stop recording until I tell you to begin again."

"Certainly, Colin."

He dragged his pants on with difficulty over his damp skin and half-walked, half-hopped to the entrance. He was tucking his shirt in when Beatrice announced, "They're at the door."

"Open," he said.

The door slid to the right, and Shalon stepped into the room. She had thrown her hood back and her cloak dripped water in a pit-pat rhythm onto his cream-colored carpet. The tall figure moved with her, head still bent forward. He realized that her arm was wrapped around the person's waist. He frowned, looking from Shalon to the figure and back again. *Her hair is different too. Blond now. And so short.*

"Shalon?"

"I'm sorry, Colin," she said, "I didn't know where else to turn."

"Who is that?"

She moved past him and sat the cloaked figure in the overstuffed chair near the door. As the head fell back, the cloak gaped open and Colin drew in a breath as he glimpsed a neatly trimmed red beard, and a face too pale to be healthy. *Chris! Of all the people I never thought I'd see again.*

"He's been shot and he contracted some kind of infection." Kneeling in front of the chair, Shalon started to undo Chris' cloak with brisk movements. *All that water will ruin the chair,* Colin thought randomly as he took a step toward her.

"He should be in a hospital."

Shalon's fingers stilled. "He should be. But I can't take him there."

"We could go to the Clinic."

She turned and looked at him, her face set in serious lines. *Why do you look so different?* he wondered. And then something in her gaze hit him and he understood everything. *Remember how she left here. Nothing's changed since then except the authorities haven't found her.* Swallowing past the sudden bitterness in the back of his throat, he asked, "Fugitives?"

She nodded. Water slid down her cheeks like tears and steam had started to rise from her self-warming cloak. "I'm sorry to do this, to just show up on your doorstep after three years and ask something like this of you, but I had no choice. Will you help us?"

Colin glanced at the unconscious Chris. *What are you still doing with this jerk?* he wanted to say. What surprised him was the thin sliver of jealousy that had slipped into his heart.

"Colin, if it's too much, we'll leave." She rose to her feet. Her cloak swung open, revealing a tasteful suit that covered her from neck to ankles in skin-tight, baby-blue glitter. It was gorgeous and nothing like what he thought she would ever wear. *Where have you been, Shalon? And what have you been doing all these years?*

"I'm sorry," Shalon said, taking his silence the wrong way, her voice brisk as she turned back to the chair. "We'll go somewhere else."

"Wait." Colin closed a hand on her shoulder. The cloak was slick and warm as blood under his fingers. She stiffened under his touch, her muscles unbending as metal. She turned her head to the right, but did not quite look over her shoulder at him. The mellow light limned her blond hair like a halo. His fingers clenched on her shoulder for a moment and then he let his hand fall away.

I can't turn you away and I can't refuse you.

"Help me get him into the bedroom," he said.

--- — — — ---

When he came out, wiping damp hands on a towel, Shalon was standing in front of the transperiwall, looking out at the storm that raged outside. Her cloak had dried and lay in a matte heap on the yellow sofa near the wall. Her suit dazzled the eye a little, but she had lowered the lights, dimming the shine. She said, "It's getting bad out there."

He stopped behind the sofa, just looking at her for a moment. *Twenty-one going on forty. You're all grown up. I wish I knew what you were thinking. And why you're here now.*

"Your face is different. You look more like I remember you now."

She shrugged. "It was a disguise. I dissolved the polymers, wiped off the makeup."

Makes sense. But that's not the important thing right now. "Shalon, he was sick before he got shot, wasn't he?" he asked.

She turned to look at him, leaning a shoulder against the wall as she folded her arms across her chest. A frown marred her smooth brow. "How did you know?"

"He has an infection all right. Spacer fever. A nasty little virus that spreads in enclosed, artificial environments. He's been off world recently?"

"A couple of weeks ago. But he said it was just the flu."

"The initial stages would have felt like that. It's not usually fatal, but if you injure yourself or develop a secondary infection, your weakened immune system causes you to go downhill very quickly."

"Can you help him?"

"It would be better if I could get him to the Clinic."

Shalon shook her head. "I'm sorry, but that's impossible. They're looking for us."

"Who's they?" *Your ruthless family? The authorities?*

She looked out at the torrents coming down outside. "It's hard to explain. You're better off not knowing too much."

"Shalon." He tossed the towel onto the back of the sofa between them and grasped the chair with both hands, leaning his weight onto them. "You show up at my apartment in the middle of the night after three years with no contact, ask me to save a very sick man who's been shot, and you think you can pull that kind of crap on me?"

She glanced at him, her green eyes amused, her lips crinkling at the edges. "Same old Colin."

Don't. Don't dredge up a past it took me so long to bury. Unexpectedly painful emotion made him grip the chair and say, "If you want my help, you'd better start talking."

She considered him, then nodded her head, just once. "Your habitat Program?"

"I dealt with her already."

Shalon turned so that her back touched the transperiwall and folded her hands behind her. "You won't like what you hear. I hope you can understand it though."

Colin sighed and sat on the sofa. "Try me."

She seemed to pull into herself, as if gathering her thoughts. "Have you watched the news today?"

"A little."

"Then you know that First Intergalactic Bank had some problems."

"Sure. They closed early."

She met his gaze. "This morning, just before lunch, Chris and I robbed their main office in PortCity."

The silence weighed on him like a stone. "You're kidding, right?"

She shook her head, never breaking eye contact.

"That's impossible!"

"That's what they thought too."

"But how?"

"It doesn't matter how."

"I have a sick bank robber in my room and I'm not about to report him, trust me."

She sighed. "The long and short of it is, the bank maintains a small overdraft account in the name of the Conway family. It's accessible, but to transfer or empty it, a Conway has to go in personally, pass the genetic ID checks and do the paperwork. Chris and I posed as Conways—husband and wife—and I transferred the account into several automatic forwarding accounts in the underworld Blacknet. From there, the money will be passed on in a rapid non-stop cycle to numerous offworld accounts for several weeks until the trail is cold and I can retrieve it. We ran out of luck on our way out, though, and he got shot." She shrugged. "I knew they would be watching all the hospitals and clinics, and I didn't know where else to go for help, so I came here."

"But how did you know where to find me? I could have changed apartments since then." He paused, reading the shift in her expression. "You spied on me?"

"After the way I left, I just wanted to be sure you were okay." She looked away.

"How often?"

"Only when I was in town."

And you never contacted me. Not once. He turned his mind away from those thoughts, aware that he didn't want to deal with the emotion behind them. The disappointment and frustration. *I wondered where you were every night. And you were right there. Close enough to touch.*

But that means she cared. Maybe as much as I did. He squashed the small voice inside him that caught and held on to that revelation, focusing on the conversation instead.

"What you're telling me—it's never been done."

"Until now." She pulled a hand out from behind her back and tugged at the collar of her suit, loosening it. "If we're found, however, their perfect record will be safe."

"Shalon."

She looked at him and he let her read his expression. She smiled, and it was like watching a ray of sunlight falling through overcast skies. "Thank you."

You're welcome.

"So, how much did you get?" he asked, trying for flippancy to lighten the charged atmosphere between them.

"A little over twenty trillion credits."

Holy shit.

Shalon's lips twitched. "I wouldn't let my face stay like that too long if I were you."

He closed his mouth. *That's a small overdraft account?*

"What the hell are you going to do with that kind of money?"

"Split it three ways between myself, Chris and Garner, our accomplice. Whatever they do with their share is their business. As for me." He saw a strange look come into her eye. "I've always wanted a spaceship."

"Well, you can certainly afford one now." He stood, smiling a little. "I should probably charge you for my services."

Shalon shrugged her shoulders. "After all you've done for me, I'd be willing to pay just about any price you name."

Her green eyes locked with his. Surprise jolted through him as he realized she wasn't necessarily talking about money, and he turned away, picking up the towel off the sofa. "So where's this Garner you mentioned?"

"Laying low. He's getting our transport off Serron ready. When Chris is better, we'll leave."

"You must trust this guy a lot. What if he runs off with the money on his own?"

"I trust him implicitly. And no one can withdraw the money but me, so there's no chance of betrayal."

"You covered all your bases."

"I try."

The soft cadence of her voice made him feel—strange. Distracted. Anxious to get away from Shalon and all the unwelcome thoughts that accompanied her presence, he said, "I can help Chris, but I will have to make a trip to the Clinic for medications and you'll have to wait here for me and make sure you keep the cooling sheets on him. Can you do that?"

"Of course."

He started toward the bedroom door.

"Colin."

He stopped.

"It's good to see you again."

He swallowed and said, "It's good to see you too."

$\cdots$ — — $\cdots$

Chris' illness was advanced and he did not immediately respond to Colin's treatments. For two days, Colin worked on him with Shalon's help. She kept constant vigil by the delirious man's bed and often held him down when Colin needed to administer medication. Sometimes, she stroked his forehead and whispered to him in the lyrical Earth language she told him was French.

"He can't speak it, but he likes how it sounds," she told him with a shift of her strong, narrow shoulders, and jealousy had caused him to excuse himself to the kitchen. When she moved, a silver tattoo on her upper left arm caught the light, and for the first time, he noticed that the unfamiliar symbol matched a smaller one on the inside of Chris' left wrist. Three dots within a circle. It made him wonder just what their relationship was.

Shalon took to wearing his clothes, mostly his shorts and any sleeveless T-shirt she could find. The first time he saw her in his clothes, he lost his train of thought for a moment. Shalon's knowing smile turned his mouth dry, but he made up an excuse about needing to check on Chris and left the room.

Ranie had called as promised, but he said nothing about Shalon and Chris. It was strange to see and hear her on the vidphone and know that a gulf separated them, even in the face of her smile and animated chatter. He was lying to her again, but there was no way that he could tell her the truth without risking Shalon's life.

On the third day, Chris' temperature fell slightly and they felt safe taking a break, heading out into the living area to watch a few mindless holos. They talked, though not the way he would have liked. Shalon found ways around most topics, but he was curious about every facet of her life since they had parted ways.

"Where have you been all this time?" he asked, tucking a hand under the side of his head as he lay on the floor. Shalon sat in a lotus position on the sofa, eating some kind of creamy concoction from a bowl.

"Around. Here and there. No one place in particular."

"What did you do all these years?'

"Colin, bless you for thinking the best of me, but I just robbed a bank." She licked her lips and grinned. "What did you think I did before that? Nursing?"

He flushed, feeling like an idiot. *Which you are, for asking that lame question.* She noticed and her grin faded. "Sorry. I can be really curt.

We mostly observed our targets. We had to work our way into the family of two of my cousins so we could pretend to be them. It took us quite a while."

"I'll bet." He sat up and leaned his back against the sofa. "What happened to that alien that was with you? Oux?"

"He's still with me. We call him Garner now."

He twisted to stare up at her. "It's your accomplice? But how?"

She shrugged and took another bite off her fork. "Things have changed a bit since you last saw us. But you—are you still with Ranie?"

He shook his head. "That ended a while ago."

She ran a pink tongue along one finger, catching a dollop of sauce. "I'm sorry to hear that. She was a good person and she tried to help me."

He turned away to stare at the holoshow. "Yes, well, I was lying to her every day, and she didn't deserve that, so I decided the best thing to do was to end it."

He did not have to specify what the lies were about. The heavy silence that followed told him she knew exactly what he was talking about.

After a while, she said, "I don't want to complicate your life, Colin. I'll be out of your hair just as soon as Chris is able to travel."

"I don't doubt that." He worried the soft fur of the cushions with his fingers. "Thanks."

"What about the Clinic?"

"I took a few days off. What the hell. I'm the boss, right?"

Softly she repeated, "You're the boss."

Feeling disturbed and uncomfortable, he cast about for something to say. "You got a tattoo, I see. Chris has the same one, right?"

She shifted behind him, and her smooth legs extended down past his head, toes burrowing into the soft carpet. She had used a lotion to change her skin back from the pale coloring of her cousin to her own natural tan. "Conways get married according to Neo-Catholic rights. That means an indelible, unfakable tattoo."

But that means… "You're married?" She must have heard the incredulity in his voice. She laughed and ruffled quick fingers through his hair in a causal gesture. Her touch traveled downward from the top of his scalp to the soles of his feet. Shalon rose to walk back to the kitchen and he watched her go, grateful she did not look back to see the effect her touch had on him.

"I wouldn't call it marriage. Let's just say, everything worked out the way it was supposed to."

- - - —— —— —— - - -

Two days later several things became clear to Colin.

Shalon wasn't the person he'd met three years before. She was harder, more focused, and more guarded. He wondered how much of that had to do with Chris. Which made him think two very uncomfortable thoughts.

Chris was on the mend and would awaken soon.

And he was hopelessly attracted to Shalon.

He left her taking a shower in his room that night, and sat on the sofa, staring out at the clear night outside, wondering what he had gotten himself into.

Of all the stupid things to do. You know you're wasting your time.

But I've always felt something between us. She feels it too, I think.

You can't act on it. It can't go anywhere.

He closed his eyes and leaned his head back against the sofa. *But she makes me feel…alive.*

"Hey."

He opened his eyes. Shalon leaned against the wall, her hands behind her back. He hadn't heard her come in. Her tanned skin looked like caramel in the dim light against her white shorts. Her slender legs were crossed at the ankle. A white cotton undershirt of his accentuated her bare, muscled arms, and he caught the silver wink of the tattoo on her left arm.

She cocked her head to the right a little and the light caught in her midnight hair. *She changed it back.*

"I didn't wake you, did I?" she asked.

He shook his head and sat up straighter. "You dyed your hair?"

She ran long fingers through it self-consciously and smiled. "Yeah. I had a quik-vial with me. I missed it."

"Nice to see it again," he said, without thinking.

"I thought you might like it," she replied.

Silence swelled between them, a pregnant bubble. He could not look away from the unspoken words in her eyes. *Don't. Don't, Shalon. I want to be stronger than that.*

He stood. "I'm getting a drink. Do you want anything?"

"Yes," she said. "But not a drink."

He broke her mesmerizing stare and went to the kitchen.

His heart beat in his chest to the rhythm of the blood pulsing through his groin. His mouth tasted like paper. When he reached the kitchen, he ordered a glass of water out of the dispenser and stood over the counter by the sink, holding the chill cylinder. He stared into the transparent depths unseeingly.

The gentle chime of the beads behind him made him close his eyes and set the glass down. He grasped the edge of the counter with both hands, the better to keep them to himself.

"Shalon."

Her arms slid around his waist and the gentle pressure of her breasts against his back made his breath come faster. The soft, moist touch of her lips brushed across the back of his neck. He clenched his fingers on the cool, rounded plastic.

"Don't tempt me like this."

"Don't run away from me," she murmured, and nuzzled his ear. Her fingers brushed higher, easing across his chest. Her tongue flicked into his ear, a secret, knee-buckling caress.

To hell with it.

He turned in the circle of her arms and slid one arm around her waist, dragging her against his chest. His mouth slammed into hers, hungry and desperate. She parted her lips willingly under the assault and he tasted mint from her mouth cleanser and the faint sweetness of her flesh. Her hand clenched on his back as she strained closer to him.

This is crazy. She's a fugitive. A married fugitive.

He let his other hand come up to tease the down-soft hair at the edge of her neck. She made a sound in her throat and he slanted his head, his cheeks hollowing as he fought to taste more of her.

Then why does this feel so right?

Shalon brought her hands forward to stroke his arms in an oddly gentle, reverent action that made his muscles quiver.

You already know the answer to that.

He tore his lips away from hers and she leaned into him, trying to recapture his mouth. Colin grasped her upper arms and held her still.

"What is this?"

"You tell me," she said, and drew a finger across his bicep. "Whatever you want. No promises beyond tonight. No strings attached."

Colin's skin jumped under her touch, and his own thumbs betrayed him, rubbing back and forth over the firm, smooth flesh of her arms. *If I go any further down this road, I'll never be able to turn back.*

Maybe it's too late anyway. I don't know. I only know she's here. Offering me what I've dreamed of for so long without even realizing it.

"Do you love him?" he asked.

Shalon pulled back a little for the first time, her face assuming that curiously blank expression it always did when she felt threatened. "Why would you ask that?"

"You brought him here at great risk to yourself. You could have just abandoned him."

"He saved my life once. I couldn't do that. Anyway, why does it matter?"

He shook her slightly. "It matters."

She smiled a sad smile. "Walk away. I won't stop you."

He stared at her, stricken, unsure what to say and knowing only what he ached to do. She moved for him, bringing his hand up to slide it under the edge of her T-shirt and touch sun-warm flesh. He let his hand rest there for a moment, just feeling her skin, absorbing her warmth.

Before he knew it, he had turned her around so that she was backed up against the counter, her leg pressed firmly between his thighs. Her tongue touched his as he grasped the back of her neck with trembling fingers, and as their lips melded, for the first time in a long time, he stopped thinking and just let himself feel.

··· — — — ···

Shalon collapsed against him, her breathing hard and erratic. Colin's heart pounded in his chest, and the sweat on his body was cold in the wake of the air-conditioning. The soft carpet caressed his legs with butterfly touches and prickled against his back and buttocks. Above him, Shalon's chest rose and fell, soft and slick against his skin. His head spun with the enormity of what he had just done.

But I wouldn't have traded that for the world. Not a single minute of it.

Shalon shifted on him, stroking her fingers over his hair. "I like this look. For once it's not falling in your eyes. You always forget to cut it until it's grown too long."

A bittersweet memory of Ranie touching him the same way crossed his mind, and made him jerk in surprise. Shalon's fingers stilled and she propped herself up on her hand. Cool air slid between them. "What is it?"

Colin caught her free hand and kissed it. "Nothing. It's not you.

It's just…" He shook his heads, lost for words. *Ghosts in the room, I guess.*

She leaned forward and kissed him, her tongue a brief caress on the seam of his lips. "I'm not sorry this happened, if that's what you're worried about."

She eased off him, leaving him staring up at the dimmed ceiling. He placed a hand behind his head as she rose up on one elbow and leaned over him.

"You've changed so much." *I feel like I hardly know you. And yet I do. The real you. The person you were before they tried to kill your spirit.* "After what happened, I never thought—"

"That I'd ever be able to be with a man?" She smiled a little at his expression, the curve of her mouth like a half-moon glimpsed behind clouds. "It's okay to talk about it. It took me a long time to learn that." She ran a hand over his bent thigh. "A friend taught me the rest."

Something in him twisted at that. "Was it Chris?"

Shalon's hand teased the line of his groin, and the flesh there jumped involuntarily. "Let's keep this between us, okay? No one else invited." She leaned in to kiss him, but he held her back with a hand splayed across her collarbone.

"My turn," he said and reminded her, "whatever I want."

She laughed, a low intimate sound. "Should I be afraid, doctor?"

"I don't know." He stroked her chin with a finger, marveling at the softness of her skin. "That was amazing, but I want something else." He rose up, kissed the delicate line of her collarbone and followed it to the column of her throat.

She sighed, touching his hair with caressing fingers as he nibbled her neck. "What do you want?"

Colin moved over her, leaning her back onto his left arm. Her hair stroked him as he spread his hand open over the soft skin of her neck. *I love touching you. I never want to stop touching you.*

"I want to make love," he said and saw the flicker of emotion that crossed her face. He had hit on the truth. Seduction was easy for her, because she was in control. But real intimacy didn't exist for her because she didn't have to let her guard down when she was the aggressor. *Well, I don't want what everyone else got. I want you.*

"Colin."

"You asked, Shalon." He kissed her chin, drawing the skin between his lips for a few seconds.

A shudder went through her body. "Colin. No."

LEX TALIONIS

He never taught you anything at all, did he?

"It's what I want," he said and pulled back to look into eyes that were uncertain for the first time. "Trust me."

"Trust." Her laugh was short, painful. "You're asking me to trust someone?"

"Yes." Colin steeled himself against the part of him that wanted to reach out and hold on to her. The part that wanted to drive out all the bad memories and replace them with memories of something new and beautiful. Instead, he nuzzled her ear and whispered, "You did before, remember?"

She pulled away from his touch ever so slightly as he touched her cheek. Her fingers clenched on his shoulders. He ignored them, parting her lips with his finger instead, feeling his stomach clench as she drew it into her hot, moist mouth. She locked gazes with him, lifting her head to follow his retreating hand.

Sorry, darling. You don't get to set the pace this time.

He pulled his finger free and replaced it with his mouth. He slowed his movements, exploring the places she had not known were sensitive, loving the gasp she made when he lifted her arm and trailed his tongue through the salty valleys between her fingers. The tremble in her back when he turned her over and drew his finger down the delicate bumps of her spine.

She turned her head away when he told her in low, intimate words how beautiful she was. How her touch made him feel. It was a long time before he got past her barriers, her need for control, her own practiced game plan to bring him pleasure, taught to her by someone who understood too little about what she really needed. But in the end, she finally understood that she deserved to feel that way. To feel loved.

He saw it in the quiver of her skin, the way her body yearned toward him. Felt it in the urgency of her lips and tongue on his. When he slid into her, she dug her fingers into his shoulders, pressing against him with everything in her, her legs wrapped around his hips. She stretched around him, tight as a closed fist, warm and welcoming as the touch of arms.

He watched her face change, meld from one expression into another, knowing that no one had ever seen that before. Not like this. That the moment was his and his alone. He felt her breath stop, then start again in a soundless, heart-wrenching rush. He watched a tear slip from the corner of her eye and disappear into the line of her dark hair.

331

I love you. It's stupid and pointless and you probably don't care, but it's the truth.

She brought her hands up to frame both sides of his face and he dragged his head around to kiss her palm with a hot, open mouth. She lifted her hips up to meet him as he thrust into her one last time and stilled.

Long minutes later, she stirred beneath him. "Colin," she murmured.

He lay on his side and pulled her against him, settling her head into the hollow of his shoulder. "What?"

"It wasn't Chris." She let her arms go around him in a soft embrace. "And I'm sorry. For all of it. I never meant to hurt you."

"We'll talk about it in the morning."

Her breath warmed his skin. "Okay."

··· —— —— —— ···

The next morning, Chris woke up.

Colin walked into the room, still pulling on his shirt after his morning shower and feeling more invigorated than he had in a long time, only to stop dead at the sight of Chris sitting up in bed. Shalon sat next to him, wearing the clothes he had taken off her the night before, one leg curled under an outstretched thigh. She turned, smiling, as he came into the room.

For the first time in his life, he wished he had not saved a patient.

"Mayfeld," Chris said in a raspy voice that had lost none of its cynicism. "I hear I have you to thank for my recovery."

"I've been telling Chris how hard you worked to save him," Shalon said.

His words stuck in his craw, so that he had to force them out. "I did what any doctor would. How do you feel?"

Later, he hardly remembered the conversation. Only the way Shalon avoided looking at him. As soon as he could, he went into the living area and poured himself a stiff drink from the little-used automatic side-bar he had installed mainly for visitors. He had his third whiskey in his hand when Shalon emerged from the room and sat beside him on the sofa. Without saying a word, she took the glass from him and placed it on the floor.

"So that's how it's going to be?"

Shalon reached out a hand toward his face and he caught her wrist. *Damn you to hell. I have some pride.* "Don't. You'll only make it worse."

"Colin." She sighed. "No promises."

"Fuck that." He let go of her wrist as though it had burned him. "We both knew what we were doing. We both knew what it meant. But you're still going to leave anyway."

"We've got a couple of days at least. He's not well enough to move yet. I'm willing to stick to the deal." She spoke softly, and it made him want to shout. *Let him hear. I don't give a damn who knows anymore.*

"This was not about a deal. I won't let you turn it into that."

She raised an eyebrow. "Not a deal? I seem to remember terms, Colin. Terms you didn't have a problem with last night."

He did not look away, enduring the hot pain that slid into his ribs, deflating him. "And that's all that matters, right? That you aren't tied down. That you can go right back to him without missing a beat."

She closed her eyes and shook her head. "You're wrong. That's not what this is about."

"Really? Are you sure you're not just kidding yourself?"

She opened her eyes. "Colin, I know how this must seem to you. But this…" She sighed. "This is all I can give you. I hope you can forgive me for that."

He started to speak, but she held up a hand. "Every day we're here makes it more dangerous for you. Garner will be here in three days. We'll be leaving with him."

Not again. Not like this. Disappointment left a bitter taste in his mouth.

"You're leaving already?"

"I am." Shalon smiled at him sadly, raising her hand to caress his face. He turned his head away from it.

She gathered him against her, her arms smooth against his neck. "I'm sorry, Colin." Her fingers stroked his hair. "I've been rather selfish in all this."

"And I've been rather foolish." He laughed against her neck. *Unrequited love. It sounds so much more romantic than it really is. The reality hurts. It hurts like hell.* "We make a great pair, don't we?"

"Yes," she replied, and he heard a tinge of sadness in her voice. "Yes we do."

··· — — — ···

When his habitat Program alerted him to someone at the door several days later, Colin opened it expecting to see the tiny green figure that was Oux.

The man in his doorway was tall and thin. His sealed black coat reached the top of his boots, but the cuffs exposed tapered hands and narrow wrists of the palest green. Straight, fine, brown hair brushed the collar of his coat, falling well past the sharp angles of his cheekbones. His mouth and nose were small, delicate, but his eyes were completely black, set like gemstones beneath heavily fringed eyelids.

"Dr. Mayfeld." The voice was smooth, but high. Like a teenager's. "It's been a while."

Colin struggled for words, trying to reconcile the butterfly-gentle appearance of this creature with the image in his mind of a monkey-like alien that could hardly say one word.

"Garner?"

The mouth smiled, exposing even teeth. "That's me. You seem surprised. Shalon didn't tell you?"

"I wanted him to see for himself," she said. Colin turned, lifting his eyebrows at her questioningly. She shrugged and smiled a little, the glitter on her blue suit flashing. *Dressed and ready to go and to hell with what happened between us.*

"What can I say?" she told him. "He grew up."

"We've got to go," Garner said with an odd, birdlike tilt of his head. "He's in the bedroom."

The alien who looked more like a human mutant brushed past him. Colin watched as Shalon pulled her cloak over herself and fastened it. He didn't know what to say, so he said nothing until Garner reappeared with Chris, supporting him with a thin arm wrapped around his waist. They paused and Chris looked from Colin to Shalon and then back again.

He knows how I feel about her.

"It was good to see you again, Mayfeld," Chris said. "Particularly good for me, of course."

"Save it. I didn't do it for you." He glanced at Shalon, who stood motionless opposite him. "She already thanked me."

"That's my Shalon all right." Chris glanced at Shalon and though his expression did not change, Colin felt some communication pass between them. "She does pay her debts."

"Garner," Shalon said, her voice soft. "Help Chris down to the car."

When the two men disappeared into the corridor, Shalon came toward him, her gaze clear and inescapable as ever. He started to say something, but her finger covered his lips in a brief, electric touch. Her lips touched his, soft as a breeze.

When she pulled back, he said what he'd wanted to say all along. "Stay."

She shook her head. "They would find me. You'd lose everything."

"Then take me with you."

She took his hand in hers. "Colin, you'll never know what you've done for me." She squeezed his hand. "But where I'm going, you wouldn't be happy. You belong here."

"So do you." He pulled her into his arms, crushing her to him and inhaling the clean soap scent of her hair.

"I owe you one, Colin. If you ever need me, I've left a secure number on your panel."

"Shalon, you deserve the kind of life that won't have you running all the time."

"Lex deserved that life," she whispered into his neck, her breath caressing his skin. "But she's gone now. I left her with the person who loved her most."

He tried to hold her back, but Shalon slipped from him as easily as air and walked out the door. And though he watched on the security holos as she went out to the waiting car and got in, she never once looked back.

··· ▬ ▬ ▬ ···

"You said you'd explain later." Chris leaned back into the plush material of the car seat. "You want to tell me what the point of all that was?"

"It worked, didn't it? He healed you and he didn't ask you any questions." She did not look around, her gaze steady on the city streets that flowed past, full of bright lights and shadowy darkness.

"I saw the way he was with you."

"And?"

"You didn't tell him you shot me."

This time she did look at him, her face still as a mask. "You deserved it. Did you really think you could hide your plans from the both of us? Did you think you could steal from me and get away with it? You're lucky I didn't kill you."

"So you rekindle an old flame to save me? That must have been torture for you. What do I have to thank for that? Some misguided sense of loyalty?"

"You saved my life once, now I've returned the favor." The tone of her voice made Garner glance at them in the rearview mirror.

"I never asked for your help. Don't think this means I owe you anything."

"What it means is the slate is clean. I did what I promised. You have your money." She paused, considering. "I believe it's time we said goodbye."

"When did you start telling me what to do?"

"Save your breath, Chris. Believe me, it's better we go our separate ways. You've had your revenge. But I'm just beginning. And you don't want to go where I'm going. Garner and I will carry on together from here."

"What do you mean, you and Garner?"

"You survived for years before him. The money should help ease the transition." She nodded her head at the front of the vehicle. "Go ahead. Ask him who he wants to stay with."

"I need him," he said through his teeth.

"Well, he doesn't need you. And I don't need you anymore either."

Chris said nothing for a while, his chest heaving as he held her gaze. "You think because your doctor patched me up, we're good now? Because we're not. You shot me. I should have sold you out to that bitch Gilene."

"You know as well as I do that if you went to the Conways, they'd kill you too, just to keep anyone else from finding out I'm alive. I took no pleasure in shooting you. You forced my hand. I warned you once to stay out of my way. You should have listened."

"I taught you everything you know. You'd be dead without me."

"I know. I'm grateful. That's why you're still alive." Shalon sighed. "Chris, we never lied to each other. I don't hold it against you for doing what was in your nature. But I won't take a snake with me where I'm going. I have enough to worry about."

Chris laughed, a bitter sound. "You know, someday you'll fuck with the wrong person."

Shalon signaled Garner and he stopped the car. "Some day, maybe. But you won't be there to see it." She pushed a button on her armrest and the door next to him opened. "Now get out."

EPILOGUE

The arc of the moral universe is long,
but it bends toward justice.
—*Dr. Martin Luther King, Jr.*
20th Century Terran Activist and Philosopher

Calen Evic stared into the flute glass in his hand, oblivious to the noise around him in the dark, laser-lit room. The pale peach liquid, with swirls of yellow, sloshed against the sides of its container and the scent of cherries tickled his nose, driving away the sweat, musk and alcohol of the crowded bar.

Here's to another mission, he thought, and drained the glass in one swift movement. He caught one of the bartender's eyes and nodded to the empty glass as he set it down on the metal counter. Uproarious laughter grated on his ears, drowning out the pounding music that had no intelligible lyrics.

More orders tomorrow, a new posting for my Group, but tonight—tonight is ours. He turned and leaned his elbows back on the hard counter, squinting into the shifting gloom with amber eyes. *Too bad I have no idea what to do with myself.* He ran one large hand through his straight, shoulder-length hair, black strands slipping forward as soon as he removed his fingers.

One of the side effects of being offworld, he thought. Home, on Orgala, every moment had been regulated. There was always something to do, something to work at. Downtime other than sleep simply did not occur. But the Groups offworld often found themselves with nothing to do for hours, even days, at a time.

New recruits became unnerved by it, and even five-year veterans like himself could be at their wits' end between missions.

What irony. We fight for our freedom, and yet don't know what to do with the smallest bit of it.

Calen turned back to the bar, post-battle ennui settling over him like a smothering hand, and picked up the refilled glass.

"Group Leader Calen Evic." *No. It wasn't possible.* The soft voice that came from his right filled his senses. He froze in the act of tipping the glass to his lips.

A throaty sound of amusement. "Has it been so long you've forgotten me?"

The glass slipped from his unfeeling fingers, and he watched as a slender hand snatched it out of the air and set it down, undamaged. He lowered his hand to the counter, spreading his palm flat, as if for support.

"Vi-Commander?"

"Ah. You remember me after all."

Eyes stinging, he let his head turn on a suddenly stiff neck. The woman that smiled at him wore a jumpsuit instead of body armor and had much shorter hair, but her green eyes were unmistakable. An empty gun belt hung low on her hips. The bar's management did not allow weapons. He'd left his own gun belt outside as well. But one thing went round and round in his head. *Alive. After all this time, alive.*

"Vi-Commander Conway," he said, shock sending a shiver through his voice. "I am grateful to find myself in your presence again." Calen began to bow but a slight shake of Shalon's head stopped him.

"We're not on Orgala anymore, Group Leader. I don't require such formality."

He stopped, unsure what to do. In the end, he grasped her upper arms with his hands. A soldier's greeting. After a moment's hesitation, she did the same.

Never in a million years. "They told us you were missing, perhaps dead."

"Wrong on one count." She shrugged a shoulder and they released each other at the same time.

"We have missed you on the battlefield," he said.

Shalon faced the bar and leaned both elbows on the counter. "I'm sure Andor has been more than adequate at his job."

He caught a trace of bitterness in her tone that surprised him.

It was general knowledge, though seldom talked about, that the Sub-Commander and Vi-Commander had been great friends. Perhaps even more than that. *But many things have changed in the last three years. Many things.*

"A drink?" he asked. She refused with an uplifted palm.

"No time for that. I have a ship waiting and I need to get my business done as soon as possible."

He frowned, sticking out an elbow in time to ward off a jostle from a passer-by. "What kind of business?"

She glanced sidelong at him. "Personal."

Unsure how to take that, he dropped his eyes and studied the swirls of his drink. *She's different. Harder. More focused. And she still knows how to make me feel like I'm a green soldier.*

"I'd like your help." Her voice startled him out of his thoughts.

"With what?"

"Calen." She turned to face him, one hand draped casually over the counter ledge. "I'm not going back home. There are things I have to deal with here that are more important. Things that have to do with my family. But for me to accomplish what I plan to, I will need help. A lot of help."

"From me?"

She nodded. "And others. I need you to find them for me. I don't know what your mission is right now, and I don't expect you to compromise your orders, but you might as well know. What I'm going to do is dangerous. It will probably take a long time—years— and you won't be able to tell anyone in Rhiannon about it."

Calen studied her calm, watchful face. "I won't betray my people."

Her lips tightened. "They're my people as well. Don't think I've forgotten that. I wouldn't dream of asking you to betray them. This is personal. I've recently come into some money, so you will be paid."

"Vi-Commander," he cut across her softly. "You forget yourself."

She paused, and a smile made her beauty obvious. "You're right. Forgive me. I didn't mean to insult you."

"Apology accepted." The answering smile that stretched his face felt odd—unnatural. *Still can't get used to it after all these years.* "You were my Vi-Commander before Niala Quemar. My duty as an Orgalian is to you as well."

Some emotion flashed in her eyes, but too quickly for him to grasp its significance. "Thank you, Calen. That's much more than I hoped for."

"What would I be required to do?"

"I'll need you to contact other Group Leaders in a similar position to yours and recruit them for me. Be honest with them, but be discreet. What I tell you must stay with a trusted few."

"Of course."

"I will need you to go on missions, but I hope to use only your downtime to accomplish them. Your obligations to Orgala will not be affected."

"Downtime." He savored the taste of the words. *Finally, something to do.* "Perhaps you should tell me what I'm going to be doing."

She grinned, her face lit up by a sudden flash of laser light. "Why, Calen. I thought that would be obvious. We're soldiers. We're going to war."

ACKNOWLEDGEMENTS

A lovely Australian lady, Edwina Harvey, helped me birth this book. I am indebted to her for showing me all my flaws and signing a contract agreeing never to reveal them to anyone else. I am grateful that I had the good luck to have her as my editor.

Anna Kashina is not only a great writer, she's a first class beta reader and friend as well. This book, literally, would not have been published without her. Thank you for never letting me give up, Anna.

Dawei Dong decided to take a chance on Lex. That makes him a hero in my book. Thank you for making my dream come true.

To all my beta readers, especially those of the OWW, thank you from the bottom of my heart. Your advice and support meant everything to me. I especially want to thank my family and friends who sacrificed peace of mind to read my work and endure my endless, frantic, probing questions. They include—but are not limited to—Andrea James, Vernice Phillip, Christon Malchan, Justin Malchan, Natalie Bazil, Edwin St. John, Wayne Cotty and my grandmother, Lyris Baptiste, who never doubted my talent. She did not live to see my book on a shelf, but she is always with me and is still the best part of my story.

Huge thanks to the Online Writing Workshop for Science Fiction, Fantasy and Horror—affectionately known as the OWW— its Yahoo chat and writing lists, the gone but not forgotten Zoo, and the wonderful people I've met in all these internet niches who helped me grow, hone my skills and prodded me in the butt when I thought I could not go on.

341

There are so many to thank, but Elizabeth Hull, Susan Curnow, Kat Allen, Elizabeth Bear, Stelios Touchtidis, David Fortier, Steve Chapman, Greg Byrne, Christine Lucas, Elizabeth Shack, Walter Williams, Jennifer Dawson, Jan Whitaker, Gio Clairval, and friends who have moved on such as Pam McNew, Kate Murray, Stella Evans, Charles "Charlie" Finlay, Clover Autrey, John Borneman, Larry, Mike the Janitor—not to mention the entire Vicious Circle and Round Table crit groups—have all given me advice and helped me on my way. I have to thank every person who ever gave me a crit on the OWW, including the amazing Nalo Hopkinson, who critted the second chapter of this book in its first draft and wrote the words that stuck with me: "I would read on".

Over ten years ago, a very famous and kind editor received an email from a new writer who had been rejected by the editor's online magazine. That editor never saw a single word the writer put to electronic paper, but she gave her the only advice that mattered. Join a crit group—specifically the OWW. It would make the new writer a better writer, no matter what stage she was at in the craft. Over ten years later, what small talent I have has been immeasurably improved simply because I took that advice. Ellen Datlow, you have never met me. But I thank you for setting me on the right path, and encouraging me to keep going. Everything I've learned has been because you took the time to give a stranger good advice.

Blessings on all of you—and anyone I forgot—for putting up with me and helping me along the way.

ABOUT THE AUTHOR

R. S. A. Garcia lives and works on the island of Trinidad in the Caribbean with a large family and too many dogs–not that any of them belong to her.

She decided to be an author when she discovered that Louisa May Alcott had been published at the age of 8. Determined to waste no more time, she finished her first collection of stories at 10. She has not stopped writing since, and indulged herself in a deep love of all speculative fiction despite the best advice of every English teacher she has ever had.

She has just signed a contract for her debut novel and is working on others in between hyperventilating over edits.

More from Dragonwell Publishing:

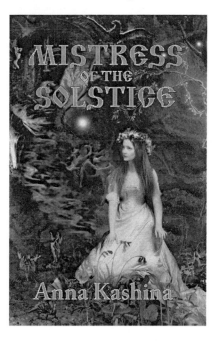

Mistress of the Solstice
by Anna Kashina

a dark romantic tale
based on Russian folklore

The Loathly Lady
by John Lawson

an Arthurian tale of
chivalry and dark magic

www.dragonwellpublishing.com

More from Dragonwell Publishing:

**The Garden
at the Roof of the World**
by W. B. J. Williams

a medieval quest
of healing, magic, and love

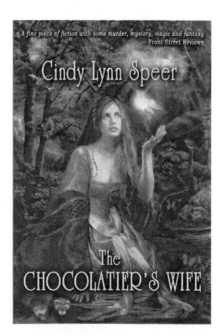

The Chocolatier's Wife
by Cindy Lynn Speer

a rich tale of romance,
magic, mystery
...and chocolate

www.dragonwellpublishing.com

More from Dragonwell Publishing:

Once Upon a Curse
by Peter Beagle
and other authors

the dark side
of fairy tales and myths

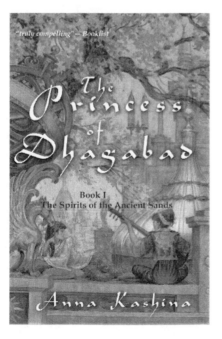

The Princess of Dhagabad
by Anna Kashina

an Arabian love story
about a princess
and an all-powerful djinn

www.dragonwellpublishing.com

CPSIA information can be obtained at www.ICGtesting.com
Printed in the USA
LVOW06s1727010714

392546LV00007B/968/P